final ACT

final ACT

a novel

C. Paul Andersen

Covenant Communications, Inc.

Covenant

Published by Covenant Communications, Inc.
American Fork, Utah

Printed in Canada
First Printing: January 2004

11 10 09 08 07 06 05 04   10 9 8 7 6 5 4 3 2 1

ISBN 1-59156-264-3

Dedication

For my wife, Kathleen, and for my children, who know their names.

Acknowledgements

*Special thanks to Nina Pykare, my teacher,
and Angela Colvin, my editor.*

Prologue

NOW

The images are so familiar that it is no struggle to recall them; in fact, the smells and tastes are almost tangible in memory—in the dream they are always overwhelming. In it I'm trying to run, but my arms and legs are lead. I silently beg myself, *Escape! She's going to find you in this forbidden place.* I'm at the top of the stairs. I must fight against something holding me from behind. A foul smell fills my nose and mouth. I sink into a blackness and I cannot claw my way out.

Then I'm choking. *Must get air.*

Even in the dream, I always remember to pray. Then, like clockwork, I see in the darkness a crack of light and struggle toward it. I breathe the life-giving air. Then someone is coming.

Sometimes, like today, I wake up at this point. I pull out of sleep almost choking on my fear. I'm sweating. I stare into the mirror before me until I recognize myself. Then I fall back on my pillow, relieved and troubled simultaneously. "How much time has to pass?" I mutter. I throw off the blankets, then squeeze my fists and tense my leg muscles just to be sure I'm completely awake.

Sometimes in the dream I get to see who's coming, and I know God has heard my prayer.

Remembering this I open my eyes, desiring to let it go for now. But I wonder if I'll ever escape the horror of those days and nights at Horstman House; if I will ever simply have the future it gave me without the past it seems shackled to.

Our bedroom is sunny and cheerful. *Not a place for bad dreams*, I reason. I see the room nearby which is now his office—the computer, his desk, and my cell phone. The phone rings, and as I go to answer it my eye catches the date on his desk calendar. It is the first day of summer 2003—the anniversary of that night is coming up. *It is over forever, isn't it?* I ask myself.

Chapter One

The freeways were relatively quiet on that June afternoon, and my roommate Jill—*former* roommate—easily found the turnoff to Colorado Boulevard and then El Molino Street, the location of the Pasadena Playhouse. She drove her new 1976 red convertible to the curb opposite the mock Spanish façade—stucco, tiled roof, and palms in the courtyard. "Well, Wendy, here it is," she said. "Looks a little run-down."

"It looks great to me—just like I imagined it," I replied.

Jill looked at her watch. "It's only one-fifteen—why don't we grab some lunch?"

"No, I'm not hungry. I'll just walk around in the courtyard in front of the theater while I wait for my ride to Horstman House. I want to soak up the mood of the place."

"Well, if you're sure. I'm going to miss you," she said, brushing away a sudden tear, then smiling.

"I'll miss you too. But I'll be back on weekends—at least as soon as I get a car."

"I'll come get you whenever you want. Maybe I'll be coming sooner than you think. You may want to come back and go to church with us on Sunday," she proposed.

"That's true," I said. I opened the door, reached behind the front seat for my luggage, and then looked closely at my blond, sun-tanned friend with a heart as sunny as her smile. "Thanks for all you've done for me. Not just today, but—"

"Yeah, I know. You'd never have made it in L.A. without me."

"That's right. I wouldn't have. You've been great."

"Hey, you sound like it's over. I'll see you next weekend. Call me tonight," she urged. "Let me know all about the Great Bella and her handsome son."

"How do you know he's handsome?"

"I saw his picture in the *L. A. Times.*"

"I've had more to do with his weird housekeeper Ingrid than with Mr. Horstman."

"Well, if it's all *too* weird—and I think it is—call me. I'm only an hour away."

I closed the door. "Yes. I'll call. Good-bye."

Jill waved and drove away. I watched her go around the corner out of sight and felt a momentary loneliness. She'd been my closest LDS friend in L.A. I hadn't always found those who shared my standards, but Jill had supported me in the gospel, and I felt lost without that companionship. I said a silent prayer of thanks for my friend.

I shook off my brooding and, hefting my luggage, jaywalked across the street, glad it was quiet at that time of day. I went up the few steps to the Playhouse courtyard to wait for my ride to Horstman House.

I was actually there—the Pasadena Playhouse—where my mother's favorite movie star, Dana Andrews, had studied, where even Dustin Hoffman had spent some time in the waning days of the school's fame, and where the great Bella Horstman had performed. The ambiance of the place captured me. I passed a circular fountain ringed by a fluted masonry edge and checked my appearance in the glass doors—not glamorous, not homely. I looked conservative enough to meet my new employers, though.

Was it really happening? Was I actually going to the private home of the great Bella Horstman, who performed at the Playhouse in its heyday? And what about Bella's son, Daniel Horstman? "Handsome," I repeated Jill's words aloud in amusement. Well, I'd probably meet him once and that would be it.

I looked up an outside stairway leading to rooms on a second floor. *Had those been the classrooms and studios of the school?* I wondered.

My secret fascination with anything related to theater and movies had brought me here, and now, I'd see it all. I'd be driven to Bella Horstman's mansion to live in her house. I'd actually be living with the great theater and film legend, tutoring Bella's grandson. Everything had fallen into place as if I'd planned it.

The woman in the ticket office looked at me quizzically, so, reluctantly, I walked out toward the street again. I sat on the steps outside the Playhouse to wait for my ride and opened my purse. Fishing out the help-wanted ad, I read it for the hundredth time:

> *Wanted. Calif. Certified Primary Grades Tchr. for Priv. Tutor, 8-yr.-Old Boy. Live-In. Ex. Sal. Right Pty. Begin 6/1/76. Call Pasadena Professionals, 1-800-965-2067.*

Had I done the right thing, leaving my secure public teaching job to teach one young boy in a new situation? But I was so glad to get out of that overcrowded classroom filled with discipline problems, that anything else would probably feel right. Certainly I could handle just one little boy.

I began to feel rather silly about choosing this somewhat romantic meeting place, but the only other location I knew in Pasadena was the Rose Bowl. Somehow the Pasadena Playhouse seemed more appropriate. Punctually at 2:00 P.M., my amazing transportation to Horstman House appeared—an old but shining limousine with a tall vertical grill and, at the rear, a luggage carrier and covered spare tire. I was startled from my wide-eyed stare when I heard my name, "Miss Wendy Wood?"

I turned to see a short, mustached, and uniformed chauffeur, and I nodded. He stood rigidly and spoke with solemn formality. "I am Helman. Mr. Horstman has sent me to drive you to Horstman House." He opened the rear door for me, then took my huge old suitcase and my makeup case and strapped them to the luggage carrier. I stepped into a spacious leather-upholstered interior, separated from the front by a carpeted expanse and a glass window. I sat back feeling more like a gawky preteen than a teacher, intimidated by both the car and Helman.

Leaving the downtown Pasadena area, which retained some of the architectural beauty of earlier decades, Helman drove past inner-city housing, through middle-class areas, to upper-class neighborhoods, and finally to the large and opulent walled estates of the very wealthy.

We came to a gated entrance flanked by columns and arched with ivy. The gates swung open for the big car, which began a winding climb to the hilltop site of Horstman House.

My breath caught when I saw the house. It was the size of half a city block; it had three stories and a flat roof like a Greek temple or a French Renaissance mansion. The impressive front entry doors were reached by a spreading half-walled terrace, and green lawns flowed downhill at the front and sides of the house.

I was relieved when Helman drove the car to a less imposing rear portico where I saw gardens filled with early June roses, a long garage, a swimming pool, and a gazebo nearby. Another small building near the gazebo appeared to have been damaged by a fire. In the distance, beyond the pool, was a little lake.

Helman retrieved my luggage, opened the car door, cleared his throat to remind me he was there, and went toward a rear entrance. *The servant's entrance?* I wondered.

I hurried to catch up, not desiring his company, but not wanting to be left behind.

He held the door for me, and I entered a narrow, dark hall that intersected another hallway—the major artery for the first floor. It was massive with high, arched ceilings. Heroic-sized paintings hung majestically on both sides of the hall. I wanted to stop to admire them, the crystal chandeliers overhead, and the sconces on gold brocade walls, but Helman's formal stride had carried him half the length of the main hall. Hurrying to catch up again, I almost ran into a marble bust on a pedestal, making me feel like the little bumbling drifter played by Charlie Chaplin in so many of his silent films.

Helman reached the halfway point at which the grand entry intersected the huge center hall. Two thickly carpeted marble stairways wound upward from either side of the entry, and he climbed to where they met at the second-floor balcony overlooking the stairs.

He glowered at me from his second-floor vantage. I was puffing when I caught up to him—he was more agile than he looked. When I caught up, he went down another corridor to the far end, where he stopped and knocked on double doors painted in gilt and ivory. This second-floor hall wasn't as luxurious as the first, but I still felt overwhelmed by the obvious wealth of the Horstmans. I glanced at myself in a floor-to-ceiling antique mirror, inhaled deeply, and prepared to meet my new employer.

From behind the double doors I heard a low and commanding, "Come in!" Helman set down my luggage and preceded me through the doorway into an ordinary room with a large wooden desk, a desk chair, a small child's desk and a child's chair—not too different from those in my public schoolroom. A tall, lean, homely woman turned when Helman said, "Miss Wood, the new tutor for Master Paul, has arrived." I was repelled by her narrow face which was dominated by a sharp nose and chin. Her small, black eyes were magnified by thick-lensed glasses. Her skin was prunelike in texture and gray in color. She wore a plain black dress and laced, narrow, pointy-toed black shoes. Her hands had long fingers. I couldn't help thinking of the witch in MGM's *Wizard of Oz*.

I reached out for a handshake and met empty space. The woman locked her hands behind her. "I am Ingrid Nourse, the Horstman's housekeeper, Miss Wood. I will take you to your room. Helman, take Miss Wood's things to her quarters."

Was it my imagination, or did Helman click his heels in response? I ventured, "I thought I would be meeting Mr. Horstman."

She eyed me coldly. "No, Mr. Horstman has checked your credentials and references carefully and is satisfied. You will, perhaps, meet him tomorrow, along with Master Paul, your pupil." She surveyed the room proudly. "I asked Helman to bring you here first. This is the schoolroom."

I looked about to see absolutely nothing that would stimulate a child's interest—a free-standing blackboard, a piece of white chalk, and the desks and chairs—that was it. I thought it looked like a nineteenth-century schoolroom—not what I'd expected in this place where money for materials and equipment shouldn't have been a problem.

Ingrid continued. "Be here tomorrow at 9:00 A.M. *sharp*." She crossed to the door. "Now, I will take you to your room. Dinner will be served at 7:00 P.M. in the servants' dining room, unless, of course, you prefer a tray in your room."

I hesitated. "I'll join the others in the dining room at seven."

Without reply, Ingrid exited the room. I had no choice but to follow.

Outside the schoolroom, I saw a stairway leading up to another story. Ingrid led me the full length of the second floor, past closed doors, the main staircase, and into a dormitory-like hall, at the end of which Ingrid stopped. She opened a door and stepped aside, ushering me into a small but not unpleasant room which I assumed was to be mine. I could make it more homey with a few personal touches. No TV and no radio, though. I'd have to bring mine from the apartment in Sherman Oaks. After all, Jill had her own. Ingrid remained in the hall. "You will use the bathroom at the center of the hall on the left. Towels and other linens are in the linen closet next to the bathroom. As I said, your dinner will be ready at seven. You may use these stairs." She gestured to a stairway at her left, which led both up to the third floor and down to the first. "The stairs go down to the servants' dining room. Please be aware that no one—I repeat *no one*—of the household staff is allowed on the third floor. I trust you'll remember that." Ingrid turned in the direction from which we had come, leaving me alone.

The plain room was not nearly as cold as the greeting I'd received. Not even a, "Hope you like it here." I examined the room more closely, finding a single bed with wooden colonial head and footboards, a small but adequate chest of drawers painted a light blue, a wooden colonial rocker without a cushion, a small writing desk which doubled as a bedside lamp table, and a wooden stool beside the desk. The curtains at the one small window were light blue lace, and a pull-down shade would provide privacy—if I needed it on the second floor. The only discordant item was the ugly rug—a moss green floral print with dark-colored vines twining around the border. The closet was small but sufficient for my limited wardrobe, but there was no mirror.

I walked to the window and raised the shade, looking past a chimney to see the rear rose garden, the blackened shell of what might have been a guesthouse, the gazebo, and one end of the pool and the small lake. The San Gabriel Mountains formed a distant backdrop. The Horstman estate was huge—the nearest neighbor must have been miles away, I thought.

I lifted my suitcase onto the bed and unpacked the few possessions I could bring on that first trip. I'd get more clothes, books, and other necessities on my days off next weekend. Now I figured I'd find the bathroom.

The rather large bathroom had a tub on high, clawlike feet. I was grateful that a shower had been added. A plain white shower curtain was drawn around the total circumference of the tub. I looked up to see a nineteenth-century toilet tank, hung high on the wall, with a chain to pull for flushing. *This will be interesting,* I thought. An old wall mirror hung above the large pedestal sink. One small bulb hung at the center of the room. There was no window and no fan. It appeared that the bathroom hadn't been changed much since the house was built, but the towels were thick and the soap was fragrant. I liked that touch of twentieth-century comfort, and decided that there would be privacy as I saw the door could be locked from inside. A skeleton key was already in the keyhole.

I washed up, then returned to my room. There was no lock on my door. I'd have to ask about that. I looked at my watch. It was only four. What could I do for three hours until dinner? I began to regret not having taken Jill's offer of lunch.

I lay on the bed. It was firm, but still comfortable. The pillow was goose down—another bit of luxury. A nap seemed like a good idea and I fell asleep.

I was awakened by the sound of my door closing. The room was growing dark. Groping for the lamp beside the bed, I found the switch and looked toward the door. No one was there. I looked at my watch and found that it was ten after seven. I was late for dinner. Maybe someone had come to my door to remind me of the dinner hour?

Straightening my hair and clothes as best I could without a mirror, I went to the head of the stairs. The stairway was rather dark, and I couldn't find a light switch. Nervously, I held the banister and made my way down the stairs, which turned at a landing partway. At the foot of the stairs, I came to a door. Opening it, I entered an all-white room, lit by a harsh overhead ceiling light. A long rectangular table was set for one. There were three covered serving dishes, a green salad, a water glass, and a napkin-covered bread basket. Was this my dinner? Had the other staff members eaten earlier?

I sat down and gave thanks to the Lord for my food, for bringing me safely to Horstman House, and for leading me to the new teaching opportunity which I so desperately needed. I spread the linen napkin on my lap, looked at each dish—baked chicken, asparagus, a baked potato, and muffins—and then ate ravenously, glad that I didn't have to worry about company manners. I hadn't learned to like California drinking water, so when I was finished, I longed for a soda. Did I dare look for one? I rose and walked to a closed door behind my chair. I knocked. There was no response, so I carefully opened the door upon a huge kitchen which looked more commercial than homey. I found a big double-doored refrigerator and searched it for a soft drink.

"May I help you with something?"

I turned to face a tall, gray-haired, and white-aproned woman, not so grave in appearance as Ingrid, but obviously unhappy with my nosing about in her kitchen. "I'm sorry," I apologized. "I was just looking for a soda."

Her back stiffened. "You won't find a soda here, young lady. We don't have them in this house."

"Well, of course. I guess not. I was still thirsty after dinner—which was very good—by the way." I tried to diffuse her hostility.

She chose to ignore the compliment. "I have cooked for the Horstmans for many years and I don't allow anyone to snoop about in my kitchen."

I offered my hand, but again it wasn't met by another. "I'm Wendy—Wendy Wood, the new—uh—teacher—tutor."

"Yes, I know. Ingrid told me to have your dinner ready at seven. I'm Blanche, Blanche Goodwin."

"Well Blanche—Ms. Goodwin—I'm pleased to meet you. And thank you for dinner. I enjoyed it but, well, if you don't mind my asking, do we always eat that late?"

"Some of the other staff members eat at five-thirty—they have evening duties. Others finish their work here, eat, and then leave Horstman House. I suppose Ingrid thought you'd rather eat alone."

Miss Nourse hadn't bothered to mention that I'd be eating alone—did *she* want it that way? And Blanche was courteous, at least, but hardly friendly. I realized I couldn't worry about that right then, as Blanche's gaze was still scrutinizing me. I saw double doors and wondered if they led to the family dining room. "When does the family eat?"

Blanche's look suggested this was not my concern. "Madame Horstman dines alone in her quarters. Mr. Horstman often dines out in the evening—since his wife's death."

"His wife died? I didn't know."

"Lisa Horstman died in a tragic fire, in the guesthouse, about seven years ago."

"How awful for the family."

"Yes." Then she changed the subject without so much as a pause. "Master Paul often dines alone."

"When?"

"At six o'clock—but in the family dining room."

I looked again at the double doors. "Is that the entrance to the family dining room?"

"Yes. It's convenient to the kitchen."

I walked toward the dining room. "Would it be possible, do you think, that I could join Paul—*Master* Paul—for dinner?" I asked, hesitantly.

She wiped an already spotless counter with a dishcloth. "That would be up to someone else."

I followed her movements about the kitchen. "Who—who should I talk to? Miss Nourse? Mr. Horstman? Madame Horstman?"

"Certainly *not* Madame Horstman! She sees no one—not even her son. Hasn't for more than twenty years. Even I haven't spoken directly to her for almost thirty years. You should probably talk with Ingrid—Miss Nourse. Mr. Horstman doesn't deal with such matters." She dismissed me, saying that she would like to clear my dishes.

"Of course. Do you mind my asking where your room is?"

"In the same hall as yours—at the other end. I have a private bathroom and sitting room," she said proudly, possibly anxious to suggest the difference in our situations.

She exited to the servants' dining room, and I followed her. "Do you suppose I could look around the house? It's too early to go to bed."

Blanche turned to me, as if to emphasize her reply. "I wouldn't suggest that. If I were you, I'd stay in your room tonight. Someone will show you around tomorrow."

"Well—would there be any problem in my walking around the grounds?"

"I wouldn't suggest that, either, but if you're that restless, I guess it would be all right. But you should return to your room at an early hour—and please use the back entrance and stairs."

"Where is the back entrance?"

"Didn't you see it at the foot of the back stairs?'

"No, I didn't. There are so many stairs in this place. I'll just go up to my room for a sweater."

"Do that, and remember, we retire early at Horstman House." Blanche returned to clearing the dishes from my meal.

I felt very unwelcome in my isolated surroundings. I climbed the stairs to my room and remembered I hadn't called Jill. The thought of calling her made me feel better, but where was a phone? I couldn't remember seeing one in the parts of the house where I'd been. There wasn't one in my room. I searched unsuccessfully on the second-floor landing near my room. Then I went down the servants' wing and, at the end by a door which probably led to Blanche's room, I found, amazingly enough, a pay phone. "A pay phone. That's just great," I muttered. Had the Horstmans borrowed this idea from another millionaire, the penny-pincher J. Paul Getty?

I returned to my room for change, but stopped outside. The door was partly open. I was certain I had closed it when I went down to dinner. I hesitated, then rapidly pushed the door open. There was no one in the room. I stopped at the closet door, then peeked inside, realizing the closet wasn't big enough for a hiding place. I laughed nervously. I was imagining things. I must have left the door open. I felt silly, kneeling to look under the bed, but I lifted the corner of the bedspread and gasped. A small figure scrambled out the other side, ran to the door, and bolted down the hall. I hurried to the hallway just in time to see a little boy dart around the corner. I ran the length of the servants' hall to the connecting second-floor corridor but could see no one there in the semidarkness. And there wasn't a sound.

Chapter Two

Returning to my room, I found my open purse on the bed where I'd left it. However, I remembered zipping the purse shut. I decided I'd have to talk to somebody about getting a lock on my door immediately, especially since there was a little prowler around. I sat on the edge of the bed, remembered my plans to call Jill, and opened the coin purse in my wallet. It was empty. Not only was my small visitor a snoop—he was a thief.

My currency was untouched, but I didn't know where to find change at that hour. I certainly didn't want to face Blanche Goodwin or Ingrid Nourse again. No call to Jill then, I realized, and tomorrow I'd have to deal with young Paul's visit to my room. Curiosity was one thing—petty theft was another; our first lesson was already planned.

Besides this new frustration, I longed to talk to someone outside Horstman House. I hadn't received the welcome I'd anticipated. Helman was formal and distant. Ingrid Nourse was cold. Blanche Goodwin had been polite but not friendly. And it seemed that my little eight-year-old student would be a handful, too. Maybe I'd made a mistake leaving my old job. Those thirty second graders didn't seem as threatening as they once had.

I decided to pray for direction and reassurance that I was doing the right thing, that I could have a positive impact on my young pupil, and that I would be able to adjust to the new environment and people with whom I would work.

After kneeling in prayer, I felt better, and I wondered if I should go to bed instead of looking over the grounds. I was glad I'd packed my scriptures and a novel, but it was only eight-thirty. I looked out the small window at the moonlit serenity of the night. I had to get some air. I searched the chest for my sweater and decided to wear a long white head scarf instead, warm enough for a June night. I missed having a mirror and checked my reflection in the window. To be safe I hid my purse under the mattress and closed the door tightly behind me.

The stairway was dimly lit now by bare bulbs overhead. Obviously the conveniences in the other parts of Horstman House had not been repeated in the servants' quarters. Using the banister, I felt my way downstairs in the semidarkness and located a rear door. When I stepped outside onto a broad lawn, I breathed the clear night air, somehow fresher at this hillside site of Horstman House above the city smog.

Where should I explore first? I wondered. I decided to wait until daylight to check out the pool and lake, and wandered instead across the grass toward the small, white gazebo. I liked the delicate wooden lace that decorated the roof. The fragrance of early June roses filled the breeze, and for a moment my spirits lifted. *This might not be such a bad place after all.*

I sat on the circular gazebo bench with my back toward the house, listening to the quiet rustle of the leaves of eucalyptus trees and palms nearby. The full moon reflected on the lake, and the tensions of the day began to ease.

Then I looked beyond the gazebo at the burned building which I'd seen earlier, and the joy of the moment was gone. I stood and walked toward the remains of the building. The roof beams were burned but still intact, and the brick walls appeared solid, so nothing appeared hazardous, but the door and window frames were blackened and scarred. The light of the moon cast shadows in the interior, which had been gutted by fire except for a few supporting brick columns for the roof. Inside were several blackened frames of furniture. Why hadn't the guesthouse been rebuilt or knocked down? I wondered. It must have been left as it was after the fire.

I returned to the gazebo, hoping to regain the peace I'd felt there. The moon lit the house, and I saw a third-floor balcony which I hadn't noticed before. Then I thought I saw a figure on the balcony. It must be Bella Horstman. *Imagine.* I was so glad I'd decided to come outside—I was actually seeing the legendary Bella.

Involuntarily, I rose and crossed to the far side of the gazebo to get a closer look at Bella, who surveyed the grounds from above. Was she looking down at me? She turned my way. To my delight, she stared at me for several moments, and I almost raised my hand to wave, but she turned and retreated as mysteriously as she had appeared. A light went on in the upper rooms, and I was mesmerized, imagining Bella wandering dreamlike in her house surrounded by the treasures of her past. My imaginings ceased when I sensed, more than heard, someone behind me.

"Lisa?" a soft voice whispered.

I turned. "No, I'm not—" I stopped. In the shadows I saw a man—tallish, slender, with dark hair. I couldn't see his face. "I'm Wendy Wood, the new teacher."

He stepped back. "Yes, of course. I'm sorry. For a moment you looked like—someone else. I'm Daniel Horstman. Sorry I disturbed you." What had he called me? Lisa? Of course, his deceased wife's name. I immediately felt sorry for him. This must have been their meeting place. Then I suddenly wondered why he had mistaken me for Lisa. Was it just his surprise at finding someone here in the gazebo? But he had acted so strangely—had his grief disturbed his sense of reality?

I could see him more clearly now: his hair blown by the breeze, a rather thin, tanned face, yet I couldn't see the color of his eyes. I suppressed my fears and walked to him, my hand extended.

He turned away abruptly. "I'm sorry to have interrupted you. I trust that Ingrid has made you comfortable?" He didn't wait for a reply. "You'll meet Paul tomorrow. Thanks for coming." He walked toward the pool and lake, disappearing in the shadows of the trees.

I lowered my hand. *Handshakes must not be the thing around here,* I thought.

I knew I probably wouldn't have the opportunity to help him through his grief, but even at this brief meeting, somehow I wanted to. I probably wouldn't even meet him again. "You'll meet Paul tomorrow," he'd said. Like the others I'd met, he was courteous and distant—and strange. I walked toward the house, disappointed and confused, but bracing myself for the next day's challenges.

In my room I knelt in prayer again, thanking the Lord for bringing me safely to Horstman House and for my new opportunity to teach and serve. I told Him there were a lot of problems in this house, a lot of sadness, and I asked that He guide me in finding a way to help. Then I sat on my bed and began my first journal entry.

Chapter Three

I set my alarm for seven, but woke earlier from a restless sleep, caused mostly by a different bed and surroundings. No one had told me when breakfast would be served, but I assumed it would be early, since I was supposed to meet Paul at "9:00 A.M. sharp."

In my morning prayer, I asked for the courage to face Paul about his stealing. I prayed I would say and do the right things. Giving thanks for my new opportunities and challenges, I prayed for help teaching, as well as evaluating the character and the abilities of my new student. Then I put on my robe and slippers, picked up my toiletries bag, and peeked out into the hall, hoping I wouldn't meet anyone and that the bathroom would be unoccupied. I closed my door, thinking again of last night's little visitor and wondering how I would handle the theft problem. The hall was quiet, and I found the bathroom unlocked and vacant. I locked the door with the skeleton key.

Arranging the shower curtain wasn't easy. I placed a bathroom mat on the cold tile floor and climbed over the high rim of the tub. *How does the shower work?* I wondered, beginning to feel frustrated.

Adjusting the water temperature to my steamy preference, I found a plunger device between the taps and pushed it down. A rattling and clanking preceded the spray, which trickled cold at first but finally produced a shower of warm water.

I enjoyed the shower, but the tub was very slippery and there were no safety rails and no safety strips in the tub. I'd have to speak to Ingrid or someone about that, too, because I was not a tub soaker. I had to have a shower.

My thoughts returned to the worries of the day, when I turned off the creaking taps and stepped out of the high tub. The bathroom towel was soft and sweet smelling, but the thought of seeing Ingrid again and of dealing with Paul almost spoiled the joy of my shower. I wondered if I would meet Mr. Horstman again.

After wiping the steam off the mirror, I completed my makeup in the bathroom, remembering there was no mirror in my room. I found a chute by the bathroom door and dropped my towels in the void, hoping they'd end up in a laundry room. I left the door open to let some of the steam escape from the fanless, windowless room.

Again no one was about. I returned to my room, relieved to see the door still closed. I dressed in a summer-white cotton blouse, and an Indian-print, navy blue and white skirt—not too stuffy, but still conservative. I decided against the white sandals. Miss Nourse would probably think it more proper that I wear hose and my low-heeled pumps. My purse and notebook in hand, I went downstairs to the servants' dining room.

The smell of bacon and eggs was irresistible. I heard voices in the dining room and saw an older gray-haired woman and a young, rather plump girl already seated at the table. They wore black dresses and white aprons and caps, so I figured they were maids. They stopped talking when I came in. I approached the older woman first. "Hi, I'm Wendy Wood. I'm the new teacher for Paul."

The woman stood and, to my surprise, extended her hand and smiled. "I'm Martha Wright." Gesturing toward the girl, she said, "And this is Angela—Angela Wood. Say, that's a coincidence, isn't it? The last name. Do you suppose you're related?"

I nodded to Angela. "I don't have many relatives. I'm from Arizona—Phoenix."

Angela didn't appear interested in a genealogical relationship with me. "I don't know," she said. "We're from Washington state, originally. I don't think we'd be related." The silence sat heavily for a moment.

Well, that bit of awkward small talk is over, I thought with chagrin. Martha appeared to be the more friendly of my new acquaintances, so I turned to her. She showed me the serving table and I loaded my plate, saying a silent blessing on my food.

She said, "Sit here by me. I'm just starting, and Angela's almost finished."

Angela agreed. "Yeah, I've got to get busy. I'm what's called a 'house maid.' I dust and I clean toilets. Gross! I took this job for the summer and, believe me, it's my last maid's job." Angela stood up, took her dishes toward the kitchen, and said without looking back, "See ya, later."

"It *is* hard to get good help these days," Martha joked, making certain Angela was out of hearing range.

Martha's gray-blue eyes reflected warmth, and the salt and pepper of her hair reminded me of my mother. I was so glad I'd found someone in the strange house that I could like and who might even like me.

"Angela's determined and college-bound, and more power to her," Martha added.

"I understand—I graduated four years ago from Arizona State University and was ready to change the world. Somehow that didn't work out."

"Why did you move to California?"

"Oh, I planned to meet Robert Redford, Clint Eastwood, and Paul Newman," I said, and laughed. However, Martha's lack of response made me wonder if she knew who they were. Then I thought I'd explain. "I mean, I'm in love with the movie and theater world—silly California dreams I guess, but I was raised on movies. My mother took me to almost every new film after my father died. It was her escape, I suppose, from her difficult life. She's gone—she died before I finished college, but in so many ways she's with me every day." I realized I'd shared something personal a little too early and there was an awkward pause. "Anyway, I didn't mean to rattle on. I just thought I'd like to try the California scene—and, with few exceptions, I like it here."

"Well, you know, you're one of thousands who've had the same dreams. This house was built on those dreams. But sometimes dreams can turn to . . ."

She didn't finish, so I tried to draw her out. "You were about to say?"

"Oh nothing, dear." She looked around as if she were afraid someone was listening. "I've said too much—I always do. You see, we're under strict orders here to mind our business regarding the family." She warned, "I've lived here long enough to know it's a very good policy to follow." She paused and clasped and unclasped her hands, seeming very concerned about something. Then she looked at me again. "I'm sorry," she said. "We were talking about you. You've been teaching?"

"Yes, but I felt like a failure. I mean, I could handle the subject matter and the preparation, but my problem was discipline. I just couldn't keep control of a roomful of thirty kids."

"I can imagine that would be difficult."

"Another teacher said I was too soft on them. So last year I tried to be a witch—but that wasn't me. When I saw the ad for a teacher of one eight-year-old boy, I thought I could still teach, but one on one."

"I hope you'll have a better experience with Master Paul. I must warn you, though, he goes through teachers in a hurry."

I tried not to look too startled. "What do you mean?"

"I mean that he's had several teachers each year for the past two years."

"Why?"

"Well, it isn't entirely his fault that his teachers leave. This big old house can be a lonely place for a single person." She looked down at her plate. "I know. But I'm used to it. This has been my home every day for almost thirty years."

"You don't ever leave?"

"No, dear, I have nowhere to go—no family or friends to visit."

"I'm sorry. I'm keeping my apartment in Sherman Oaks. I plan to go there on weekends."

"Well that sounds quite ideal for you then, but Horstman House is my home. It's my *only* security." She sighed and stood. "I have some duties upstairs. Maybe we'll meet again—sometime."

"I hope so. Thanks for talking with me. You're the first friendly person I've met here," I said.

"Well, don't let Ingrid get you down." She looked behind her, then spoke in a whisper, "She's been a thorn in the side of others in your position. I'm sure she thinks that no one else is good enough to teach Master Paul."

"Thanks for the warning. I'll try not to let her get to me."

"Thatta girl," Martha said, gathering her dishes and going toward the kitchen.

I stood. "Just one more question, Miss Wright."

Martha stopped in the kitchen doorway. "Call me Martha, and I'll call you Wendy. Okay?"

"Yes, fine. Is your room located near mine?" I asked.

"Yes, I'm right across the hall. If you need something, just knock. Of course, I'm only there at night."

"What exactly do you do?"

"I'm assigned to the third floor."

"But I thought no one was allowed to go there."

"Oh, I have little contact with Madame Horstman. I'm not allowed in her private chambers, except to clean her rooms at specified times. She 'vants to be alone.'"

I laughed, glad to find someone with a sense of humor. "All you do is clean her bathroom?"

"No, I dust and vacuum. I pick up her food trays sent up from the kitchen on the dumbwaiter—then I set them on a table beside her door and knock. I do the same with linens and clothing she sends out to be cleaned. The rest of the time I am required to wait in a small sitting room at the top of the third-floor back stairs—for her summons."

"It must be boring."

"It is sometimes," she said as she got up to leave. "I just wait in case I'm ever needed. But I rarely am. I do my needlework, watch television, and read to pass the time."

"A television set? Do you suppose I could join you sometime?"

Martha hurried back into the room. "Oh, no—*absolutely no!*"

She seemed so alarmed at my suggestion that I wanted to withdraw it. "I didn't mean to intrude on . . ."

"Oh, I'm sorry, dear. I didn't intend to be rude. It's just that—I'm sure Ingrid must have told you—no staff member is allowed on the third floor. It's a strict rule. I go there only with specific orders which I follow faithfully. And, of course, I've been here for a long time . . . perhaps too long," she said absently.

"Yes, of course, Ingrid told me about the third floor, and I wouldn't want to get you in trouble."

I thought it odd how frightened she had seemed, and then how very relieved. "Thanks, dear," she whispered. Then she glanced about furtively and tried to smile, but her worried eyes belied her smile. She exited to the kitchen, leaving me wondering about Martha's real feelings regarding Horstman House and its inhabitants.

I tried to shake my own worried mood and finished my breakfast. The information about Paul and my "supervisor," Ingrid, upset me. I wondered how long I'd last as Paul's teacher. I carried my dishes to the kitchen. There was no sign of Blanche, so I followed the others' example and put my dishes in the big sink.

I climbed the back stairs to the second floor, stopped in the bathroom to make certain there was no egg on my face, and went to the main hall. It was eight-fifty; I was on time. I walked down the long hall toward the schoolroom feeling like a little girl again.

Martha had told me not to let Ingrid get me down. I said another silent prayer for courage, insight, and self-control. Then I breathed deeply, lifted my shoulders, and repeated Martha's "Thatta girl!" with the same humor *and* my own determination not to let this strange house get to me.

The classroom door was closed. *Should I knock? No, after all this is my classroom.* I opened the door, finding the room empty. I stepped inside the darkened, musty space and went to the window. Locating a draw cord for the heavy drapes, I opened them wide. I tried the window, but it was either fastened or stuck shut. Another thing I'd have to discuss with Ingrid—*Miss Nourse*, I corrected myself. The room needed an airing in more than one way.

At exactly nine Ingrid entered, reluctantly followed by Paul—a thin, pale, dark-haired boy, with big brown-black eyes. He was small for his age, and was dressed in a gray suit with short pants, a white shirt, a black tie, and black knee-high stockings. *Well, he looks like a proper schoolboy*, I thought with sarcasm. It seemed obvious that Paul hadn't had much say in selecting his clothing. He was dressed like a nineteenth-century English boy and he didn't look happy about it. My kids in public school, with their longer hair and flare-legged pants, would have teased him mercilessly.

Ingrid made formal introductions, pulling me from my thoughts. "Miss Wood, this is Master Paul. Paul, what do you say to your tutor, Miss Wood?"

Paul didn't move or look up. He said quietly, "How do you do, Miss Wood."

"Hello, Paul," I responded, wanting to say more, but not knowing how to break the ice with Ingrid present. I found myself pitying him instead of being angry that he'd snuck into my room.

Ingrid crossed to behind the teacher's desk to show me its contents. "There are paper and pencils in the desk and chalk in the blackboard tray. Paul's books are in his desk. You will teach the basic subjects—reading, writing, and arithmetic. On occasion, for diversion, you may read history and scientific texts which I will provide from the first-floor library. No children's or adult literature, no art, no music need be taught. Master Paul studies piano with a private tutor who comes to Horstman House each Saturday morning."

I interrupted, "But Ingrid—Miss Nourse—I'd like to organize our curriculum after I've done some evaluation of Paul's abilities, of course. I'd assumed that I'd be doing the planning."

"Miss Wood," Ingrid condescended, "I am well acquainted with modern ideas about education. But I wish you to know that I was governess and teacher to Paul's father, Mr. Horstman, and he has given strict orders that my recommendations regarding Paul's training be followed."

"Well, of course, I'll do as you ask." I had said too much, I realized, so I changed the subject. "I was wondering, could we get that window fixed so that it will open, and could I hang a few pictures to brighten up this room a bit?"

Paul looked up for the first time.

"Miss Wood, the schoolroom is a place for concentration without distraction," Ingrid insisted. "It will remain as it is. But I will have someone check the window. It must be stuck with paint."

It must have been stuck for years, then. The cold gray paint looked very faded. "Well, we'll just have to get by with some fresh air," I said. "Won't we, Paul?"

Paul looked down again. Maybe he thought that taking sides with me against Ingrid wasn't a good idea. He said nothing. He seemed very restrained in Ingrid's presence.

Ingrid continued. "As I said before, the specified curriculum will be followed as will your instructional schedule for each day, Monday through Friday, nine to three. It's in the center desk drawer. Follow it implicitly. Again if you need books or materials, please contact me."

"Where will I find you?"

"My office and private quarters are on this floor, to the right just before the central stairways. Knock! Now, Master Paul, please step out in the hallway. There are some private instructions for Miss Wood."

Paul left dutifully without looking back. Ingrid moved to close the door, where she remained standing.

"Miss Wood, Mr. Horstman has instructed me to tell you that several subjects are forbidden in your conversation with Master Paul."

"But I—"

"You will listen carefully. Others have failed to follow these instructions and have, in due course, been relieved of their teaching assignments here. Mr. Horstman is paying you well and expects to be obeyed—as do I."

"Well, of course, I'll do all I can to satisfy you and Mr. Horstman."

"Good. Then listen carefully. There must be no discussion with Master Paul of his deceased mother or the circumstances of her death."

"But I would think it would be good for him to talk about her— under the circumstances. Any child who has suffered that kind of loss needs to—"

"I am giving you instructions which must be followed. If you cannot, then pack your suitcase!"

I said nothing more in protest, feeling certain that I wouldn't be able to tolerate this woman or this job.

"There is one more subject, Miss Wood, which you will *not* discuss with Master Paul—his grandmother, Madame Horstman. She requires complete privacy, both from outsiders and those whom she permits inside her house." She stepped closer to me and looked directly in my eyes. "You will not discuss Madame Horstman with Master Paul!"

"Surely, his own grandmother wouldn't want to avoid her grandson. Isn't it natural that Paul would be curious about her, living in the same house but kept from knowing her?"

She stepped closer. "That is none of your affair. The question is, are you willing to follow these restrictions?"

"Well, yes—if that's what Mr. Horstman wants."

"I assure you it is." She returned to her post by the door.

"But how will I avoid the subjects if Paul brings them up?"

"I suggest that you simply ignore personal questions and stay with the curriculum. That's your job."

In disgust I thought, *Teachers teach human beings, not robots,* but I knew it would do no good telling her that.

Ingrid rested her hand on the doorknob, suggesting that our conversation was over. "I trust we understand each other. Now, I will invite Master Paul to come in and you may begin teaching. Lunch will be served here in the schoolroom at twelve noon."

I'd hoped for a break at noon so that I could call Jill, but Paul was apparently to be my responsibility throughout the day.

Ingrid led Paul in and turned to leave.

Without thinking of Paul's possible reaction, I said, "Oh, just one more thing. I need some change for the pay phone, unless there's another phone I can use."

Paul crossed sheepishly to the window. I really hadn't meant to bring up the missing change that way.

Ingrid surprised me by opening an old-fashioned coin purse attached to her apron strings. "How much change do you need?"

"Oh, I guess—about two dollars in nickels and dimes should do," I stammered, pulling dollar bills from my purse. I realized that I would indeed be using the pay phone on a regular basis since it was evident that all employees had to use the pay phone. Ingrid clicked out the coins like a penny-arcade change maker, and then she carefully folded my one-dollar bills in her change purse. She counted out the money in my hand, then turned to leave.

"Miss Nourse, is there a phone number I can give to people who want to reach me here? I don't expect that anyone would answer the ringing pay phone in the hall."

"Yes, they may call my office. I'll write down the number." She took a notepad from her apron pocket and a pencil from behind her ear, wrote down the number, and thrust the paper at me. "I trust that outsiders won't be calling often."

"No, for now I just wanted to give my roommate—former roommate—a number in case of emergency. There may be a few others who will want to call later, but for now, that's all." I didn't think this was the time to explain that my bishop and home teachers from

Sherman Oaks might want to call. I was sure she wouldn't understand the need. I'd wait for another time when she wasn't so irritated.

Ingrid opened the door, but I remembered one more thing. "Could I make one more request before you go? The tub in the servants' bathroom is very slippery. Could you talk to someone about getting a safety rail installed or placing some safety strips in the tub?"

"Humph! I'll see what I can do." Ingrid nodded curtly and left, closing the door behind her.

I sighed with relief. Now, how to bridge the gap between Paul and me? I couldn't ignore the problem of his visit to my room. I crossed to behind him at the window, leaning back on the edge of my desk. "Paul, I'm excited about our chance to learn together. Do you have anything you'd like to say to me before we start?"

Paul didn't turn to me. His shoulders were shaking, and I heard his quiet sobs.

I took him by the shoulders and turned him around. Those dark eyes were bright with tears. "Paul, I want to be your friend and your teacher, so we have to talk about your visit to my room last night."

"Thanks," he said quietly, then sighed and turned away, averting his eyes.

I waited patiently for him to continue, but he said nothing. "What do you mean—thanks?" He still didn't respond. I stood, moved to between him and the window, and sat on the window sill to get down to his level. "Paul, I'm not angry. I just want you to explain your actions."

He didn't turn from me again and finally spoke. "Well, I meant . . . thanks . . . for not telling Ingrid," he whispered.
"Well, I thought you and I should discuss it privately."

He slowly reached his hand into the pocket of his coat and brought out a handful of change. "This is the money I took from your purse. I'm sorry." He put the coins in my hand, still looking down at the floor.

"Thanks for returning the money, Paul, and for your apology. It's accepted. But we still have a problem. Why did you come into my room and why did you take the money?"

He was silent for a moment, then turned away. "Paul, as I said, I'm not angry but I do need an explanation for your behavior."

"Well—I went there to see you—to look at you. My last teacher looked a lot like Ingrid."

I almost smiled, but controlled myself and turning him around, looked directly into his eyes. "But my door was closed."

He squirmed and lightly kicked the floor nervously with the toe of his shoe. "I know. I knocked, and the door just opened. So I looked in. You weren't there, and then I saw your purse on the bed."

"Yes, go on."

"It was wrong, I know, but I wanted to see if there was a picture of you in your wallet. I opened the purse and found your wallet with a picture on your driver's license. I was glad—you're pretty."

I couldn't help being pleased at his compliment. "Okay, I understand why you came into my room and why you opened my purse. Now, how about the money?"

"Well, I hadn't seen that much money all at once. I wasn't going to steal it. I was just holding it. Then I heard you coming, so I got scared and jumped under your bed. When you looked under the bed, I . . . ran. I didn't remember the money in my hand until I got to my room." He looked as if he were about to cry again. "I was afraid you'd tell Ingrid or my father. Ingrid would punish me if she knew I'd gone into your room."

"Have you learned anything from all this?"

"Yes, I won't ever go into someone's room when they're not there."

"And?"

"And I won't ever get into anyone's things again." He looked up at me. "I really wasn't going to take anything."

I stood. "I know, you were just *too* curious for your own good."

Paul moved to his desk and sat down. He looked relieved. "I couldn't sleep all night worrying about what you'd do," he said.

"I didn't sleep so well, myself. But we can't leave this problem until I'm sure you know you did wrong."

"I promise I've learned a lesson." He ducked his head, sheepishly.

"Well, I believe you." I sat at my desk. Interesting that I was calling the depressing-looking thing, mine. "Do you want to tell me more about yourself? Do you like to read?"

"Yeah, I *like* to read," he said, "but I'm not very good at it."

"Who told you that?"

"Oh, Ingrid—and my last three teachers."

"How many teachers have you had?"

"Only five—in two years," he finished, red-faced and looking up to see my reaction.

I remembered Martha's comment about Paul's having had a lot of teachers, but I was shocked to hear he'd had five. "Five teachers in two years. I might have thought you'd had as many as two—but five?"

"Yeah, I know. Father and Ingrid are mad at me. Father says I purposely try to get rid of them, and Ingrid thinks I'm a spoiled brat."

"Well, *did* you drive them away?" *Poor kid thinks it's all his fault,* I thought angrily while keeping the frustration out of my tone.

"No, but I didn't like any of them. They were too much like Ingrid. All they wanted to do was please her."

"I can understand that, can't you?" I asked, thinking of my own need to please her.

"Yes, but why did they have to make everything so boring?"

"Learning can't always be play, you know. Sometimes it takes hard work."

He stood at the front of his desk. "Oh, I don't mind that. It's better than sitting alone all day. But can't we have *any* fun?"

"Learning's the greatest fun there is, and I still have a lot to learn about teaching. It would be great if we could learn together, wouldn't it?"

He looked startled at my suggestion. "Yeah, that sounds better, anyway."

I felt better too. The dreaded encounter with Paul was over. Now, if I could help him . . . If I could be his friend. But could I keep Ingrid from interfering?

Chapter Four

The first day of teaching Paul went rather well. I didn't have formal testing instruments but realized that Paul did, indeed, have some problems with reading. He had an excellent speaking vocabulary, however, and a natural aptitude for mathematics—or arithmetic, as Ingrid called it—and probably was working math problems at a third-grade level. When I asked Paul to write a few sentences about something he enjoyed doing, it took him a long time to think and even longer to write about it. His subject? Playing Solitaire. Apparently Angela, the temporary housemaid, had kindly taught him something that he could play—alone.

Paul and I ate lunch together in the classroom; it was delivered by Blanche at noon on a tray. Blanche was still polite but impersonal. The food was good—lean ham sandwiches and a green salad, juice for me, and milk for Paul. After lunch, more evaluation of Paul's strengths and weaknesses consumed the hours. Before I knew it, it was three.

Paul interrupted my thoughts, shyly asking, "Could I use the bathroom?"

I realized we hadn't had a break. "I would guess so! Do you know we've been in this room since nine o'clock? Will you show me where a rest room is?"

"Oh, there isn't one for everyone to use. You have to go back to your bathroom. So do I." He stood and hurried toward the door.

I followed. "By the way, where is your room, Paul?"

"On this floor. The first door on the left when you leave the servants' hall. That's why—" He looked at the floor.

I smiled. "Yes, I know—that's why you were able to get away so fast last night."

"Yeah, right." He smiled, but with just enough guilt to keep me from being angry.

We walked together down the long hall. "Maybe you could show me around the house, Paul—the first and second floors?"

"Sure," he said, more concerned about getting to the bathroom than about conversation.

We met no one in the corridor, and I left Paul at his room, instructing him to meet me there in ten minutes. I went to the bathroom in the servants' hall to freshen up. Then I hurried to my room. This job had one perk, I realized as I opened the door—maid service. My bed had been made, and the room tidied up. *How can this continue if I get a lock on my door?* I wondered.

I left my room and, passing the pay phone, looked forward to the chance to call Jill and tell her about my first twenty-four hours at Horstman House. I found Paul waiting outside his door.

"That was a relief," he said.

"I agree. From now on we'll plan a ten-minute break each morning and afternoon. Remind me, and if you need a break at anytime, just ask. Okay?"

"Okay."

I was pleased to sense him walking close beside me. We'd be friends after all, and he seemed to need a friend. "Now, Paul, it would be great if you could give me a tour so I won't get lost in this big place."

"Well, there are a lot of places where I—where we—can't go. I can't go up on the third floor."

"I've been told that, Paul. So let's not worry about it. Okay?"

"Here are my father's rooms, just across from Ingrid's. He has a whole lot of rooms in the front of the house. We can't go in there when he's away, and I don't want to go in Ingrid's office, do you?"

"No, I don't. Just so I know where it is."

"Well, that's all, the servants' rooms, my room, Ingrid's office, and Dad's place—oh, and the schoolroom—but that's the second floor. The first floor's better." He took my hand and pulled me back toward the central stairways leading down to the first floor.

"You said 'Dad' just now, when you were talking about your father's rooms."

"Oh, I'm not supposed to call him that unless we're alone. Ingrid says I must call him Father."

"Well, that's fine, so long as you can call him Dad when you're together."

"I can. He doesn't mind."

Mind? Why would a father mind being called "Dad"? Paul's father wasn't on the forbidden discussion list, so as we wound down the long, heavily carpeted marble stairs to the first floor, I asked, "Do you and your father—your dad—spend much time together?"

"No," he replied without emotion. "He's very busy." Then he bounced down the last few stairs. Paul seemed happier just being with someone who treated him as if he had worth, like a human being—a child.

"Do you have any special times together?"

"Sometimes at night—not very often—he calls me into his place and we talk."

"That's good. Do you ever have special outings? Do you have fun times?"

"Well, last spring he took me to his office."

"And?"

"That's all. He's very busy."

Too busy to realize that his eight-year-old son is a very lonely little boy, I thought, in frustration. "I'll have to talk to him about that when I see him again," I said.

"Oh, have you met my father? Most of my teachers don't, you know."

"Yes, we've met." I realized I couldn't tell him the circumstances of the meeting.

Paul stopped on the first floor at the foot of the stairs. "Well, what do you want to see first?" he asked.

"Oh, I don't know. Why don't we just start at one end of this main hall and move to the other?"

"Okay, let's go to the dining room." We went down the long, elegant corridor, which had so impressed me when I'd arrived.

"Do you know anything about these lovely paintings?" I asked.

"No, I just look at them. Some of them I like—some I don't."

"Well, you have a real art collection here, Paul," I said, looking at a Gainesborough portrait. "I think it might be fun to learn something about the artists and their paintings. Would you like that?"

"Yes, but Ingrid wouldn't."

"Oh, we'll find a way to tie art to history—In fact, I studied art history as one of my minor fields in college and learned that every artist lived in a special time period, and their paintings reveal their world, so we can learn some history too. Do you think that might make it all right?"

"Well, I guess so, but maybe it better be our secret."

"Okay—our secret, for now at least." I didn't see why I had to justify including the arts in our studies, but so be it, I decided.

We reached the arched doorway of a formal dining room located at the end of the corridor. I gasped at the beauty of the room. Long, narrow windows were hung with Prussian curtains in a soft rose-color that draped the outside wall. The walls were pale green, decorated by ivory and gold chair rail and crown moldings. On the wall opposite the windows was a huge marble fireplace, and above it hung a large oil portrait. I recognized at once that it was the great Bella. I was drawn by her wild eyes, her blown hair, the sultry pose, and the ancient Greek costume. I silently read the engraved plate at the base of the painting: *The Glittering Counterfeit.* *Bella Horstman as Phaedra. Hippolytus: "Great Zeus, why didst thou Place women, evil counterfeits, to glitter in the light of the sun?"*

"The Glittering Counterfeit," I whispered. *Strange,* I thought, *that Bella chose to entitle her portrait this way. Maybe it's how she felt about her life as an actress . . .*

My fascination with the portrait was broken by Paul's words, "That's my grandmother."

"Yes, I know, Paul. It's exciting, isn't it?"

"I—I don't like it."

I looked at him in surprise. "Why? Why don't you like it?"

"It scares me. Every painting of her in this house scares me."

"There are others?"

"Yes, there's one in almost every room on this floor. I wish Dad would take them down."

I knew we were starting to tread on forbidden ground so I spoke quietly and chose my words carefully. "Hmm, but you understand that your grandmother is—was—an actress? This painting is not your grandmother in real life. She was painted as a character in a play."

"I know but I've never seen her in real life. The paintings are the only way I know her, and she looks mean in all of them."

"Well, I'm sure she isn't mean. She just acted the roles of evil women. They were her specialty."

He asked, "Don't you think some of those actors play people who are like them?"

His insight surprised me. "Well, it's possible, but there are many nice people who are actors. I'm sure your grandmother is one of them."

"But why won't she see anyone? Why won't she see me? Or Dad? Why can't we go into her part of the house?" The pent-up questions came flooding out.

I was now firmly footed on forbidden ground and began trying to end the conversation without hurting Paul's feelings. "Well, I don't have answers to those questions, Paul. Your grandmother is very old, and I'm sure she must have good reasons for her actions. Sometimes when people have spent their lives in the public eye, they crave solitude more than anything."

"I don't know what you mean."

"I mean that she spent her life before the public, both as an actress and in her everyday life. Everyone knew all sorts of personal things about her. Now, she doesn't want everyone watching her and interfering in her business anymore. She wants to be alone." I smiled at my unconscious quoting of a Garbo character, as Martha had earlier, but when I looked at Paul's sad face it didn't seem funny anymore. "I'm sorry, Paul. I understand you would like to know your grandmother. Maybe that's something you should tell your father."

"I have."

"I guess we'll have to leave it at that, then. Let's talk about something happier. You were going to show me the rest of the first floor."

He seemed reluctant to change the subject, but returned his attention to the dining room. "Well, this is where I eat dinner. Blanche or Angela bring my breakfast to my room. You know about lunch."

I admired the long, dark mahogany table with ornate chairs for fourteen places. A big, lonely table for one little boy. A magnificent silver service was set on a mahogany buffet at one end of the room. A large china cabinet displayed crystal and china at the opposite end where double doors led to Blanche's kitchen. I glanced at the massive crystal chandelier above the table and then looked down at Paul.

"Let's continue the tour," I suggested.

"Okay, these rooms are all open." He led me into the main hall and opened a tall door. "They're all about the same, except for this one. It has a desk. I guess it belonged to my Grandfather Horstman. This was his office when he was home. He's dead now."

I wanted to ask more about his grandfather, Bella's former husband, but decided that questions might again lead to taboo subjects. I already knew that the great Daniel Horstman II, whose portrait was labeled in his office, had inherited a mining fortune and then added oil and railroad holdings to his wealth. I had learned that much from a brief newspaper clip about his divorce from Bella. I looked at his portrait very closely—a somber thin-faced man, like his son Daniel, with dark hair that was gray at the temples, and a mustache. A conservative contrast to the fiery, exotic painting of Bella in the dining room. Maybe that's why he left her—a poor match? I then wondered which parent Daniel Horstman III took after. *He resembles his handsome father, but which is he more like in his temperament? And why should you care so much?* I suddenly asked myself.

Paul touched my hand, bringing me back to the present. "I like this room but I can't play in it," he said.

I looked at a billiard table and the large, old leather chairs and sofa, which must have provided a comfortable retreat for Daniel II and his guests. A bar, presently unfurnished, was at one end of the sofa. Behind the straight-backed, wood-and-leather desk chair, one long window competed with another portrait of Bella, this time as Lady Macbeth holding a candle. Had Bella been an ambitious Lady Macbeth, driving her husband to heights and depths? Was that how he had seen her? Had *he* chosen the portrait for his office, or had Bella?

"Let's go to the library," Paul suggested, going out into the main corridor. "We could look in these other rooms, but they just have chairs and tables—and more paintings of Grandmother."

We passed a formally furnished drawing room, the grand front entry hall and stairways, and came to double doors opposite the narrow hall where only yesterday I had followed the driver, Helman.

Paul pushed down a gilt handle that opened a door revealing one of the most beautiful rooms I had seen—a Louis XIV library with antique chairs, sofas, desk, and tables. The walls were lined with book collections in marvelously varied bindings. Tall windows, draped only at the sides, provided abundant reading light and views of the gardens. A ladder was mounted on a railing encircling the entire room, promising access to all the books. There was a warmth here that I had seen nowhere else in the house.

"Oh, Paul!" I exclaimed. "This is a wonderful library. It's my favorite room in the house."

"Dad says it's his favorite place too. He comes here a lot when he's home but he's told me not to bother him when he's in here."

He's not supposed to bother him? When is he allowed to bother his father? My concern grew to anger. How could such a sweet little boy be kept at a distance from the only family he had? There were all the possibilities of a full life here, but Paul was kept from taking advantage of it by an uncaring, self-centered father and grandmother—and by their devoted Ingrid.

I turned to Paul, knelt, put my hands on his shoulders, and looked at him directly. "I'm sorry, Paul, that your life has been so lonely. Maybe we can change that."

Paul seemed surprised at my expression of concern and started to pull away. Then he smiled happily and, before I could stop him, reached out and hugged me around the neck—just as Ingrid entered the library.

Chapter Five

Ingrid stopped in the doorway. "What is going on here?" she fumed.

Paul jumped at the sound of Ingrid's voice and ran behind me. I looked up to see Ingrid, with Helman standing behind her. I stood and asked, "What do you mean 'what is going on here?' I was expressing concern for Paul's welfare, and he gave me a hug. That's all there was to it. There's nothing to be upset about."

Paul moved closely behind me for protection from Ingrid's stare.

Ingrid walked directly toward me. "I gave explicit instructions that you were to remain in the schoolroom and that, if necessary, I would bring books and materials to you."

"Paul was just showing me the house. We quit the schoolroom at about three; it's three-thirty now. We're touring on our own time."

"Perhaps I did not make myself clear. You are to remain on the second floor. And this display of affection between teacher and pupil is most inappropriate."

I was about to defend myself when I was shocked to see Mr. Horstman in the doorway behind Helman and Ingrid. Obviously he had heard Ingrid's last remark.

"Ingrid, is there some problem here?" he asked.

Helman stepped back to clear the way, and Ingrid, taken off guard at first, turned quickly to see Mr. Horstman. "Yes, sir, there *is* a problem. I gave instructions to Miss Wood to keep her activities to the second floor and to be discreet in her relationship with Master Paul. I not only found her here in the library but found her embracing your son."

"But that's not true," I protested.

"That will be all for now, Ingrid," Mr. Horstman said, dismissing her. "I'll discuss this matter with you later, after I have talked with Miss Wood."

Ingrid left in a huff, followed submissively by Helman.

Pausing, perhaps to make certain that Ingrid was out of earshot, Mr. Horstman looked sternly, first at Paul, then at me. "Now, could you explain, Miss Wood, why you didn't follow Ingrid's instructions?"

"Well, maybe I didn't understand them," I began. "I understood that the third floor was off limits but had no idea that I was restricted entirely to the second-floor schoolroom and my room."

"Yes, I believe I saw you exploring the grounds on your first evening here."

"I'm sorry. I just needed some fresh air and—"

"Oh, never mind. I suppose we're so accustomed to our sedate lives here that we've become overprotective," he added, speaking quietly so that Paul wouldn't hear. "And Ingrid tends to be a rather firm disciplinarian with *all* of us."

"Well, I certainly meant no harm, but I don't think I can live and teach here without some degree of freedom."

He asked, "Should that freedom extend to embracing my son?"

Paul stepped from behind me. "Dad—Father, I hugged her because she was trying to make me feel better."

"I'm discussing this matter with Miss Wood, Paul. It might be better if you go to your room for a while before dinner."

Paul looked at me. "It will be all right, Paul," I said. "I'll see you later."

"You—you won't leave, will you?"

"No, I won't leave, at least not tonight. Don't worry, I'll be in the classroom tomorrow at nine if I don't see you sooner."

"Okay, if you promise." Paul backed toward the door, disappearing down the hall.

Paul was so lonely and so insecure. I'd have to defend him *and* myself, I realized. There was an awkward silence, which I broke, my anger giving me courage. "It's true, you know. Your son is a *very* lonely little boy. I was just trying to cheer him up."

"Is that the way teachers behave in the public schools now?" he asked, more quizzically than seriously.

"Well, this situation is a bit different from a school. I'm alone with Paul all day and I appear to be the only friend he has."

"Oh, you needn't defend yourself on that score. I personally checked your references. You see I *do* care for my son. You're wondering about that, aren't you? I'm simply surprised that you became so close so soon. Hugging the first day?" He smiled, more amused than sincere.

"We *have* become good friends already. I'm glad of that."

He gestured toward a sofa. "Should we sit?" he asked.

I walked to the sofa, then turned back to look at him. In daylight I could see his dark eyes—Paul's eyes—and his narrow, strong face. Jill was right; he was very handsome. "I know that you care for Paul," I said, sitting. "And he obviously idolizes you. It's just that this big house, with its many rules, seems a very cold place for a young boy."

"Believe me, I know all about that." He relaxed across from me in an armchair.

"Have you considered a private school, or even public school, for Paul?"

He sat upright. "Certainly not. I believe in tutorial training in the primary years. When Paul is older, he will, of course, attend the best private school and have the best university training available. In the meantime, you would do well to concentrate on being his tutor and following Ingrid's directions."

"Miss Nourse was your teacher, too, I assume."

"Yes, she was. My mother hired her about thirty-five years ago, as a housekeeper. Then, when another teacher suddenly left Horstman House, Ingrid began tutoring me, when I was five."

"Then you were happy with her instructional approaches?"

"Happy? Happiness has nothing to do with it, does it? I simply want Paul to learn the basics he'll need for life. That's what Ingrid emphasizes."

"Do you think those basics are learned only in the classroom?"

He looked at me with irritation. "I'm tiring of this discussion, Miss Wood. Simply follow Ingrid's directions, and you'll have no further problems."

"Then we can't use the library? Also, I was going to ask permission to eat my evening meal with Paul."

"Oh, I really see no valid reason why you can't have the run of the first floor, but why do you want to eat with Paul?"

"Well, I understand that you often eat out in the evening. That big dining room is a very lonely place for a little boy to eat by himself," I said with more reproach than I intended.

He looked down at his hands. "I see. Well, I find no problem in your joining Paul for dinner, but, remember, I don't want him spoiled."

"Do you think love and companionship spoil a child, Mr. Horstman?"

He looked at me and spoke softly, almost to himself. "Hmm. Well, yes, they can, especially if one grows up expecting love and then realizes that *no one* really has the capacity to give it fully. The love of self seems to rule the world, I'm afraid, and I think Paul needs to understand that—in order to survive."

I wanted to say more, to tell him what I really thought about his distancing himself from his son, but I had won a battle, at least. I decided to let well enough alone—for the time being.

"Then will you tell Miss Nourse that I have permission to use the library—and to eat with Paul in the evening?"

"Yes, I'll tell her. She won't like it, however, and Ingrid can be formidable. She's fired five teachers in the past two years, you know."

"Paul told me. That certainly can't be good for him either. He thinks he's totally responsible. But Miss Nourse may have met her match in me, Mr. Horstman. I already care about your son and I don't believe a constant change in teachers is what he needs." I stood. "May I ask one more thing? Will you promise me just one more thing?"

"What is that?"

I stepped toward him. "Please don't allow Ingrid to fire me summarily. If she decides that my work is unsatisfactory, will you discuss it with me and dismiss me yourself, if you find it necessary?"

He rose and walked away toward the windows. "I haven't handled those matters in the past. Ingrid directs the affairs of this house. She has since my mother . . . since my mother decided to become a recluse. I can't manage without Ingrid."

"But surely you could grant me that one thing—the privilege of talking with you before you'd fire me?"

He turned to me. "You're a very tenacious woman, Miss Wood. Yes, I'll explain your situation to Ingrid." He moved toward the door. "Now, if you'll excuse me, I have an appointment in town." Stopping in the doorway, he looked back at me and then down at my legs. He smiled, then left.

My eyes followed his to my stockings. I had a run from my knee to my ankle. *Well, so much for thinking he was admiring my legs.* I almost laughed out loud.

I felt some of the anxiety that had been with me since my arrival lift a little. I wasn't overjoyed by the small gains I'd made, but I hadn't done badly for one day.

I made my way to the stairs, planning to freshen up before dinner—this time at six, not seven—with my new friend, Paul.

Now, to call Jill, I thought excitedly, *but first, I'd better tell Blanche about the new dinner arrangements.*

Chapter Six

I went to Blanche's kitchen and she wasn't pleased with the news that dinner should be set for two in the family dining room. She rushed about complaining, "How do they think I can manage all these changes? Bring a tray here, Blanche. Set another place there, Blanche. I don't have enough help in this big kitchen as it is."

"I'm sorry," I offered, "but we, Mr. Horstman and I, decided that Paul shouldn't have to eat alone. I'll be glad to eat whatever you fix for him."

"Humph! If you ate what he wants, it would be peanut butter and jelly sandwiches every night." She threw her hands up in the air in disgust.

I smiled at her and stepped closer. "Well, I even like peanut butter and jelly, Blanche, and I'll help with our meals if you'd like."

"No one cooks in my kitchen but me," Blanche insisted, contradicting her earlier complaint about not enough help. She sighed. "It will be all right, I suppose. I'm sure you're right about the boy. He's alone too much."

"Thanks, Blanche." Responding to her unexpected moment of understanding, I pressed her hand, then headed for the back stairs and to the second-floor pay phone.

Climbing the stairs, I hoped Jill was home from work. I dropped a dime and nickel in the coin slot, dialed Jill's number, and added the coins requested by the operator. Jill's machine answered. It was the male voice of one of our friends she'd had record the message so no one would suspect that women lived there alone. When I heard the beep I said, "Jill, sorry I couldn't call last night. I'll explain later.

Things are fine here—not great, but okay." I gave Jill the number to call to leave a message. "I'll try to call back later. Love you." At least Jill would know that I was all right.

I went to my room. *I have nothing to do*, I thought, feeling extremely restless. It was only 5:00 P.M. I decided to write in my journal, and suddenly, it seemed, it was almost six. I closed my journal, straightened my clothes, and went to the bathroom to wash up. Then I went downstairs using the second-floor corridor and descending the main stairway. I made a grand *Gone With The Wind* entrance like Scarlett O'Hara. *There I go, always fantasizing*, I chided myself in good humor. I crossed the long main hall to the dining room where I found Paul, still dressed in his formal gray suit, seated at the head of the long table. My place had been set beside him to the right.

He smiled broadly when I entered and he stood up, pulling back my chair and holding it while I sat.

"Thank you, kind sir," I said. "You are indeed a gentleman."

"Yeah, Dad, I mean Father, taught me to be polite."

"Then he *has* taken some time with you?"

"Well, not exactly. He just told me to watch him when we have guests. I saw him do that for a lady who comes here sometimes. He said I should always be polite."

I was bothered at my level of interest in Paul's reference to a lady guest. "Does your father have guests—lady guests—often?"

"Oh, no. She's the wife of a friend of Dad's who died—the friend died, I mean, not the lady."

"Do you—like her?"

"Oh, she is okay. Kind of stuck-up though."

I felt an unexpected and momentary relief that the woman wasn't a regular visitor. Then I chastised myself for even entertaining the thought of a possible relationship with Daniel, not just because of the difference in our ages and situations, but because he didn't seem to know how to be a father. And he wasn't LDS I reminded myself. I knew better than to allow a physical attraction to influence my emotions. Besides, I guessed I should be glad that Paul had contact with someone, with anyone, from the outside. I decided to leave it at that. "Well, the salad is served. It looks good. Shall we give thanks and say a blessing on the food?"

He looked surprised. "Yeah, I guess. We've never done that before," he said.

"I'm sorry, Paul. Prayer is so much a part of my life I sometimes forget that others may not find it customary."

Was I encroaching on another taboo in suggesting that we offer grace at our meals? No one had ruled that we shouldn't pray in this house, but would it be inappropriate to introduce Paul to prayer without consulting with his father first? After all, I'd been given permission to dine with Paul and I certainly had the right and the need to pray. In answer to my doubts, a sweet spirit of peace, accompanied by Paul's innocent, questioning eyes, told me that praying with him that evening could do no harm. I'd talk with Mr. Horstman about his views on prayer at the first opportunity.

Paul seemed to be waiting for me to act. "It's okay. I didn't say that I don't want to pray. I just don't know how to do it," he explained.

"Well, if it's all right with you, I'll pray then."

"Yeah, it's okay," he said with obvious curiosity.

Paul followed my example, bowing his head and folding his arms. He seemed awed by the new experience. I offered a simple prayer of thanks and asked the Lord to bless our food and to bless us.

When I was finished, he asked, "Do you always pray when you eat?"

"Yes, if I can. Sometimes I pray silently when I'm in public situations," I said. "And I also pray night and morning—and whenever I feel I need the Lord's help."

"Does He really help you?" he asked.

"Yes, He does, Paul. He answers my prayers—and I believe that He would answer yours too."

He didn't respond but sat quietly thinking. I decided I might have said too much and returned my attention to our meal. "Shall we eat?"

He looked up and smiled. "Yes. I'm sure glad Dad let us eat together."

"I am too. I didn't like waiting till seven to eat and I had to eat alone last night."

"It's no fun eating alone." He dug into the salad with enthusiasm.

"If all goes well, we can keep company every weekday evening except Fridays."

"Why not Fridays?"

"Well, I've kept my place in Sherman Oaks, and I'll leave Friday afternoons. Then I'll go to church Sunday mornings and return late on Sunday evenings."

He was downcast. "Sherman Oaks? How far away is that?"

"It's only about an hour away on the freeways. Unless traffic is heavy." I tried to reassure him that it wasn't too far away but he didn't seem convinced.

"I've only been on a freeway once," he said.

"You have?"

"The only time I left Pasadena was to go to Dad's work in L.A."

I was shocked to realize that Paul had seen less of his world than many less fortunate children. "Well, maybe we can do something about that."

"Could we? Do you think I could go with you to Sherman Oaks?"

"I don't know about that, Paul. We'll have to take it slowly. I wouldn't want to upset Ingrid—or your father. Maybe sometime, in the future, you could come on a Sunday and go to church with us."

"Church? I've never been to church either. Why do you go?" he asked.

"Well, it's very important to me. I go there to show my Savior—Jesus Christ—that I love Him and want to obey His commandments. I go there to take His sacrament. Do you know about that?"

"No. I've read some stories about Jesus, but no one has ever really told me anything about Him. I know that Christmas is supposed to be His birthday. But we don't even celebrate Christmas that much," he said.

"Paul, I don't want to do or say anything that your father wouldn't approve of. If I stay here long enough, maybe I can talk with him about how he feels regarding religion in your life. But I'd have to have his permission to teach you about that. Okay? I hope that you understand."

"Yeah, I understand," he said, dropping his chin.

"I was able to talk your father into letting us use the library and eat together. Later on, I'll talk to him about church and about some field trips."

"What are field trips?"

"That just means that we travel to some special places to experience new things firsthand. Libraries, or museums, or parks. Maybe even church-related experiences. But don't get your hopes too high. I'll work on it, okay?"

He brightened. "Yeah, that's great. I'll try to wait."

We finished our salads, and Paul rang a little bell at his side. Instead of Blanche, to my surprise, Angela appeared to gather our plates. "You two eating together now, huh? Well that's a first."

"Angela, I didn't know you help out in the kitchen, too," I said.

"Well, I'm usually gone before now. But Blanche complained that she needed help, so I was recruited." Angela didn't seem too happy about her new duty. "Well, I guess it's okay. I can use the extra money, and it's just for the summer. That's what keeps me going." She left with our salad plates and returned with hot rolls, a marvelous chicken entree, and French-cut green beans.

"Just ring, when you're ready for dessert, *Master* Paul." Angela giggled, exiting to the kitchen.

Paul pulled a face. "She knows I don't like it when they call me 'Master Paul,'" he explained.

"I was a bit surprised at that formal title, too, but I suppose it's your father's way of making you feel grown-up."

"No, it's Ingrid's idea. She called Dad 'Master Daniel' when he was little."

Ingrid was living in the past, I thought. "Well, then in Ingrid's presence I'll call you Master Paul, but when she's not around, it will be Paul, okay?" I returned to our delicious meal.

When Paul rang the little bell again, Angela brought a luscious strawberry dessert, bowed with mock formality, and left. We both ate every bite.

"That was really good," Paul said, wiping his mouth on the linen napkin. "Things do taste better when you don't have to eat alone." He jumped from his chair. "Let's go up to my room and play a game."

"Oh, Paul, I'd really like to, but maybe we'd—"

"I know, maybe we'd better not. Ingrid wouldn't like it." He went toward the doorway, then turned and ran back to me. "This has been the most fun I've had in a long time. Thanks!" He ran down the hall to the stairs, looked back at me, and waved. I waved back, glad that he couldn't see my tears.

I turned to the kitchen and was confronted by an irate Ingrid standing with her hands on her hips.

"Well, Miss Wood. In just one day you've managed to turn this house topsy-turvy. I hope you're pleased with yourself!"

"Well, I am, really," I responded truthfully.

"For the first time in my memory, Mr. Horstman has countered my instructions. I was forced to accept your freedom to gallivant about the house and to dine with a family member. You seem to have forgotten that you're an employee here."

"No, I haven't forgotten. My job is to do what is best for *Master Paul*," I protested, showing more bravery than I was feeling.

Ingrid stepped closer to emphasize her point. "If you really cared about Master Paul's future, you wouldn't lead him to expect that his teacher can substitute for his family."

This time I didn't back down. "If I don't substitute, who will? Will you?"

"Certainly not. I know my place. I am in charge here but I wouldn't presume to a personal relationship with a member of the Horstman family. It's disgraceful!"

Her words and hate-filled eyes actually frightened me, but I had to stand up for Paul. "Well, for now, at least, Mr. Horstman has given me permission to get to know Paul. I don't intend to abuse that relationship."

"See that you don't. I'm warning you, I will not permit this household to fall apart as it did when Lisa—" She stopped midsentence, possibly feeling she had said too much.

She looked at me, emphasizing her threat once more, then walked past me into the corridor, her heels clacking on the marble floors. I didn't turn to watch her go. Shaken by this confrontation and Ingrid's negative reference to Lisa, Paul's mother, I hurried through the kitchen and up the back stairs to my room.

Opening the door, I found a folded sheet of type paper on the floor inside, as if it had been shoved under the door. Absently picking it up, I sat on my bed to regain my composure after my conflict with Ingrid. I'd never met anyone like her. I couldn't believe that she had actually warned me to back off in my relationship with my student.

Then I remembered the paper in my hand and slowly unfolded it. I read: LEAVE THIS HOUSE. The note had been typed with such an old, faded ribbon that I could hardly see the words, and I couldn't believe what I read—*Leave this house?* Who could have—who *would* have written this note? I read it again and was so shocked that I began shaking. I examined the faded typing. The typewriter's misaligned keys seemed to emphasize the crudity and brutality of the message.

I had left my door open, and rose with shaking knees to close it and to lean against it for support.

Chapter Seven

I didn't know what to do about the note. Ignore it? Call it to Ingrid's attention or Mr. Horstman's? Or would Ingrid already know about it, having typed it herself? Would Mr. Horstman think I was hysterical if I went running to him with a silly piece of paper? Or would he even help me, even if he did take the note seriously? I had no one to talk to.

But I was frightened. In Sherman Oaks I'd answered disturbing prank calls but I'd never actually received a threat. Was someone playing a practical joke? *Would Paul—of course not,* I assured myself. After our first encounter I might have suspected him, but not now. We'd already grown too close, and I knew he wanted me to stay.

Who else was in the house during dinner? Blanche? Martha? Bella? It was absurd to think that any of those mature women would write a hate note and sneak it under my door. Blanche wasn't outright friendly, but she wasn't hostile. Martha was kind. And, of course, the aging Bella never left her quarters on the third floor. Could Helman have disliked me enough to write it after one encounter? It did appear that he followed Ingrid's orders. I hadn't included Daniel in my inventory, but then, all he had to do to get rid of me was fire me.

I didn't know all of the staff of course. I'd seen men working on the grounds. There would have to be at least one full-time gardener, I reasoned. And there were maids or housekeeping workers in the house at various times. Since I hadn't actually met any of them, there was no logic in thinking that some other unknown staff member would want me gone.

All my worrying led to the conclusion that the most likely person to have typed the note was Ingrid. She couldn't fire me. I had seen to that. She had certainly been angry enough that she might resort to other means to get rid of me. It was probable that she used an old typewriter for household correspondence since change was something she seemed to reject. I would have to find some way to compare the typed note with the typeface on Ingrid's typewriter.

In the meantime, what to do with the note? I decided the safest place was in my purse, which I resolved to carry with me at all times at least until I could get a lock on my door. I rose from my bed, found my purse, and carefully hid the note inside.

Should I just leave? That certainly seemed the easy way out. But what about Paul? If I left now, he'd suffer another disappointment from an adult. Also, I reminded myself, I didn't have another job. I had to make good here or else start over. After thinking awhile, I was resolute. I wasn't going to let some nasty, bitter person drive me away.

I looked at my watch—9:00 P.M. I could go to bed and read myself to sleep, but I was too tense, too preoccupied. *Maybe a hot shower will help*, I thought. I hoped everyone else in the servants' wing had retired by now.

I changed into my robe and found my slippers, shampoo, and a hairbrush. The hall was empty and quiet. I closed my door and almost ran to the bathroom midway down the hall. The door was unlocked, and the bathroom was unoccupied.

Nervously, I closed the door and reached for the skeleton key. It wasn't there. I looked on the floor to see if it had fallen out of the lock. It was nowhere to be found. *Strange. Should I forget the shower? No.* I persuaded myself that steamy, relaxing water was just what I needed.

There was nothing in the bathroom to use as a wedge to hold the door shut, so I hurriedly removed my robe and slippers, and decided the chance of being interrupted was remote.

I set the temperature of the water while standing outside the tub. Then, climbing over the high rim, I pulled the encircling shower curtain around the tub tucking it so that the water wouldn't leak on the floor. I checked for the soap and then pushed down the plunger. The pipes clanked. Then the rushing water felt wonderful. I shampooed my hair, getting soap in my eye, but the tensions of the day began to drain away with the water. The steam filled the enclosure and the entire room, and the slippery tub caused me to grasp for the tub rim just in time to avoid slipping.

Strong hands suddenly came from behind, pushing down forcefully so that my feet slipped forward. I screamed and the back of my head struck the tub. Then I remembered nothing until I found myself lying on my side in my bed, with Martha and Blanche standing over me.

I was relieved that I was wrapped in my robe, but the dull ache at the back of my head brought back the fright of my fall.

"I—I fell," was all I could say.

"Hush, dear," Martha whispered, holding my hand. "The doctor is on the way. I called him myself." She gestured toward my head. "You have a nasty cut on the back of your head which may require stitches." She covered me with a blanket. "Now just lie still until the doctor comes."

Blanche stood sternly at the foot of the bed. "You're not the only one to complain about that slippery tub," she said. "It's too bad we have to have a nasty accident to get some attention."

Martha stroked my forehead. "Now don't excite yourself, dear. I heard your scream from my room and came right out. The bathroom door was closed but fortunately unlocked. There was no one about. Then I went to Blanche's room to get her to help with you."

"I—I don't remember any of that. I just remember feeling hands pushing down on my shoulders." I found the strength to blurt the truth out, but the force of my words made my head ache.

Blanche opened her mouth in disbelief, moving to the side of the bed opposite Martha. "That's foolishness, Miss Wood. Why would anyone want to do that? That kind of thing couldn't happen here."

Why, indeed? I wondered, but I didn't say it.

The doctor's arrival interrupted our discussion. Martha made hurried introductions, "Wendy, this is Dr. Richardson. He's been the Horstman family doctor ever since I can remember. Doctor, she hit the back of her head on the edge of the tub, as I explained on the phone."

The old doctor was balding, wore thick owlish glasses, and had a neatly trimmed gray mustache to match the rim of his hair. "I was just leaving home when you reached me. Otherwise, I'd have suggested calling an ambulance." Gesturing for the women to step back, he replaced Martha at my side. Taking an instrument and flashlight from his bag, he looked into my eyes. "Well, the pupils aren't dilated abnormally, so concussion doesn't appear likely. Do you feel dizzy or sense any other signs of imbalance or nausea?"

"No," I answered slowly.

"Now, if you can stay on your right side, I'll take a look at your head." He gently patted my shoulder.

I winced at the sharp head pain.

"Well, young lady, you've lost some blood," he said, looking at the bloody towel and pillowcase. "I need to clean up that wound. This may sting a bit," he cautioned, washing the wound with gauze and a cleansing agent.

It stung, all right, and I gritted my teeth to keep from yelling.

"Well," the doctor decided, "the bleeding is worse than the wound. I don't think stitches are needed. The head sometimes bleeds rather profusely even when the lesion isn't deep. I'll just clean this up and bandage it."

He finished the dressing and cleaned up his tools and hands, then, turning to Martha, said, "She'll need this dressing changed daily for a few days, Martha. Can you help?"

"Of course, doctor," Martha replied. "Are there any precautions?"

Closing his bag and leaving some antibiotic ointment on my desk, he directed his response to me. "Well, I would rest tomorrow if I were you. And if you become dizzy or have any vision problems, please let me know. Otherwise you should be all right." He started toward the door, then stopped. "But, for heaven's sake, get Mr. Horstman to put some safety rails around that old, slippery tub."

"We will, doctor," Blanche said with resolve.

I asked, "Should I take anything for the pain?"

"Just some aspirin should do," the doctor prescribed in his old-fashioned manner. He added, "If I don't hear of any complications, I'll telephone tomorrow before noon to see how you're doing." He patted my shoulder, "Good night, now."

Martha followed him to the door. "Can you find your way out, Doctor?"

"I found my way in, didn't I? It's been awhile since I've been here, but I probably know this house as well as you do, Martha." At that, he exited down the hall.

Martha returned to my side. "Will you be all right now, dear? Can we get you anything else?"

"Blanche," I spoke slowly so as not to increase my headache, "would you mind getting me a glass of water from the bathroom?" I requested.

"Of course, I will." Blanche seemed relieved to go. "While I'm there I'll tidy up the bathroom a bit and get rid of this bloody towel. And I'll bring back a clean pillow slip."

When Blanche had gone, I said quietly, "Martha, she doesn't believe me. I *was* pushed."

Martha tried to cover her reaction, but seemed not to believe me either. "Well, I was the one who—found you, and there was *no one* else about. Of course, I'll report what you've said to Ingrid."

"No, please don't. Just tell her I had an accident and might not be able to teach Paul tomorrow. I need some time to think—to recover."

I debated about showing Martha the threatening note, then decided to keep it to myself. Someone wanted me out of Horstman House, and Ingrid seemed the most likely candidate. I began to wonder what really scared away Paul's other teachers.

"As you wish, dear. But Mr. Horstman should be told. I didn't notify anyone tonight. I—I just rushed to call the doctor." Martha almost seemed as if she were trying to convince me of her concern for my welfare. Something about her tone seemed a little too forced. She began the same furtive looking about and behind that I'd seen at breakfast, her calm manner disappearing.

"Yes, tell Mr. Horstman I had an *accident,* so that he won't think I'm neglecting Paul. And someone will need to explain to Paul."

"I'm sure Ingrid will tell the others." She looked up. "Here's Blanche with the water. Do you want an aspirin now?"

"I think I have some in my purse." I looked for it. "It was right here on the table."

Blanche passed the glass to Martha. "You probably forgot where you set it. Never mind, I'll get some aspirin from my room." Blanche left again, setting the clean pillow slip on the foot of the bed.

I was frantic. My purse—I knew I'd left it on the table. I realized I should have taken it with me to the bathroom. "Martha, I know my purse was here."

Martha looked around the room. "Could I check your closet and drawers," she asked, proceeding to do so without waiting for my reply. Without difficulty, she found the purse on the floor of the closet. "See, here it is." She handed it to me, and I looked inside.

"It isn't here," I said without thinking. The note was gone.

"What isn't there?" Martha asked. But her innocent manner wasn't entirely convincing me. Something was going on behind those questioning eyes.

"Uh—the aspirin," I answered slowly. "I thought I had some in my purse." I decided not to mention the note until I knew who wrote it, who delivered it, *and* who took it. I was beginning to think that I couldn't trust anyone at Horstman House.

"Well, no matter, Blanche is bringing some." Martha picked up the pillow slip. "Now, if you can hold up your head I'll change that pillow cover."

I raised my head, wincing as I moved. Martha seemed to have regained her calm, as she skillfully cared for me, quickly removing the soiled pillow case and replacing it with the new one. "Now you can lie back again," she ordered.

"Martha, thank you for helping me. I'm glad you were here."

She looked directly at me before answering. Did I detect a fleeting look of distress in her eyes? I wondered. "I'm glad I was—here too," she said, "or it could have been worse. I mean—Blanche wouldn't have heard you. She's slightly deaf, you know."

"No, I didn't notice. Maybe that explains her, uh, distant manner?"

"Oh, yes, she's a good enough soul. She's just a very private person."

Blanche interrupted, bringing the aspirin. "Here you are," she said. "Anything else before I go? I have to get up early to cook breakfast."

"No, but thank you, Blanche—Mrs. Goodwin."

"Oh, I think you should call me Blanche after tonight. I'll bring a tray up to you for breakfast." She was gone before I could object.

"Well, I'll get back to bed too, unless you need something else," Martha offered.

"There is just one thing. You'll think it silly, I know, but would you mind leaving your door ajar? Just for tonight. In case I—need you."

She hesitated. "Well—of course I won't mind." She quickly looked toward the hallway. "I'll leave the lights on in the hall, too." She turned to go, then looked back. "Good night, now. I hope—you feel better in the morning."

When she rushed away, I turned out the lamp on the bedside writing desk. I knew with certainty that someone really did want me out of Horstman House. But without the threatening note, who would believe me? I closed my eyes, sure that the shocks and worries of the night wouldn't allow me to sleep. Then I turned to the Lord for help, asking Him to comfort me, protect me, and help me to make the right decisions about my future at Horstman House. Shortly after praying, my anxiety was replaced with a calm reassurance, and my favorite psalm, Psalm 23, which I'd memorized as a child, crept into my thoughts. *The Lord is my shepherd; I shall not want. He maketh me to lie down in green pastures; he leadeth me beside the still waters. He restoreth my soul: he leadeth me in the paths of righteousness for his name's sake. Yea, though I walk through the valley of the shadow of death, I will fear no evil: for thou art with me; thy rod and thy staff they comfort me. Thou preparest a table before me in the presence of mine enemies . . .* The words ran through my mind again and again until I fell asleep.

Chapter Eight

Throughout the night I dozed, but each time I turned, the pain in my head woke me. I couldn't find a comfortable position. It hurt when I lay back on the pillow. When I turned on my side I felt as if the wound was reopening. I tried sleeping face-down, but that didn't work either.

Along with the physical pain came a nagging fear. Had I imagined that someone pushed me down in the tub? I'd complained to Ingrid about the lack of safety rails. Had Ingrid thought of that complaint and used that very tactic to try to frighten me into leaving? Or had someone really wanted to hurt me—or even kill me?

Somewhere among these conscious night thoughts, I dreamed that someone came to my door and peered in. Then the figure left as quickly as it had appeared. A nightmare, I told myself when I awakened fully, though somewhat unconvincingly.

A more pleasant dream seemed so real that I did have to convince myself it didn't happen. I was outside in the rear gardens, which were lit by the stars and moon and I came to the gazebo where Daniel was sitting in the shadows. He appeared despondent. Then he looked up and called me. His face was without expression, but his eyes suggested sadness. I sat beside him and asked, "Daniel, what can I do to help you?" His reply was brief, "Help Paul. I have failed him. Please, help Paul."

Then I awoke when Blanche brought in my breakfast tray. "I hope I didn't wake you. I waited until nine knowing you needed a rest."

"Oh, that's fine," I mumbled. "I've spent a strange night—half asleep, half awake—nightmares and dreams." I suddenly remembered

Daniel's fervent plea, *Please, help Paul.* Was this an answer to my prayers for guidance?

Blanche crossed to the bedside desk with the tray. "Well, you ought to eat something to build your strength, but there's nothing here that has to be eaten right away."

"Thank you, Blanche."

"Can I help you sit up?"

"Yes, that might be a good idea. I'll just sit on the edge of the bed."

It hurt to move, and I felt a momentary spinning and nausea, but it passed when I placed my feet on the floor.

"I'll check again in about half an hour. Eat what you can." Blanche turned to leave.

"Blanche, thanks for your help—last night and this morning."

"You're welcome. We *servants* have to look out for each other—no one else will." She smiled at her attempt at humor.

"I guess you're right."

Blanche left me with the wonderful food—several frosted croissants, fresh orange slices, and juice. I was amazed at my appetite. *Well, as Blanche said, I must keep up my strength,* I thought, justifying my intent to gorge myself. I was pleased that Blanche seemed to have accepted me—as one of the staff—and maybe as a friend.

I was aware of someone at my door and turned to see a long-faced Paul.

"That's a great big bandage," he said, looking at my head. "Ingrid told me. She didn't want me to come, but when she went to her office I ran out of the schoolroom and down the hall." He came closer. "Your bandage has blood on it."

"I must look awful, Paul, but it really isn't as bad as it looks. I—I fell in the tub."

"I know."

"The doctor came and said that I'll be all right—no stitches."

"That's good. Stitches hurt."

"Oh, have you had stitches?"

"Yes. Once I fell down the stairs and had to have five stitches in my forehead." He lifted his hair to show me a small scar.

"Well, my fall wasn't that bad I'm glad to say."

"Can I help you?" he asked.

"Thank you, Paul. I appreciate your concern. I really do."

I thought a moment, then made a decision to tell Mr. Horstman what happened to me—what really happened. "Would you tell your father about my accident, if you see him, Paul?"

"Yes, I will." He sounded pleased to be given a grown-up responsibility. "Dad told me he'd be at home today sometime. I'll tell him. Guess we won't have school today?"

"No, but I should be better tomorrow. I'm going to try to rest today to make up for a bad night. I couldn't sleep very well and when I did, I dreamed or had nightmares."

He sat on the edge of my bed. "I didn't know grown-ups have nightmares."

"Oh, yes, we try to sort things out in our sleep, just as children do."

"Sort things out? What do you mean?"

"Well, our dreams and nightmares are our mind's way of making our problems into stories we have to figure out. But, in dreams, the problems are sometimes disguised—the people, places, or things may not seem exactly as they do when we're awake," I explained, hoping that he'd understand that dreams weren't necessarily to be feared. Perhaps I was trying to convince myself of that too. "Sometimes the answer to our problems is hidden in the story, or at least the story is our mind trying to figure out the answer."

"I get it. That makes me feel better. I have some bad dreams but I don't tell anybody about them." He looked at my tray. "Your breakfast looks good."

"Would you like a croissant? I thought I'd eat all of them but I can't."

"Yes—Yes!" He snatched it up as if he hadn't had breakfast.

"Didn't you eat this morning?" I asked, clearly surprised at his uncustomary exuberance.

"Yes, but I'm hungrier since you came."

"I've never had that effect on anyone," I laughed, "but I have a very good appetite myself. Do you think you'd better get back to the classroom soon, before—"

"It's too late for that, Miss Wood."

We turned to see Ingrid, hands on hips, standing in the doorway.

"I'm sorry," Paul said quietly. "I just had to make sure she was okay." He backed to the wall beside my bed, as far from Ingrid as he could get.

"I told you to stay in the schoolroom," Ingrid lectured. "I also told you that I would report Miss Wood's condition to you." She came into the room and took Paul by the shoulders. "Now, come with me. You're not to bother Miss Wood again today."

"Oh, Paul's no bother," I protested. "Of course, he shouldn't have disobeyed you," I added calmly, "but no harm's done."

Ingrid responded by urging Paul toward the door. "We'll discuss this matter later, Miss Wood." She moved to go, then turned back. "I trust that you are feeling better after your accident."

"I feel better than I did last night, but I would appreciate your following through with arrangements for some safety rails and strips in that bathroom."

"Well, of course. I intend to do that today."

"Thank you," I said with sincere relief.

Paul waved good-bye. He walked slowly, at first, then I heard his running footsteps down the hall. He was either running from her or demonstrating his newfound courage, I thought, and smiled.

"You will be staying on then?" Ingrid asked. "You haven't let this occurrence change your mind?"

"What do you mean?"

"I simply mean that some might be reluctant to stay in a position where things began so badly."

I tried to stand but changed my mind. "Well, let me make something very clear, Miss Nourse. It will take more than an—accident to scare me off. And I want a lock installed on my bedroom door and a better lock installed in the bathroom."

Ingrid's face reddened. "Well, of course I'll have to discuss those requests with Mr. Horstman."

"Do that, please, at your earliest opportunity. I insist on privacy in my room and bathroom. That's not too much to ask."

"But the bathroom has a lock," she protested.

"The key was missing when I went there last night."

"Well, it probably fell on the floor when someone else closed the door."

"No, I looked for it. The key was gone. I think someone took it—deliberately."

She stood tall, the controlled superior again. "You're just unstrung by all that's happened. No one took the key. It's there now."

"How do you know that?"

"The door was open when I came down the hall. I checked the bathroom, as I inspect all the rooms from time to time, to see that the housemaids have done their jobs. The key was in the lock," she insisted.

"Please talk to Mr. Horstman about my requests—today, if possible."

She dismissed further discussion and started to leave, then remembered, "Will you be able to teach Master Paul tomorrow?"

"Yes, I'm feeling much better. I may even spend some time in the library today."

"Do you think that's wise?" she asked, obviously disapproving the idea.

"Yes, I do. There are some questions I want answered. Maybe I'll find the answers there—in the library."

Striking her schoolmistress pose, she relented. "Well, of course, since Mr. Horstman has given his approval, there is no way I can keep you from the library. But please be careful. There are many valuable books and documents there."

"Miss Nourse, I assure you that my teacher training included the use and care of a library. I won't damage anything."

"Yes, well, I'll go to Master Paul then and set him to studying again." She moved to leave, but I stopped her with another request.

"Just one more thing, Miss Nourse. If you have a typewriter in your office, could I use it?"

She turned abruptly. "No! No one uses my office. There is a portable machine in the library. Use that."

So much for my attempt to check the typeface on Ingrid's typewriter. I'd have to find a more subtle approach, I decided.

"Is there anything else, Miss Wood?" she asked sarcastically. She sounded fed up with my demands, but I was beyond caring.

"Oh, yes. Have I had any phone messages? I was expecting a call from my friend Jill."

"No one has called. I will tell you if they do." She left, muttering to herself.

I'd have to call Jill again but I couldn't tell her about last night. She'd be right here to drag me away. The thought of Jill warmed me, but she seemed so far away; not only in distance but in time. Had I really been at Horstman House less than a week?

Blanche interrupted my thoughts when she returned for the tray. "Did you eat something?"

"Yes, I did. It was delicious. And Paul came by to help eat the croissants. He couldn't resist."

She seemed pleased. "His appetite has improved remarkably. You must be good for him."

I settled back in the bed. "I hope so, but I don't feel much good to anyone today."

"I'll take the tray if you're finished. I'll bring some lunch to your room later."

"Oh, don't bother, Blanche. I'll come down. I'm going to get dressed if I can. In fact, I plan to spend some time in the library today."

She picked up the tray. "Well, don't overdo it."

"I won't. I feel much better after eating. Thanks again, Blanche."

She almost bumped into Martha, who was entering my room.

"Whoops, sorry, Blanche. I see you've had some breakfast," Martha observed.

"Yes, I feel better."

Martha went to my desk. Today she was acting more like the Martha I'd first met than the nervous woman she had been last night. "Well, I only have a second," she said. "I came downstairs to help change that dressing. Looks like it needs it. Turn sideways, will you, and I'll try to take this off without hurting you too much." She loosened the tape from my scalp.

"Ouch!"

"I'm sorry, but the wound bled quite a lot during the night, and Doctor Richardson said—"

"I know—change the dressing daily. I'm grateful, really, but I'm like a little girl when it comes to hurts."

Martha laughed, making a new bandage from the materials the doctor had left on the desk. "I'll put some of this antibiotic ointment on the wound, so it won't get infected."

"Martha, you remind me a lot of my mother. I appreciate all you've done."

She stopped what she was doing and seemed about to say something. I thought I saw tears, but then she went back to her duties as if nothing had touched her, placing the first-aid supplies on the desk. "Well, speaking of mothers," she said, "I've got to go *mother* that child upstairs. She'll be banging on the door for me to remove her breakfast tray if I don't get up there. She does make her presence known."

"To you, maybe. What a strange life—up there away from the world."

Martha hesitated before answering, looking toward the hall, then said in a hushed voice, "Yes, strange indeed." She seemed anxious to avoid saying more.

"I'd really like to know more about her so that I can understand Paul a little better."

Martha moved to the door. "I know you've been told that subject is taboo."

"I have," I agreed, but I wanted to get more from Martha. "I'm not suggesting that you tell me about her present life. I know she was an actress, and I can't help being fascinated with her past."

"Yes—an actress," she said, seeming caught up in her thoughts. "Theater, silents, then the talkies."

"Her husband left her? I guess all that fame and fortune didn't bring them happiness?"

I sensed that she warmed to talking about the past, perhaps reminiscing about a somewhat happier time. "Oh, the money wasn't the problem. After the birth of Daniel, Bella wanted little to do with either her husband or her baby. She was almost forty when Daniel was born, and her career was waning just when World War II broke out. She searched for someone or something to blame for her lessening popularity. Her husband's wartime industrial efforts added to their fortune, but she turned over the rearing of her child and the care of her husband to—others."

She paused and looked nervously toward the hall again, so I prompted her. "Mr. Horstman said something about his lonely childhood."

"Yes, well, I've said too much and taken too much time," she said, abruptly ending her revelations. She put the soiled bandage in the wastebasket by the desk and moved again to the door. "Rest as much as you can. If I can sneak away again, I'll check on you later." She started to leave, then turned back again. "Are you sure you want to stay here?" she asked. "We're not the best company for a young girl."

I was surprised, moved, and then concerned at Martha's unexpected suggestion. "Well, I have to give it a fair trial," I said. "I didn't come here to fail—and I think Paul needs me."

"Well—if you're sure," she said again preoccupied with her thoughts.

I was disappointed that she wouldn't keep talking about the Horstmans, but couldn't press it further. "Thanks again, Martha, for your help and concern. I think I'll spend some time in the library today."

"Well, if you think that wise." That phrase again, I thought. Everyone seemed intent on cautioning me about the wisdom of my decisions.

I was left alone. I was sure that Martha had a lot more to tell and resolved to try to get her talking again. Feeling a bit shaky, I managed to get to my closet and found a peasant blouse with a wide neck and a pair of old jeans. I located my slippers and a hair brush. Taking my purse with me, I made my way to the hall and then to the bathroom.

There was no sign of last night's occurrence. The bathroom was spotless. I saw in the mirror my pale face and stringy hair. Maybe I should have stayed in my room, but I wanted to look for the portable typewriter Ingrid had mentioned. I hadn't seen it.

I did my best to clean up, and adding some color to my lips helped. I decided on a part in the middle of my hair and two pony-tails; easy to fix without removing the bandage. I refused to look like an accident victim all day.

Somewhat refreshed, I was determined to use my free time searching the library for the typewriter, and possibly for some infor-mation about the Horstmans. Going down the grand stairway, I tightly grasped the handrail for support. I reflected again on the huge house filled with art treasures and antiques—a cold, formal place with everyone keeping to himself or herself—and a little boy trying his utmost to survive this loneliness. This house was not a home, and the people in it were responsible.

I found myself at the library, opened the high double door, and was overwhelmed again by the warmth and beauty of the room. It was spacious, but the arrangement of the furniture made it seem almost cozy. The varied colors of the books and furnishings, the light from the windows, and the view of the rolling green lawns made this room so different from the rest of the house. No wonder this was Paul's favorite place.

I surveyed the books, finding they were arranged both by content and by authors' last names. Someone had spent a lot of time and effort collecting and arranging this library which was heavy on classics and history. But I was looking for something more personal; something autobiographical or biographical like journals or scrapbooks or photo albums kept by the Horstmans. I found a Bible, but it contained no family data.

I felt I was snooping, but I was motivated both by the mystique of the family and by my real desire to understand them for Paul's sake—and my own.

I found several books dealing with mining, oil, and railroad barons, and read the information on Daniel Horstman II, but it was all impersonal narrative about his business involvements and accomplishments—nothing about his wife, Bella, or about his son, Daniel III. I replaced the books carefully and had about decided that nothing private or personal had been saved by the family, or at least that it was elsewhere in the house.

Deciding to look for the typewriter I was drawn to a large map table that was covered with plate glass. Beneath the glass were a world map and a map of the United States. Both would be helpful in teaching Paul.

I leaned on the edge of the table looking more closely at the maps, and the top moved slightly. Adjusting the glass to its former position, I felt hinges just under the rim. The table had a lift top. I opened the table expecting to find more maps inside.

Instead, I was delighted to see hundreds of clippings and photos, some bound by rubber bands and others by large metal clips. Obviously someone had carefully and thoughtfully organized them.

I propped open the tabletop using a built-in wooden dowel. Examining the newspaper and magazine clippings, I noted that Bella was the subject of most of them. But there was also a smaller bundle of clippings topped by a photo of her son Daniel—Daniel on his wedding day, with his lovely dark-haired bride in her elegant wedding dress, coming down the steps of a church surrounded by a crowd of guests and photographers. Daniel, younger of course, was smiling and open in a manner I hadn't seen. He would have been happy then with his new bride, before her death—before the fire.

I found a comfortable chair and read excitedly each clipping about Bella. They were reviews of her plays—*Hippolytus, Hedda Gabler, Medea*—and of her performances as Clytemnestra and Lady Macbeth—all great and powerful classic women whom she had portrayed onstage before being lured to film.

Her movie roles had been written or tailored for these same strong female talents. *Magnificent Heiress, The Tigress, A Woman Scorned*—all melodramatic titles in which the power of her performances had made the movies greater than the scripts, at least according to the critical reviews accompanying the photos.

There were also clippings from the early movie magazines: "Bella Speaks as 'The Enchantress'" and "Bella Rises to New Heights in Talkies." Undoubtedly, her stage training had paid off, I reasoned, when talking films became more than moving pictures.

It appeared that the legend of Bella had been carefully constructed by the Hollywood publicity machines, playing up her marriage to Daniel Horstman II. Her fame had combined with wealth and power to create a royal image, worshiped by the masses of moviegoers during the depression.

I was mesmerized by the words and photos, believing the fantasy as I read, and momentarily forgetting that I was actually sitting in Bella Horstman's library. The hours passed quickly while I relived Bella's past.

Somewhat reluctantly I set aside the numerous clippings about Bella and picked up those dealing with Daniel's life. The first clipping beneath the wedding shot was a photo story about Daniel and Lisa honeymooning in Paris, the Eiffel Tower in the background. He still wore the smile of a happy newlywed.

Subsequent stories dealt with Daniel's work as a corporate lawyer and with his joining a prestigious banking firm in Los Angeles and with other successful business dealings. There were a few photos from the society pages showing Daniel and Lisa at various functions. Was there a reflection of boredom in their faces in these later pictures? But how could that have been, when they had been so caught up in an exciting social life?

There were no more clippings dealing with Daniel or Lisa until the birth of Paul. "Horstman Heir Born Today," the caption read beneath a photo of a serious Daniel and a weary-looking Lisa, holding their newborn son.

Then nothing until the story of Lisa's death in the fire: "Mrs. Daniel Horstman III Dies Tragically in Fire." I looked at the photo of the burning guesthouse, then read the story of Daniel's unsuccessful attempts to get inside the fire-ravaged building, the late arrival of the fire trucks, and the subsequent discovery of the charred and unrecognizable remains of the body. It was reported that Dr. Ernest Richardson, county coroner, had determined that Lisa had died in the fire. I realized, then, that Dr. Richardson, who had treated me, had been both the Horstman's physician and the coroner at the time of Lisa's death. The story revealed further that Dr. Richardson had termed Lisa's death "accidental" and that funeral arrangements were to be announced. Investigators decided the fire had indeed been accidental, probably caused by spilling of turpentine, which Lisa was using in her oil painting. The turpentine had spread across the floor into an open fireplace.

That tragic accident destroyed a storybook life and marriage, I reflected. Daniel lost a beloved wife, and Paul lost his mother. Neither had been able to accept the loss, I reasoned, but it seemed that Paul suffered more than Daniel because he'd never known a mother. Unable to shake a sense of sadness, I replaced the clippings in the map table, checking to see that all appeared as I had found it. I was lowering the tabletop when Daniel entered the library.

Chapter Nine

He had caught me with my hand in the cookie jar, and I was embarrassed.

"I went to your room to talk with you about your accident," he said. "Blanche told me where I might find you. I hope you're okay." He held out a tray. "She sent me with your lunch."

I finished closing the map table. "Thanks, I didn't feel like being cooped up in a sick room all day, so I came here to—uh—get acquainted—with the library," I said, trying to justify my snooping. Again I felt like a schoolgirl, conscious of my clothes and hair.

I noted that he was dressed less formally than when I'd first met him, in a soft tan turtleneck and brown herringbone pants. Coming toward me, he looked less imposing and was actually smiling. "I see you've found the secret of the map table." He put the tray on a low table by a sofa.

"Yes, I—found the hinges and thought I'd find more maps inside. I'm sorry if I—"

"Oh, I suppose there's no harm done. I don't think anyone has lifted that lid since—since Lisa went—away. Collecting and organizing the clippings was her obsession."

I moved toward the sofa and sat, trying to distance myself from the evidence of my snooping. "I did look through the clippings. I was excited by the stories about Bella—your mother."

"Oh, yes, the great Bella, loved by all the world," he said rather sarcastically.

"Well, one of my passions is theater and film, so I found the information fascinating."

He moved away from me toward the window. "A lot of Hollywood hoopla and gossip. Nothing to do with the real Bella."

"Yes, well, I also read some of the clippings about you—and Lisa. She was beautiful. And you appeared in the photos to have been very happy."

He turned to me, seeming almost surprised at this observation, "Oh, I was!"

"I'm sorry it all had to end so tragically, sorry for you and for Paul."

"Oh, Paul hardly knew his mother. Didn't you realize that?"

"Well, even so, he misses *having* his mother, I'm sure."

He walked toward the door, seeming anxious to change the subject. "I guess that he does, but I can tell you that having a mother doesn't guarantee happiness either. He gets by, just as we all do."

I rose and went toward him. "But is getting by enough?" I asked. "I mean, he's a very lucky little boy in many ways, but—"

"But his father doesn't spend enough time with him. Right?"

"Well, you said it, but it's more than spending time. He's really hurting."

He reentered the room, talking more to himself than to me. "I rail at myself about it. I feel guilty, but I just can't bring myself to—"

"To what? To give him the love and attention he needs? To make time for him? To stop avoiding him? To really become his father?" I stopped, almost out of breath. After releasing all the questions I had stored in my thoughts, I wondered if I'd said too much.

Daniel didn't react with anger, however. Instead, he seemed humbled by my attack. "He reminds me so much of his mother," he said quietly. "He even looks like her . . . her dark eyes . . . the shape of his face."

I followed him to the center of the room, propelled by my concern for Paul. "But he also looks like you. He's *your* son too."

Daniel went to a table bar at the far side of the library and poured a drink. Without looking up or turning, he asked, "Will you join me?"

"No, thanks, I don't drink," I said, perhaps too rudely.

He sat on a sofa, facing me. "Isn't it strange how we repeat the behavior of our parents? You'd think it would be the opposite."

I found an armchair across from him. "Yes, child neglect can be like a virus. If you feel your mother treated you badly, why don't you try *not* to do that to Paul?"

"I hope I'm not entirely guilty of that. I hope Paul knows I love him."

"Oh, he might, but it wouldn't hurt for you to tell him," I said. "I know that he loves you."

"Why—why do relationships have to be so—painful? I can't look at him without thinking of his mother."

"But that's natural. Maybe you could begin by talking to him about his grandmother. She's still here. I really can't understand why you don't—"

He stood, obviously considering leaving again. "That's right, you don't understand," he said, angrily. Then he sighed and regained control. "Why talk with him about a grandmother who was *never* a mother to me and could *never* be a grandmother to him?"

"Never? You mean you were never close to her?"

"Never! I was reared by Ingrid, with help from Helman, when she thought I needed some—physical discipline." He turned away and walked toward the windows at the front of the house. "My mother didn't want me. She had already driven my father away. He left before I was born. She even tried to hide her pregnancy from him and from everyone. She went into temporary retirement for a year. Then, after I was born, she seemed to blame my existence for the failure of her comeback."

I moved behind him. "Yes, Martha told me something about that," I said sympathetically.

He turned abruptly. "Martha is paid to keep her opinions to herself."

"Oh, please don't blame her. I suppose I was prying. Martha seems very devoted to her duties. It was my urging that got her talking."

"Nevertheless, I'll speak to Martha about her chatty nature. The Great Bella always demanded total privacy."

"Total? You mean you don't visit her—see her?"

"No I didn't—don't. She began withdrawing from the world in the early forties, and by the time I was Paul's age she communicated with me only through others or through her written notes."

"That must have been horrible for you," I said, empathizing with his hurt. "I was so close to my mother—I could never have handled that. How painful, knowing that your mother was right here in this house but was unwilling to see you, to recognize you. It must have been awful."

"Yes, it was horrible. I envy what you must have had with your mother. But I learned to deal with it. After all, she was a total recluse for about thirty years. As a child, if I wanted to see her, I would hide in the gazebo and watch for her to step out on her third-floor balcony."

"Yes, I think I saw her there the night we—met in the gazebo." I was immediately embarrassed at having recalled that brief incident.

"Well, yes, that was a rather difficult moment for me." He sat on the wide window sill. "I don't know why I've been telling you all of this. I guess I'm trying to justify my actions, or maybe my lack of action, related to Paul. I'm sorry if I've used you as a listening post. I don't usually talk about myself this much."

I wanted him to continue talking because I was learning a lot about the Horstman family that I could use in helping Paul—and possibly Daniel too. I asked, "Was the gazebo a private meeting place for you—you and Lisa?"

"Well, yes, for a while it was," he said quietly. There was a brief silence in which neither of us knew what to say. "But seeing you there—it was—well, frankly, you look a lot like Lisa, and you were wearing a head scarf much like hers."

I was flattered and yet bothered by his comparisons between Lisa and me. "Then I'm sorry I wore it," I said. "I'm sorry to have brought back tender memories for you. I'm sorry, too, that your life has been so difficult."

I moved involuntarily toward him, then stopped with another question. "Don't you try to make contact with your mother—even now?"

He seemed unduly agitated by my question. "It's impossible!"

"Does she communicate with you?"

"She always used typewritten notes," he replied.

Typewritten notes? Could she have had someone deliver the typewritten message directing me to leave? Further consideration of the possibility was interrupted by Daniel's coming close to me.

"There's something different about you. I've told you more about myself in these few minutes than I've ever told anyone, except Lisa. But she was never sympathetic."

"Well, I'm sorry about that, too, Daniel—I mean, Mr. Horstman."

"I think calling me Daniel is okay—out of Ingrid's earshot, of course." He led me back to the sofa and sat beside me. "I didn't come here planning to talk about myself and my problems," he said. "Paul found me to tell me about your accident and asked if I'd check to see that you're really all right. That *is* a big bandage on the back of your head. Paul told me about it."

"Yes, it looks worse than it is, but the fall scared me."

"I was glad to hear that Martha came to your aid."

"Yes, I guess she heard me cry out. I'm glad she did. I blacked out."

"Dr. Richardson said that you'll be all right?" he asked with a concern so sincere that I was touched.

"He said that he'd call later to see if I have any symptoms of concussion. As you can see, I don't have any."

"You should rest, don't you think?"

Somewhat reluctantly, I rose from the sofa. "I suppose I should lie down for a while." I started to leave, then remembered my other errand. "Oh, Ingrid said that there's a portable typewriter here. I haven't found it."

"I haven't seen that old thing for years. Ingrid has a typewriter in her office. Couldn't you use that?"

"Apparently not," I said with the same finality that Ingrid had expressed. "I asked, but she said I should use the portable."

"She guards that office like Fort Knox. Do you need a typewriter to use regularly?"

"Yes, I do," I realized aloud.

"Well, I'll bring a good one from the office tomorrow. Is it more urgent than that?"

"Well, yes, I wanted to prepare some materials for teaching Paul tomorrow." I was determined to get a look at Ingrid's typewriter.

"Let's go right now. If Ingrid's in her office, I'll intercede for you. If not, you can go to work, and I'll leave a note explaining that I gave you permission—just *once*—to use her typewriter. Okay?"

"Yes, thank you."

"But what about your lunch?" he asked.

I hurried back and grabbed a sandwich from the tray. "I'll eat on the way," I said.

Daniel placed his glass on a hall table outside the library and walked with me to the grand stairway and then past it.

I stopped at the foot of the stairs. "Isn't this the fastest way?"

"No. Didn't anyone show you the elevator?"

"Paul didn't mention it when he gave me the grand tour."

"I guess he's been told so often not to use the elevator for amusement that he didn't think to show you. Come on, it's this way." He continued down the hall.

At the end of the main floor hall, just before the entrance to the dining room, was a door like all the others. Daniel opened it. "They installed this elevator in the late '30s," he said. "But it's checked regularly. It's small, but safe for two or three people."

He gestured me into a closetlike cubicle lit by a small fixture, then closed the door behind us. He pressed a button marked "2," and I noted there was a button for the third floor, but said nothing about it. The elevator creaked, then shuddered to a stop.

"Wasn't that better than climbing those stairs in your condition?" Daniel ventured.

"Well, the stairs create a chance to exercise, but yes, it was easier today, and it's closer to my room, too. I need to get a textbook."

"Then I'll go with you," he offered.

We entered the hall leading to my room. Passing the bathroom, I remembered the lock problem and stopped. "Did Ingrid mention that I'd asked for a lock on my room door and a better lock for the bathroom?"

"No, but I saw her for only a moment. Why?"

"Then I'm glad I mentioned it. Because there's no lock on my door, and the bathroom locks with an old skeleton key. I couldn't find it last night, when I went to shower, and I had to leave the door unlocked."

"But aren't you the only one who uses that bathroom?" he asked. "There shouldn't be a need for locks here."

"I don't know who uses the bathroom, but I would feel safer with better locks."

"Safer? Where in the world could you feel safer? We're surrounded by walled grounds and we have a security system. The supervisor of the grounds also doubles as a night watchman. He puts the men to work on the grounds in the morning, tries to sleep during the day, and then watches over the place at night."

"I know I sound like a scared little girl, but—"

"No, but you do *look* like a little girl, with those ponytails and jeans."

I blushed. "I know. I thought I wouldn't see anyone today."

"Oh, you look fine. It's a refreshing change from Ingrid's uniformed staff."

"Well, of course I dress more formally when I'm teaching."

"Too bad!" Daniel smiled. "I'll get some locks installed. Now get that book, will you?"

"Of course." I hurried to my room, found a math workbook I'd brought along, and returned to find Daniel leaning against the wall. I showed him the workbook. "Here it is."

"Then let us invade Ingrid's stockade," he said, in military voice. I laughed, and he ushered me down the hall toward Ingrid's office.

I felt more welcome at Horstman House and found myself liking Daniel more than in our earlier meetings. I hadn't mentioned the note that was left in my room and then taken from my purse. Perhaps I'd simply misplaced it. Neither had I told Daniel that my fall wasn't an accident. But he was planning to arrange for door locks, and I felt relieved just to know that. Also, I was seeing a softer, more vulnerable, more caring side of him. *He could be ten years older than me . . . Why even think of that!* I pulled myself from my silly thoughts. He wasn't LDS anyway. Something prompted me to remember my mother's warning words about guarding my heart when interacting with young men that weren't Mormon. *But Daniel's not a "young" man . . .* I imagined teasing my mother. I almost sighed aloud. Young or not, my mother was right—Daniel just wasn't a candidate.

Ingrid's office door was locked. Daniel knocked to no response and then drew a key ring from his pants pocket. "I have a master key," he explained.

"Do you really think we should?"

"This is my house, remember. We're not breaking in—just using the typewriter."

"Okay, if you're sure, but I'll hurry. I don't want to face Ingrid again today."

"Her bark is worse than her bite," he said reassuringly.

"Are you certain? She doesn't seem to like me very much, and—"

I was about to mention the note but decided to do my detective work instead. "I'll just type this work sheet for Paul." I sat at a small typing stand and found some typing paper on a nearby shelf.

"We probably ought to get a small duplicating machine in the schoolroom," he suggested, watching me from the doorway.

"That would be nice, but I can get by with a typewriter for now." I rolled the paper over the platen of Ingrid's ancient machine, wishing that I still had the note for comparison. But the first letters I typed were evenly spaced vertically and horizontally. The type style was different, too, smaller and more clear than that used to type the note. That settled one question. Ingrid didn't type the note, or if she did, she didn't use her typewriter.

Daniel stood straight and announced, "Well, I'll leave you to your work. Think I might see if Paul's done with school for the day."

I smiled up at him without rising. "That sounds like a great idea."

"See you later?"

It was a question, not a statement, so I answered, "That would be nice."

"Maybe I'll join you and Paul for dinner?"

"That would be wonderful—for Paul."

He turned and headed down the hall toward the classroom.

Realizing that Ingrid was probably there with Paul, I quickly gathered up the used paper and my book. I'd done what I had planned. Now all I wanted was to get out of Ingrid's office.

I reached for the light switch and saw them by Ingrid's phone—two messages from Jill. I picked up the papers seeing that one message was dated Monday, 7:00 P.M., and the other, Tuesday, 8:00 A.M. Jill had called twice but Ingrid hadn't told me, and I'd asked her specifically whether Jill had called. What reason could she have for not giving me the messages? She certainly wasn't the careless, forgetful type. I'd have to call Jill and explain, and I'd consider confronting Ingrid about the messages when no one else was present.

Chapter Ten

With mixed feelings I returned to my room, glad to have seen Daniel's better self, but still concerned about the threat, my fall, and Ingrid's failure to give me my messages.

I decided that a rest would be good and, after closing the door firmly, I lay down on my bed. I slept soundly until four in the afternoon, just in time to freshen up for dinner.

My head felt somewhat better, and my spirits rose remembering Daniel's suggestion that he might join us for the evening meal. I knew that would please Paul.

Since I'd packed nothing more formal, I chose a pretty, light blue cotton dress, then took my makeup bag along to the bathroom, thinking once again that I really needed a mirror in my room.

The hallway was rather dark for late afternoon, suggesting an overcast sky outside. In the darkened quiet I was startled by the ringing of the pay phone at the far end of the hall. *Should I answer it?* I wondered. It seemed unlikely that the call would be for me. I decided that someone should respond either way, and neither Martha nor Blanche was about.

I hurried down the hall and lifted the receiver, not knowing exactly how to answer a Horstman House pay phone. I decided on "Hello." There was no response for a moment, but the line was open—no dial tone.

I was about to hang up when a whispered voice I couldn't identify slowly repeated the words of the threatening note, "Leave this house." Then the line went dead.

I held the receiver for stunned seconds before hanging up. Who could be so concerned by my presence here to resort to such terrorizing?

Immediately my thoughts went to Ingrid. She couldn't fire me without Daniel's consent, and I knew that she didn't approve of my teaching methods or of my growing relationship with Paul and his father. But how was my presence a threat warranting that kind of response? There was no one else to suspect, but even for her the motive seemed shaky. What was she trying to hide?

I almost ran back to my room. I had fully intended to dress, pack my suitcase, call a cab, and then get out of Horstman House. The events of the past few days did not bode well for my future there. I'd think of it as a learning experience and move on. Maybe I'd return to Arizona and forget my romantic California dreams.

Then I heard a timid voice behind me. "Wendy—Miss Wood— did you hear? Dad's going to join us for dinner?"

I turned to see Paul's beaming face. He came closer, looked at me and said, "What's the matter? You don't look happy."

When I spoke, I tried to control my shaking voice and hands, but he probably sensed my fears from my breathing. "I—I just had an upsetting phone call. I'll be all right."

"But you're scared," he said. "What scared you?"

"No, I'm not exactly scared. It's just that—" I couldn't tell him. It would do no good to upset him when he couldn't help. "I'm okay. It's just my—accident. I guess I'm not feeling as well as I thought."

He stepped back. "Then you won't come to dinner?" His disappointment was so touching that my resolve to leave melted—at least for that night. Maybe I'd tell Daniel about the note and the call. He'd know what to do, surely.

"Oh, yes, I'll be there for dinner," I assured him. "I wouldn't miss it. Now run along and get ready, and I'll do the same."

Paul smiled again and ran down the hall toward his room. I thought, *What a small thing to make him so happy—dinner with his father.* I hoped it would go as well as Paul wanted. Maybe this would be a new beginning for Paul and Daniel. I had to do my part in making it happen. Then maybe it would be enough and I could leave.

I looked into the bathroom, still apprehensive about the happenings of the night before. It was vacant, as always, and I hurried to fix up my hair and face for dinner. I wanted to look the best I could for the occasion. I reminded myself that I was being silly, and upon reflection my spirits sank again. Tonight would be a happy time, I hoped, but there were some realities I had to face. My foolish self would have to be held in check if I was to convince Daniel that someone was threatening me. I had no proof. If only I had that typewritten note.

Paul was already in the dining room when I arrived—but no Daniel. Paul stood when I entered, pulling out my chair and waiting to speak until I was seated. "Dad isn't here yet."

"Well, I'm sure he'll come," I said, trying to sound more certain than I felt. Was Paul in for another disappointment?

"He's awfully busy, you know," Paul said, already preparing himself, and me, for another letdown.

"Well, let's wait until he comes," I suggested. I was hungry, but Paul's feelings were more important.

We sat in silence, neither of us knowing what to say to excuse Daniel's absence. I was unable to pretend lightheartedness. My head was hurting again. My anxiety grew, and my concern for Paul depressed me.

"Do you still feel bad?" Paul asked.

"I guess my accident took more out of me than I thought," I said, avoiding mention of the real cause for my behavior.

There was another long silence, and Paul kept looking toward the hall for his father's arrival.

I couldn't take the silence and broke it with a lame joke. "The salad smells good enough to eat," I said.

Paul tried to laugh but couldn't hide his hurt. "I thought he'd come. He's the one who said he wanted to." He curled his lower lip, hung his head, and pouted—behavior I hadn't seen in him before.

"I'll see what's keeping him," I offered. "You wait right here in case he comes." I stood and went into Blanche's kitchen, where I found Blanche and Angela preparing baked salmon for the main course. They looked up when I entered.

"Oh, Wendy. We'll be right there with the dinner," Blanche said, rather defensively.

"I wasn't coming to check on dinner, Blanche. Mr. Horstman hasn't come. I wondered if you know why."

Blanche looked at Angela, who shook her head in negative response. "No," Blanche answered. "Neither of us has heard anything from him."

"Well, something probably detained him," I said, without conviction. "We'll start without him, I guess."

Angela looked at Blanche and shrugged her shoulders. "What else is new?" she asked.

"You must mind your business, Angela," Blanche cautioned. "It's not our place to comment on Mr. Horstman's actions."

Blanche's censure was directed as much to me as to Angela, I realized, so I returned to the dining room, hoping that Daniel might be there. He wasn't. Paul stared at his salad, lost in his thoughts.

"Are you getting ready to devour that salad?" I asked playfully, knowing that he wasn't thinking of food.

"No, I'm not hungry anymore," he said, sulking. Then he kicked the chair at his left side, knocking it over.

I was surprised but understood his frustration. "Did that make you feel better?" He shook his head. "Well then, pick up the chair, Paul. I'm guessing your father has been delayed, so we'll start without him," I finished, trying to reassure him. "I understand that you're disappointed, but don't take it out on the chair."

"I don't want this salad," Paul said grumpily. He stood and picked up the chair, returning it to its former place by the table.

"Well, I need the vegetables and I think you do too," I encouraged.

Then I thought of Brigham Young's advice about the need to pray even when you least feel like it. The mood didn't seem exactly right, and I hadn't discussed with Daniel his feelings about prayer, but I thought it might be a good idea right then to ask for the Lord's help. So even though Paul was unhappy—or maybe because he was unhappy—I said a blessing on the food and also asked the Lord to bless Paul and his father. Paul didn't join me. Instead he began playing with a tomato slice.

Although Blanche's meal was excellent, as usual, there was no way to rescue the occasion. Daniel didn't come and Paul was downcast for the remainder of the meal. And my earlier fears were replaced with anger—at Daniel, at Ingrid, and at myself. But I resolved not to be frightened away. Paul needed me, even if no one else at Horstman House wanted me here.

At his door I said good night to a saddened Paul and went to the pay phone to try to reach Jill. I got her phone answering machine again and explained that her earlier messages had been delayed. When

I started to say that I was all right, I couldn't help the trembling in my voice. But I regained control to tell her that I missed her and would try to call again tomorrow.

Chapter Eleven

The next morning I rose early with a strong determination to help Paul in any way I could. He needed a mother—or a father—but a friend would have to do. I knelt and again asked that the Lord guide me in my decisions, protect me from harm, and direct me in my attempts to help Paul. I thanked Him for blessings of the past, including my own wonderful mother. Then I asked Him to bless Paul and Daniel that they would find a way to improve their relationship and that I could find ways to help them become a family.

Standing after my prayer, I thought on my feelings of peace as opposed to the fear I had felt earlier at Horstman House. Somehow I sensed that my own desires to stay were warring with my fears, and it seemed the Lord was supporting my desire to stay. If Paul and his needs were not in the equation, it would have been easier to leave. But I also reminded myself that I didn't have another teaching job. I'd burned my bridges in California public schools, at least for the present.

Returning to immediate tasks, I set out the same blue dress I'd worn the night before. I realized that if I stayed I'd have to bring more clothes.

After leaving my room, I was amazed to find that an early riser had installed a safety rail and some safety strips in the bathroom. I locked the door with the old skeleton key. The locksmith hadn't been there, but I was encouraged to find that either Daniel or Ingrid had arranged to make the tub safer. It felt good to wash out the stickiness from my hair, and the wound had stopped bleeding so that I didn't need to bandage it. After getting dressed and then arranging my hair as best I could, I went down the back stairs to Blanche's kitchen and dining room.

No one was there, but the breakfast buffet was ready, so I helped myself to scrambled eggs, toast, and orange juice.

Blanche entered from the kitchen. "Oh, I was planning to bring a tray to your room," she said.

"Thanks, Blanche, but I'm feeling much better this morning. I'm going to teach Paul today." I said this not only to inform Blanche but also to let her spread the news, to anyone who might be interested, that I wouldn't be scared off.

"Well, that's wonderful. But don't overdo it. That was a nasty accident."

I was about to directly contradict her choice of term but thought better. Instead I said, "Someone has put some safety strips and a rail in the bathroom. If I can get the lock fixed, I won't have to worry about another . . . accident."

Blanche didn't respond to my insinuation. She went to check the buffet, then turned toward her kitchen. "I'll plan your lunch for the schoolroom, then," she said, closing the kitchen door behind her.

I said another prayer of thanks and blessing over the food, and repeated my need for help in making decisions that day. Then, finishing breakfast and returning up the back stairway to my room, I was surprised to find a gray-haired man kneeling by my door. He didn't look up when I approached, but continued his work on the lock.

"You're installing a lock?" I asked, realizing the answer was obvious.

"Ya can see that, can't ya?" he replied, abruptly. He was drilling a hole in the door for the lock and seemed disinterested in me. "Locksmith is just one of my many hats," he said without looking up.

He was wearing an old felt hat and a well-worn denim jumpsuit. Unshaven, his wrinkled face suggested the man was in his late sixties. But he had little trouble standing to get the lock that he'd left on a nearby table.

He looked at me then, but just briefly. "This *your* room?" he asked.

"Yes, and I'm glad to get a lock on it," I said.

"If I didn't have so many jobs to do, there'd be no need for locks 'round here," he complained. "I can't be a jack-of-all-trades and a good watchman, too."

"Oh, then you work full-time at Horstman House?"

"Yes, I work here. That's all I do—work," he grumbled, returning to his job at my door. "Handyman, groundskeeper, and security guard. Too much for one old geezer."

"Well, I'm Wendy Wood, the new teacher for Master Paul."

"I know who ya are," he said. "I just didn't know where they'd put ya."

"And you are?"

Either he was too grumpy or too busy to answer, so after a moment of waiting for his response, I squeezed past him into my room.

After a moment, he grumbled, "I'm John, John O'Connor."

"I'm glad to meet you, Mr. O'Connor," I said as I found the workbook I needed to teach Paul. Then, moving past Mr. O'Connor, I said, "Well, I'm off to work too. Will I see you again?"

"Ingrid will give ya a key to this lock," he said. "I'll lock it when I'm finished."

I stopped. "Thank you." I didn't like the fact that Ingrid would still have a key to my room if she was the keeper of the keys.

"Keep your door locked," Mr. O'Connor warned.

"Oh, I intend to, but who will have a duplicate of my key?" I asked, then wondered why he'd emphasized the need to lock it.

"Ingrid has a master key for the whole estate. So does Mr. Daniel, of course."

"Of course," I said, feeling less certain of the possibility of securing my room.

"Thanks, Mr. O'Connor."

"Sure," he said, smiling for the first time, a warmth entering his brown eyes. "I fixed up the bathroom for ya, too. I'll put a lock on it, when I'm done with this one. Use the same key." He returned to his work, seeming less grumpy, when he added, "Ya can call me John."

"I will—and thanks again, John, for your help."

I went down the hall toward the classroom thinking that John was one of the more friendly people I'd met here. Approaching the classroom door, I thought happily that maybe Paul and I could begin again without Ingrid's interference.

Paul was alone, waiting in the classroom. He brightened to see me. "Hi! I thought maybe you wouldn't come," he said.

"Well, I feel much better today, Paul, and I couldn't wait for us to get started again."

"I'm sorry," he said.

"Sorry?"

"That I acted like a brat last night at dinner. I don't want you to be mad at me."

"Well, that's a nice apology, Paul, but I understood that you were disappointed. It's just that neither the chair nor I could help the situation. Anyway, I'm grateful that you kicked the *chair*, not me," I said, laughing.

He smiled shyly. "Sometimes I just feel like kicking something," he explained.

"As I said, it's great that you didn't kick me." I smiled. "Let's forget it for now. Maybe we can talk more about your feelings later. Under the circumstances they were quite normal. Okay?"

Paul seemed relieved that I didn't lecture him, so I taught, avoiding further discussion of his father's failure to join us for dinner the previous evening. But I was determined to have it out with Daniel when I saw him.

When we returned from our morning break, I saw that Ingrid had left my room and bathroom key on my desk. I was glad I didn't have to deal directly with her.

Paul and I spent several uneventful days, but our learning together progressed, and I was getting a handle on his learning needs and strengths. I told him over and over what a great job he was doing, and I resolved again that he would get some enriching experiences beyond Ingrid's prescribed reading, writing, and arithmetic. But I didn't promise anything to Paul, not wanting to cause him further disappointment if I couldn't convince Ingrid to give us more freedom.

I decided that Daniel was purposely avoiding both Paul and me, either ashamed at having disappointed Paul again or not wanting to face my evaluation—spoken or unspoken—of his behavior.

The weekend, my first since coming to Horstman House, arrived. I had at last been successful, in reaching Jill by phone. She said that she could come to Pasadena to pick me up on Saturday, not Friday, so that I could return to Sherman Oaks to get more of my things and go to church.

I had confused feelings about leaving; I was glad to get away and to get more clothes, a mirror, my television, my radio, and more books to help me pass all my empty hours at Horstman House, but I was very worried about leaving Paul, who had made no secret of his concerns about my going. I knew that he feared I wouldn't return, deserting him as so many others had. I reassured him as best I could, trying to reassure myself at the same time.

I needed to reflect on my new situation without the stresses that I felt here. I needed to review all that had happened in this past week and decide whether I really wanted to stay. But in just one week, I realized, Paul's needs and his future had become my highest priority.

I gave Jill detailed directions to find the Horstman estate and arranged to meet her at the front gates at nine on Saturday morning. Her voice on the phone suggested that she was unhappy at not being able to see the house, but I assured her that she would have an opportunity in the future. For the time being I thought it best to postpone Jill's introduction to Horstman House and its occupants.

When I left by the rear entrance, which I'd used when I first came to Horstman House, Helman gave me instructions for opening the gate. Leaving him at the rear portico, I looked up at the third-floor balcony where I had seen the Great Bella. Then my eyes roamed once again over the beauties of the grounds at the rear of the mansion, marred only by the burned remains of the guesthouse. I looked back once more at Bella's windows and was startled to see the draperies move.

Then I saw Paul waving from the second-floor schoolroom window and I threw him a kiss. His sweet farewell made me forget the eeriness of Bella's reclusive life.

I walked down the winding road toward the gates, getting a closer look at the entry grounds. Everything was manicured beautifully. Roses and other spring flowers were in bloom everywhere, their fragrance filling the air. I thought of John O'Connor and his crew. He really knew what he was doing where landscaping was concerned. I hoped that he was just as good at being a night watchman. Maybe I could enlist his help in watching over me.

My spirits lifted as I escaped from the oppression and events of the past week. I hadn't realized just how isolated and threatened I'd felt. Then I saw Jill's car parked by the gate. Behind one of the gateway's supporting pillars, I found the switch that Helman had mentioned, and the gates swept open for my departure.

Seeing Jill was a joy, and I loved the drive in her convertible to Sherman Oaks, feeling a sense of abandon and freedom that I hadn't experienced in days. Jill questioned me about my week, and I told her about Ingrid, Martha, Blanche, and others, omitting details of the "accident" and brushing off Jill's concerns about my fall. Also, fielding her questions about Mr. Horstman, I didn't admit to her, or even to myself, my growing interest in the problematic Daniel, focusing instead on explaining Paul's needs.

The weekend seemed too short, but I managed to eat a lot, to prepare my belongings for transport to Pasadena, and to take in the new Steven Spielberg thriller *Jaws*. Somehow the terror of the characters in the film allowed me to purge some of my own fears.

The best part of the weekend was Sunday, when we went to Church meetings. In sacrament meeting I felt a sense of peace and was grateful to renew my vows to follow the Savior by taking His sacrament. The speaker, a sweet-faced, middle-aged sister, was introduced to the congregation by the bishop. She was new in the ward, but she confidently approached the lectern, emanating a strong spirit in her posture and stance. Her resonant voice supported my first impression of her, and her subject, about the need to be patient in seeking answers to our prayers, seemed to be directed to me. She suggested the scripture in Doctrine and Covenants 101:16: "Be still and know that I am God." I opened my triple combination and turned to that scripture, marking it for future reference, as I felt almost certain that I would be referring to it often in the near future. In that moment, I suddenly felt it was right to believe the Lord would keep me alive and make his purpose for me clear. I was to return to Horstman House and to help Paul, believing that the Lord would guide me and protect me, spiritually and physically.

Of course, I spent some time worrying about my return to Horstman House, its problems, and possibly its dangers, but I tried not to let Jill see my fears. I knew that I had to go back both for emotional and practical reasons. My thoughts became resolutions. I couldn't let Paul down. And I had to prove myself—to myself. I couldn't fail in another job. In fact, I desperately needed the job. I thought again of the scripture cited in sacrament meeting, *Be still and know that I am God.* It would be difficult to be "still," fearing that my life might be threatened, but I had an answer, at least for now.

Jill very kindly faced the Sunday evening freeway traffic to deliver me once again at Horstman House. Pulling up to the gates, she said, "I know how you got out, but how do you get back in?"

"Well, I wasn't entirely sure they'd want me back, but I managed to pry another secret from Helman."

"Who's that?" Jill asked.

"I told you about him. He's the chauffeur who brought me here. Naturally he has to know all about getting in and out," I explained. "He said that there's a bell and an intercom on the right side of the gate, hidden behind one of the support pillars."

I got out of the car, began looking for the secreted communication system, and found it in a brick column behind a climbing rose bush. Obviously the intercom was not in common use since I was required to part the bush to find the speaker and a button marked "press." I pressed it, waited for a response, then pressed it again—and again. Finally, Helman's voice ordered: "Please state your name and business."

Startled at the military-sounding command, I said, "Uh, this is Wendy Wood. I've returned." Somehow saying the words made me both wary and sad. I looked over at Jill, waiting patiently in her car, and fought an urge to hop in, tell her to floor it, and get me back to my life before Horstman House.

My thoughts were interrupted by another barked command from Helman. "The gates will open. Drive directly to the porte cochere at the rear of the house. Your driver will not leave the car. I will meet you there."

I returned to Jill's car and, forcing a lighthearted manner, said, "Our *orders* are to wait for the gate to open, drive to the rear of the house, and wait in the car." I laughed, but felt again that I was surrendering my freedom upon reentering that walled estate. The gates swung open as if by royal decree, and Jill drove up the hill to Horstman House and whatever was in store for me. Then I remembered Paul. He wanted and needed me to be there. That was my reason for returning. And that would be my reason for staying—if I did.

"Some digs," Jill observed, when we reached a point where she could see the full breadth of Horstman House.

"Yes," I replied, "but it's more a museum than a home, I'm sad to say."

"Well, I guess I'll have to pay the admission fee if I'm ever going to get inside," Jill quipped.

"I'm sorry I can't be more hospitable," I apologized. "Maybe things will change after I've been here awhile, but I've been told over and over that the Great Bella 'vants to be alone.' They really are very protective of her privacy. There are even parts of the house where no one but Bella is allowed."

"You're kidding?" Jill would have said more, I'm sure, but we had reached the house and Helman—waiting in his military stance.

When Jill stopped, Helman moved directly to open my door. "Do you have baggage with which you need help?" he asked curtly.

"Yes, thank you, Helman. I have a lot of things in the trunk," I explained.

Jill started to get out to open the trunk but was stopped by Helman. "I have no need of assistance. Allow me to use your keys to open the trunk." He went to the driver's side, holding out his hand for the keys, then opened the trunk and began unloading my things onto the porch.

I shrugged at Jill, apologizing with my facial expression rather than words. "Thanks," I said. "I'll try to get a car soon so you won't have to keep facing the freeways. I appreciate your help so much."

"I don't mind the freeways," she said with a nod toward the house, "but I really don't understand why you want to stay here." Jill finished loudly, unconcerned that Helman could hear her. "I wish you'd tell them all to go fly a kite and come back with me. You can find another job—I'm sure you can."

I spoke quietly, "I have to give it a fair try and I've told you about Paul. He's had so many teachers disappoint him. Not to mention his so-called family."

"Well, I'd hoped at least there'd be some romantic interest here for you—the eligible Daniel Horstman. Maybe you can convert him! How about it?" she hinted.

"Jill!" I protested.

"Miss Wood," Helman interrupted.

"Yes, I'm coming," I responded. "We'll have to talk about that another time, Jill. I guess Helman's ready, and no one keeps him waiting. Thanks again. I think Helman will open the gates for you. Drive carefully."

"Call me," Jill said. "You do have change for the pay phone, I take it?" She laughed and was gone, and I felt very much alone. I turned back from watching Jill drive off and saw a curtain move in a third-floor window. *She* had been watching my return.

Helman moved one of my boxes inside the rear door, pressed a button, waited long enough for Jill to escape the estate, and then closed the gates. He then proceeded to carry more of my belongings inside, without a word.

I picked up a suitcase and one small box and followed Helman into the ominous atmosphere of the dark hall. For better or worse, I was once again in Horstman House.

Chapter Twelve

My first Sunday evening at Horstman House was much like my first night there—alone again, and wondering what to do with myself. I had unpacked and found a place on the bedside table for my small TV and my radio. But I really wasn't in the mood to kick back; I'd done enough of that over the weekend. I went down to the servants' dining room, but it was deserted. It appeared there was to be no evening meal on Sundays. Blanche probably took dinner to family members' rooms, and the staff probably had to fend for themselves, I reasoned. Well, I wasn't hungry anyway, I figured, just bored.

I returned to my room and turned on the radio, trying to find some spiritually satisfying music, but heard instead the Bee Gees. Another station was playing an early Carpenter's hit, which only added to my loneliness. I tried the TV, but the built-in rabbit ears provided poor reception, so I gave up on the news about Nixon. Then I reviewed the scriptures which had been stressed in Church meetings that day, but concentration was impossible. The house was so oppressive and dreary that I had to escape. I decided to go outside to enjoy the spring weather and further explore the grounds. I found my white cardigan and, after locking my door carefully, started down the back stairs toward the dining room, kitchen, and a first-floor exit. The dimly lit stairwell combined with the silence was eerie. My heart raced when I thought I heard a noise behind me. But when I turned I could see no one. *Just the creaky big house,* I supposed, laughing at myself for being so jumpy. But I held the handrail tightly and hurriedly escaped to the rear door.

It was a relief to step outside into the twilight beauty of the grounds. I walked through the rose gardens and looked toward the gazebo and the pool, thinking of going that way. However, a wind had come up from the north, and I decided to head the opposite way toward the garage. There were lights above the six-car building, and I wondered if Helman lived there. A path led beyond the cobblestone driveway toward the woods and small lake. It was light enough to pick my way along the path, but even so I wished I had a flashlight.

I was about to turn back while I could still see the lights of the main house because I had an eerie feeling that someone was following me. But I continued along the path and stepped through a parting of the thickly growing trees to discover the courtyard of a small cottage. The house, hidden by the trees, was such a surprise and was so charming that I was drawn to the lighted porch. On the front door a nameplate invited, "John and Mary O'Connor. Welcome."

Welcome. I'd seldom seen or heard that word at Horstman House. I responded automatically by lifting my hand to knock. Then reason controlled impulse. I realized that a late Sunday intrusion of an unexpected and unfamiliar guest might not be so welcome, after all.

Instinctively, I looked through an undraped window to see if anyone was about, but the comfortable-looking living room appeared empty. They might be eating dinner in another room, I thought. I'd come back another time, after becoming better acquainted with Mr. O'Connor.

I had decided to return to Horstman House when I heard it—a wailing sound coming from the direction of the lake. It sounded like a tomcat pining for an amorous female, or maybe an animal crying in pain. Something told me to run the other way, but I couldn't ignore a cry for help, even from an animal. Ignoring that inner warning, I pushed through a wall of fir-tree limbs, ducking under one low bough and another. The aroma of the trees was pungent when I brushed against the needles. Then I caught my sweater sleeve on a jagged, broken limb and, trying to pull it loose, fell backward down a slight incline. My hand was wet and muddy. Obviously I had reached the lake. And the caterwauling cries continued, sounding even more desperate.

So I picked myself up and turned in the direction of the noise. In the growing darkness I could see a shed at the edge of the lake, and the sounds seemed to be coming from there. I carefully approached an open, heavy, wooden door and reached inside hoping to find a light switch. The animal noises were even louder and more frantic. I found the switch, and the shed was lit by one overhead bulb.

A big snarling, angry black cat was trapped in an old piece of fish netting, trying to claw its way out. The cat's distress had brought me to what I realized was a boathouse, where a dusty old Chris-Craft inboard boat was berthed.

How could I release the animal without getting scratched or bitten? There was a workbench along one wall. Maybe I could find a knife or some other cutting tool. There were flowerpots and garden tools everywhere, and among them I found an old pair of gloves. I hurriedly shook them to get rid of bugs or spiders, before putting my hands inside. I didn't find a knife, but there was a rusty pair of garden shears hanging on a nail.

Hesitantly I approached the hissing cat, which calmed some when I began to remove the netting, possibly sensing my attempts to help. The second I had cut a hole large enough, the cat jumped out, hissed, and escaped through the open door.

I turned back to return the gloves and shears, and the lights went out! At the same instant the door banged shut, and I thought I heard a locking-bar drop into place. Feeling my way in the darkness, I ran into the door and tried to open it, but it wouldn't budge. Who could have shut me in? Was someone playing games? I found the light switch again and then looked for another door or window but found only a folding, overhead garage door. It was padlocked in place.

Then I saw smoke coming under the entry door and flames through the cracks between the roof boards. The building was on fire! I screamed but realized that no one was likely to hear me. *Keep your head!* I commanded myself. I had to get out! I slid into the water beside the boat and, holding to the railing on the boat, edged toward the garage door. But the overhead door was closed to the edge of the water and beneath it were iron bars.

I dove under to try to swim out but found the iron bar gates were mired in mud and locked with a padlock and chain. I swam to the surface, avoiding the hull of the boat. Would someone see the fire? Would someone come to my rescue? It seemed impossible that anyone would come in time.

Smoke filled the shed, so I stayed in the water below the floor line. Then I began worrying about an explosion if the fire were to spread to the boat. I was coughing and becoming exhausted. Fear created a desperate and futile hope. I climbed into the cabin of the boat and was relieved to see a key in the ignition. Could I start the boat and use the motor to push the boat through the door? I said a frantic prayer for help.

The engine cranked but would not start. I tried it again and again, making a mighty noise but accomplishing nothing. Then I felt it—a blast of hot air followed by a cool wind. Someone yelled, "Is anyone in here?" My prayer had been answered.

I was coughing and gasping but managed to start climbing out of the cabin. "I'm here," I choked. "Help me! Help me!"

Apparently I passed out at that point, because the next thing I was aware of was that I lay on a sofa with John O'Connor leaning over me, washing my face with a cold cloth.

"Good, good, you're comin' around now," he said with genuine concern. "I was afraid for a moment I might lose ya."

I tried to respond but began coughing again.

"I got ya out before ya were burned and brought ya on that old wheelbarrow to the house, but your breathing scared me for a while," he added.

Finally I was able to croak a reply, "Thanks—thanks for getting me—out."

"Well, I smelled the fire. Then I heard ya trying to start that old engine. That's how I knew someone was in there. Otherwise I wouldn't have tried to get in. The wind must have blown the door shut, and the fire spread mainly up to the roof, eating up those old wood shingles."

I tried talking again. "Could I have some water?"

"Sure, sure, I have it right here. Let me help ya." He held a glass to my lips, and I gulped the cooling liquid.

"Thanks—thanks again," I managed to say.

"I called the main house. They've sent some men to watch the fire, but decided to just let the old boathouse burn down." He sounded regretful about it, but then he turned his focus to me, patted my arm and said, "I'm sure someone's on the way to see how ya are."

The water seemed to restore my voice. "The wind may have blown the door shut, but who—who could have started the fire?"

"Well, I'm afraid I'm guilty," he apologized. "Ya see, this afternoon I was burning some dry leaves and weeds back in the trees by the lake—they didn't get cleaned out last fall. I thought I'd put the fire out, but there must have been a spark or two left. And that wind fanned the flames. I'm sorry. It was an accident."

That word again. I wondered, how was it that the accidents of the past week all seemed to involve me? But I didn't say that to John. He seemed so genuinely sorry.

"I think they sent for old Doc Richardson," he said, looking at the clock on the wall.

"Oh, tell them not to bother him. I'm all right. I just feel shaken—and frightened."

We were interrupted by a loud knock at the door, followed by the entrance of Daniel Horstman, who didn't wait for John to show him in. Seeing me on the sofa, he said to John, "Is she okay?" Then he rushed to me and kneeled by my side. "Are you—are you hurt?"

"No, no. I was just telling John that I'm more shaken up than hurt," I said quietly. I tried to control my feelings but began to cry. Somehow I was relieved to have Daniel at my side and I couldn't stop the emotional release.

I was surprised when Daniel embraced me, like someone comforting a frightened child. "There now, let it out. You're in shock. But thank heaven you weren't burned." Then, realizing that he was holding me, he became self-conscious and carefully laid me back on the sofa pillow.

He said to John, "Your workmen got the boat out and are watching the fire to make sure it doesn't spread." Turning back to me, he explained, "We're just letting it burn out. No one has used that old boat for years, and the boathouse should have been torn down long ago." He looked in my eyes. "You're sure you don't need a doctor?"

"No. please, no! I'm all right," I urged.

"We tried to reach Dr. Richardson but couldn't. John said that you seemed okay, but I rushed here to make certain—to see if we should call emergency services." He seemed anxious and very concerned.

"I'm sorry. I'm sure this brings back some bad memories from the other—the earlier fire," I said.

"Well, yes, it does. But this time no one was burned—hurt." He sounded sincerely relieved. "We'll get you back to the house when you're ready."

I felt like asking to stay in John's cottage, where I definitely felt more secure and at home than at Horstman House. I asked, "John, is Mary—is your wife—here?"

There was a silence, broken by John. "I'm sure no one has told ya. Mary's been dead for almost ten years. She always used the boathouse as a potting shed, so I'm kind of sad to see it go. I found her there one day—among her plants. She was gone."

"So my actions have brought back sad memories for you, too. I'm so sorry," I said, and I meant it.

"No need to feel sorry," John reassured. "It's been a long time, but it's one of the reasons I haven't kept up that boathouse. I didn't like going there, to tell ya the truth."

"I understand." I felt I had to explain why I'd gone there. "I was just exploring the grounds earlier and came to your house. That's when I saw her name—Mary's—on the door. Then I heard a cat wailing. It sounded as if it were in pain. I found it trapped in a net in the boathouse."

"Was it a black tom?" John asked.

"Yes, it was," I replied. "Is he yours?"

"No, he's a stray, but he's been around for a while. He's a good mouser. That's why I keep him," John said. "Those old nets were never used for fishing. Mary used them for roses and vines to climb on. There's no fish in the lake now."

"Well, thanks again, John. I apologize for having caused so much trouble for you." I looked at Daniel. "For everybody." I tried to sit up. "I guess I'm ready to go back now." Both men hurried to help me.

"Now, take it easy," Daniel cautioned. "We could get a car for you."

"No, don't be silly. I can walk that far, if you'll help me find the way back. I'm feeling rather disoriented."

"Of course, I wouldn't let you walk back alone—especially in the dark. Thanks, John, for taking care of her. I'm glad you heard her in time." He looked at me, then back at John. "The men will watch the fire. Why don't you call it a night?" He walked me toward the door.

"Take that afghan with ya, Miss Wood." John went to the sofa and returned with a crocheted afghan, putting it round my shoulders. "Ya don't want to get a chill. Ya can bring it back another time. We'll have a happy visit next time."

"Thanks, I'd like that," I said.

"I'll meet with you tomorrow, John," Daniel said in a strangely stern tone. And we left for Horstman House.

We said little while walking toward the house. In truth, I was too wet, cold, and tired to talk. Daniel saw me up the stairs to my room and suggested that I get into some dry, warm things and lock my door. He said good night and that he hoped I'd be better after a good night's sleep. Then he left down the second-floor hall.

Only two things were keeping me from fleeing Horstman House right then—I had to see Paul again, and I was going to have a good, long talk with Daniel Horstman in the morning.

Chapter Thirteen

Despite the trauma of the evening, I slept soundly and awakened early. I was ravenous. I hadn't eaten since noon on Sunday, and filling my stomach seemed paramount—until my aches and pains reminded me of having been trapped in the burning shed. I felt sick, knowing now with certainty that someone was determined to hurt me, kill me, or at the least frighten me into leaving Horstman House. I knew that the wind and an errant spark were not the cause of last night's incident. I found that I desired to be more in tune with the Spirit, as I recalled with some clarity that I hadn't felt good about going into the shed, but had followed my own will rather than those feelings. I expressed gratitude to the Lord for preserving my life, when I knelt at my bedside in the morning. I also asked that I might be more in tune with His will. When I finished my prayer I felt a strong impression that there was something more I had to accomplish here. Was the Lord directing me to stay? I thought once again of the Lord's commandment to be still and let Him direct my life. I also felt that I needed help and perspective.

The time had come to tell Daniel of my suspicions and to demand that he help me find the perpetrator. Two serious attacks in a few days ought to be sufficient proof. But while preparing to shower, I realized that I still had no genuine evidence.

I locked the bathroom door, using the manual deadbolt which John had installed. I felt more secure than I had before, but my memories of slipping and banging my head were coupled with my more recent brush with death by fire. I found myself shaking all over, regardless of the usually soothing effect of the warm shower.

I calmed down a bit by the time I dried off. There were bruises and scrapes on my arms and legs. They were only minor injuries, but they served as reminders of my ordeal.

I returned to my room, unlocked my door, and then wondered what to do with the wet clothing I had dropped to the floor. No one had mentioned handling of my personal laundry, so I'd taken it back to Sherman Oaks with me last Saturday. But I couldn't keep these wet clothes in a laundry bag. I supposed I'd have to ask Ingrid.

The thought of Ingrid rekindled my anger. Our conflicts regarding Paul had become the focus of my rage, and I was certain that she was involved somehow in everything unpleasant and dangerous that had happened to me. I'd accuse her when I talked with Daniel, I decided. But what proof of her other involvements did I have? My fears surely wouldn't be enough to convince him. Without the threatening note and without a witness to the threatening phone call, he'd dismiss my charges as hysteria. I'd have to find some way to persuade him that my experiences weren't mere accidents.

I dressed in a black crepe dress, wanting to appear as mature and businesslike as possible so that Daniel wouldn't look at me as the young, ponytailed girl he'd seen the past week.

Then I suddenly asked my reflection, why am I even worrying about what Daniel thinks or believes? A soft knock at my door interrupted these frustrating thoughts, and I answered it, wanting to lash out arbitrarily at whomever was there. Upon opening the door, I was greeted by the sweet, worried eyes of Paul.

"Paul, what are you doing here so early?" I asked in surprise.

"This time I listened at the door before I knocked. I could hear you moving around in here," he explained.

"Well, I'm very glad to see you, but shouldn't you be at breakfast? Blanche will be wondering where you are."

"I just had to come to see if you're okay. I heard Dad talking about what happened to you last night."

He looked so upset that I wanted to bend down and hug him. But I thought better, remembering Ingrid's scoldings about becoming too familiar with the family. So I took his hands and said, "I'm all right, Paul. I don't want you to worry about me. Okay?"

"Well, okay, but I had to see if you were here—and all right."
Then he asked hopefully, "Are you going to teach me today?"

"I had planned to, maybe later. Okay? I have to talk with your
father about what happened and . . . some other things."

Trying to find a way to stay, he said, "I know what. We could eat
breakfast together." He grabbed my hand to pull me along with him.

"Well, I don't know. Ingrid might not be happy about that and
she'll expect you at the schoolroom at nine," I reminded.

He whined, "But I won't be late for school." He held out his
wristwatch. "Look, it's only eight. We can eat fast, and then I can
hurry to the schoolroom. She won't even know." He smiled mischie-
vously in anticipation of my agreeing.

"No, Paul, on second thought, we won't sneak about. If we eat
together, we'll just say that we did. There's nothing to hide." I decided
at that moment that I was through bowing to Ingrid's tyranny. If she
didn't like it, then I'd take it up with her boss, Daniel. "Let's go down
and ask Blanche where she'd prefer to serve us—your dining room or
mine."

Blanche wasn't too happy about setting another place beside Paul
in the main dining room, but certainly thought it more appropriate
than allowing Master Paul to dine in the servants' eating area. So Paul
and I started a big breakfast of pancakes, eggs, and bacon in the
hallowed room usually reserved for the Horstmans, or more
accurately, for Paul.

I had forgotten temporarily what lay ahead of me, but was
reminded by the unexpected entrance of Daniel.

"Well, what have we here?" Daniel asked in greeting. "I've been
looking for both of you."

Paul spoke first, "I talked Wendy—I mean Miss Wood—into
having breakfast with me."

"I hope it's all right," I added. "Paul was concerned about me, and
neither of us had eaten yet, so we just came here together."

"Well, then, I guess we'll have to be together facing Ingrid's
wrath," Daniel said. His easy manner was disarming, as I'd spent the
early morning bracing for a confrontation and was still feeling
combative. He seemed less authoritative dressed informally in jeans
and a chambray shirt.

He went into Blanche's kitchen, then quickly returned. "Blanche will set another place for me if you'll let me join you." He sat down across from me without giving us a chance to react. Blanche bustled in and set a place for him, then left.

Paul said abruptly, "Hey, this makes up for that night you didn't come to dinner last week."

Daniel looked sheepishly at each of us. "Yes, I guess it does. I'm sorry," he explained. "I got involved in some business on the phone and forgot until it was too late to come. I apologize to both of you."

Paul's youthful candor had taken care of one of the matters I'd planned to discuss with Daniel—his need to apologize or to make up to Paul for his failure to show for dinner. So my anger subsided a bit. But I still had to make it clear that I wanted his help in preventing more threats or attempts to harm me. Looking at Paul, I decided that would have to wait until he wasn't present.

Conversation was awkward. We tried to make the breakfast chatter light, but it all seemed forced and unnatural. Even small talk had to have a starting point, and we couldn't find one. The occurrence of the night before was an unsatisfactory subject. After his initial outburst, Paul seemed constrained in his father's presence. And I couldn't bring up my concerns. *What's left, the weather?* I thought in frustration. Somehow we made it through the meal, but no one watched the time—a sure recipe for disaster. And it came, in the form of Ingrid, disaster incarnate.

She pushed through the kitchen doors, took one look at the gathering, and ordered, "Master Paul, you are late. To the schoolroom at once."

Paul jumped up to attention and, looking to me, then to his father for support, pleaded, "But we're having a special breakfast."

"We will discuss that with Miss Wood later," Ingrid retorted. "In the meantime, rules are rules." She pointed with her long index finger. "To the schoolroom."

Paul said quietly, "Okay," and moving out of Ingrid's sight, he stuck out his tongue, backed out of the room, and plodded down the hall.

Involuntarily, I stood. "Was that necessary?" I asked her.

"Necessary? Indeed it was mandatory. I will not allow this house to fall apart because of your liberal attitudes," she stated sharply.

Daniel, neutral up to this point in the argument, stood and explained, "It's my fault, Ingrid. I joined them for breakfast and we weren't aware of the time."

"That's right," I added, looking accusingly at Ingrid. "Also, the events of last night do call for a slight change in routine." I took a breath and plunged ahead. "I need to talk *privately* with Mr. Horstman, so if possible, could you teach Paul or excuse him from school until we're finished?"

Ingrid began to object, but Daniel stopped her. "Yes, do that, will you, Ingrid?"

"But I have other duties to attend to," she complained, in a rather shocked voice.

"Thank you," Daniel said in dismissal. "I'll speak with you later."

Ingrid drew a deep breath and rose to her toes. Then, suppressing her anger, she lowered her heels, looked hatefully at me, and went down the hall expressing fury in every step.

I turned to Daniel. "Thank you. I'm sorry to be such a constant disruption to your life."

"Well, it has been quite a week," he agreed, smiling.

"Can we stay here to talk?" I asked, moving back to my chair.

"Yes, I guess this is as good a place as any." Always the gentleman, he waited for me to sit and then returned to his chair opposite of me. The situation felt too formal, like a negotiation at a conference table. *But maybe that's suitable,* I thought.

I was searching for a way to begin when Blanche and Angela entered. "Excuse us," Blanche said. "Could we get the dishes out of your way if you're finished?"

Daniel replied, "Of course, Blanche, thank you." He seemed relieved at the interruption.

Angela looked at Daniel, at me, and then raised her eyebrows as if to say, "What's this all about?" She smiled, but Blanche was all business, rushing Angela out to the kitchen with the remains of breakfast.

Their leaving was followed by another awkward silence. Finally, I decided to dive in. "I'm glad you came and that you apologized—to Paul. It meant a lot to him."

"I was apologizing to you too. I just couldn't get rid of that woman—the one who called me," he blurted out. He hurried to explain, "It was business, at least her business. Carolyn Reinhart is quite a talker when she wants something. And she wants to use my mother's name and film work to raise money for a charity."

I was interested, both in this other woman and the reference to Bella, but said only, "You don't need to elaborate. I understand that you have a busy life. It was just that—"

"I know, I promised," he admitted.

"Well, that was number one on my discussion list—Paul. In fact," I said, "he's the *main* reason I'm still here. In the short week I've known him I've become very concerned about his future. And I've become very attached to him—as a pupil."

"And he to you, I've noticed, but not just as his teacher." He paused and winked. "I think he's fallen for you."

"I sense that too." I smiled and shook my head in amusement, then became serious. "But it comes from his great need to be loved— to know that someone loves him. He wants a family. He wants a father." There, I'd said it clearly.

"And he needs a mother," Daniel said, lowering his eyes to the tabletop.

I couldn't help urging, "Well, we know that isn't possible right now, but the rest is. He has you. He has a grandmother—"

He looked up. "No, he doesn't have a grandmother." He waited a moment, then continued, "But he does have me. I do love him and I want him to know that." He paused, thinking. "Will you help me?" he questioned.

I was so overjoyed at hearing this sincere expression of his love for Paul, and of his determination to change, that I couldn't control my response. "Yes, yes I will. I'll do everything I can to bring the two of you together." I was surprised to find that my eyes had teared up. I was clearly more emotional after my attack, but the force of my feelings about Paul and Daniel was surprising even to me. I hadn't thought of myself as the emotional type before.

Daniel rose from his chair and came behind me. He turned me about and said, "I know you've had a difficult time here—with Ingrid and with the accidents—but you've already blessed this house. You've helped me—us—more than you know. There's new life here because of you."

His words warmed me and his body language caught me off guard. *He's going to hold me.* Of course, I would have stopped him, but then he abruptly stepped back.

I reflected that the morning has been filled with awkward moments—now another one. I turned toward him in my chair and felt the same desire to show affection, but checked my emotions as he had done. Instead, I said, "Well, we've resolved one of my concerns, but you've brought up the others—Ingrid and the accidents. We have to talk about them, too. I want to stay here for Paul, but I can't continue to argue with Ingrid." I turned away. "I can't continue to be afraid."

"Afraid? I know you've been hurt, but you shouldn't be afraid here. I've already explained that—"

I stopped him. "But you don't know *everything* that's happened. You know only part of it."

"Well, tell me the rest. I can't help you if I'm in the dark," he said.

"But I feel so foolish and I don't—didn't—know you well enough to confide in you."

"You do now. Go on. You can tell me." He sat at my side in Paul's place at the table.

I gathered courage to let it all out. "To begin with, I didn't just fall in the tub. I was pushed."

"Martha told me you said that, but she assured me it was impossible. When you screamed, she came immediately to help. She would have seen anyone trying to escape the bathroom," he reasoned.

"I know what I felt—hands on my shoulders pushing me down. But there's more." I was hesitant to go on having no proof, but I had to get it out. "There was a note slipped under my door. I kept it in my purse, but it disappeared."

"A note? What did it say?" he asked. His voice was calm, but his physical movements appeared agitated, like he was suppressing something.

"It was very clear. It said, 'leave this house.' I was so shaken at finding it, but I kept it, in case I needed it for proof."

"Don't think I'm doubting you, but I have to know everything. Please go on," he said, rising and pacing.

"Yes, I want you to know," I stressed. "The note was typed. That's why I wanted to find the typewriters in this house, to compare the typeface, but someone took the note—maybe so I couldn't find out who wrote it."

"Well, I'll find out—"

"Wait, there's more. I received a threatening phone call. I heard the pay phone ringing in the hall. I couldn't recognize the voice, but when I answered, someone—I think it was a woman—repeated the same message as the note and hung up."

Daniel was very agitated by my revelations. He came back to the table, leaned in and looked directly at me. "Could you have imagined it? Because of the stress you were under?"

"No, I didn't imagine it." I was irritated by his reluctance to believe me. "What reason would I have to imagine that—or to make it up? I haven't been here long enough to develop ulterior motives. *Someone* wants me out of here badly enough to try to frighten me away, or failing that, to kill me."

He moved beside my chair. "Well, this is my house. And I don't want you to leave. When you're around Paul seems happier than I've ever seen him. And I want you to stay."

"Well, then, please talk with Ingrid," I begged. "I don't like pointing fingers because I have no proof, but she's the main source of conflict here. She doesn't like me and she doesn't want me here."

He sat at the head of the table. "I understand your feelings. But her reactions aren't directed only at you. She's made life difficult for others in your position. She's very jealous of her relationship with Paul—with the family."

"Yes, Martha mentioned that to me, but I don't think the other teachers were quite as determined, quite as vocal, as I've been—but it's only because of Paul's needs."

"Several of our household staff have been here for many years. Ingrid, Martha, Blanche, Helman and John almost seem like family. In many ways, they're the only family I've known. I've depended on them for everything," he explained. "I'm going to meet with all of them and make clear my wishes as far as you're concerned. That should end any debate about your standing here. They'll be ordered to take good care of you, I promise you. And I'm going to look out for you."

"Thank you." I stood, feeling genuinely relieved. "That does make me feel better—to have your support. I'll try to earn it, to be worthy of your trust in me. I really believe I can help Paul."

"You have already, and you've helped me—to start to bridge the gap between us. He likes you more than anyone we've brought here." Looking up to me, he said, "I do too." He paused, seeming to reflect on his words. "I'm sorry, that wasn't appropriate."

"I—I don't mind being told that I'm liked and needed," I said quietly.

"I've been wanting to tell you how *badly* we need you since the first time we talked in the library." There was another awkward pause. "I'm sorry, I'm forgetting—our situation. Forgive me," he said. "It's just that I want to get to know you on a more personal basis, and . . . well, I sense you do too." He hesitated. "Though now might not be the appropiate time."

I wasn't sure what he was getting at, but I had concerns of my own. "I guess I have to remember why I'm here—to teach your son. I don't want anything to interfere with that. But there are other differences between us which do matter."

"What do you mean? Our ages?" he asked.

"Well, you need to understand that I don't believe in casual relationships. I want to know someone *very* well before I lose my head. And, there's something else."

"Yes? What?"

I stood and moved away from the table, turning my back to him. "I'm very inexperienced, where men are concerned. In fact, I'm as naive as a country girl can be."

"Maybe that's what makes you so appealing," he suggested, smiling.

I turned toward him. "There's more."

"Okay, tell me," he urged.

"I'm a Mormon girl. I have some very strict standards when it comes to relationships. So I move *very* slowly and I try to keep my head on straight."

He became rather defensive. "Well, I know about your background. In fact, that's one of the reasons I wanted to hire you—your reputation and the reputation of your church. Believe me, I checked carefully into your past. And several of my acquaintances have hired Mormon nannies. As I've said, I *do* care about what happens to my son. And I'm not rushing you into—anything," he said. "Especially not now."

"I know that. But I just wanted you to know that there are differences which go beyond our ages. I'm sure I'm not like other women you've known."

"Other women? It's obvious you don't know me either. Believe me, I haven't known a lot of other women. Before I was married, I was as naive and inexperienced as you say you are when it came to the opposite sex. I lived a very monastic and secluded life within these hallowed Horstman halls."

"Well, I guess that's what I needed to say, and what I needed to hear." I sat at the table again.

"For the time being?" he asked.

"Yes, for the time being," I agreed. "But there is one more question."

"Of course, what is it?"

I sighed, then asked, "Do you really believe I was accidentally locked in the boathouse?"

"Well, I have to rely on John's report of the situation since I wasn't there. He said that the wind must have blown the door shut and that old locking bar was hanging on a loose bolt. He figured the bar just fell into place when the door slammed shut. I questioned him thoroughly about it and about the cause of the fire," he assured me.

"I guess I'll have to accept that explanation then," I said, and Daniel appeared relieved. I added, "But it seems very odd that so many unusual circumstances would occur just as I happened into the shed. And why did the lights go out?"

He looked shocked at my question and paused as if trying to phrase a response. Then, not answering, he looked at me closely. "Let's just be glad that John found you and you weren't hurt. That's enough, isn't it?" he persuaded.

"I guess it will have to be—for the time being."

Chapter Fourteen

After my talk with Daniel, I went to the schoolroom. Paul was there, sitting at his desk and reading an ancient second-grade reader. "That's great that you're already working, Paul!"

He looked up and smiled happily. "I didn't think you'd come," he said.

"Your father and I finished our talk, for now, so I came to eat lunch with you when it's time." I looked at my watch; it was ten-thirty.

"I was scared because Ingrid was so mad. She went back to see Dad, and I thought maybe you'd have to leave—like the others."

"Did she say something about that, Paul?"

"Well, she didn't think I heard her but she told Helman that she wanted you out of this house and the sooner the better. That scared me," he said, coming to me.

"Your father says that her bark is worse than her bite," I explained, not entirely convinced myself. Paul looked puzzled so I clarified. "I don't mean to be disrespectful. It was just a way of making the idea clear. What your father really said was that I shouldn't worry about Ingrid and we should just go on with our work. It's good advice, so let's do it, okay?" I went to the desk.

"I know what you mean. Sometimes she's so bossy and mean but she doesn't really hurt us," Paul said.

"Yes, that's right," I agreed without real conviction.

Paul read aloud to me for the minutes remaining before lunch, and I realized once more that he really needed help building his skills. Too many teachers and too little continuity in his learning, I thought.

"It's twelve-fifteen, and Blanche hasn't brought lunch," I said.

"I know but I need to use the rest room," Paul said, pulling a face and gritting his teeth.

"Oh, I'm sorry, Paul," I apologized. "We're off schedule again. Let's go down the hall, then check on lunch. Maybe Blanche's schedule has been interrupted too."

We found that true. Paul went to his room, and I to the hall bathroom. Then we met in the servants' hall. Deciding to take a shortcut to the kitchen, we went down the back stairs, and I was surprised to see, for the first time, the servants' dining room in full use. Martha waved, and I waved to her and to John. The other employees looked up and some smiled, then went about finishing their meals. I hadn't seen Martha since the previous Friday, so I asked Paul to wait at the foot of the stairs. I slid between the wall and the workers to talk with Martha and to thank John again for his help the night before.

Martha greeted me warmly, "Oh, Wendy, I'm so glad to see you."

John, seated across from her, stood. "Ya look a lot better than ya did last night," he observed. "Ya feeling all right?"

"Yes, thanks." I said. "It's nice to see friends—to know I have some here. Both of you have rescued me this past week. I'm grateful and I hope you won't have to again."

"Well, I'm certain we won't," Martha reassured me. "We're all going to take better care of you."

"Yah, we are," John added.

It was obvious that Daniel had met with them already, since they were echoing his words. I hoped that at least Martha and John wanted to and weren't just following orders.

"Well, you've both been good to me." I remembered Paul was waiting for me. "Paul and I came down to find some lunch. Is Blanche around?" I asked.

"Oh, no," Martha explained. "After we met with Mr. Horstman this morning, she went right up to her room. Angela's taken over the serving for today. I think she's in the kitchen."

"Thanks, I'll check with her. I'll see you later," I said, and returned to Paul.

Together we went into the kitchen where a frantic Angela and another girl, whom I hadn't met, were up to their ears in food and dishes. Without appearing to look up, she said, "I hired on as a maid, not a cook's helper. This is worse than cleaning."

"Is there something we can do to help?" I asked.

"Oh, no," Angela replied. "Everything looks a mess, but everybody's been fed—Oh, I forgot. I was supposed to get a tray to the schoolroom for you. Dang! I thought I'd done it all."

"Well, we don't mind eating here if there's anything left."

"Yeah, there are some turkey sandwiches there on the counter. Will that do?" Angela asked.

"Sure," Paul said. "Can we eat in here?"

"The sandwiches look good, Angela, but I think we'd better not let Blanche catch us eating in her kitchen."

"No, she'd have a fit," Angela agreed. "Take them up to your schoolroom, will you? Then she won't know I forgot." She ran to the refrigerator. "Here, take these cartons of milk, too." She handed us the milk and a tray, and we loaded the sandwiches on a plate.

This time the shortcut was through the main dining room, so Paul opened the double doors and we barged in together only to meet Daniel and Ingrid, seated at the table in serious discussion. They looked up.

"I'm sorry," I apologized. "We didn't realize anyone was here."

"You see what I mean," Ingrid said with satisfaction. "A total disregard for routine and my directions." She raised her chin in defiance.

I hurried to explain, but became more and more annoyed as I did. "Apparently Blanche had to go to her room, and Angela was very busy, so we came down for our tray." I resented having to make excuses for such an easily understood situation.

"We were hungry," Paul said.

Ingrid was not to be kept from pressing the point, however. "This is just another example of interruptions in our orderly household. Blanche is upset, and mealtime doesn't go as it should."

"Ingrid, let's not make mountains out of molehills," Daniel suggested. "Things will get back to normal now."

"I wish I could be that certain," Ingrid countered, shaking her head. "But, of course, we'll do as you wish, Mr. Horstman. I'm just warning that—"

"That's enough for now. Let's just get back to our duties," Daniel proposed.

Ingrid stood to leave. Daniel also rose. Then, seeing the futility of further protest, Ingrid left without a word through the kitchen.

"So long as you're here, why not sit at the table for lunch?" Daniel asked.

"That's a great idea," Paul said, running to his usual chair.

"Then we wouldn't have to take the tray upstairs," I agreed, and moved with the tray to the chair Ingrid just vacated.

"I've talked with the household staff, as you may have noticed. I think they understand what's expected from now on," he said.

"Yes, I thought you must have met with them. John and Martha were almost *too* anxious to please. But Blanche and Ingrid don't seem to have taken your orders—your suggestions—quite so well," I observed.

"Oh, Blanche was upset by everything that's been happening, and we expected Ingrid's response, didn't we?" Daniel asked, smiling.

"Yes, but—" I looked to see how Paul was reacting. "I wish things could be different—that we didn't have conflict over every decision I make regarding—" I stopped before referring to Paul, gesturing toward him with my head instead.

"You'll have free rein regarding your teaching from now on. I've asked Ingrid to give you total freedom in those decisions. If you have any problems, I hope you'll let me know," Daniel said firmly.

"Well, thank you. As I said before, I'll do everything I can to earn that trust."

Daniel smiled at me, then gathered some papers from the table, saying, "I'm going to leave you to eat your lunch. I have to check on the clean-up at the lake. Then I have a meeting in town this afternoon." He stood to go. "Can you two get along without me for a while?" He tousled Paul's hair and then put his hands on Paul's shoulders. Paul looked up and back in happy disbelief at the unusual attention. And I smiled my approval.

"We'll try," I said. "Have a good afternoon."

"I will. You too." He held up his open palm in parting, and Paul and I watched him leave. I knew from Paul's smile that he too could see that the man walking down the hall was beginning to change.

After lunch we returned to the schoolroom and began making plans to make learning more interesting. Pictures and new books would be a start, but plans to take advantage of the library, the gardens, the lake, and the art collection were anxiously anticipated. I couldn't wait to add some real-world experience to our textbook learning.

The day ended more happily than it had begun for at least two occupants of Horstman House, Paul and his teacher. I hoped, too, that Daniel's efforts to halt the threats and so-called accidents would end my fears.

Chapter Fifteen

A very welcome, uneventful evening followed our school day. Paul and I had a pleasant meal and experienced at least a degree of normalcy, uninterrupted by Ingrid's tirades or other unsettling events.

I went to bed early, tired from the preceding twenty-four hours. I prayed fervently that night, thanking the Lord for helping me communicate with Daniel and for Daniel's active response to my pleas. I also thanked Him for the privilege of being a teacher and for the things which Paul and I had accomplished together. I thanked Him for my student, Paul, and asked Him to aid me in the challenges related to helping Paul in his learning and in his personal life. I pleaded for His protecting hand that night especially. Then, more secure behind a locked door, I slept well.

The next morning, my activities began to seem more routine, and I went to the schoolroom more optimistically than I had before. Paul also seemed more at ease, with me more permanently in his life.

During the ensuing weeks we set up a new schedule including the basics that Ingrid wanted taught, but we revised the reading program to include opportunities for self-expression in writing and discussion of what we had read. The reading subject matter was selected to tie in to current events, history, literature, and art; this way the verbally oriented curriculum was correlated rather than categorized in unrelated tasks. We did the same with mathematics, trying to relate addition, subtraction, short division, and multiplication to life experiences in simple budgeting and numerical problem solving.

We often read or studied in the library, both for a change in atmosphere and to make access to its treasures more readily available.

The arts were not forgotten. We toured the rooms and halls of the first and second floors, experiencing works of art from the ancients to modernists thanks to a marvelous exhibit of paintings and sculpture which the Horstmans had collected.

I made reference to the Horstman family as I taught, giving them credit for their foresight and wisdom in creating within their home a truly excellent experience with the visual arts. Personal references to the Horstmans were, of course, kept to a minimum in deference to Ingrid's and Daniel's wishes.

We walked a lot inside and outside the house, and this exercise, combined with Paul's improved appetite, led to a healthier-looking little man. I resolved that in the future we'd get outdoors even more, studying science in nature's laboratory; but I hadn't recovered entirely from my experience at the boathouse, so I avoided the lake and pool.

I began to feel exhilaration in my teaching that I hadn't felt in public schools. Of course, Paul was an anxious and receptive pupil, responding positively to our real adventures in learning. As a result, I saw steady improvement in his skills and growth in his breadth of knowledge.

Several weeks passed, enlivened by an occasional evening meal with Daniel and Paul. Daniel was always kind, but apparently had decided to recreate the imaginary line separating employer and employee. In some ways I hoped it was just "for the time being" and that we, too, could become friends.

During this period I became aware of a subtle change in the household. I met John O'Connor several times in the evenings. He was just strolling the halls, he had explained, but it was reassuring to think it might be a result of Daniel's orders to take better care of me.

There were infrequent visits from Ingrid, just to let me know she hadn't completely let go of the reins. She used body language to convey her disdain for my teaching methods. The most she ever said was, "Humph, a waste of time" or "Your spending for materials has gone way over budget." But we had no major conflicts or quarrels, and I began to think that life at Horstman House could be good.

Of course, I left on the weekends since Jill insisted on driving to pick me up. These brief sojourns outside the Horstman world were pleasant diversions, but I began to feel guiltier each time I left Paul. He'd go into a blue mood, and each Monday he acted out and took half a day to cheer up. Also, I felt I was imposing on Jill, though she said otherwise. I was saving money, however, and hoped I could soon buy a car.

I knew that Daniel was trying to come closer to Paul, but they had developed so few common interests. The dinners were nice but still seemed rather formal. My desire to bring them closer made me impatient both with Daniel and myself. I needed some way to get them to have some fun together—and I couldn't help wishing to be included—Horstman House was not the fun place I'd envisioned before coming there.

Then an event, which at first seemed more likely to distance than unite us, led to an interesting experience outside Horstman House. Daniel announced to Paul and me that he would have a dinner guest on a Wednesday evening and asked that we join them. When I heard that the guest was to be Carolyn Reinhart, I remembered Daniel's complaints about her tenacity and their lengthy telephone conversation on the eve of Daniel's missed dinner appointment with Paul. I remembered, too, that she had wanted to talk about a Bella Horstman Festival for charity. *Is that her purpose in coming?* I wondered.

I didn't get opportunity to talk further with Daniel about her, but was surprised to learn from Paul that Carolyn Reinhart was that "kind of stuck-up" widowed lady who previously had come to dinner at Horstman House. *So theirs isn't just a business relationship*, I thought somewhat suspiciously. Although her visits to Horstman House may have been infrequent, Carolyn's influence over Daniel probably went beyond that of a casual acquaintance. I realized that I had no real reason to be upset about her visit. After all, Daniel's relationships were no business of mine.

Undoubtedly, Mrs. Reinhart was glamorous and sophisticated. I was sure she'd make me look like a country bumpkin. *That's what you are—a teacher from rural Arizona*, I reminded myself. That awareness served to jog my memory regarding my real mission—teaching Paul.

I decided that I couldn't and wouldn't try to compete with Carolyn Reinhart for Daniel's attention. But as the night of the dinner approached, I found myself worrying that I didn't have a thing to wear.

When the big date arrived, I settled on basic black—the same old silk jersey dress I wore for every special occasion. But I tried to dress it up with the faux pearl necklace and earrings which had been my mother's.

At the wish of our illustrious guest, dinner was scheduled at eight, instead of our usual six. At seven forty-five, Paul knocked on my bedroom door. When I responded, he asked, "Do I look okay?" He was dressed in a dark gray gabardine suit and a black tie.

"You look very handsome," I said and meant it. "But we both look very serious in our dark clothes—not the best for a July night? I hope it's not an omen."

"Omen? What's that?"

"Oh, just a silly, superstitious warning of bad things to come," I explained. "But I'm just kidding. I'm sure we'll have a pleasant time. Anyway, we have to try to make it that for your father and his guest."

"Well, you don't need to worry about her. She won't bite. And you're prettier than she is—she looks old."

I could have kissed him. *They say children tell the truth,* I reminded myself. I hoped he was doing just that.

"Well, thank you, sir," I said. "Will you escort me to the dining room?" I took his proffered arm, and we descended to the first floor.

Daniel was waiting at the foot of the stairs in the main entry hall. "Well, you two look nice," he said. I couldn't help feeling flattered at his approving stare.

"You look rather distinguished yourself," I said, observing how handsome he was in his white dinner jacket and black tie.

"Yeah, Dad, you look great," Daniel added.

I was so happy to see the growing freedom in Paul's interaction with his father. And I couldn't help wishing that just the three of us were going out to some marvelous, atmospheric restaurant.

"Carolyn—Mrs. Reinhart—hasn't arrived. She believes in being fashionably late. I warned Blanche to plan that way," Daniel said.

"Oh, Blanche says she knows Mrs. Reinhart's always late for dinner," Paul said.

Daniel, aware that Paul's candid remark had revealed Mrs. Reinhart's previous visits, laughed and agreed, "Yes, she is Paul. Well, Helman is playing butler tonight, so let's wait in the drawing room, shall we?" He took my arm and Paul's hand and led us to the first-floor drawing room which I had only peeked at previously.

It was another elegant room. Like the library, it was furnished with authentic French pieces and decor. It, too, was a formal but comfortable gathering place, its spaciousness made more cozy by the conversational groupings of furniture, upholstered in rose and blue print or plain fabric with ivory and gilded wood.

The warm lighting from crystal chandeliers and lamps added to the hospitable feeling. Though the fireplace wasn't lit, the gilded, framed mirror above it and the polished wood of the mantle made it a focal centerpiece.

The grand piano that Paul practiced on sat on a raised dais inviting a player to perform. Trying to forestall an awkward waiting period, I asked, "Paul, will you play for us while we're waiting?"

"I can't," he said shyly, offering as an excuse, "I don't have any music."

"You can't fool me," I responded. "You practice in the late afternoon without music—I've spied on you. You have several pieces memorized." I hoped his father would hear him play and then praise him for his abilities. I wished the words into Daniel's mouth.

I was pleased when Daniel joined in the persuasion. "Paul, I'd like to hear you too. It's been a long time since you've played for me."

"I don't think I've ever played for you," Paul said. "You never asked me to."

"Well, I'm asking you now," Daniel said, awkwardly. "Please play for us."

"Well, okay, but don't expect too much. Professor Lawrence says I don't practice enough."

"Professor Lawrence?" I asked.

"He's Paul's piano teacher. He comes on Saturdays, so you haven't met him," Daniel said. "In fact, I can hardly remember him. Ingrid hired him when Paul was six."

"Yeah, I've only been playing for two years. I'm not that good," Paul said while moving to the piano bench. He sat down, removed the cover from the keyboard, and waited for us to gather around.

We sat together on a sofa facing the piano and waited expectantly. Paul eyed us, and said "I'll play 'Moonlight Sonata.'" He began a simplified version of Beethoven's masterpiece, and we shared amazement at the depth of emotion he expressed in his playing. *His sensitivity is a real gift*, I thought in awe.

"Thank you," Daniel said when Paul had finished. Daniel had tears in his eyes and I wanted to hug him for this caring response to Paul's efforts.

"That was beautiful, Paul. You definitely should continue studying and practicing," I urged. "You have a real talent in music."

Helman entered and, in his formal attire and manner, announced, "Mrs. Reinhart has arrived."

Fluttering past Helman, the overwhelming presence of Carolyn Reinhart, in her peacock-blue feathered dress, was bestowed upon us. Like a bird alighting, she flew straight for Daniel, paying no attention to either Paul or me, and embracing him, kissed him full on the mouth. The blond-dyed and coiffured bird of prey had claimed her possession.

Of course, my reaction was colored somewhat by my insecurities, but I was both chagrined and amused. The latter response was enforced by Daniel's surprise. He was openmouthed and speechless, which Carolyn seemed to interpret as a positive reaction to her arrival. I thought Daniel's behavior quite funny and covered my mouth to hide a smile. Paul just stared wide-eyed.

"I'm so delighted to see you, darling," she said. "Thank you for inviting me—*again*." Apparently she had seen me when she entered. I supposed she wanted to make clear her special status here.

Daniel recovered, "I'd like you to meet Paul's teacher, Miss Wood. Miss Wood—Mrs. Reinhart."

"Oh, call me Carolyn. *Everyone* does." She sized me up again. "And your name?"

"Wendy," I answered. I could think of nothing else to say.

Paul, seeing Helman waiting in the doorway, saved the moment. "I think dinner's ready," he said, taking my hand and leading us to the hall.

The dining table was beautifully set for four, one place at the head, two on one side, and a single place setting on the other. Carolyn quickly claimed the latter, allowing Daniel to hold her chair. Daniel then stood at the head of the table, and Paul sat nearest his father after seating me. *I'm the third man out*, I realized. But Carolyn seemed pleased, having assumed her place at Daniel's right.

Daniel nodded to Helman, who then went to the kitchen to signal Blanche. The formality seemed strange to me, but the others took it in stride. Blanche and a girl whom I hadn't met served the appetizer, a marvelous shrimp cocktail. Helman poured the white wine for Carolyn and Daniel. I declined, and he ignored Paul completely.

I smiled at Blanche and reflected that I hadn't seen much of her in the weeks past. Had she been avoiding me? I'd seen Martha at breakfast most mornings but hadn't really had much contact with her or anyone in the house except Paul. Maybe that was the way it would be from then on.

I was brought back to the present when I realized that Daniel was asking me a question. "I'm sorry," I said. "I guess I was daydreaming. What did you ask?"

"Carolyn was talking about art education, one of her passions, and I asked if that was also one of your interests?" he repeated.

"Well, yes, one of my minors was in art, but I'm neither an artist nor a critic I'm afraid. I enjoy art and art history, however," I explained.

Blanche's assistant removed the appetizer and then served a delicious clam chowder and a green salad. I loved seafood even if I wasn't so pleased with Daniel's dinner guest. I'd just concentrate on Blanche's excellent food and get through this some way.

"Then you may be interested in my invitation," Daniel said. "In connection with one of her charities, Carolyn is co-hosting a buffet luncheon at the Norton Simon Gallery on Saturday. When I talked with her earlier, I suggested to Carolyn that you and Paul join us since you've been wanting to get Paul out into the world a little more."

Carolyn was not so enthusiastic about our coming. "Well, I'm sure that would be fine, but children usually aren't invited to these affairs," she said.

But Daniel was persistent. "Oh, Wendy will be with Paul, and besides, he's a real gentleman—*very* mature for his age."

Paul smiled at his father's praise, and although I was not certain I really wanted to go, I wasn't about to disappoint Paul—or Daniel. "We'd love to come," I said. "Wouldn't we, Paul?"

"Yeah, that would be great," Paul exclaimed, picking up a phrase which I so often used.

"Then it's settled," Daniel said. "We'll be there on Saturday, Carolyn."

Her response was interrupted by the serving of the entree. We busied ourselves with the special tools provided for eating lobster and, for the most part, ate in silence, enjoying Blanche's wonderful seafood dinner.

We chose to skip dessert, and Carolyn, probably motivated to get Daniel to herself, said, "Well, it's been lovely. Now Daniel, could we talk *privately* about that matter I proposed in our telephone conversation?"

"Oh, yes, the Bella Horstman Festival. What do you think, Wendy, would people come to a revival of my mother's old films?" he asked, ignoring Carolyn's attempt to get rid of us.

Carolyn bristled. "Oh, don't bother her with our plans. You see, dear," she condescended to me, "I have an entire staff of volunteers to assist me with this project."

Daniel pressed on, "But Wendy is a film buff of sorts, and I think her opinion would be valuable in gauging whether the festival would attract an audience." He turned to me again. "Frankly, I'm very reluctant to revive anything to do with that period in our lives—or, rather, Bella's life. We've moved past that and—"

Carolyn interrupted with, "But darling, the whole idea is a natural. We'll stage the revival at the Pasadena Playhouse where Bella performed in live theater. They're willing to mount a screen for the films and are even considering a live production of *Hippolytus*, staged just as it was when Bella played Phaedra. Daniel, it would help both the Playhouse and my arts in education project. You simply must persuade Bella to give us permission to go forward." *She's attempting to dismiss my opinion,* I noted with interest. *But Daniel isn't.* I couldn't help feeling good about his regard for my thoughts.

"What do you think, Wendy? Should we pursue this?"

"Well, it sounds very exciting, but that's just my personal reaction. I really know nothing about organizing a festival," I said.

"That's what I was after—your personal opinion," Daniel clarified. Turning to Carolyn, he said, "I'm still not sure I want to stir up the past, Carolyn."

"But Bella's fans are still out there, and a whole new generation has curiosity about her work," Carolyn insisted. "I'm sure we'll attract a huge crowd—and my charities will benefit greatly. Please, Daniel, you've just *got* to help me." She placed her hand over his and leaned in intimately, using the full force of her persuasive feminine appeal.

"We'll think about it, but I make no promises," Daniel said, firmly withdrawing his hand.

"Well, when you come to the Norton Simon affair I'll send Jennifer after you. This was her idea after all, and she won't take no for an answer."

"Who's Jennifer?" Paul asked, echoing my thoughts.

"Why, Jennifer Jones, darling," Carolyn answered. "Surely you've heard of the great film actress, Jennifer Jones. She married Norton Simon."

"I thought we were going *to* Norton Simon," Paul said. "Are we just going to see some old man?"

"No, Paul," Daniel explained. "The building and gallery are named after Mr. Simon. It's his art collection, and he's opened it to the public. We're going to his museum."

"Your father knows Mr. Simon through business associations, dear," Carolyn said, drooling over Daniel and dismissing Paul. "And now that Jennifer isn't acting full-time, her energies are directed toward the gallery and her other charitable work. I admire her greatly," she effused.

I was overjoyed at the prospect of seeing Jennifer Jones, whose films both my mother and I had loved. But I tried not to act like a starstruck schoolgirl, keeping my excitement in check. Even the prospect of seeing Carolyn again couldn't dim the potential excitement of the coming event.

Daniel said, "Alright then. We'll go to the charity exhibit and luncheon." He stood and moved behind his chair. "But I remind you, Carolyn, I can be as stubborn as you and your friends are determined. I really don't want to dredge up my mother's past, and it will take a lot to convince me otherwise."

"A lot of what?" she asked and giggled.

"A lot of convincing," Daniel countered dryly.

"Well, let's find someplace comfy where we can be alone, and I'll convince you," she said, rising from her chair. "It was nice to have met you—uh—Wendy." She took Daniel's arm and began to lead him back toward the drawing room.

"Good night, Dad," Paul said.

"Good night," I added.

Daniel turned, held out his open palms, and shrugged his shoulders as if to say, "I give up." I just smiled and raised my hand in parting.

Paul and I went upstairs together. I sensed that he too felt somewhat let down at having our evening cut short.

I tried to adopt a more lighthearted mood. "The exhibit sounds fun. Guess I'll be staying here for the weekend then."

"Oh, yeah, I didn't think of that. That sounds great. I can't wait," Paul exclaimed.

We parted at the door to his room, and I asked myself what would be next? Then I went to the pay phone to call Jill and tell her that I'd be staying the weekend at Horstman House.

Chapter Sixteen

Saturday came quickly, and again I was faced with finding something to wear. The basic black wouldn't work for the charity luncheon, and my blue cotton dress was too everyday. Finally I settled on an off-white linen pants suit, decorated in Native American motif. My Navajo turquoise necklace and ring completed the effect. Simple, but unusual enough to be special, I hoped.

Horstman House was even more quiet on that Saturday morning than on a weekday. There was a skeleton staff at breakfast, mostly full-time employees. I sat with Martha and John and was hurt to find their manner still somewhat distant—not uncordial, but for some time they had treated me differently. *News sure travels rapidly in this little Horstman-House world. They probably already know that Daniel has invited Paul and me to the charity luncheon. I wonder if it makes them feel like I'm not one of them anymore?* I didn't want that since they'd befriended me, and I certainly had no idea where I stood with Daniel. I tried to make conversation, but both Martha and John must have had other plans. They were off in a hurry.

I finished breakfast, put my dishes in the kitchen, as was our custom, and wondered again about not seeing Blanche more regularly. In fact, everyone seemed to be keeping to themselves of late. Strangely, I hadn't even seen Ingrid or Helman very often.

With nothing else to do that morning, I returned to my room and settled on an hour or so of scripture reading to pass the time until eleven when we were scheduled to leave for the gallery. But I couldn't concentrate, finding myself reading the same page again and again with little comprehension.

Instead, I was thinking of going with Daniel and Paul. I was excited to visit the Norton Simon, aware of its reputation but never having been there. Even the unpleasant prospect of seeing Carolyn Reinhart wasn't enough to dampen my enthusiasm for the total experience— seeing the art works, rubbing shoulders with movie celebrities, and getting Paul and Daniel out of their Horstman-House rut.

Paul knocked on my door just before eleven. "Let's go," he called. I opened the door to see him more casually dressed than usual in a light tan shirt and light brown slacks. His tie was more colorful than those of his usual uniform.

"You look pretty," he said, giving a much-needed boost to my ego.

"Thank you, Paul," I said. "We're both looking more relaxed today. I hope we've chosen well for the occasion."

"Dad told me what to wear, and you look great," he said. "Let's go."

I didn't really know where we were to meet Daniel, but Paul didn't hesitate in leading me to the front entrance where Helman waited near the same ancient, classic limousine which had brought me to Horstman House. He held the rear door for us, and I slid across to the opposite side. Paul joined me, sitting in the middle.

After only a moment's wait, Daniel arrived. He too had dressed for the heat in a summer-weight beige sports jacket and light brown slacks. His tie was a contrasting blend of darker tans and browns. Climbing in beside Paul, he was his handsome, poised self. "We're ready," he said to Helman. "I believe you know the way."

"Yes, I do, sir," Helman replied. I was surprised at Helman's courtesy. He hadn't said a word to Paul or me when we arrived.

"We won't have to stay long," Daniel said, somewhat hopefully.

"I want to stay, Dad. I can't wait," Paul countered.

"Well, you may not find it that exciting, Paul—finger foods and adult chitchat," Daniel warned.

"I'm not going to see the adults," Paul continued. "I really want to see the art."

"Well, that sounds very grown-up, Paul. Are you responsible for that, Miss Wood?" he asked, smiling at me.

I was glad for the chance to show him just how much Paul had learned. "We've studied art history and the painters and sculptors of most of the art works in your house."

"Yeah," Paul added, proudly, "I could give you a tour of our own house. But Miss Wood says there's lots of modern art at Norton Simon. I want to see that because most of ours—of Grandmother's—is so old."

"The museum has a big collection of Picasso's works and some sculpture pieces by Rodin. That should satisfy your curiosity," Daniel said.

"Yeah, I like that one Picasso in our place. It's weird." We laughed at Paul's excellent description that captured a typical first reaction to Picasso.

As we drove, Paul craned his neck to look out the window, saying, "Look at that" and "Did you see that?" He was clearly enjoying his first trip away from Horstman House in a long time.

Before we knew it, we'd left Colorado Boulevard and merged onto Orange Grove. We then took a right and eased into the parking lot of the Norton Simon museum. Helman drove to the foot of the stairs leading to the main entry, and we joined others who were arriving for the luncheon and exhibit.

Daniel jumped out of the car without waiting for assistance from Helman and came around to open the door for Paul and me. He looked at me more closely when I stood. "That's a very enchanting outfit, Wendy—Miss *Wood*. From Arizona?"

"Yes. I found it there on my last visit." I was flattered by his attention.

Daniel asked Helman to come back for us in three hours. I'd hoped we would have more time in the exhibits but as Daniel's guest, I wasn't in a position to suggest it.

Paul had squeezed past us and was already taking the steps two at a time, exhilarated by his newfound freedom and the new experience.

"Hold on," Daniel called. "Wait for us."

Paul stopped and turned. "Hurry up," he urged. He headed for one of the modern sculptures by the entry walk, and I held my breath when he climbed on. It wasn't something I expected of him, and realized that for all his solemnity and maturity, he was still a little boy. I ran to get him off and said, "Paul, the sculptures may look like toys but they're not."

"Those sculptures are too valuable to climb on, son," Daniel remonstrated. I noticed that Daniel had amazing self-control, and I was pleased that he had corrected Paul rather than berated him.

Paul seemed momentarily anxious; then, when he realized he wasn't going to be punished, he smiled. After apologizing he stood back, studied the sculptures, then said, "They're neat."

That was as good an evaluation of Rodin's work as I'd heard. "Yes," I agreed, "neat and simple."

The reception line was just inside the main entry, and beyond it I could see the buffet laid on long, linen-covered tables. I felt a bit self-conscious with all those important people. Then, at the head of the line I saw Jennifer Jones, just as beautiful in life as in her films.

My mouth was dry, and my hands shook, when Daniel formally introduced us. "Jennifer, this is my son, Paul, and his teacher, Wendy Wood." He then turned to us. "Wendy and Paul, Ms. Jennifer Jones—now Mrs. Norton Simon."

She held Paul by the shoulders. "What a fine young man he is, Daniel. And Wendy, is it?" She held out her hand and grasped mine warmly. "I'm glad to meet both of you." Turning to a distinguished man at her left, she said, "This is Mr. Simon, my husband."

I felt as if I should curtsey, but controlled the impulse, saying, "It's an honor to meet both of you."

"Hi, this is a great place," Paul said, his eyes alight with excitement.

Mr. Simon smiled and said, "Nothing pleases me more than to have you say that, young man. That's the reason for this *place*, as you call it, for bright people like yourself to enjoy it and learn from it."

Mr. Simon was interrupted by the fluttering, loud entrance of Carolyn Reinhart, plumed for this occasion like a pink flamingo. She left her place at the end of the reception line and descended upon Daniel. "I've been watching for you," she said, grabbing his arm and leading a protesting Daniel along the line and then out of sight, leaving Paul and me to fend for ourselves—which we did.

At the end of a brief, but pleasant conversation, the Simons were called away by other guests. "Ms. Wood," Mrs. Simon said, "I'm sure we'll meet again. I hope you'll have a wonderful time here."

"We will," I said. "Thank you." And we proceeded through the remainder of the line, meeting others whose names I'd heard before. I was so nervous and excited at meeting all of the celebrities that I didn't realize Daniel had completely disappeared.

We reached the end of the line, and Paul said, "The food looks good. Maybe we should eat first. Then we can see the art."

"Well, do you think we should wait for your father?" I asked, looking for Daniel.

"Oh, Carolyn's got him. She'll probably talk and talk like she always does, so let's not wait," he begged.

"Okay, I guess we don't have much time. We should make the best of it."

I was rather upset at Daniel's leaving us, I realized. I wasn't at all hungry until I saw the selection of food—delicious looking appetizers, hors d'oeuvres, finger sandwiches, breads, salads, and finally caviar and champagne. Skipping the latter, we unashamedly loaded our plates and searched for a place to sit. We found a marble bench away from the crowd but still in the reception area. Paul ate without comment but with enough energy to suggest that he liked the food.

I kept watching for Daniel's return, then decided to forget him and enjoy the experience with Paul. We finished eating, returned our plates to an attendant at the tables, and then moved to the information desk to pick up a pamphlet which would direct us to the various exhibits.

The modern art which Paul was so anxious to see was on a lower level, so we descended a wide, winding staircase to a very modern, expertly lit gallery. I was amazed at the breadth of the Picasso collection, and Paul kept repeating, "Neat! Neat!"

We spent about an hour enjoying that area, then I suggested, "We'd better save some time for the Impressionists and the American artists. They're located upstairs," I finished, checking the brochure.

On the main level we went first to the exhibit of American painters. Winslow Homer, John Singer Sargent, and Andrew Wyeth appealed to Paul. Then, noting that we had only a half hour before Helman came for us, we crossed the reception area to the wing where the Impressionists were displayed.

The luncheon was over, it appeared, and the caterers were cleaning up. The reception line had been replaced by a woman seated at a table collecting donations from the departing guests, most of whom were writing checks.

Daniel was still out of sight, so we spent time with Renoir, Monet, Manet, and Mary Cassat. I loved Cassat's paintings of children. Her beautiful, young subjects stirred my maternal instincts.

Just as we wound our way toward the exit, Daniel joined us. "I'm so sorry," he said. "Carolyn cornered me in an office and would not let up until I talked with Jennifer about the Bella Horstman Festival. I lost track of time." He looked at Paul. "Paul, I'm sorry. I'd planned to see the exhibits with you."

"Oh, that's okay," Paul said resignedly. "Anyway, we had fun *without* you." He took my hand as if to emphasize his point.

"Yes, we enjoyed the food and the art, but we would have liked to have had you along," I said, trying to soften Paul's reaction to being disappointed by his father again.

Daniel winced at Paul's candid reaction, then offered a plan for future outings. "Well, next time we go somewhere, I'll drive," Daniel suggested. "Then we won't have to worry about Helman's schedule."

"Yeah, that's a good idea," Paul agreed. "Next time, let's go in *your* car."

I looked out the glass doors and windows of the foyer. "Speaking of Helman, he's just driven up," I announced, trying to hide my own disappointment that our time together had been so brief—and only partially successful.

Daniel stopped at the table to write a check, seeming in a hurry to leave. The secretary at the table smiled and said, "Thank you so much, Mr. Horstman. You've been very generous. Here is your receipt."

We were moving to the exit doors, when Carolyn appeared again. "Daniel," she called. Then, hovering near him and clasping him by the hand, she whispered, "Don't forget our agreement."

Daniel looked directly at her and whispered in rather menacing tones, "Your *blackmail* has worked, Carolyn, for now at least." He pulled his hand away and hurried us outside, leaving a stone-faced Carolyn watching from behind.

"Blackmail?" I asked, rather startled at his words and actions.

"Yes, blackmail," he answered conclusively. "I'll cooperate with the Festival. Then we'll be rid of her—for good."

The trip home was quiet and somewhat anticlimactic, but at least Paul seemed happy to have gotten out of Horstman House, even for a short time. And Daniel had mentioned the prospect of another outing and the possibility of the Bella Horstman Festival coming about, so I had to be satisfied. Also, I couldn't help feeling pleased that Carolyn Reinhart might not be a permanent fixture at Horstman House. *How did he put it?* I asked myself. *Oh, yes.* *"We'll be rid of her—for good."* I had to admit the thought was delicious.

Chapter Seventeen

Tired from the day's events, I went to my room, removed my jacket and shoes, and had a short nap. I awakened in time for dinner and joined Paul as on weekdays. Apparently, Blanche had come to expect that, since the table was set for two.

Paul anticipated our saying a blessing as if he'd always done it. I had asked Daniel if he would allow Paul to participate in prayer, and he had smiled at me and said, "I don't see what it could hurt. We can use a little help with our problems—from whatever source it comes." Then he had dismissed the subject. So, having received permission, I asked Paul if he would like to pray. He agreed to try and said a humble, sweet prayer of thanks, ending with, ". . . and please bless my Dad."

We ate lightly—a crisp green salad, a delicious cold potato soup, and newly baked bread—just right for a summer evening. Paul was still chattering about the things he'd seen. I was glad he was so happy.

We parted at the door to Paul's room, and I walked away thinking that the remainder of the weekend would be pretty dull. I wondered if there was an LDS ward or branch nearby. *But, then, I have no transportation*, I reminded myself. I really would miss going to church. Sundays had always created an opportunity for me to recharge my faith and hope, and I always attended if I could. I'd ask my bishop in Sherman Oaks to find out where I should attend in Pasadena, now that I was more certain I'd be here for a while.

Instead of going to my room, I decided to go outside, intent on staying near the house. Even after all those weeks, I still hadn't forgotten the horror of being trapped in that burning boathouse.

The moon was full, the night was warm, and a gentle breeze stirred the perfumes from the flowers. I found myself walking toward the gazebo, remembering the night I'd first met Daniel there.

So much had happened since then. Some experiences had been unpleasant—others downright frightening. But on the positive side, I had won the right to teach Paul as he deserved to be taught, I had helped bring Paul and his father closer, and I had become better acquainted with Daniel than I had expected when I first came to Horstman House.

What would the future bring? I reminded myself of the wisdom in taking things as they come—a day at a time and not expecting too much. I remembered, too, that Daniel wasn't LDS *First things first*, I lectured myself.

I sat on the gazebo bench, listening to the rustling leaves of the eucalyptus and savoring the scented breeze. I closed my eyes and leaned back against a post.

"Wendy?" a voice said.

I opened my eyes to see Daniel standing over me. "Oh, you scared me," I said, feeling foolish at my reaction.

"I didn't mean to surprise you. I didn't see you at first," Daniel said. "I often come here in the evening."

"Yes, you told me this was a meeting place for you and . . . Lisa. I'm sorry if I've intruded on your memories again."

He sat beside me. "Oh, no." He sighed, then said, "That was all so long ago. As you said, just memories, nothing more."

"Well, I mean that I didn't think before coming here—about this spot being your special place," I explained. "I didn't think I'd see you here—or anywhere—tonight."

"I come here to think." He paused, seeming to have forgotten for a moment that I was there. Then he began again, as if he hadn't stopped, suggesting his need to explain their relationship to me. "You need to understand that Lisa and I had grown apart years before the—fire. She had become someone quite different from the person I thought I'd married."

"You mean you weren't in love anymore?" I asked.

"Well, this is difficult to put into words, but I meant that *she* wasn't in love with *me*. In fact, I'm not sure she was ever in love with me. You see, she'd become totally obsessed with Horstman House, and the legend of the Great Bella. You saw the clippings she'd gathered in the library. I guess the aura of Bella's world was what attracted her to me in the first place. And gradually she distanced herself entirely from our reality and started to live in her own romantic view of the past. She began to reject not just me but her son. It hurt! It wasn't what I wanted. In fact, it felt like a repetition of my earlier life—the rejection. But she didn't seem to care about either of us."

"I understand your hurt," I said. Then, without thinking, I covered his hand with mine.

"I did hurt. I thought I'd found someone who loved me—someone to love. But her turning away from me was a confirmation of my feelings and . . . my fears."

"Your fears?" I asked, not entirely comprehending.

"It all seems a bit melodramatic—even childish, I suppose." He stood and walked to the other side of the gazebo and onto the grass, turning away from me.

I followed behind him. "Go on," I urged. "I'm not here to judge you. I'm glad you can confide in me."

"Well, I'd never felt love from my mother or my father. I began to fear that I—I don't know how to say it without sounding self-absorbed."

"Tell me," I said.

He turned, still looking down, then said, "I began to think no one could ever really care for me."

Sympathetically, I said, "Paul loves you. Why can't you focus on that?" I asked.

"I'm sorry," he said. "I have no right to burden you with my problems—past or present."

"But . . . I think I want you to," I said. "I want to help you—and Paul."

"I know. That's exactly why I shouldn't. I have no right to try to make you—care about me."

"I—I do care about you—and Paul. I can't think of you separately. I'd like to help both of you have a happier, better life."

He said nothing, just looked past me.

"Are you in love with—Carolyn?" I asked, and immediately regretted it.

"No, of course not. I once thought—maybe even hoped—there might be something between us someday. But in her own way Carolyn is as phony as Lisa. She's more concerned about Carolyn than about anyone else."

He looked above and beyond me again, and I turned to see what he had seen. There, on the third-floor balcony, was Bella, staring in our direction. When I turned, she looked at me, as she had on my first night at Horstman House, then moved slowly away and reentered her third-floor domain.

"I guess I'll call it a night," Daniel said, rather abruptly. "See you tomorrow?"

"I hope so," I responded, a bit mystified by his changing moods. "I'll be teaching Paul, of course, but you could join us for lunch."

"I'll see," he said. "I'd like to." He started to walk toward the pool and lake, then stopped and turned. "I think maybe I'll walk down by the lake. Would you like to join me?"

In a way I wanted to go with him, but something in his manner and the thought of seeing the charred boathouse made me shudder. "No, I'm not too anxious to go near the lake," I said, truthfully. "Maybe another time. Later, when I've had time to forget the—accident at the boathouse." Was this feeling another warning about future problems—future dangers? I wondered. If so, I planned to listen this time.

"Of course. It was thoughtless of me to suggest it." He turned to leave, then stopped again. "I do need your help with something."

"I'll be glad to help you if I can," I said.

He came back toward me. "I can't face all the preparations and hoopla of this Bella Horstman Festival. Will you help me get through it?" he asked.

"But I know nothing about that kind of organizing and entertaining," I said.

"Oh, believe me, Carolyn will do all the organizing. I just need your emotional support. I can't face reviving that period in our lives. It was not a happy time for me—or for anyone here," he said.

"Well, of course, I'll try to help, if you really need me. It's nice to be needed." A warm feeling overtook me and I realized how alone I had felt for so much of my life. I paused before asking a question about something that was worrying me. "But why did you let Carolyn *pressure* you into this festival, if you really don't want to do it?"

"Well, it's a long story—which I can't share right now. Maybe someday I can make things different." He took me by the shoulders and said, "For now, will you just accept the fact that I have to see this through and I need your help?"

I thought of Bella's appearance on her balcony and looked there furtively. "Yes. But has Bella—has your mother—agreed to all of this?"

He dropped his hands to his sides. "The studios own the rights to her films. Carolyn and her committee will make arrangements for their showing. They just want to come here for a closing event—a ball, she calls it. I own the house now, so that isn't a problem. All that I have to arrange is the use of Bella's *great* name and the protection of physical privacy. I think I can handle that."

"Then how can I help?" I asked.

"I just need your support during the coming weeks. I need someone to talk to, and someone to help me remember Paul and my goals with him. And your help with Paul—Paul needs you."

"Well that's enough for me. I've decided I'm not going anywhere—for the present. I'm very pleased with the progress Paul's making in learning and in self-confidence. I certainly don't want anything to interfere with that."

"Then you'll stay on?" Daniel pleaded.

"Yes, I've already made up my mind that I can't just leave Paul. He does need me, as a teacher and as a friend," I said.

". . . or, as a *mother someday*," Daniel suggested. I couldn't tell if he was serious or teasing me, so I simply stared back. "Thank you, Wendy. I'll try to make you happy for your decision." Then he turned and walked toward the lake, leaving me still questioning my place and future at Horstman House and Daniel's secretive and evasive behavior.

Chapter Eighteen

I spent my time on Sunday studying the scriptures, napping, and walking the grounds. It passed quickly, and Monday morning came before I knew it. The events of the preceding Saturday with Daniel seemed almost as if I had imagined them. But the reality of the weekday routine intruded on those musings, with breakfast served in Blanche's everyday style—a buffet laden with eggs prepared in various ways, choices of several meats, and a wide assortment of breads and rolls. Various hot and cold beverages were always available. No one could say that employees didn't eat well at Horstman House. *Certainly I'm eating better than when I was cooking for myself,* I thought. *Not necessarily healthier—but better.*

I had, however, lost one of the Horstman House employee perks—maid service. My insistence upon a locked room, with limited issuance of keys, had left me to make my own bed and tidy my room. Someone—one of the housemaids, I supposed—had picked up my dirty linens and left clean sheets by my door.

I had also almost grown accustomed to the lukewarm social atmosphere which had become even more obvious of late. Martha, John, and Blanche were always courteous but in an impersonal way. I had no more private meetings or conversations with any of them and wished daily that the promise of friendships could have materialized. I resolved to make an effort to talk with one of them. I wanted to know why their attitudes toward me had changed.

Of course both Ingrid and Helman displayed an even more open hostility by speaking to me only when absolutely necessary and then only in icy tones.

I could only assume that my growing involvement with Paul and Daniel had, indeed, isolated me from others at Horstman House. This hurt me as I had never intended that result. In fact, I realized, I was longing to be part of the staff and to feel like I belonged—somewhere.

I met Paul at the schoolroom. His happy glow had diminished somewhat, but I sensed that he still felt a new promise and freedom in his life.

"Hi," he said, accompanying his greeting with a wide grin. "What'll we do today?"

"Well, it's back to the books, I'm afraid—back to reality." I opened the curtains and the schoolroom window, which was no longer stuck, I noticed. I silently gave thanks to John O'Connor's handiwork. Then I went to my desk and Paul followed to his. We could hear the birds chirping and the noises from the gardeners' tools. The warm sun filled the room and I thought the day was too nice to spend inside.

But I still wanted to avoid confrontation with Ingrid, so we disciplined ourselves to do some serious reading and study until breaktime. Afterwards, we returned to study mathematics until lunchtime, when we were interrupted by the arrival of our tray, delivered by none other than Blanche, herself.

"Blanche." I couldn't conceal my surprise. "I—uh—expected Angela to bring the tray."

Blanche's hurried manner suggested that she really didn't want to be detained. "Oh, Angela didn't come in today, and I had no one else to bring your food."

"We would have come down if we'd known," I said. "I'm sorry you had to come all that way."

"I used the elevator," she explained, quickly setting down the tray and moving to leave.

I decided to take advantage of her unexpected arrival. "Blanche, could we talk for a moment?"

"Well, I have a lot to do in the kitchen," she said, crossing toward the door.

I stood and followed her. "I won't keep you—just a question."

"Well, all right, but I do need to hurry," she said.

"Paul, go ahead and eat your lunch. I'll join you in a moment."

I opened the door for Blanche and went after her into the hall, closing the door behind me. "Blanche, I don't know just how to say this. I feel that you've—that everyone's been avoiding me. Can you tell me why?" I asked.

"Well, you must be imagining that," Blanche answered nervously. "I can't think of anyone who's avoiding you."

"Blanche, I'm not imagining it. During the past month or so, since a short time after the accident at the boathouse, you, Martha, and John have been very distant. In fact, I've hardly seen you."

She looked down the hall. Then, turning back to me, she whispered, "If you say I said it, I'll deny it. Mr. Horstman made it clear that our conversations with you should be limited to our work. I mean, I can only talk to you when serving your food—nothing personal. We're supposed to take care of you—of your needs. That's all."

"But why? I can't understand why he would do that," I said, puzzled and angered by Blanche's revelation.

"Well, I suppose he wants you left alone he doesn't want us talking with you about—anything that goes on here. He—"

She was interrupted by the noise of Ingrid's heels striking the marble floor. We looked up to see her churning toward us.

Blanche said, "I have to go. I've said too much." She started down the hall toward the approaching Ingrid.

I couldn't hear what Ingrid said to Blanche, but her manner suggested that she was delivering a tongue lashing. Blanche, red-faced, quickly looked back at me, then hurried past the central stairs toward the elevator.

Ingrid glared at me, then turned away, stalking to her office.

"Miss Nourse," I called, remembering not to call her by her first name.

She stopped. "Yes," she replied officiously.

I hurried toward her. "Had Blanche done something you didn't approve of?" I asked.

"I simply reminded her to go about her duties. It's none of your affair," she answered curtly.

"Well, it wasn't Blanche's fault she was detained," I explained.

"I know that," she retorted. "In the future, don't keep other employees from their work. We've too much to do here."

"I like Blanche and I hadn't talked with her for ages," I said.

"We don't have time here for exchange of pleasantries. In fact, you should be in the schoolroom now."

"But it's my lunch break," I protested.

"You don't have a 'lunch break,' as you call it. Your responsibility is with Master Paul throughout the day." She went to her office without further comment, and I was left with resentment that I hadn't felt for some time.

This place was cold enough without restricting the "exchange of pleasantries," as Ingrid had put it. *Talk about a police state*, I thought. I couldn't wait to give Daniel a piece of my mind. If what Blanche had said was true, he was the cause of the estrangement I had felt from the other employees—Ingrid was just his enforcer. Why had he done that? I asked myself. Why had he alienated the others from me? It didn't seem right or fair.

Daniel hadn't shown for lunch. *Big surprise*, I thought, sarcasm getting the better of me. But I intended to find him before the close of the day.

I returned to Paul, trying not to appear agitated. We ate our lunch in silence, however, and Paul sensed that something was wrong. Finally, he asked, "What's wrong?"

"Oh, everything's fine," I said.

"I was afraid Ingrid had told you we couldn't go on any more field trips or something. I heard her. She has a loud voice," he said

"Don't worry, Paul. She can't keep us from going on field trips. In fact, she can't interfere in any way with our learning as long as I'm here."

"Well then I hope you won't leave like my other teachers did. I hope you'll stay here," Paul said. "I don't want to go back to the way it was before you came."

"Oh, Paul," I said, "I don't want you to worry about that anymore. I've made up my mind to stay despite the—" I caught myself before saying what I was thinking about the negative things at Horstman House.

"Despite what?" Paul asked.

Before replying, I wondered if I should be truthful, or if it would burden him too much to know I was still afraid—afraid of not belonging, afraid of not being able to trust anyone, even afraid of being physically or emotionally hurt. I paused too long before answering.

"What?" Paul insisted.

"Despite my feelings that I *really* don't belong here," I said, trying to be truthful without saying too much.

"But you do. I want you to stay, and Dad wants you to stay. I'm sure he does," Paul pleaded, coming close to me and taking my hand. There was a panic in his eyes.

"Oh, I know that, Paul, and I want to stay—for you and for your father." I sat at my desk. "But let's not spoil a beautiful day. The weather is perfect. And I'm all right. I just need to talk with your father again."

"Maybe he'll come to dinner," he said hopefully. "Then you could talk."

"I was hoping the same thing," I said. "Now, why don't we plan another field trip right now," I suggested, trying to change the subject and the mood.

"Yeah, that sounds great. Where should we go?" Paul asked, sitting at his desk.

"Well, this time I think we ought to get outdoors—see some of nature's creations."

"That sounds great," Paul said again, making me realize that I needed to teach him some new ways of expressing his excitement. "Where should we go?"

"I've heard some wonderful things about the Huntington Gardens. Apparently the grounds have numerous botanical exhibits and gardens, and then there's the Huntington Library and the many Huntington art collections. It's a gigantic place, I'm told. We'll have to do a lot of walking, and it would be an all-day outing."

"That sounds great," Paul repeated again, and I thought he was right. It did sound great.

"Do you think Dad will go with us?" Paul asked.

"I don't know. We'll talk to him—tonight if we see him," I said.

"And we'll have to decide when to go—how about Saturday?" he proposed.

"Well, that's rather short notice, but I guess I could stay the weekend again, if your father can arrange his schedule to go."

"Well, if he can't, let's go *without* him," he said, jumping up and begging like a puppy.

"But I don't have a car," I reminded him.

"We've got lots of cars. Do you know how to drive?"

"Yes, of course. I suppose I could find the way there."

"You could—I know you could. We could get a map."

"But what about your piano lesson on Saturday?" I asked.

"Last week my teacher came early. Maybe we could get him to again." Paul was almost bouncing up and down from excitement.

"But last Saturday we didn't leave until 11:00 A.M. We probably should get to the Huntington earlier, so we'll have more time."

"Well, maybe we could just skip my lesson one week," Paul suggested cautiously.

"I don't think Ingrid would be too happy if you did that."

"I thought you said she can't interfere." He sat again, his fists supporting his chin, pouting.

"But that applies to the regular weekday. Ingrid made arrangements for your piano lessons on Saturdays. She hasn't agreed to give up her planning of your weekend schedule," I reminded.

"Maybe Dad could talk with her," he said.

"Maybe he could," I agreed. "But for now we'd better get back to some studying. Let's see what happens tonight with your father."

We returned to our reading and writing, trying to concentrate on that instead of the anticipated holiday.

At dinnertime, I arrived at the dining room before Paul since I hadn't bothered to change for dinner. The pink-and-white print skirt and pink cotton blouse that I'd worn all day were cool and comfortable—just right for the warm summer evening. Besides, I liked what pink did for my complexion.

I sat at my customary place at the table and found myself thinking again of the meeting with Daniel Saturday night. He had only said that he needed me—needed my help. *Why does that bother me?* I wondered.

I reviewed our conversation. All he had talked of was his lack of love from others and his hard life. He'd apologized for sounding self-absorbed, but I reflected that the focus was indeed upon *him* and *his* problems. But then again, was I simply revealing my own insecurities in doubting him—being so bothered because it meant he didn't think about me enough? Why was I even letting myself think about him in terms of me? My thoughts started flying at that point. Maybe it wasn't just me—was the Spirit warning me to back away? Why did he tell the employees to avoid me? What did he really want from me? Did he even think on me at all, or was it all about him with no concern for my feelings, or even Paul's? This made me angry all over again. All these problems continued to dominate my thoughts, while I waited for Paul and for dinner to be served.

Moments later Paul came bouncing in. "Dad didn't come?" he asked.

"No, but it's only a few minutes after six. He may come yet," I said.

Blanche served a salad, baked halibut, and wild rice. I said the blessing, and we began eating without further reference to Daniel, but I knew that Paul shared my disappointment.

We were halfway through our meal when Daniel, still dressed in a gray business suit, arrived. Paul jumped up to greet him. "Dad, we thought you weren't coming."

"I'm sorry. I'd planned to be here for lunch and dinner, but my appointments in town ran longer than planned. In fact, I had to take a colleague to dinner." He looked at me, smiling apologetically.

"I'm glad you came, even late." I stood. "I was—*Paul*—was—anxious to see you," I said, trying to cover my vacillating emotions. I was happy that he'd come but I was still angry about what I had learned from Blanche. "I need to talk with you after dinner," I said, firmly.

"Of course," he said, seeming a bit surprised by my tone. He held my chair, inviting me to sit again. "I think I saved room for dessert. What is Blanche serving, do you know?" He sat across from me.

"She hasn't brought it, yet," Paul said. "But it'll be good. It always is."

"Yes, Blanche is a great cook," Daniel agreed. "Your dinner looked better than mine was."

"She does have a way with seafood," I said. "I like the emphasis on fish and poultry in her menus."

Small talk, I thought, with some frustration. *Why do I want more?* Fortunately, we were interrupted by Blanche's coming to clear the dishes.

"Blanche, what's for dessert?" Daniel asked.

"Nothing too fancy, I'm afraid. I was just going to ask if they wanted some sherbet or ice-cream sundaes."

"I want a sundae—with lots of cherries and caramel topping," Paul said without hesitation.

"That sounds good to me too. But only one cherry, please, Blanche. How about you, Wendy?" Daniel asked.

"The sherbet sounds good," I said. "Have to watch my waistline." I turned to Blanche. "The dinner was wonderful, Blanche, as always. Thank you."

Blanche smiled at the praise but looked quickly at Daniel and said only, "Thank you." She rushed out with a tray loaded with dishes, then returned with our desserts. "Will that be all, Mr. Horstman?" she asked.

"Yes, thanks Blanche. Why don't you call it a night? We'll put our dessert dishes in the kitchen," Daniel offered.

"Well, thank you, sir. I'll put a few things away. Then I'll go up to my room. I have had a big day." Without pause, she went to her kitchen.

Paul made quick work of his sundae, then dived right into another anticipated treat—the trip to Huntington Gardens. "Dad, Wendy—Miss Wood—and I are planning another field trip." He looked at me for help in asking Daniel to go, but Daniel interrupted.

"Planning so soon? And just when are you thinking of going?" he asked.

"Saturday. Will you take us?" Paul begged.

"We thought we'd go early," I added. "I've checked, and the Huntington opens at ten-thirty on Saturdays."

Daniel looked at Paul. "I'm so sorry, Paul—Wendy—I have to attend Carolyn's committee meeting on Saturday morning, to get Carolyn off my back."

"Well then we'll just go *without* you," Paul said, more impertinently than he would have dared several months before.

The ball was in Daniel's court, I thought, and I said nothing, waiting for his reaction.

"I suppose I could join you for lunch," he offered. Neither of us responded. "Oh, I know what you're thinking—you've heard that before. Right?"

"Right, Dad," Paul said, "but that'd be good. Wouldn't it Miss Wood?"

"Yes, yes it would," was all I said, not wanting to appear too eager.

"Wendy says she can drive," Paul said.

"Have you been to the Huntington?" Daniel asked.

"No, and I'm not insisting on driving, but that's an option. I think I could find it if you'll give me directions," I said.

"Well, why don't we have Helman take you there," Daniel suggested. "Then I can drive us back and we won't have to worry about having two cars to bring home."

"Yeah, that sounds great. That way you'd *have* to come—to take us home. Maybe we could go somewhere else Saturday night," Paul proposed, really taking advantage of Daniel's awkward defensive position.

"What do you think, Wendy? Shall we make it a day?" Daniel asked. "We could take in a movie."

"It all sounds wonderful to me," I answered. And it did. I could hardly believe what I was hearing.

Paul bounced off his chair, "Yippee!" he yelled. "Things are really lookin' up around here. I'm so glad you came here, Wendy—Miss Wood."

"I'm glad too Paul. And let's settle this 'Wendy—Miss Wood' thing, shall we? Why don't both of you call me Wendy—outside the classroom—and you can call me Miss Wood when I'm teaching." I almost added, "for *Ingrid's* sake," but thought better.

"That sounds like a good plan," Daniel agreed. "Now, Paul, off to your room. Put your dishes in the kitchen, first. Okay?"

"Sure—all right," Paul said, going to the kitchen with his dessert dish. "Good night Miss—Wendy, good night, Dad." He disappeared into the kitchen, before we could say anything, then returned immediately and said, "There's just one other thing—my piano lesson?"

Daniel made it easy. "I'll tell Ingrid to cancel it—just this *one* time."

"Thanks, Dad." Paul grinned, waved, and then skipped down the hall to the stairs. I was so glad to see him happy. He was quite different from the Paul I'd met last spring.

Daniel, smiling, echoed my thoughts. "He's a changed boy, Wendy. Thank you."

"Well, as long as Ingrid doesn't catch him skipping through the house," I responded, pleased at his praise.

"You look pretty in pink," he said, surprising me with the change of subject.

"Thank you." I was glad he noticed, even though his words weren't very original.

An awkward pause followed, neither of us knowing where to take our conversation or our relationship—employer-employee, host-guest, friend-friend? It was an embarrassingly confused situation, and I really didn't know how to proceed.

Daniel broke the silence. "I'll take our dishes to the kitchen."

"Let me go with you," I said, rising from my chair. "Then I can use the back stairs to my room."

We went together through the double doors to the kitchen and placed our dishes in Blanche's sink. I looked about at her spotless kitchen, already deserted by Blanche and the other employees. "I don't know how Blanche does it at her age," I observed.

"Yes, she has always been a valuable employee," Daniel agreed. He paused in thought, then said, "She probably could use more help. I'll talk to Ingrid about it."

"Oh, I didn't mean to suggest—"

"I know you didn't," he assured, "but Blanche has served us long and well. We owe her—*I* owe—her a lot."

"Angela has helped her some, I guess, but she's really supposed to be a housemaid, isn't she? And won't she be leaving for school in mid-August?" I asked.

"I really don't know but I'll talk to Ingrid," he promised. "This Bella Horstman Festival coming up will make more work for everyone. The food will be catered, of course, but Blanche will want to supervise, I'm sure."

"Is the date set then—for the festival?" I asked.

"Yes, Carolyn wants to hold it the last week in August—before Labor Day when everyone will be out of town."

"That gives you about a month to prepare," I said.

"I won't be doing much planning or preparing, thank heaven. Carolyn and her committee will do all that. All we have to do is have the house ready for the big final event—the 'ball,'" he said in mock imitation of Carolyn's affected voice.

I laughed, feeling somewhat guilty afterward. I couldn't help feeling glad that Carolyn hadn't overwhelmed him—that he could see through her. Then I reminded myself to stop thinking that way. I knew he was off-limits for more reasons than I cared to count. "I guess I'll go up to my room," I said, not really wanting the evening to end. Then I remembered I had a bone to pick with him, and smiled at the thought of my mother's description of a sticky confrontation. "Oh, I just remembered a question that I wanted to ask—a—problem that's bothering me," I said haltingly.

"Of course, what is it?"

"Well, it's hard to express my feelings about . . ."

"Go on," he said. "I want to help if I can. Let's sit and talk." He led me to a kitchen worktable and pulled out a chair for me, sitting next to me.

"I'm afraid you may think I'm being silly—too sensitive," I began, "but I've felt that the other employees here have been treating me like I have a communicable disease—or like I'm a porcelain doll. Either way, they have very little to do with me. It bothers me. It makes me feel that I don't belong—"

"Don't belong? How can you say that? You know how much Paul needs you—how much I—"

I cut him off before I lost the courage to confront him. "I talked with one of your trusted employees—told her how I felt."

"Who?" he asked.

"I can't say, because she asked me not to." Then my frustration came full force. "She said that you'd given orders that I should be well taken care of but that they were to have no personal relationships with me," I blurted out.

"Well, what she said may be true," he responded defensively. "But you're reacting without regard of context. Remember two things, please. The rules of this house were established long ago by the *Great* Bella, and they are privacy and formality in *all* relationships. And I was also reacting to your accidents. I told you I was directing our staff to take better care of you—to watch out for you. I told you I was going to do that." He took my hands in his. "I wasn't trying to isolate you. I just wanted to—protect you." He looked down at our joined hands and suddenly let go. "I'm sorry if you've been treated badly. That wasn't my intent."

I felt he was probably right not to hold my hand, and said, "No, Daniel, I'm not saying that. But I do need to feel a part of the staff family here. I live, eat, and work with them. I can't be walking on eggshells all the time, wondering what people are thinking—wondering why they don't seem to like me."

He took a long time in phrasing his reply. I was about to stand and leave, becoming more frustrated by his delay, when he said, "I'm sorry. I didn't realize the position in which I'd placed you, Wendy."

"I'm not saying that you have deliberately tried to make me unhappy—"

"No, I haven't," he said. "Horstman House has *never* been a happy place—for anyone. And there are some things that can't be changed until—"

He stopped again, so I urged, "Until what?"

"I've explained all that I can. I've told you about our family relationships—or *lack* of them. I've explained that I can't change all of that. I've tried to change my relationship with Paul, with your help, but that's all I can do—for now."

He was being evasive and he used those words again: "for now." Everything seemed on hold—for now.

"Well, at least I know better where I stand. That's become very important." I rose and turned away from him. "For now, as you've put it, I guess I'll have to be satisfied with that. And I'll try not to be oversensitive to others' reactions to me."

He stood and moved around to face me. "You've been more than patient, and I'm grateful," he said.

"Will you do just one thing for me?" I asked.

"You know I will—if I can."

"Then will you tell Martha, Blanche, and John that it's all right to talk to me, even if they have to avoid discussing the Horstman taboos. Could they talk to me about—the—the weather—or something equally non-threatening?"

Daniel seemed deep in thought. Another long silence ensued, so I started to leave. "I think I'll go to my room now," I said, becoming very impatient.

Daniel stopped me. "I'm so sorry, Wendy. Horstman House has not been good to you, I'm afraid. As I said, it's not a happy place."

I pulled my hands away. "People are about as happy as they make up their minds to be," I stated, quoting Lincoln unintentionally.

"I really *wish* it were that *simple*," Daniel said, then turned and exited without another word through the dining room doors.

I was left alone, staring at empty space. Then from the direction of the servants' dining room door I heard a creaking sound followed by footsteps. I crept in the direction of the sound but could see no one. I closed and opened the door to the servant's dining room, trying to reproduce the creaking sound. No noise, but behind the door I discovered another. I tried the newly discovered door, turning the knob. Nothing happened, so I pushed the door with all my strength. The creaking sound occurred again, and the door opened inward, revealing a black void. A dank, damp, cellarlike odor emanated from the darkness. Reaching unsuccessfully for a light switch, I stepped out and down onto a stair. Then, from the blackness below, I heard the same whispery voice that I'd heard months before on the upstairs pay phone, repeating those same threatening words: "Leave this house." A flicker of light in the distance revealed a long wooden stairway, then it moved away leaving all in darkness.

In my determination to make out the figure, I slowly stepped down another stair, and the boards beneath my foot gave way. My flailing right arm caught on some sort of rope or insulated wire, and I hung by my elbow, reaching out with my other hand to keep from lurching forward down the stairs. The cord which had caught my arm held, and I found the wall on the other side, steadying myself while I stepped backward and upward onto the first solid stair. Extricating my arm from its hold, I pushed my way up into the safety of the kitchen.

I looked about and then seeing no one, found my way cautiously up the back stairs to my room, clutching the banister all the way. I made it to my room, slammed and locked the door, and sat on the edge of my bed. I was physically secure, but was shaking inside and out.

My thoughts were racing. Curiosity had almost done me in again. The near accident could have been avoided if I'd simply gone to my room instead of nosing about. But I hadn't imagined that warning voice. And what of the breaking stair? Did the wood just give way, or had someone arranged for it to break? Had the person who spoke been listening to my conversation with Daniel? Had he or she planned to lure me into the stairwell?

This time there were no physical injuries, just a few scratches on my arms and legs, but the wounds to my heart, soul, and sense of security were deep. I lay back on my bed, squeezing my eyes, and asked the Lord to calm me. Then I plead for assurance about whether I should remain at Horstman House. I also asked Him to protect me from whatever or whomever was trying to frighten or harm me. I pled for direction in knowing how I could find courage to stay and to help Paul and Daniel. I felt frustrated praying for the same things, over and over again, but I still clung to the promise of an answer with my patience and faith.

After my prayer I calmed down and thought more clearly, remembering that scripture which had guided me throughout the summer, "Be still and know that I am God." I hadn't interpreted this scripture as suggesting that I simply sit back and do nothing, leaving it all to the Lord. Rather, I realized, I had to continue to do what I could.

Carefully reviewing my situation, I was so moved that new resolve came over me. The greatest talent which the Lord had given me was my sensitivity to the feelings and needs of others, I thought. I would stay and continue to reach out to Paul. I would try to help his father come to love him. In my own defense, I would become a more wary detective. This time I wouldn't announce my *accident* to anyone. I wouldn't depend on anyone in Horstman House to defend or protect me. I'd find out for myself who was trying to get rid of me. Those attempts had backfired—this time I was going to fight back. I felt a new peace, sensing that this was the divine guidance for which I had so frequently prayed.

Chapter Nineteen

The next morning I rose early, planning to go to Blanche's kitchen before the breakfast crowd arrived. I wanted to inspect the door, the stairway, and the area where it led without interference from anyone.

However, Blanche was there already preparing breakfast. The door to the stairwell was closed. After greeting her and trying to field her questions about my early arrival, I asked her point-blank, "What's behind that door, Blanche?"

"Oh, that leads to the laundry, but the door is never used. It's bolted shut from the other side," she said.

"Isn't the laundry in use anymore?" I asked.

"Oh, yes. The workers use those double doors at the rear of the house. Haven't you noticed them?"

"No, I haven't," I said.

"Well, they're hidden behind some tall shrubbery. The laundress and maids haul laundry in and out that way but they also use the dumbwaiter to move laundry from one floor to another. Then there's the chute for soiled linens. I'm sure you've seen it in our wing. I sometimes use the dumbwaiter to send food up to—" She stopped abruptly, but I could have finished for her, . . . *up to Madame Horstman.* I remembered Martha's explanation that she picked up Madame Horstman's food from the dumbwaiter.

I started to contradict Blanche's statement that the basement door was bolted shut but decided instead to try it myself. I walked toward the door, as if approaching the servants' dining room. Then, when Blanche turned back to her cooking, I pushed hard on the basement door. It was locked, just as Blanche had said. I didn't say anything to her but left the kitchen, then exited through the rear door into the gardens behind the house. I decided I was going to take a look at the laundry and its two entrances for myself.

Finding the open double doors behind several tall evergreens, I stepped inside to a ground-level laundry containing several commercial-size washers and dryers, ironing and pressing tables. The lights were on and some machines were running, but no one was there. I walked toward an iron railing at the rear of the large, steamy area. I could smell again the damp odor I'd noticed the night before in the stairwell. I looked over the railing to a dark lower level and then saw a metal stairway leading downward. I pressed a light switch which I found at the head of the stairs. Dim lights revealed a large room stacked with boxes, old furniture, and barrels—a storage area. At the far side of that room I could see the foot of the wooden stairway.

I checked behind me to see a still unoccupied laundry room, then started down the metal stairs. My heels clanked on the steps, echoing off the masonry walls, so I removed my shoes and carried them to the bottom, replacing them when I felt the damp basement floor.

I crept toward the wooden stairs, avoiding the dusty stored items as best I could. The wooden stairway was quite dark, but I could see footprints in the lint dust going both up and down the stairs, suggesting that the steps were safe enough to hold my weight. I climbed carefully, startled by the hanging wire which had stopped my fall the night before. The wire had ripped free of its fastenings when it had caught my arm. I crept forward seeing a crack of light beneath Blanche's kitchen door. I stopped when I found the broken step, visible in this light. Mixed with the dust on the step was new sawdust from a sawed board.

I caught my breath at the realization that someone had, in fact, intended that I would step on the sawed board and fall down the stairwell. I looked about for a saw while stepping backward down the stairs, trying to avoid disturbing the footprints which someone had made last night. My eyes had become more accustomed to the semi-darkness, and at the foot of the stairs I could see additional footprints in the dust leading to and coming from beneath the stairs. Studying them, I realized they were prints of a woman's long, narrow shoe.

Behind the stairs I found the saw, probably placed in haste behind the bottom step. I avoided picking it up but kicked it further out of view. Then my foot struck another object, which rolled along the cement floor into view—a flashlight; it was obviously the source of the flickering light which I had seen last night. The person who had set the trap for me and who was the owner of the whispered voice had hidden beneath the stairs, luring me there and waiting for my fall.

I heard a sudden noise behind me, the lights in the basement went out, and I was pushed hard from behind and fell forward to my hands and knees on the cement floor. Then I heard cautious footsteps in the direction of the laundry room stairs and exit. I was disoriented in the darkness, and my hands and knees stung. I knew I hadn't imagined *this* push and I fought panic, trying to remember my resolve to fight back.

I tried to pull myself up, hanging on a wooden stair for support, but was unsuccessful. I sat for a moment, trying to adjust to the surroundings. On the second try I managed to get to my feet by leaning on a wooden pole. I didn't want to be found in the basement. Someone again would try to explain away my injuries as just another accident caused by my foolish snooping. But this time I had evidence. I reached and felt about for the saw and flashlight. They were gone. But the footprints and the sawed step would remain as proof of my story when I chose to tell it.

I slowly made my way in what seemed the direction of the metal stairs, leaning on various stored objects to steady myself. A light switched on in the upper laundry and I jumped. I could see one of the maids loading clean linens onto a cart. Then I heard squeaking wheels moving away toward the outside doors.

I didn't remove my shoes but stepped lightly and slowly up the stairs, pulling myself along the banister. When I finally reached the top, the laundry level was deserted. I brushed the dust from my clothing as best I could, then examined my smarting hands and knees. They were reddened and scratched but there was no blood.

I made my way to the exit and headed for the rear door accessing the stairs to my room. I heard noise in the dining room, but fortunately no one was on the stairs. I went to my room, locking the door behind me. I checked the time—eight. I had left my room at seven that morning.

I sat on my bed and felt a renewed urgency to get out of Horstman House. Besides, I rationalized, how could I be of help to

Paul, when someone was so determined to get me out of the way? I trembled, recognizing how narrowly I'd escaped. How could I stay?

I didn't have time to pray or to dwell on the answer, because there was a knock on my door.

"Yes," I said, attempting a normal-sounding voice.

"It's Blanche. You didn't stay for breakfast. I wondered if something's wrong."

Determined to control my anxiety, or at least to make everyone think I was in control, I lifted myself from the bed and moved to the door. "No, no," I said, opening the door a crack to look out. "I just didn't—eat breakfast this morning."

"Well, you came down so early, and when I turned around you had gone. You're sure nothing's the matter?"

"I'm all right, Blanche, but thanks for your concern. I'll be very ready for lunch, when it's time," I said.

"Well, I'll go back to the kitchen, then. Let me know if I can do anything," she said, moving to the stairs.

"Thanks again, Blanche." I couldn't keep from looking after her at her feet. I realized that she must wear a size six—too small to match the footprints in the basement. Of course, she couldn't have been down there, busy as she was in the kitchen. I closed my door without locking it and sat on my bed again.

This really was no way to live—always the victim and the amateur detective. The experience of the past twelve hours had left me exhausted and hurting again. How could I teach Paul, let alone help him, in this condition?

The thought of escaping Horstman House still nagged at me, but my anger was returning, and besides, both Paul and Daniel had declared their need for me. Whoever wanted me out didn't have a father and son's best interests in mind either. I also had to admit that I'd never been needed like I was needed at Horstman House. I'd never felt that important to someone else, I realized. But could that realization balance the fears—the realities—of my situation? One thing was certain, Daniel's efforts to take care of me weren't working.

I had to make a decision; either change my clothes and go to the schoolroom, or, more difficult, pack my things and make arrangements to leave. It was almost nine o'clock. Paul would be waiting for me. I prayed for help.

Then, trying to regain the feeling of assurance I'd felt earlier, I was interrupted by a quiet tapping on my door. Again I answered, "Yes."

Paul said in a quiet voice, "It's me. Are you okay?"

I went to the door, opening it to see Paul's gentle, sweet look of concern. Was he the answer to my prayer? "You didn't come to the schoolroom," he said, "so I came to find you. You're all dusty."

"I—uh—know. I went down in the dusty basement, but please don't mention that to anyone, okay? I'm just going to change my clothes."

"Why did you go down there?" he asked.

"I can't explain right now, Paul. Please, just let it go. I was looking for something," I said.

"Well, okay," he said, his curiosity unsatisfied and looking a little hurt. "I'll wait for you to get cleaned up."

"I'm sorry Paul. I didn't mean to be short with you. Maybe you'd better go back to the schoolroom. I'll change my clothes and wash up a bit. Then I'll come along. Why don't you start reading in your workbook. Okay?"

"Sure," he answered, brightening. "If Ingrid comes I'll just tell her you're coming."

"Okay, thanks, Paul. I'll be there as soon as I can."

He strolled down the hall, possibly accepting my silence on the matter.

Locking my door, I took a clean blouse, skirt, and nylons to the hall bathroom. I checked my sore hands and knees. Fortunately the abrasions weren't bleeding—just skinned knees and palms, which might be difficult enough to explain. Then I removed the dusty clothing, washed up, and fixed my hair. I put on the clean clothes, wiped the dust from my shoes, and felt almost whole again. I knew I wouldn't be able to concentrate on teaching this morning. I'd keep Paul busy and take time to consider my future—and the secrets of Horstman House.

To make my morning complete I met Ingrid coming out of her office. "Well," she said, looking at her watch. "You're bending the rules again I see—it's nine-twenty."

I looked her in the eye, then slowly swept my eyes down her skinny frame to her shoes—long, narrow, and a very possible match for the footprints in the dusty basement. Of course, they were cleaned to their usual dull black—no dust.

I said nothing but went straight to the schoolroom, leaving an open-mouthed, ignored Ingrid staring after me. I was too angry to make "pleasantries" or to banter with her that morning. It felt good to slam the schoolroom door behind me.

I realized that this moment of defiance was a landmark—a simple demonstration to Ingrid and to myself that I was no longer in bondage to her restrictions and rules. I didn't care anymore what she thought of me and I wouldn't be afraid of what she might try to do to me. I would fight back.

Then I decided, once and for all, I'd stay here for Paul and Daniel and I'd find out who was trying to harm me. *Whoever you are, you're dealing with a new Wendy.* I smiled at the thought and said to Paul, "Let's get to work, and this afternoon we'll finalize our plans for the weekend trip to Huntington Gardens."

"That sounds great," came Paul's usual reply.

Chapter Twenty

When I wasn't teaching Paul I spent the days before our Saturday excursion looking at people's shoes and keeping out of dark, lonely places. My resolution to go on the offensive empowered me to a degree. I was regaining a sense of humor and developing a less morose attitude about my future. No matter what happened here, I could make it—somehow.

I would continue to help Paul, I determined. I would worry less about Daniel and his feelings about me, and come what may, I would be ready for anything. I rehearsed these attitudes again and again, feeling that through my frightening experiences, the Lord had blessed me with new strength.

I called Jill to tell her I'd be spending the weekend at Horstman House. She became very interested when she learned that Paul and I would be joined in our plans by *the* Daniel Horstman III.

"I told you something might come of this, didn't I?" she teased, taking credit for first mentioning Daniel to me. Then she got serious. "Have you brought up the Church?"

"It's not like that—yet," I insisted. "He's going along to be with his son."

"Sure he is. You don't think he could be with his son some other time and place—without you along?" she asked. "Be careful, Wendy."

"Well, it's too complicated to explain right now but I will. Anyway, I have a favor to ask."

"Sure, go ahead," she responded.

"I've saved enough for a down payment and I'd like to look for a used car next week. Do you suppose you'd have time to help me?" I asked.

"I've got an even better idea. Have your fun with Daniel and Paul on Saturday, then I'll come early Sunday morning and we'll look for a chapel in your area. Maybe my bishop can find where your ward or branch would be. I'll check with him. Then we can go together to church on Sunday. How about it?" she asked.

"Please deposit fifteen cents for the next three minutes," the operator interrupted, reminding me again of my restricted living situation.

"I can't believe you have to use a pay phone all the time," Jill said after I'd deposited the coins.

"I can't believe it either, but this is a strange place."

Jill read a bit of truth in my choice of words. "Strange?" she asked. "Explain."

"Oh, nothing. I just meant the living arrangements are a bit strange." I still hadn't told her or anyone outside Horstman House the details of my so-called accidents and threats because up to now I'd had no proof, and I had even wondered at times if I really was just being hysterical.

"Well, then, I'll pick you up on Sunday. What time?" Jill asked.

"That would be nice. As early as you can get here," I said.

"Okay, I'll be there at nine. Then we'll decide on a day to go shopping for your car. How's that?"

"Sounds wonderful. I can't wait to see you." I paused for a moment, then suggested, "Would it be too much trouble for you to come again on Tuesday, after work? I'm sorry to be such a bother all the time, but I do need a car. Tuesday would be good for me."

"Oh, Tuesday will be fine. It isn't that difficult to come there after work. After all, my work is closer to Pasadena than our apartment is," she said.

"Could you come as early as you can after work? Some dealers will be closed, I'm sure, but I hope I can buy a car in one evening. I really want to have my own transportation. And it will make it so you don't have to travel so much," I said. I thought, but didn't mention, that it would also provide me a means of escape if I had to leave here in a hurry.

"I haven't minded it, really," Jill said. "I've seen some scenery I wouldn't have—and I've had a chance to rub shoulders with the other half." She laughed. "Of course, it would have been nice to have been invited inside," she pointed out again.

"I know. I'm sorry. I promise to bring you here for a tour of the house before I leave."

"You mean on Tuesday?" she asked, anxiously.

"Oh, no. I mean before I leave for good," I explained, realizing that I had stated the possibility for the first time.

"Are you thinking of that?" Jill asked.

"Every day," I admitted. "But I've told you about Paul, and—"

"And there's Daniel," she teased.

"No, that's not what I was going to say."

"Well, you can tell me more—I expect you to tell me more—on Sunday. Okay?"

"That sounds great," I said.

Despite my declarations of newfound independence and strength, I didn't return to the basement storage area to reexamine the broken stair and footprints or to look for the saw and flashlight. My poor body had been banged up enough, and I found myself doubting I could get help. My choices were few, too; take Daniel there to show him the evidence of my prearranged fall, or wait until I could determine who had planned it. I suppose I was afraid that my accusations would again fall on deaf ears. "Another accident," Daniel would say. He would tell me that I shouldn't have gone down there, that the stairs were in disrepair, and that the locked door must have been left open—accidentally. Somehow I couldn't face that. But this time I had proof. I still didn't know for certain the identity of my enemy—but I did have strong suspicions. Then another thought came. *Could Daniel be protecting someone—directing my suspicions elsewhere?*

The rest of the week I tried to concentrate on the trip to Huntington Gardens and to match Paul's excitement. But I felt a premonition that all wouldn't go well. I attempted to shake this anxiety, but couldn't, and I prayed often for equanimity.

Neither Paul nor I had seen Daniel since Wednesday night, and the Friday evening meal approached without indication that he had made arrangements for our transport to the Huntington in San Marino. We were both relieved when Daniel unexpectedly arrived for dinner.

"Hello," he said shyly.

Paul and I had already begun eating, so we looked up and said in surprised unison, "Hello."

"May I join you?" Daniel asked.

"Yeah, Dad," Paul responded. "We were getting worried about tomorrow."

Daniel moved to his customary chair. "Oh, I've followed through. I told Helman to be ready to drive you at nine-thirty—will that be okay?" Daniel asked, looking at me.

"Yes, that will work nicely," I said. "We wanted to be there when it opens."

"Are you still gonna come?" Paul asked.

"Yes, I told Carolyn that I *have* to leave her meeting at eleven-thirty—so I should be able to get there by about noon. Then we can have lunch at the Tea Room."

"The Tea Room?" Paul asked. "Do they have food—or just tea?"

"Oh, they have food, and it's very good. Good desserts, as I remember," Daniel reassured him.

"That sounds great," Paul exclaimed.

Daniel turned to me. "What do you think, Wendy? Will that be all right?"

"I—*we* can't wait," I said.

"I want to see the cactuses first," Paul said.

"Cacti," I corrected and smiled. "We've been reading about the desert garden."

"Well, don't get lost in it," Daniel said. "It's huge. Actually, you could spend the whole day in just that area."

"Really?" Paul asked, wide-eyed.

"Yes, really. You'll be amazed at how big it is and how old and tall some of the desert plants are," Daniel added. "Go there first, as Paul suggested, and spend about an hour. Then, climb back up the hill to the reception area. I'll meet you there at about noon."

There was a pause, then I said, "Thanks for coming along. I think we'll enjoy it. And we'll learn a lot, won't we, Paul?"

"Yeah, this is the kind of learning I like—not just books," Paul said.

"Well, we've read about the gardens. Now we can see them—the real thing," I agreed.

"Is Blanche still in the kitchen?" Daniel asked.

"I'm not sure but I think so," I said.

"I'll go see," Paul said, running off before Daniel could protest. "I'll get her to bring your dinner, Dad."

It had been days since Daniel and I had our private talk in the kitchen, though much had transpired between us, I felt almost as awkward with him at the present moment as I had at our first meeting. I was reviewing these thoughts, when Daniel spoke. "I've been very busy the past few days—and nights. Sorry I haven't come around."

"Paul's the one you should apologize to. As for me, I don't expect you to change your life just because I'm here—because I teach here," I said, suddenly defensive. "All I've asked of you is a change in your attitude toward Paul."

"I've made some progress there, I think—with your help," he suggested.

"Yes, yes, you have, and that pleases both of us, Paul and me," I said.

"But?" Daniel asked.

"I didn't say 'but'—"

"You didn't have to say it. I sensed it in your manner. Let me finish it for you. You wanted to ask—but what about us?"

"No, I didn't want—I *wasn't* going to ask that," I said firmly. "I have other things to worry—to think about. Besides, I've clarified that our differences, our backgrounds, present some real concerns for me."

"I guess I've presumed too much, then," he said.

"Presumed? What do you mean presumed? All we've discussed is your need of my help," I said with a little more bitterness than I thought I'd felt.

He didn't respond, so I sighed and said, "Let's just lighten up. Can we just be friends? We'll focus our energies on improving Paul's life instead of worrying about *us*. From now on, that's where I intend to concentrate—that's what I'm here for after all."

"Yes, that's what you're here for," he said quietly. "It's just that I'd hoped someday that—"

I cut him off. "I have to face realities. I'm an employee. You have your life, and—"

"And?" he urged.

"—And I think we'd better leave it at that," I said.

"For now?" he suggested.

"No, not just for now," I lectured. "Relationships develop—or they don't. A personal relationship between us doesn't seem possible or probable anyway. We're too different. We come from totally different backgrounds. I'm devoted to my church and to my teaching. You're devoted to your past and your business and social life. So let's focus on Paul's needs. Tomorrow let's just try to have a good time. Okay?"

Daniel's answer was interrupted by Paul's return. He held the door for Blanche, who was carrying Daniel's dinner.

"Blanche still had some chicken for you," Paul said. "It's really good, Dad," he said, returning to his chair.

"It tasted wonderful, Blanche," I said.

"Well, I try," Blanche responded, setting a filled plate before Daniel.

"You do better than try, Blanche," Daniel said. "The food is always excellent. The employees say that too—and that's quite a compliment. In most places employees complain about the food, you know." He paused for a moment, looked at Blanche, then said, "Blanche, before you go, I've decided—I've had it pointed out to me—that you need more help," Daniel suggested.

"Oh no, sir. I'm doing fine," Blanche protested.

"Oh, I know you're doing fine, but we're going to have to host that Horstman Festival Ball I've mentioned, and Angela and some of the other summer help will have left. So why don't you tell Ingrid that I suggested hiring two permanent kitchen helpers. You can train them to do whatever you wish."

"Well, thank you, sir—but could you mention it to Ingrid, so that she won't think I've been complaining?" Blanche asked.

"Well of course. I'll make it clear that it's my idea," Daniel said.

Blanche left with a relieved smile on her face.

"That was very nice," I said.

"Well, thank you for pointing out Blanche's needs. I tend to over-look those things—to leave them to Ingrid, and Ingrid . . . " He stopped, so I finished for him.

". . . isn't too sensitive to others' needs," I added.

"Well, I guess you're right," he said. "That's a generous way to put it."

"She is right, Dad," Paul chirped. "Wendy's always right."

"Yes, she probably is, but please don't report our conversation about Ingrid," Daniel said.

"Oh, I won't. I'm smarter than that," Paul boasted.

Daniel finished his dinner while we ate dessert. Then Paul left, saying, "I can't wait till tomorrow. I don't think I can sleep."

Daniel stood and watched him skip down the hall to the stairs, smiling after him but saying nothing. Then he sat, accidentally bumping my sore knee under the table.

"Ow!" I yelped. He jumped up as if he'd been slapped. I turned to see his bewildered expression.

"I'm *so* sorry," he said.

I stood and turned to him. "I didn't mean to scare you," I said. "I—hurt my knees—and hands," I explained, displaying my reddened palms.

"Hurt your knees and hands? How?" he asked, covering a smile with his hand.

"It may sound funny but it isn't," I said, sounding like I was pouting.

"No, forgive me. It just seems unusual for a grown-up to have skinned knees and hands," he explained.

"Well, it hurts just as badly as it did when I was a kid," I said, defensively. Then I thought, *I should tell him now. I should finally make accusations—just let it all out.* But I didn't—I wasn't sure why. Instead I said, "I went down in the laundry room to look for something and . . . I fell down . . . under the stairs."

"Under the stairs? What were you doing down there?" he asked.

"Oh—come with me. I'll show you," I blurted out, without thinking.

"Show me what?" he asked.

"Show you what really happened to me." I led him through Blanche's kitchen and outside to the laundry entrance. No one was there at that time of night, but the door was unlocked. "Do you know where the light switch is?" I asked.

"Well, I haven't been down here in a long time," he said. "But it should be just inside the door." He felt for it, and the overhead lights came on. "Now what in the world do you want to show me?"

"How and where I got skinned up," I said, holding out my hands again.

"Let me look at them," he said, and I obliged. "There are no cuts or scratches on your hands. How about your knees?" he asked, smiling.

"I'm not about to show you my knees," I said.

"Well, then, what did you want to show me?"

"I wasn't going to tell you until—"

"Until?" he urged.

"Until—later. I didn't want you to think it was just another klutzy accident—caused by my snooping."

"Come on now. What did you want to show me?"

I took him to the storage area stairs where I knew the location of the light switch. I pressed it, and to my amazement, the lower area was filled with fluorescent light—the dim basement no more.

"But it was so dark when I was here before," I exclaimed. I looked down to see a completely changed room. The furniture and storage items were still there but they were stacked neatly and were dust free. "This place was so dirty," I said. "My clothes were covered with dust after I'd been here."

I started down the stairs and Daniel followed. At the bottom, I ran toward the location of the wooden stairway leading down from the kitchen. It had been replaced with newly painted metal stairs and railings. The wooden stairwell was gone, as were, of course, the sawn-through boards and the footprints in the dust. "Nothing is the same," I protested.

"I think I can explain that," Daniel said. "Weeks ago I asked John to have his crew clean up this area and replace the old wooden stairs. After the fire in the boathouse, John looked around for other fire hazards and suggested that this basement was a real fire trap. He was waiting for the metal stairs to arrive. I guess they came this week."

"But I wanted to show you—I had proof—" I stammered.

"Proof? Proof of what?" he asked.

"Proof that someone is trying to hurt me—or kill me!" I practically yelled in frustration.

He came to me, concerned. "What are you talking about?" he asked.

I pushed him away. *Here I go again, the babbling idiot*, I thought. "Someone sawed through the wooden stairs and I almost fell down them—from the kitchen."

"But that door from the kitchen has always been bolted shut—from this side," he said.

I sat on the newly installed stairs, trying to compose myself. "Blanche told me that, but the other night, when you left me alone in the kitchen, I heard that door open. When I stepped in, the boards gave way and I barely escaped falling all the way to the bottom."

He sat beside me, trying to comfort me. "Is that when you hurt your hands and knees?" he asked.

"No, I came down the next morning through the outside doors, I saw footprints in the dust, and the second step down had been sawed through."

He looked at me in disbelief, so I went on. "I even found the saw and a flashlight. The night before someone had tried to lure me down the stairs so that I would fall. Whoever it was warned me to leave."

"You mean, the accident was a warning?"

"No, I mean I heard a voice telling me to leave." Somehow it all sounded so unlikely now and my embarrassment and frustration levels rose. "Then, when I came here the next morning to investigate, someone pushed me down and then sneaked away. I wanted to show you what I'd found—the sawed stairs and the footprints. Now, they're gone—my proof is gone."

"I'll talk to John. He can tell me about the stairs and footprints. I'm sure he or his men would have seen them when they did the work." He looked at me sympathetically, then he took my hands in his. "I believe you, Wendy."

Those words meant so much to me—they were so unexpected that I began sobbing in relief. "Thank you—thank you," I whispered.

Daniel looked into my eyes and said, "I'm going to do something about this, Wendy." He sounded as if he really meant it, and for the moment, at least, my future seemed a little brighter.

Chapter Twenty-One

Daniel took me to my room and waited while I went to the hall bathroom to change into my summer-weight nightgown and robe. Then he walked me to my door, unlocked it, and said, "Sleep well. Think about tomorrow. We'll have a good time, I promise." He paused, then whispered, "Sweet dreams," and locked my door from the outside with his master key. I knelt down, turned off the bedside lamp, and said a brief prayer. Then, relieved, I lay down and fell asleep almost instantly.

The next morning I awoke eagerly anticipating the day's outing. I was determined to leave Horstman House behind—to forget the bad experiences and remember the good just for one day. I showered, then dressed in a silky tan-and-white paisley jumpsuit and white sandals comfortable for walking in.

Limiting breakfast to toast and juice, I took the opportunity to sit by Martha, whom I hadn't talked with for weeks.

"Off for a holiday, then," she said, smiling in her old way—the way she had when I first met her.

"Yes, Paul is anxious to see the Huntington Gardens. Have you been there?" I asked.

"No, I'm sorry to say I haven't. As I explained, I never get a chance to leave Horstman House, and if I did, I wouldn't really have anywhere to go—no one to visit and no one to go with," she said somewhat resignedly, if not regretfully.

"Well, maybe I could change that," I offered. "I'm going to buy a car so I'll have my own transportation. We could go somewhere together some weekend."

She seemed almost shocked at my offer. "But I never really have a day off because of—" She stopped midsentence, then nervously rephrased her reply. "When I came here, I was required to be on call seven days a week. I did it willingly because they offered me something I'd never had—a home and security. I suppose I might have changed things after Lisa—after the fire . . ." Martha appeared caught up in her memories and didn't finish, looking furtively toward the door.

"Oh, I understand that Madame Horstman requires someone always to be available, but surely, just once, another person could sit in for you," I suggested.

"No—no that's impossible. I promised, in return for my home here, that I would be the sole caretaker. I can't say more." She hurriedly stood and gathered her dishes. "But, thank you, Wendy. You're the first person in recent memory to have expressed concern for my welfare. It makes me wish—" She stopped abruptly.

"Yes, wish what?" I asked.

"Oh, never mind. I *can't* change things. But thanks again." She smiled and I thought I saw tears. Then she said, "Good-bye, Wendy," and exited to the kitchen.

"Good-bye" sounded rather too final and made me wonder if Martha knew something I didn't. But I shook off these thoughts, still determined to have a happy day with Paul—and maybe with Daniel.

After breakfast I went to my room and bathroom to brush my teeth and check my makeup. Then, noting the sunny day, I grabbed a wide-brimmed straw hat and walked downstairs to find Paul and Helman waiting outside. Paul literally jumped up and down with excitement. Helman, to my surprise, greeted me rather cordially. "Good morning, Miss Wood. Are you ready?" he asked.

"Yes, thank you, we're ready." I took Paul's hand and we walked to the car. Helman hurried ahead to hold the door for us.

His change in attitude was further suggested by his next words, "I've chosen the fastest route, Miss Wood, so that you will arrive when the Huntington opens."

"Thank you, Helman," I said, wondering what had created Helman's uncharacteristic concern and good humor.

The drive was pleasant, and Paul's eyes were glued to the window. He said, "Look at that—" and "Did you see that?" in response to each of the many sights that were new to him.

We reached San Marino, which was an obviously upscale residential community. The homes were beautiful and increasingly impressive along Allen Avenue close to the entrance to Huntington Gardens. A beautiful two-story house with a realtor's sign on the front lawn caught my eye—a colonial style surrounded by trees and shrubbery. I found myself wishing for a home of my own like that someday—so different from the cold expanse of Horstman House.

My daydreaming was interrupted by our arrival at the entry gates of Huntington Gardens. After stopping at a small guardhouse, we climbed a hill to the parking area. I was surprised at the natural and informal look of the acres just inside the walled estate. I had expected the same formal landscaping as that at Horstman House.

Helman drove to a curb before a wide, bench-lined walkway, stopped the car, and came to open my door. "You will enter here, Miss Wood. The information office, gift shop, and other visitor amenities are in the reception area," Helman explained.

"Thank you, Helman," I said, still amazed at his courtesy. Paul and I exited the car and were confronted by hordes of school-age children disembarking from buses. Paul looked at them wistfully, as if wanting to be included in a way of life he'd never experienced. He'd never known other children or even really played.

Helman brought me back to the present with the reminder, "Mr. Horstman says that he will join you here and will drive you home. Is there anything else, Miss Wood?"

"No, no thank you, Helman."

"Good day then," he said, returning to the car. He stopped for a moment, opened the rear door on the driver's side, leaned in, then called, "Miss Wood, you forgot your purse." He held up the purse and brought it to me.

"Oh, thank you, Helman. We'll need that," I said, chastising myself for being so careless.

Helman drove away in that beautiful, classic car, and we found ourselves watched by the children and others lining the walkway. I realized our arrival in the Horstman's limousine had caused quite a stir. I felt both conspicuous and pleased. *They must think we're somebody important—celebrities, even.* My star-struck past caused me to revel, just a bit, at this unaccustomed attention. But Paul was not so silly. He had run ahead wasting no time in getting to the "good stuff," as he called it.

I caught up to him. "Maybe we'd better find a rest room before we go on our hike," I suggested.

"Good idea," Paul agreed.

I waited outside the men's room for him, telling him not to talk with anyone. *I'm thinking like a mother warning her child about strangers,* I thought in surprise. *But Paul has had so little experience with the world—wonderful naiveté, but also dangerous in a real world where trust is so often violated.* I was becoming quite philosophical when Paul returned.

"Let's go," he said, grabbing my hand.

We passed the very tempting gift and bookshop, but I urged myself onward, after picking up a brochure on the desert gardens from a kiosk on the reception patio.

We looked at the map and moved down some stairs to the beauty of manicured grounds, which I had expected to see. Summer annuals and perennials were in colorful profusion. Off to the right was the impressive Huntington Library, which I'd heard was a prestigious center for scholarship, and to our left was the paved, downward trail to the desert gardens. Huntington really was an enchanted place, an ideal world. My spirits lifted, as I breathed the flower-scented air.

We wound downward, Paul racing ahead. I warned him to stay in sight. "Wait for me," I called, laughing at Paul's joy and exuberance. He seemed as happy as I to be free of Horstman House and to be experiencing a new adventure.

About halfway down the trail we passed a large greenhouse and then came to a side trail which led into the desert gardens.

Paul was already inside when I walked into another world. I had been accustomed to the deserts and plants in my native Arizona, but this was something quite different. The cacti and other succulents were very numerous and varied in size from low growing plants to huge, tree-high monsters. Signs pointed out that they came from all over the earth. I realized Paul and I were alone in a magnificent, mysterious, but also threatening environment.

Of course, Paul was not reacting as I was. He was examining things at his level, finding birds, lizards, and other creatures living in their habitat. Once in a while he'd look up and say things like, "Wow, look at that big cactus," but for the most part, his fascination was at ground level.

Some of the cacti were in flower, and I tried to adopt Paul's point of view, looking at the details at my height. But the farther we went into the labyrinth of desert foliage, the more eerie it felt. I could hear children's laughter in the distance, but Paul and I seemed isolated from that outside world, and I began longing for the open spaces of the main walkway.

Suddenly I realized that I had lost sight of Paul. I called his name quietly at first. Then, when there was no answer, I began to panic. "Paul, Paul, where are you? Get back here and stay with me!"

Still no response, and I found myself almost running. "Paul, answer me!" The trail branched off in several directions. I chose one and rounded a bend to find Paul on his hands and knees, examining a colorful spider in its web.

"Paul, you frightened me. I couldn't find you."

He looked up. "I'm sorry. I just got so excited running after a little lizard that I forgot everything else. Then I saw this spider."

"Didn't you hear me calling you?" I asked in exasperation.

"No, I'm sorry. I didn't mean to leave you. I just got so excited," he repeated.

"Well, take my hand and stay with me. I don't want to lose you." I didn't want him to know, but this exploration into the realm of giant plants was really frightening me for some reason.

Then I reasoned that Paul was seeing everything I'd hoped he would—nature in all its wonder and beauty. After all, that was the real reason for our trip, I reminded myself.

A small bench appeared at another bend in the trail and I suggested that we sit for a moment. "It's warm," I said, "or else I'm heated up from chasing you." I smiled at Paul, sat down, and patted the bench for him to sit beside me. I fanned myself with my straw hat.

"But I'm not tired," Paul complained.

"Just a short stop—then we'll make our way out of this forest. We'll just have time to trudge up the hill to meet your father." I opened my purse to get a tissue to mop my brow and was surprised to find a small envelope inside. The typed address simply read "Wendy."

"What's that?" Paul asked.

"I—I don't know. And I don't know how it got into my purse." I hesitated to open the envelope but couldn't just ignore it. Slowly I tore it open and withdrew a plain sheet of stationery. Typed in that all-too-familiar, irregular-spaced type was an even more familiar message: "Leave Horstman House." But there was more: "Final Warning!"

My hands were shaking and I was nauseous. Paul could tell something was wrong. "Are you okay?" he asked.

"Yes—yes, I'm okay." I didn't want him to know the content of the message.

"What did it say?" he asked.

"Oh, it's nothing—just a—reminder," I said, all too truthfully. It truly was a reminder of my tenuous situation at Horstman House.

I sat quietly, lost in my questions. Who had put the note in my purse? Who had opportunity to do it? I had been fairly sure that I knew who was behind all of my negative experiences at Horstman House, but Ingrid hadn't been near my purse. Of course, she could have come into my room using her master key. But I had put my keys in my purse just before going down to meet Paul and Helman. The envelope was not in my purse then.

Helman. He'd handled my purse at the car, I remembered. Had he been looking for some way to get the note to me? Had my leaving my purse in the car provided that opportunity? Why Helman? He and Ingrid seemed to have some kind of understanding, but what would he have against me?

Paul interrupted my frantic thoughts. "You ready to go yet?" he asked anxiously. "I want to eat—I'm hungry."

"Yes, yes, let's go." I stood and tried to decide which path to take, then saw a sign indicating the exit trail. We walked together, at my insistence, and finally made our way out into the open area and the main path.

"Hey, we came a long way," Paul said.

He was right, I realized. The hill to the reception area was quite a distance from where we'd entered the desert gardens.

"The going is always easier than the coming back," I remarked. "That hill looks longer and steeper than it did coming down."

The noonday sun was bright, so I put on my hat and sunglasses. Paul didn't seem to mind the walk, and I tried not to complain.

"That was neat," he said. "I've never seen so many cactuses—*cacti*, I mean." He had corrected himself before I could speak.

I didn't enjoy the hike up the hill, but the exertion was what I needed to release the tension created by the warning note. Also, the walk gave me time to think and to remember my resolution to be on the offensive, rather than the defensive. I resolved again that I wasn't going to let anyone or anything ruin this day, or drive me away—at least not until I was ready.

I had concrete proof of the threats and I wouldn't lose it this time. I'd show this note to Daniel when he arrived, I decided.

Then I remembered Daniel's words that he believed me. That recollection relieved me. I realized I wasn't alone in fighting my enemy.

We reached the reception area and searched for a drinking fountain, which Paul found near the rest rooms. Then we sat on a bench in the shade of the covered pavilion and waited for Daniel's arrival. Paul became restless after a fifteen-minute wait, so I consented to let him explore the gift shop near where I was seated. I could see the entry door and decided it would be safe for him to go alone. I didn't want to miss Daniel.

"Don't touch—just look," I cautioned, "and come back in ten minutes."

"Okay, I just want to see if they have some neat books or toys." He was off and almost inside before he finished talking.

I went to the kiosk and found a guide to all of the gardens, then returned to my bench. I was hungry too after our walk, but found myself thinking again about the note—and the warning. If it weren't for Paul's needs, I reflected, I'd have left Horstman House after my first few days there. *And that's still my reason for staying*, I assured myself. But could I risk staying after that final warning? Whoever wanted me to leave was an expert in creating "accidents," and I had no doubt that person was also capable of arranging my final, fatal departure.

Paul returned, excited about a puzzle and some three-dimensional cutout books he'd seen. "Do you think I could buy something for a souvenir?" he asked.

"Oh, I wouldn't be surprised if your father would go along with that," I said.

"Good. I like that book with the dinosaurs that stand up when you open the page," Paul said. "Where's Dad?"

"Well, I don't know. He said he'd be here at noon but he might have been held up in traffic," I suggested.

"Or Carolyn tried to keep him from leaving her *stupid* meeting," he whined.

"There is the possibility that the meeting ran longer than expected." I guess we were preparing ourselves for another disappointment.

"I'm hungry," Paul said.

"So am I, but I don't want to miss your father." I looked at my watch. "It's twelve-thirty. Let's wait another fifteen minutes. Then, if he hasn't come, we'll look for the Tea Room and hope he joins us there."

The fifteen minutes passed with no sign of Daniel and Paul couldn't sit still any longer. "Let's go eat," he said.

"Well, okay. I hope your father will know where we've gone."

We started to walk toward the stairs when I had an idea. "I'll go back and leave a message at the information desk. Maybe your father will think to check there when he can't find us."

"Good idea," Paul said.

We went back to the kiosk at the center of the pavilion. The lady at the desk thought it unlikely that anyone would inquire, but when I mentioned Daniel Horstman, her attitude changed immediately.

"Oh, I know who he is," she effused. "I'll watch for him and tell him you're at the Tea Room." *It's amazing what the Horstman name can do*, I thought.

"Could you direct us to the Tea Room?" I asked.

"Of course. Go down the stairs and past the library. Then go behind the Huntington mansion to the Elizabethan Garden. Then toward the Rose Garden, turn right, and you'll see the sign directing you to the Tea Room. Have a wonderful time," she said.

"Thank you. We will."

Paul took off in the direction of the stairs, and I rushed to catch up. "Wait for me, Paul."

"I'm sorry," he said. "I'm just so hungry."

I reflected on the improvement in Paul's appetite and the positive changes in his behavior. His health had improved, too. And this realization diminished the weight of my problems somewhat. But I was still hoping that Daniel would follow through and come. Paul didn't seem too concerned about it, but I knew he'd be disappointed later if his father didn't show.

We followed the directions we'd been given, crossing behind the mansion—now an art gallery—and stopping for just a moment to see the sculpture garden, which I recognized as the setting for several movies. Then we came to the Elizabethan Garden filled with herb plants and English garden varieties.

We passed through an arch into an arbor covered with delicate climbing roses. Beyond were the beautiful roses for which this California area was famous, because of the Pasadena Rose Parade. I wanted to linger, but after finding the signpost, Paul was headed for the Tea Room.

We went into the cafeteria, opting to eat outside under the trees rather than going into the formal Tea Room. The food choices were excellent; I decided on a chicken-salad sandwich on a croissant. Paul wanted a hamburger, so we waited for it to be cooked. Then he asked for a root beer. With mental apologies to Blanche for daring to drink soda, I ordered one too. We didn't choose desserts from the many cakes, pies, and other pastries displayed, thinking that we'd save that for later—when and if Daniel arrived. We went outside and found a table under a spreading California oak.

Squirrels played and foraged about us, and birds came looking for handouts. Eating outdoors was fun, and the meal would have been perfect if only Daniel had arrived. Paul was experiencing nature and enjoying every minute.

"I love hamburgers," Paul exclaimed. "We never have them."

"Blanche fixed hamburgers on one evening that I remember," I said.

"Yeah, but she just puts it on two slices of bread—no buns. This is lots better."

By the time we finished eating there was still no Daniel.

"Should we wait here for your father or go back to the entry?" I asked.

"I want to see some more. Let's not waste time," Paul urged.

"But what if he comes and can't find us?"

"He'll know we're here someplace. Remember, we don't have a car to go back," he reasoned.

"Well, that's what worries me, but I guess you're right." I checked my watch. "It's one-thirty. He's an hour and a half late. Maybe we should go on," I said.

"Yeah, where shall we go?" He stood, and I followed, gathering our leftovers on a tray and depositing them in a garbage container.

"I think you'd enjoy the Japanese Garden," I suggested. "Let's go that way."

We walked through the rose garden, noting roses named after the famous—Red Skelton, Esther Williams, John F. Kennedy, and many others. I could have stayed there smelling the roses, but Paul was more interested in finding the Japanese gong, the bridge, and the goldfish we'd read about in the brochure.

We went down some stone steps to covered seating, and then found, or rather *heard*, the gong. Children were taking turns drawing back the striker, which, when released, struck the bell, causing it to resound throughout the area. Paul had to wait his turn, until the school group had reluctantly moved on at the insistence of their teachers. But it was worth the wait. He had the gong to himself and took advantage of that. I had to move away to protect my hearing but decided to let him have at it. He was enjoying himself so much that I didn't have the heart to stop him. I sat in the shade of a vine-covered arbor and reviewed our situation. It would have been nice to have shared this experience with Daniel, I thought, but I'd have to be satisfied with Paul's happiness. The thought of the threatening note returned, but I didn't have time to dwell on it, before my thoughts were interrupted.

"Well, hello."

I turned, surprised to see Daniel behind me. He was his ever-handsome self in a tan summer suit and tie.

"Hello, yourself," I said, standing. "We hoped you'd find us."

"I just followed the gong," he said. "When you weren't at the Tea Room, somehow I knew that's where Paul would be." He laughed.

"He's having a great time," I said, deciding to let Daniel broach the subject of his late arrival.

"I'm always apologizing for being late," he said. "Carolyn's meeting was never ending and I couldn't get away."

"Well, we were concerned but figured you wouldn't leave us stranded here." I tried to sound more good-natured than I felt.

"No, I wouldn't forget you. I'm really trying to be more dependable."

"No harm done, I guess. Paul will be happy to see you."

We found Paul still gonging away. He saw his father and grinned. "Dad," he yelled, "this bell is neat. We've been having fun." He gave the gong one final swing.

"I'm sorry I missed it, Paul. But I'm here now. What's next?" Daniel asked.

"We're gonna go on that Japanese bridge," he said as he pointed. "And see the big goldfish."

He took off down the stairs and headed for the bridge and the lily pond, which I also recognized as a setting for several movies.

Fortunately there was no time for the awkward small talk which seemed to plague my every reunion with Daniel. We were too busy keeping up with Paul who was running from one visual delight to another. The Japanese garden was an idyllic setting, and the goldfish were fun to watch from the bridge. Paul could have played there all afternoon, I was sure, but we lured him up the hill to see the Japanese house and then the peace garden.

We sat on large rocks overlooking the gravel and sand which had been raked carefully into patterns simulating land and water. The patterns were hypnotic, and, for a moment, I felt the tranquility which they were designed to create. All of us sat quietly, feeling a temporary peace in this beautiful place.

"Wendy, this is fun. We never went on family outings when I was young. In fact, I don't remember doing much of anything together. This is what Paul needs—what I need. Family," Daniel said.

I was surprised at his reference to "family," but this situation was certainly more familial than any I'd experienced since coming to Horstman House.

"It has been good for Paul," I agreed. "He's learning a lot, too," I added, reminding both of us of my teacher-pupil relationship to the "family."

There was a rather long silence, which I broke with the question, "How did the meeting go?"

"Carolyn's agenda was lengthy," Daniel answered. "There were a lot of details to iron out." He paused. "I really wish I hadn't agreed to all of this. I hate the thought of all the publicity and the crowds. Why did I agree to let them plan this festival?"

"Well, for one thing, Carolyn is very persuasive. I've seen her in action."

He nodded. "Yes, but she's more pushy than persuasive and she isn't afraid to use every card up her sleeve."

"And she appealed to your humanitarian side—it's *all* for charity, for the children," I said, too sarcastically.

"We both know that's a minor part of it. Carolyn does most things for Carolyn—she loves the limelight. And I hate it."

"Another weekend and it will all be over. 'This, too, shall pass,' as my mother used to say."

"You've mentioned your mother, but you really haven't told me much about your family," he said.

"There's not much to tell. My father died when I was five years old. My mother raised me. We lived in a trailer in the desert for a while. Then we found a little rental house in Apache Junction, close to our Mormon meeting house. Mom loved the Church, and she held tight to the gospel's promises of eternal life—eternal marriage. That's what kept her going, living without Dad for all those years."

"Yes, I know about some of your beliefs," he said. "One of my business colleagues is LDS When we were in Westwood participating in a business conference at U.C.L.A. he took me for a brief visit to the Los Angeles Temple Visitors' Center." He paused, as if he were evaluating something. "But, if you don't mind my saying so, the concept of eternal marriage sounds a little like a fantasy."

"Well, it isn't!" I said, my defenses on the rise. At his surprised expression I calmed down. "You're basing your opinion on your own bad experiences. The ordinances in LDS temples *do* bind in heaven what is bound on earth. You can read about that in your Bible—I know you have one, I've seen it in your library. Anyway, I'll tell you more about it someday, if you're *really* interested."

"It may surprise you to learn that I do read that Bible in the library. It wasn't dusty, was it?" He laughed. "And I *am* interested. You know why?" he asked.

"Yes, the Holy Spirit is touching your heart," I said, smiling.

"That may be, but *you* are touching my heart too," he said shyly. There's something very special about you, Wendy. I see it. Paul sees it.

The first time I saw you I knew that you were different from anyone I've ever known."

"Well, thank you. But I'm really just an unsophisticated girl from Apache Junction, Arizona."

"Then it must be an interesting place," he remarked.

"Well, it is and it isn't. The view of the Superstition Mountains is great. But poverty is still quite evident there. I know, we lived in it."

"Then how were you able to go to college?" he asked.

"In some ways I had to grow up in a hurry. In others, I'm still, I've realized, pretty naive. I had to work part-time throughout high school and then continued that during college. And I had a grant and a loan—so I went straight through each year and graduated in three years."

"I admire you," he said sincerely. "Everything was handed to me on a silver platter, as they say—everything except the things which really count. You loved your mother, didn't you?"

"Yes, I did—very much. And she loved me," I said quietly. My throat was beginning to constrict and I spoke more slowly. "We were close, and her death was hard for me. The gospel of Jesus Christ helped me—it helped me endure her death."

I swallowed and waited until I could gain control of my feelings. Daniel held my hand. After a moment I continued, "When I finished college, there was really nothing to keep me in Arizona, so the offer of a teaching job in California looked like a real escape—but it wasn't."

"Then you came to teach for us, and we haven't made you happy either." He looked away, then stood suddenly looking around. "Where's Paul?"

I rose and looked right, then left. "Oh, he's running over there in the area just past the Japanese gate—it almost looks like a pasture."

"Guess we'd better go after him," he said. We walked through the gate, surrounded by Japanese pines.

I looked at my watch. "It's three-fifteen. We'd better move if we want to see more. The gardens close at four-thirty."

"Time flies when you're having fun," Daniel quipped.

"Yes, or when you come late," I replied, wanting to bite my tongue as soon as I'd said it.

"I've apologized—again. But we have the whole evening. That is, if you're still interested."

"Oh, I am—*Paul* is. He's still hoping to see a movie," I reminded him.

"You're wonderful," he said.

"Just what does that mean?" I asked, smiling.

"It means that you've become very special—to Paul—and to me," he said, looking into my eyes. "But—we—I—have to be patient. I have to ask you to be patient," he said.

"Patient? I'm a very patient person, but I have to have a direction—I have to know what I'm waiting for," I said.

"I have—I want to get to know you better. But I have to take care of some problems—to make some arrangements. I'm committed to do that, and it may take awhile."

"Well, I have some problems, too, related to what you've been *hinting* at—my background and my Church, so I agree that we need some time. Several things *have* to change." I'd planned to bring out the threatening note at the end of the day, but this moment was too opportune, I decided. "I need to show you something—something I found in my purse." I opened it, drew out the note, and handed it to him.

He read it, then sat on a bench, saying nothing.

I sat beside him. "It wasn't in my purse when I left this morning. Somehow someone put it there, after Paul and I entered the car."

"How could that happen?" he asked, incredulously.

"I think Helman did it when he found I'd left my purse in the car. He dropped us off, returned to the driver's side, and saw my purse on the backseat. He retrieved it and called me back to get it. He had time to slip the note into my purse—he's the only one who handled it."

"I'm confused," he said. "Why would Helman deliver a message like that?"

"I've told you—I've received notes before with the same message. But I was able to hold onto this one. There *is* a difference in the message, however—*final* warning—that's more than an implied threat," I emphasized. "I can't simply wait around for something else to happen to me."

"Then what do you intend to do?" he asked solemnly.

"I'm going with Jill on Tuesday to buy a car—in case I need to leave. I was still debating that, but today's threat has made it seem more likely—more urgent."

"Wendy, I said that I believed you when you told me of the first threat and happenings in the laundry," he said sincerely. "I also told you I'd do something about it. Please believe me when I say that I will. I *will*," he emphasized, pleading for me to trust him.

I didn't have a chance to ask him exactly what he could do, because Paul returned. "I've been chasing a little squirrel. At least, I think it's a squirrel, but it kept digging holes in the dirt—then it went into a hole in the long grass. I couldn't find him," Paul rattled on, returning our attention to the real purpose of our outing.

"Maybe a groundhog or a gopher?" I ventured. "We had prairie dogs in Arizona."

"Could be," Paul said. "Anyway, it's fun."

Daniel stood. "I don't want to spoil your fun, Paul, but we'd better move on. Do you want to see the art collection, or should we save that for another time?"

"I wanted Paul to see Gainesborough's *Blue Boy*, but maybe we could come back some other time," I agreed.

"Does that mean you're planning to stick around?" Daniel asked quietly.

"We'll talk about it later," I answered. "Why don't we walk through the camellia garden," I suggested, consulting the brochure. "That should take us into the sculpture garden, and we can walk from there to the parking lot."

"Are we still going to the movies?" Paul asked, anxiously.

"Yes, if you want to," Daniel said. "We'll have to get a newspaper and see what's playing."

"I've done that," I said. "How would you like to see *The Bad News Bears*, Paul?"

"Are there bears in it?" he asked.

"No, that's the name of a Little League baseball team. They aren't playing well, but with the help of the coach and a girl pitcher, they get it all together."

"Cool," Paul said. I smiled at Paul's new favorite word. He'd heard it on our last outing, and after hearing me use it once, he'd taken it up along with "great."

"What do you think, Dad?"

"Sounds good, son. Like what's happened to us—a *girl* helps them out of their rut." He smiled at me.

Our afternoon and evening planned, we set off on our adventure determined to have a good time. I realized we had set aside any attempts to resolve my dilemma, but the promise of a resolution was there.

Chapter Twenty-Two

The camellias were abundant, but rather withered and browned by the late summer sun. *I'd like to see them again in early spring.*

Just beyond the camellia garden we reentered the grassy expanse ringed by classic sculpture and balanced by an ornate fountain in the center. Again I wanted to linger, but Paul looked briefly at the statuary, then ran down the green field headed for the exit and the promise of dinner and a movie. The day seemed a total success for him, just as I'd hoped.

We stopped at the bookstore to purchase Paul's souvenir dinosaur book, laughing to ourselves at the illogical association of dinosaurs and Huntington Gardens. But that didn't matter—Paul was happy.

Daniel's gleaming black Jaguar convertible waited in the parking lot, and we set off for the next leg in our journey.

"This really is a beautiful area," I said when we drove slowly down Allen Avenue.

"Yes, it is," Daniel agreed. "It's a nice residential community."

"I actually saw my dream house on the way here," I said, making conversation.

"Oh, really. Where is it?"

"Another block or two—on your side. It's a colonial with natural rock, white brick, and a rail fence."

"What, no white pickets?" Daniel joked.

"No—but the rails are white. I guess I sound like a daydreamer."

"No, no. Not at all. I've sometimes thought of a place like that for myself. You know, Horstman House isn't a home. It's more like a mausoleum," he said.

"Well, I wouldn't have said that, but since you have, I agree with you. I couldn't live there for long—but then, I grew up in a trailer." I pointed. "There it is—on your left."

"You didn't mention it was for sale," he said, seeing the realtor's sign.

"No, I didn't."

"Let's stop and see it." He braked and swung left into the driveway before I could protest.

"But don't you need a realtor to show you the house?" I asked.

"Oh, I'll bet the owners won't mind. I'll tell them we saw the sign and can't come back soon. They'll let us in. Come on."

"Let's do it, Wendy," Paul urged, following his dad out the driver's side door.

Daniel was already at my door. "Come on, let's just take a look—for fun."

"Well, I guess it won't hurt to—look at it," I agreed.

Paul pressed the doorbell, and a sweet-sounding chime provided a welcome.

"Some nice shade trees," Daniel observed, looking at the front yard.

"Yes, it's ideal," I said, feeling both excited and embarrassed.

A pretty white-haired lady in her midseventies came to the door. "Hello," she said, adjusting her housedress and patting the bun at the nape of her neck.

Paul blurted out, "Could we look at your house?"

Daniel interceded. "We know we should have arranged for an appointment through your realtor, but we saw the house and the for-sale sign and couldn't resist asking."

"Well, I'm really not supposed to show the house on my own." She hesitated, looked us over, then looked at Daniel's car. "But I suppose it would be all right. The place is a mess though. You'll have to excuse that." She held a screen door open wide and ushered us in.

Contrary to what she had said, the interior was spotless and as well cared for as the grounds. "Your home is lovely," I complimented.

"Well, thank you, dear, but it's just become too much house for me since Harold died—Harold was my husband," she explained.

She led us through the center entry hall. On the left was a comfortable living room with a cozy fireplace, and on the right was a large dining room. The color scheme throughout included shades and tints of blue, avocado, and gold against walnut woodwork and pristine white walls. I loved it.

"Come back through here. There's a family kitchen with another fireplace, and a service area and half bathroom lead to the garage over there. The four bedrooms and two full bathrooms are upstairs," she added. "Those stairs are getting to be too difficult for me, too."

"When are you hoping to move out?" Daniel asked.

"Oh, whenever I can sell the house," she answered. "My married daughter lives in Santa Monica, and they have a guesthouse on their property which they're willing to call a mother-in-law house for a while. They say that I need to have someone nearby to look out for me. Oh, I don't know how it will work out, but I *would* be closer to my grandchildren and the temple and that would be good."

"The temple—you mean the Mormon temple?" I asked, astonished at the possibility that we had stopped at an LDS home.

"Well, yes, dear. The Los Angeles Temple on Santa Monica Boulevard. You've seen it, I'm sure," she said.

"Yes, I have. I'm LDS too," I explained.

"Well, I somehow thought you looked like a special family," she said smiling. "I'm so glad that you stopped to see the place. Harold would have been happy to think that someone from our Church would be living in our place."

I didn't know how to respond to that, but decided it best to keep quiet.

"Well, come and see the backyard while we're back here," she suggested.

"Yeah," Paul responded, shooting ahead of her through French doors that opened onto a covered patio, so that I didn't get a chance to try to explain that our "family" was not what it seemed.

"We haven't had our children around for years," she explained, "but I still have the pool cleaned, and the old swing set is still out there." She stepped ahead of us to the outside.

"Isn't this neat, Dad?" Paul exclaimed, already in the swing.

"It is neat, Paul," Daniel agreed.

"Oh, your backyard is wonderful," I said, walking across the stone patio floor to the lawn.

Just then a little blond head popped through an opening in a hedge. "Sister Martin, can I come over and play?" a young boy asked. He had called her "Sister." *Could the neighbors be Mormon too?* I wondered, but didn't get an opportunity to ask.

Sister Martin turned to see him. "Surely, Tommy. Come over for a minute. These folks are just looking at my house."

Blue-eyed Tommy, who appeared to be about Paul's age, was not shy. He went directly to Paul and said, "Can I swing too?"

"Sure," Paul said, "if it's all right with her—with Mrs.—?"

"I'm Sister Martin," she kindly replied. "But you folks haven't introduced yourselves either."

"I'm Daniel," he said, offering his hand. "And that is Paul in the swing, and this is Wendy."

"How do you do," she said. "You folks are a lovely family. I can tell. Would you like to see the upstairs?"

Daniel didn't correct Sister Martin's reference to "our" family. Instead, he said, "Yes, we would." I thought I'd explain our situation before we left.

The bedrooms were spacious, and the bathrooms were large and sparkling. The master bedroom had a fireplace and an adjoining sitting room. "Harold used that room for his hobbies. He loved genealogy," she said. "In fact, that's what brought us into the Church. Harold started to correspond with the LDS genealogy center. Then we traveled to Salt Lake City and loved the spirit we found there on the Salt Lake Temple tour. The rest is history," she said, laughing.

She continued telling us about the hobby room. "You could use it as a playroom, or a TV room, or even a nursery." She smiled at me. I felt guilty deceiving her about our relationships and intruding on her hospitality.

But Daniel seemed unconcerned and went right on. "Well, it's an ideal house," he said. "I imagine you're not anxious to leave it."

"Oh, I'll miss our home and our Mormon neighbors, but I'll take my memories with me," she said. "Anyway, one has to move on. One thing is certain in life—change. That's true for all of us."

We moved slowly down the stairs, following Sister Martin. She had answered my question about the neighbors and I felt strangely excited.

"I'll get Paul," I offered, and went out the rear doors. "Paul, we have to go if we want to see the movie," I called. I watched him say his reluctant good-byes to Tommy. He stopped when he reached me and waved to Tommy, who was escaping through the hedge.

"I wish I had a friend like Tommy," Paul said.

"Someday you will," I assured him. I thought that unlikely, unless there were some big changes at Horstman House. But I remembered Sister Martin's words, *change is certain,* and agreed.

Paul and I reentered the house through the patio doors. Sister Martin was talking with Daniel in the front entry hall, and I approached them. "Sister Martin, thank you for showing us your beautiful house. I hope that you'll be very happy living by your daughter. She's a lucky girl," I said, thinking of how much I missed my mother.

Daniel also thanked Mrs. Martin for showing us the house, and I didn't get opportunity to say more because Paul was dragging me out the front door. "Let's go," he said. "I'm hungry." I followed Paul to the car, waving good-bye to Sister Martin as she stepped out with Daniel.

"Good-bye," she mouthed and waved.

Then Paul and I got in the car, waiting for Daniel, who was still talking with Sister Martin at the door.

We waved to her again when Daniel finally joined us and backed out of the driveway. I felt a heart tug when we drove away, almost as if I were leaving my own mother. Sister Martin reminded me of how much my home and mother had meant to me.

Daniel remarked, "Nice lady," but said nothing more about the house. Instead, he asked, "Where shall we eat?"

"You know Pasadena better than I. You decide." I wondered what had happened between Daniel and Sister Martin and why he was looking so pleased with himself.

"Well, we've done Japan and Europe today. How about Chinese for dinner?" he proposed.

"I've never had Chinese food," Paul said. "Let's eat that."

"Agreed?" Daniel asked.

"Sounds good to me," I said.

"I know a little place in town that has *authentic* Chinese-American cuisine," he said, laughing at the misnomer.

"That's good," I replied. "I couldn't eat a carp after watching all those goldfish."

Daniel turned onto Colorado Boulevard and headed downtown.

Our dinner was good. The atmosphere was as Chinese-American as the food, but Daniel showed off his genuine expertise with chopsticks, and Paul and I entertained him, in turn, with our feeble efforts to use them.

The movie theater was nearby, so we walked in an area which was a gathering place for teenagers and college students. Everywhere there were open-air sidewalk cafes and shops. I smiled at the flashy flare-legged pants, big collars, and bright colors which most of the teenagers were wearing. There were a few kids dressed in holdovers from the 60s hippy generation, but in the main, the fun atmosphere appeared wholesome and harmless.

Paul was spellbound by the movie, and I found it refreshing and fun. Daniel lost his usual reserve, laughing and cheering with Paul when the Bad News Bears were victorious. Popcorn and sodas made the experience complete.

After, Daniel and Paul walked happily back to the car, but my spirits were dampened by the prospect of going back to face the realities of life at Horstman House.

Chapter Twenty-Three

Upon our return to Horstman House, Daniel parked his car outside the big garage and saw Paul and me to our rooms.

"I don't think I can sleep," Paul said. "I've had so much fun."

"I bet you'll go right to sleep. You've had a big day," Daniel countered.

"I'm glad you had fun, Paul. Did you also learn something?" I asked, trying to reemphasize the educational aspects of our trip, just in case Ingrid asked Paul for a report.

"Yes—I learned there's a lot more out there than what's here where we live," Paul said.

"That's good, Paul," Daniel praised. "I'm sorry it's taken so long to show you some of—what's out there. But I promise I'll make it up to you." He leaned over and hugged Paul. Paul hugged Daniel back and smiled his joy.

I thought that happy sight made everything I'd been through here seem almost worth it. "Good night, Paul," I said. "I'm going to church tomorrow with my friend Jill, but I'll see you Monday morning, okay?"

Paul looked surprised but said, "Okay. Bye, Wendy. Thanks—" He paused for a moment, then ran to me and hugged me. "I'm so glad you came here," he said and went happily into his room.

Daniel and I walked in silence to my door. Then he said, "I'm so glad too." He smiled, held up his palm to say good-bye, and moved away toward his quarters.

I changed into my nightgown and robe and went to the bathroom, locking the doors behind me. I hadn't forgotten the day's threatening note and I was going to be wary of any further attacks.

Returning to my room, I locked my door and placed the stool against it. I reasoned that if anyone opened my door the stool would tip over and wake me. I wouldn't panic but I'd be ready.

All our walking and activity had tired me, too. I knelt and said a brief prayer of thanks for the progress of the day. I asked again for His protecting care, then lay on my bed and fell asleep.

I rose early the next morning, and dressed for church. Walking downhill to the front gates to meet Jill, I almost couldn't believe all that had happened to me in three short months. Later, after church, I'd write in my journal and try to reevaluate my position with regard to Paul, Daniel, and the other occupants of Horstman House.

Jill waited at the front gates, as she'd promised, and I was overjoyed to see her. I pressed the button to open the gates and literally ran to Jill's car, hopping in beside her. She asked numerous questions about our trip to Huntington Gardens, and I told her every detail of our day, skipping only the note which I'd found in my purse.

Jill hadn't been able to reach our Sherman Oaks bishop to get an address for an LDS chapel, but we had no trouble locating one in residential Pasadena. The architecture of the building so closely resembled our Sherman Oaks chapel that we knew it was an LDS building the moment we saw it.

The sunday school service was just beginning when we arrived at about ten, so we found seats in the back of the room. The ward members were older—there were few children—and there was a great spirit of reverence. I found comfort in taking the Lord's sacrament. We returned later for testimony meeting, and the testimonies of Jesus Christ expressed by the speakers increased my faith and reinforced my resolve to endure.

Because Jill was coming back so soon on Tuesday evening, we returned directly to Horstman House, saying good-bye at the estate entrance. I pressed the intercom bell, requested readmittance, and the gates swung open.

I spent the remainder of the evening reading scripture and catching up in my journal. It had been a real day of rest, especially from my cares at Horstman House.

On Monday and Tuesday, the school hours seemed to drag on forever. I was looking forward to the prospect of another evening away from Horstman House on Tuesday, and despite the fun I'd had with Paul and Daniel on Saturday, I wanted more time to think about the future—a future which might not include them. I had accomplished one of my goals—the reunion of Paul and his father. I doubted that their relationship would ever deteriorate to its previous level, even if I weren't around to nurture it. At least I prayed that was true.

For car shopping, I wore denim flared pants, a pullover navy-blue-and-white-striped shirt, and some white walking shoes. I went out the rear door and walked down the long drive to meet Jill at the gates at five that evening. The birds were still chirping, and the petunias and pansies planted along the roadway combined to make the summer evening feel like spring. My mood lifted in that familiar feeling of escape, which seemed to come each time I left Horstman House. I thought that one day, someday, I probably wouldn't come back.

Jill was waiting dutifully for me when I came to the gates. I waved, then found the button which opened them. "Oh, Jill, it's so good to see you again" I said, leaning over to hug her. "Thanks so much for coming so often to help me."

"You're very welcome. I enjoyed the drive, even in the heavy traffic." She looked me over. "You look great." She laughed, displaying perfect white teeth and a smile as sunny as her yellow outfit. "Let's go," she said charmingly. There was a reason she dated so much, I reminded myself, and felt momentarily lost in thoughts about whether I'd be found beautiful and charming to a good man someday.

I climbed in beside her, brushing off my wistful thoughts. "I'm not sure exactly where to look for a car," I admitted.

"I saw a huge row of car dealerships just off the Pasadena Freeway. I know right where to find it—so why don't we start there?" Jill suggested.

"Have you had dinner?" I asked, hoping that she hadn't since I was hungry.

"No, I haven't, but we'll have to eat fast. You'll need some time to look if you're going to buy a car tonight." She turned her convertible around and headed toward the freeway.

"How have things been since Sunday?" she asked.

"Oh, up and down. Paul is happier and he and his father are getting along much better."

"That's good, but I'm not asking about *them*. How are *you*?"

I really didn't want to rehearse all that had happened to me at Horstman House. After all, she would just insist that I leave immediately, and I wasn't ready to give up—yet. Instead, I said, "The job is okay, because of Paul. I've grown very fond of him. But I'm not sure I can stay there. That's why I want to get a car, so—"

"So what?" she urged.

"So, if I make up my mind to leave I can just pack my things and go."

"Well, your room in our apartment is still waiting if you want to come back," she offered.

"I know. That's reassuring, but I'd have to find another job. I'm still not sure I want to go back to the classroom, even if I could find a teaching position this close to the start of the school year."

"There are other things you could do."

I didn't get a chance to ask what was in my head, *Like what?*

"Hey, there's a restaurant." Jill pulled in and parked. We went inside, found a booth, and ordered.

During dinner Jill tried to get me to talk about Daniel, saying, "You promised to tell me some details about what's been going on in your life. It's time."

"Well, with few exceptions, I still don't like the people at Horstman House. And the place has too many restrictions, too many taboos, too many places and people that are off limits. I'm not used to living like that—"

"And—?" Jill asked, wanting me to continue.

"And—I have gotten to know Mr. Horstman—Daniel—better. But I don't know about a—serious relationship with him. I still have some concerns about him, not the least of which is that he's not Mormon. I find myself wishing that things were different though. It's frustrating because he's made it clear that he's interested in getting to know me better, and he's shown some interest in religion."

"Really, wow!" Then she checked her excitement, wisdom taking over. "Hmm . . . Remember, you've only been there about three months," she cautioned, spreading mustard on her ham sandwich.

"Is that all? Somehow it seems like a year."

"Well, it isn't. Maybe you're rushing things. Just because he's handsome and rich doesn't mean he's a good catch." She laughed. "Seriously, you *do* need to know him better, and there is the difference in your backgrounds—the Church," she reminded.

"I know. I haven't forgotten that." I stared out the window.

"Hey, you'd better eat your soup. It's getting cold."

"I suppose you're right. I guess I have too much time to think—to daydream."

"Nothing wrong with that."

"I feel an urgency to get on with something—maybe it's to get out of there," I admitted.

"To get away from Daniel?" she asked, looking at me with real concern.

"I just don't like the house—the place." I toyed with my soup. Somehow I had lost my appetite.

"You sound almost afraid!" she said, alarmed at my admission.

"I have been—at times. Oh, it's silly, I guess." I took a deep breath. "Anyway, let's finish up and go car shopping. I'm buying dinner," I said, "and I want to pay for your gas."

She tried to protest, but I wouldn't have it. "You have been so good to me," I reminded her. "Let me do something to repay you."

"Okay—but I just want you to know that if you ever need me, I'm still as close as the phone."

"The *pay phone*, you mean," I said, trying to laugh at the absurdity of my situation.

Jill drove along the freeway until she spotted the row of car dealerships she'd seen earlier. Taking the next off-ramp, we landed in a car-shopping haven. She turned into the first dealership on the right and found a parking spot.

The salesman there was too pushy for me—I wanted some time to look on my own. We left the overbearing salesman with his used cars and walked, rather than drove, to the dealer next door.

And there it was—my car! A 1972 two-door Plymouth hardtop with a white vinyl roof and a sunshine-yellow body. It was only four years old. *I love it!* I decided. The white vinyl interior matched the roof, and the faux wood on the dashboard added warmth. It was in such good shape that I thought it must have been owned by the proverbial "little old lady from Pasadena."

The salesman was busy with another customer but he let us take the car for a test drive. I checked everything out and thought—since the mileage was low, the tires were good and the oil was clean—I'd have to have it.

We returned to the dealership where I paid a fifteen-hundred-dollar down payment, signed some papers, and the car was mine.

"I can't believe you bought almost the first car you looked at," Jill teased. "And you know what they say about buying a car at night—the paint looks better under the lights," she warned good-humoredly.

"I know, but that's the way I've always been. I pretty much know what I want and when I see it, I go for it."

"That doesn't seem true when it comes to men," she remarked, half teasing, half serious.

"As you know, I haven't had much experience with men," I said, truthfully.

"Or with cars, for that matter," Jill added with a wink.

"Well, I guess you can get rid of a car if it's a lemon. Relationships aren't quite that simple, are they?"

"No, they're not, and I should be talking. If Mike doesn't marry me soon, I'll be an old maid," Jill said

"Is he still elders quorum president?" I asked. "Maybe he's too caught up in his calling to think about marriage."

"That's the one thing I like about him, his dedication to his calling," Jill admitted. "Do you want me to follow you back—to make sure you get there?"

"I can find the way. You just go one direction, and I'll know to take the other. Thanks, Jill. Somehow having this car makes me feel a lot more secure. Now if I can just make the payments."

"You will. I'm glad you have the car. Do you plan to come next weekend?" she asked.

"Well, no. We have a big event next Thursday through late Saturday—The Bella Horstman Festival."

"Hey, now that you mention it, I've seen posters in the Hollywood area and heard it advertised on TV and radio. Somehow I didn't make the connection—I didn't know you'd be involved."

"Well, I'm not really. A big committee did the organizing and promotion. But I will be going—to the revival of Bella's movies and to the play at least. They're doing a live production similar to Bella's appearance in *Hippolytus*—at the Pasadena Playhouse."

"The Pasadena Playhouse—where it all began," she said in mock romantic tones, batting her long eyelashes.

"Yes, you're right. At least that's where Bella's live theater career began."

"That's not what I mean, and you know it. That's where I dropped you off."

"I know and I wouldn't have guessed then that . . ."

"Go on," she said.

"Oh, nothing. There's also a festival dinner and ball on Saturday night at Horstman House—then it will all be over, and I can decide what's next for me."

"Cinderella at the ball. It's all just too romantic," she sighed, jabbing me with her elbow. "I wish I could come—but I guess I'm just the ugly stepsister, left at home."

"That's not the way the story goes, but I wish you could be there. Unfortunately, this servant girl can't invite anyone. I'm not even sure I'm going. I'm sorry."

"Oh, it's all right. Anyway, I don't have anything to wear and I don't have a fairy godmother." *Neither do I*, I thought.

I walked her back to her car. "Thanks again, Jill. I really am grateful for all you've done—and for your friendship. It's meant a lot to me these past few months. You've kept me going."

"I still think you're holding something back," she said. "But if I can't pry it out of you, I'll feel better knowing you have a getaway car." She laughed, hugged me, then drove away, again leaving me to face the problems at Horstman House.

My pace quickened as I walked back to my car. *Well, my car and the bank's,* I thought. But I couldn't help feeling the elation that comes with purchasing that first car—the embodiment of freedom and mobility. And, I realized, it represented an accomplishment. I'd earned it.

Now to endure the coming week. I looked forward to the movie revival and to seeing the play, but the Festival Ball didn't hold much appeal for me. I figured if I ended up going, I'd be stuck with the company of Carolyn Reinhart and her pretentious crowd. That thought was unappealing. But I had promised Daniel to help him through the hoopla, as he'd called it, and I couldn't renege if he invited me to go.

I prayed with all my heart that the busy pace and the crowds which were to descend on Horstman House would keep my unknown enemy at bay, at least until the festival was over. But I'd watch my back at all times.

I got lost only once on the way back, exiting the freeway too soon. When I finally approached Horstman House, and Helman opened the gates, I drove my car up the hill and realized I'd have no place to park it. But, of course, Helman took control of the situation.

He was waiting at the rear portico. "I see that you have purchased a car," he said, noting the temporary license in the car window. "Did you consult Mr. Horstman regarding housing it?" he asked, having reverted to his usual condescending manner.

"No, I'm sorry, I really didn't think about that. I could just park it at the side of the garage," I suggested.

"That will not do at all," he replied disdainfully. "One of the garages is not in current use. We'll house it there—for now. Follow me," he commanded. He walked briskly along the driveway to the garage, and I followed slowly, quelling an urge to gun the motor and run him down. I laughed at the absurdity of the thought, but realized these kinds of feelings were foreign to me, and I reflected on my changing attitudes since coming to Horstman House. I was sure that Helman had placed the most recent warning note in my purse, so he was involved at least indirectly in the threat.

Helman opened the heavy wooden garage doors and stepped aside to usher me in. My car was rather wide for the narrow garage, built for cars of the 1920s, but I eased it in—then squeezed out of the car door.

Helman said, "The garage doors lock with a padlock, but I will leave it unlocked until I can get a key for you."

"Thank you, Helman," I said, gritting my teeth to hold back what I really wanted to say. Without looking back, I left Helman to close the garage doors and headed for the rear door and stairway to my room. Again I had a strange feeling that someone was watching me walk to the rear of the house.

Even my elation at having a car couldn't lessen the gloom which descended upon me as I entered Horstman House.

Chapter Twenty~Four

The few days before the Bella Horstman Festival were generally uneventful for me, but the preparations for the ball seemed to require a constant stream of workers both out of doors and on the first floor.

Paul and I remained in our second-floor domain, and, of course, no one ventured into the third-floor sanctuary. The main stairways to the second floor and the stairs leading to the third floor had been cordoned and blocked off to remind strangers to stay on the first floor. Regular members of the household were forced to use the elevator or the rear stairway to access the second floor. But everywhere else were groundskeepers, builders creating a platform at the foot of the main stairways, decorators transforming the drawing room and entry into a grand ballroom, and workers festooning the terrace.

The kitchen and dining room were also taken over by cooks and caterers, so Paul and I moved into the servants' dining area for our meals. Blanche tried to keep the household staff fed but otherwise made way for the caterers. And Daniel simply stayed away, totally avoiding the confusion and hubbub, I supposed.

Paul and I tried to concentrate on his studies, peeking at times at the mess—then at the progress—of the preparations. But most important to me right then, my prayers had been answered—the relentless activity in the house had forestalled any threatening action against me.

Daniel finally appeared on Thursday, the morning of the opening event, which was the revival showing of several of Bella's movies. He joined Paul and me for breakfast in the servants' dining room, or rather, he watched us eat.

"Hi, Dad," Paul said happily. "We haven't seen you since Saturday."

"Yes, son, I've been very busy. I'm sorry, if I've neglected you—both of you," Daniel said, looking at me. He sat across from me at the table.

"Well, the big event has come at last," I said, making safe conversation.

"Yes, and it can't be over too soon for me," he replied.

"It's been decided," he explained, "to show the films all day at a downtown Pasadena movie theater to avoid conflict with play rehearsals and preparations at the Pasadena Playhouse."

I realized he'd taken for granted my going to the screening because he'd made no formal invitation. "We'll leave at six-thirty tonight," he said. "At eight o'clock they're showing *The Grand Duchess*, one of Bella's earliest films. I *have* to make an appearance, Carolyn tells me, and I think I can stomach watching that one."

I was surprised at Daniel's negative attitude toward his mother's films, but I supposed he couldn't be objective in separating the real Bella from the actress Bella. "I've seen only one of Bella's talking pictures," I said, "so I was looking forward to this one. Has the attendance at the other films been good?" I asked.

"Yes, sell-out crowds, Carolyn informed me. She's already bubbling over with the success of the festival."

"I can imagine," I said. "But you'd rather see it succeed than fail, wouldn't you, since the committee has worked so hard to make it happen?"

"I really don't care about that. I'll just be glad when it's over," he repeated.

"Am I going too?" Paul asked quietly, breaking a long silence.

"Well, of course, Paul," his father replied. "I just assumed you knew you were invited. I'm sorry."

"Well, I'd really like to see what Grandmother was like—in her movies, I mean," Paul said. "Is this movie scary?"

"What makes you ask that?" Daniel asked.

"I explained that to you, Paul," I interrupted, "when we were looking at your grandmother's portraits. She played evil characters, but that doesn't mean she was like them."

"No, it won't be scary," Daniel added. "The character Bella plays is a strong, evil woman, as Wendy says, but the story shouldn't be frightening for you."

I reflected while Daniel was trying to reassure Paul about the elusive woman who had also been a stranger to him in his own home. *She is evil*, I thought.

Daniel abruptly changed the subject. "Well, if you two have finished breakfast I have some things to show both of you."

"But it's time for school to begin," I pointed out. "It's almost nine."

"Oh, why don't we forget school this morning," Daniel suggested, to Paul's delight.

"You mean it, Dad?" he asked. "What will Ingrid say?"

"Yes, what will Ingrid say?" I echoed.

"With all there is going on around here, I doubt she'll even notice you're not in the schoolroom. But if she says anything, refer her to me. Okay?"

"Sounds good to me too." I said. "How about the rest of the week?"

"Well, let's not overdo a good thing," he suggested, smiling. "How about a half day of school today and a half day tomorrow on Friday?"

"Dad, you're the greatest," Paul said. "Isn't that a cool idea, Wendy?"

I smiled my agreement. Then, followed by Daniel, Paul and I took our dishes to the kitchen where we found Blanche, who appeared more than a little distressed.

"Blanche, are you all right?" I asked.

She looked up from a pile of breakfast dishes in her sink to see Daniel. Immediately trying to compose herself, she said, "Yes, yes, of course. I'm fine." She began to rinse off dishes and load them in her commercial dishwasher.

"You don't seem fine," Daniel observed. "Is all of this festival thing too much for you?"

"No—no. My work hasn't increased." But she couldn't hold back her feelings. "It's just that—I can't *stand* having all of these people—these strangers—in and out of my kitchen asking questions and ordering me around."

She was extremely agitated, and I couldn't help wondering if she wasn't as emotionally sound as she had seemed when I first met her.

Then I felt guilty for even thinking that, as she began to respond positively to Daniel's kindness.

"It's all right, Blanche," Daniel said. "It will soon be over, and until it is, I'm going to tell Ingrid to inform our staff that after today they're on their own for meals until next Monday morning."

"Oh, we can't ask them to do that," she protested.

"Oh, yes we can," he said. "Take care of lunch and dinner today. Then we'll give the grounds people and the maids the day off on Friday. That will leave the main household staff on duty for a three-day weekend—just Ingrid, Helman, John, Martha, and yourself, unless you'd like to take off for a few days."

"Oh, no. I've got to be here to oversee the kitchen and dining room when those caterers move in," Blanche insisted. "And *she* will need meals." Blanche clarified her reference with a nod toward the third floor.

"Yes, but by the end of today everything should be ready—the house and the grounds. And, of course, the caterers will bring in most of the food already prepared," Daniel said.

"I know, I know, but I must be here to—supervise," she said. "Thank you, anyway, Mr. Horstman. You've relieved me just by letting me blow off some steam."

"Blanche, if I can be of help to you, please don't hesitate to ask," I offered, again feeling guilty about my earlier suspicions.

"Well, thank you, Wendy—but I'll be fine now." She went back to her dishes, and Daniel led us up the back stairway to the second floor.

"I have surprises for you. I left them on the table by the elevator," Daniel said.

Paul ran on ahead, and we hurried down the servants' hall, trying to match his speed.

"That was very kind," I said. "What you did for Blanche."

"Well, I can't turn back the clock—we have to go ahead with this thing now. But maybe it will be easier for her if she's not having to feed all of us at the same time she's trying to guard her kitchen."

"She's a good soul," I said.

"That she is," he agreed.

Paul had already found some packages on a table near the elevator door. "Are these the surprises, Dad?" he asked.

"Yes, you found them," Daniel said, moving to distribute two flat boxes, one to Paul and one to me.

"What in the world?" I asked. "Paul, you go first."

Paul set his box on the table again and removed the lid. He held it up. "What is it?"

"Well, not the most exciting thing a boy could wish for, I'm sure, but I wanted you to feel dressed up for tonight. It's a tuxedo—just your size," Daniel said, smiling.

"Gee, it's neat, Dad," Paul said, obviously not knowing quite how to react. "I'll look great."

"See I hadn't forgotten you. I *had* planned to take you to the film. Of course, it won't be quite the same as Saturday night—but at least we'll be together."

"You'll be very handsome, Paul. You should try it on to see how it fits," I suggested.

"Okay, I will, but someone will have to help me. The shirt doesn't have any buttons. And what's this thing?" he asked, holding up a cummerbund.

"That goes around your waist, and this little box has studs and cuff links." He opened the box to display the gold jewelry. "These go in the button holes and those go in the cuffs," Daniel said, pointing to each item.

"Oh, sure. Now I remember seeing yours. Okay. I'll go in my room and try to put all this stuff on." He was gone with his dubious treasure in hand.

"Well, now open yours," Daniel said.

I set the box on the table, lifted the lid, and inside found the most elegant white evening dress I'd ever seen. I held it up. "It's beautiful, Daniel—too beautiful—I really can't accept this," I said.

"Of course you can. I know you haven't had a chance to shop, so while I was in L.A. I found something for you. I hope you like it."

"Oh, I do, but it's too elegant for a movie theater," I suggested.

"Well, it's not for tonight. It's for Saturday night—for the ball. I hope you'll wear it then."

"But I really hadn't planned to go to the ball. You hadn't said any more about it."

"I know. That's one of my failings, I'm afraid. Because I've thought it through, I tend to think I've communicated my thoughts—too many years being alone, I guess. I apologize—as always," he said.

"Well, you shouldn't have to apologize for being so generous. I suppose I should try it on, then."

"Yes, please do. I'll wait here in case Paul needs some help."

I walked slowly to my room, still not sure that I should accept the dress. My mother had always told me not to take personal gifts from men, particularly strangers. But did Daniel fit that category? He was still a stranger in many ways—I never knew what to expect from him. When he stayed away for a few days I decided there really could be nothing between us. Then he returned and did something sweet— like buying this dress—and I'd be confused again.

Then I reminded myself that he hadn't done the most important thing—he hadn't inquired about my welfare. He hadn't referred to that threatening note I'd shown him. He hadn't asked if anything had happened since I received the threat. Did he doubt the threat was real, or did he just put it out of his mind, as he'd learned to do with so many other personal matters?

Reaching my room, I unlocked the door, then locked it behind me. I was still being very careful. I held the dress at full length, unable to see it in entirety in the small mirror I'd brought from Jill's apartment. I thought, *This dress seems familiar to me.* Somewhere I'd seen one like it. Of course, it was very similar to one that Lisa wore in a newspaper photo I saw in the library—both white, both with cap sleeves, and both gathered in an empire waist below the bustline.

My first reaction was to give him benefit of the doubt. I told myself Daniel couldn't be blamed for choosing a dress like one Lisa had worn. He probably did it subconsciously, choosing something he liked without realizing the reason. Then doubts crept in. Was Daniel so obsessed with the memory of Lisa that he had tried to set me up as her replacement? Or maybe someone else that might . . . was Bella involved in this and the other strange things which had happened to me? I almost began to panic, but I remembered my firm resolution to take control of my life at Horstman House. I determined again not to say anything about my suspicions. I wouldn't allow fears to chase me away.

I tried on the dress. It hung beautifully—an exact fit. I felt that few men could have chosen that well. Perhaps Daniel had told the saleslady I was about the same size as Lisa. *I do look a lot like Lisa's photos*, I realized with a shudder. Even Daniel had remarked on that. Then, that upsetting thought returned that I was perhaps being groomed as Lisa's replacement. *But that's foolish—Daniel is simply being nice because of Paul—and because of his need to have someone along . . . to give him reason to avoid Carolyn and her crew.*

Temporarily shaking off my reservations, I put on my white, medium-heel shoes, then went reluctantly down the hall to exhibit Daniel's gift.

Paul, already dressed in his new duds, was with Daniel. They both turned when I approached.

"Wow, you look great," Paul said.

"I have to agree—wow! You look more beautiful than I'd imagined," Daniel added.

"Thank you, both. Well, we're all dressed up with no place to go. Think we'd better change?" I asked, feeling an urgency to remove the dress.

"Yeah, I want to get out of this stiff shirt," Paul said, and we all laughed.

"Formality does exact a price—discomfort," Daniel agreed. "I have an idea," he added. "Why don't we go for a ride and find someplace to eat lunch."

"That's a great idea, Dad," Paul said. "I'll hurry." He ran to his room, removing clothes as he went.

I was less energetic in my departure but I was very anxious to change, and the thought of getting away from there for even a short time was pleasant. I left Daniel standing alone by the elevator.

When we were ready we went down the back stairway and out to the garage.

"I hear you found a car. I haven't seen it," Daniel said.

"Oh, it's nothing compared to yours," I said, "but I love it."

"Where is it parked?" he asked.

"Helman insisted that I park it in a garage. I think he wanted it out of sight—it's too colorful. Not sedate enough. It's in the first one on this end," I explained when we neared it.

"Can we see it?" Daniel asked. "Do you have a key to the padlock?"

"No, Helman said it would be left unlocked until he could get a key for me."

He opened each heavy garage door and propped it back with weights.

"Hey, that is a pretty sporty model," Daniel remarked. "Sunny—just like you." He smiled.

"I've hardly been sunny around here, but I do like the yellow—a happy color," I agreed.

"Well, it looks to me as if you're a pretty good car shopper. It appears to have been well taken care of," he observed, walking around the rear of my car and looking inside.

"I haven't driven it since I brought it here, but it seems to run well. I hope I did all right." I thought, *Actually, I'm quite proud of myself.*

"Would you like me to drive it—to check it out?" he asked.

"Why not? But I guess it's mine—even if it's a lemon."

"No it's not. Even with a used car, you have a few days to decide if it's what you want. Shall we drive it to the restaurant?"

"Yeah, let's do, Dad. I like it." Paul was already squeezing into the backseat.

I handed Daniel the keys, and he squeezed in, too, offering to back the car out so that I could get in more easily. Then we were off.

"Hey, this is very nice," Daniel said, making me feel good about my decision.

"I really don't know much about cars, but I liked it the moment I saw it," I said.

"I like it too. It's just right for me back here," Paul said from the backseat.

Daniel drove to the freeway, then took an off-ramp to an area where several food places were clustered. We chose a spot that Paul saw first—it advertised California burgers. "I want a California burger," Paul insisted.

"Well, I don't know what a California burger is, but we'll try it," Daniel said good-naturedly.

I loved the feeling of normalcy when we were away from Horstman House. No pressures, no disagreeable people, and no threats. *It would be wonderful if we could live this everyday life every day,* I thought.

We went inside and found a booth in the Kelly-green-and-white vinyl interior. It turned out that the California burger featured avocado and roasted green peppers. Each of us ordered one with California fries and sodas and settled back to see how quickly the food would come.

Paul abruptly announced, "I have to go to the bathroom. Where is it?"

The rest room was nearby, so we decided it was safe to let him go alone. "Wash your hands," we said simultaneously. Daniel and I smiled at each other.

After a silent pause, Daniel said, "I've been wanting to talk to you alone. But we'll need more time. Perhaps tonight—after the show?"

"That's fine," I said, "if it isn't too late when we get back. What are we going to talk about?" I asked, hoping that he planned to get around to how he was going to help me with my problem—the threat.

"Well, as I said, it will take more time than we have today, but I want to explain some things to you. I want to tell you what I've been doing this week—and I have several *huge* favors to ask of you."

"That all sounds very ominous," I said and laughed, trying to add a lighter touch to Daniel's very serious pronouncement.

"It's not ominous, I hope, but it will require a lot of—understanding . . . and acceptance on your part," he said quietly.

"I told you once before that I'm usually very patient. But I do have a problem I'd like to resolve today—the threats on my life."

"Well I assure you I haven't forgotten that. I'm hoping to solve your problems too," he said.

"You're making me anxious. Can't you just come out and tell me what this is all about?" I asked.

"Not here—not now," he replied.

Paul returned, interrupting any further pleading on my part or any explanation from Daniel. I was left wondering and worrying about what Daniel had in mind.

We ate rather quietly. Daniel and I had said all that could be said right then, and Paul was busy munching his now favorite food—a hamburger.

I drove on the return trip to Horstman House. I let Paul and Daniel climb out before I garaged the car.

"Well, that was fun, and you did very well in buying your car," Daniel said. "It should last you for quite a while." He shut the garage doors, and we walked together to the rear entrance and back stairway.

Leaving me at my bedroom door, Daniel said, "We'll meet out front at six-thirty, then?"

"Great, Dad, but will you come to my room before you go down?" Paul asked. "I need some help with those studs."

"Sure, I'll help you," Daniel said.

"I'll see you in the schoolroom in a few minutes, Paul," I reminded.

"Okay, I guess we have to," he replied.

"Yes, we have to."

Daniel and Paul waved and walked down the hall together to Paul's room. I smiled after them, happy in their newfound closeness. But my concern about Daniel's motivations and my worries about his plans seemed to overshadow any momentary happiness.

Chapter Twenty-Five

Paul and I finished our half day of school at about four-thirty, leaving me time to eat a quick supper at the five-o'clock serving, take a quick shower, and decide what to wear.

Actually, the choice of a dress was simplified by the fact that I had only three which were suitable for the black-tie affair. I rejected the first two, since I'd worn them before, and they were too hot for a late summer evening. I had a pink—my mother would have called it dusty rose—cocktail dress which seemed right. Also, I remembered that Daniel had complimented me when I wore pink on another occasion. The dress was three-quarter length and short sleeved. I added my matching pink satin heels and my mother's pearls.

At six-twenty I took the elevator to the first floor and walked through the halls to the huge front entry, which had been transformed into an art-deco ballroom for the Saturday night party.

Going outside, I was disappointed to see that Helman was to drive us in the limousine. His brooding presence put a damper on our outing. Paul and Daniel were already seated in the back, and Daniel got out to allow me to slide into the middle.

"You look beautiful, Wendy," he said. "I haven't seen that dress."

"That's partly why I wore it," I admitted. Daniel smiled.

Helman drove slowly to the theater in fairly heavy traffic. Our conversation was limited to small talk about the coming event, partly because of Helman's presence.

Because it was still light I hadn't seen from a distance the searchlights traveling the sky. But when we turned onto the Colorado

Boulevard—site of the old movie palace—I thought I was attending a 1930s or 1940s movie premiere.

Both sides of the street were lined for a block with movie fans, gathered, I supposed, to catch a glimpse of arriving stars, would-be stars, and dignitaries. Helman pulled the classic limousine to the red-carpeted curb, and the crowd cheered—at the car, I guessed.

My heart was beating rapidly, and Paul expressed my feelings. "Gee, look at all those people. What are they cheering about, Dad?"

He didn't have time to answer. A doorman opened the rear door, and Daniel stepped out onto the red carpet, helping me to climb out, which I tried to do with a degree of dignity. Paul wasn't concerned with making an impression—he was too impressed himself when he jumped out of the car to applause, whistles, and cheers.

I realized Daniel's face was familiar to Southern Californians, and being the Great Bella's son enhanced his celebrity status at this event. He smiled and waved to the crowds, then grabbed Paul and me by opposite hands and hurried us into the theater as Helman drove away.

Reporters and television cameramen assaulted Daniel at the theater entrance, deluging him with questions. "How does it feel, Mr. Horstman, to have your mother's films revived?" "Is Bella coming?" "How's her health?" "We hear she's still a hermit—any truth in that?" "Who's the pretty lady, Mr. Horstman?" "Is this your son?"

Daniel tried to answer all the questions with one brief comment. "We're all very happy to be here." Then he pushed our way into the lobby, where we, or rather he, was greeted by the ever-fluttering Carolyn, dressed as the bluebird of happiness in blue sequins and blue-dyed ostrich feathers.

"Oh, Daniel, you've come at last," she gushed. "Follow me. We're seated on the front row." Throwing kisses right and left, she dragged Daniel down the aisle, and Paul and I followed conspicuously, feeling like uninvited shirttail cousins.

Carolyn manipulated the seating so that Daniel was on the end of the row. She sat next to him, with Paul at her right, and I was left to sit by Paul.

Oh well, I thought. I knew Daniel's true feelings about Carolyn. I decided to ignore her and enjoy the excitement of the evening.

When the theater was filled, the houselights dimmed, and a spot-light shone on Carolyn. She stood, then pulled Daniel from his seat and toward the stage. The spotlight followed them up the stairs to the ornate proscenium where a stagehand gave her a hand microphone.

"Ladies and gentlemen, fans of the Great Bella, honored guests," Carolyn began. "It is my great pleasure to present my dear friend, Mr. Daniel Horstman the Third, the son of the legendary Bella whom we've gathered to honor. Mr. Horstman—"

She handed the mic to Daniel, and he had no choice but to respond. "We're pleased that you have come and hope that you will enjoy the revival of Bella's film, *The Grand Duchess*, and the other events of the festival. We're grateful for your contributions to these fund-raising activities for the arts in education. Our thanks to Carolyn Reinhart and her committee." He quickly returned the mic to Carolyn, who bowed in response to Daniel's praise and the applause she loved.

Daniel left the stage ahead of Carolyn, while she remained basking in the limelight, by blowing kisses to the audience and repeatedly mouthing "thank you."

Daniel hurried to us, pulled Paul to his feet, sat him down in the seat which Carolyn had occupied, and then sat between us. I smiled to myself at this demonstration of his preference to be seated by Paul—and by me.

Carolyn, followed by the spotlight, left the stage and returned to her seat, startled to find it occupied by Paul. Since she was still in the spotlight, literally, she had to accept Daniel's maneuver without protest. But she was obviously chagrined when the lights went out. I could feel daggers in her stare.

Then, the curtains opened, and Bella's old film flickered to life.

Although no title credits were given, I soon realized that Bella's *Duchess* was patterned after John Webster's *The Duchess of Malfi*, a revenge tragedy I'd read in a college dramatic literature class. The Duchess was not so much a villainess as she was a victim of her brothers' lust for revenge, so Paul's first view and impression of his grandmother did not entirely confirm the fears created by her portraits. I was glad of that, since it appeared that would be Paul's only opportunity to meet his grandmother—as a figure captured on celluloid.

The movie was dated in technique, script, and acting style, but it still displayed the undeniable talent and charisma of the Great Bella.

Daniel watched with alternating anxiety and boredom. Paul appeared spellbound by the strange characters, settings, and moods of the story—and by his grandmother. And I was fascinated at being transported back to the heyday of Bella the Great—the movie goddess.

Toward the end of the picture, Daniel leaned over to me and whispered, "I told Helman to meet us at the rear of the theater building so that we could escape the crowds. I'm going out that closest exit before the film ends. When it's over, grab Paul and head for that same exit. I'll meet you in the side alley and we'll rush for the car."

"Okay," I said. "Did you hear that, Paul?"

"Yeah, sounds fun," he said, with a big grin.

Daniel stood and walked quickly to the exit nearest the stage, and as the final credits began to roll, Paul and I followed, to the consternation and muttering of several patrons, offended that we didn't stay to the end.

Daniel was waiting anxiously at the outside door, and we ran together to the alley at the rear where Helman was waiting as ordered. We jumped in and were off.

"Well, that's the first time I've sneaked *out* of a movie theater," I said, laughing.

"It was more fun than facing those reporters again," Daniel agreed. "Well, that's over. Two more events and we can get back to normal."

Get back to normal? That's the last thing I wanted—the normal life at Horstman House.

Paul expressed the same thoughts. "I don't want to get back to normal," he said. "I like what's happened. I'm glad Wendy came to change things."

Helman cleared his throat, inadvertently reminding us that he could hear all that we said. His response reminded me of Helman's involvement in all that had happened.

"I don't mean I want to get back to the way things were, Paul," Daniel clarified. "I'm glad that Wendy came into our lives too. And I'm glad that we've gotten to know each other better."

"Me too, Dad."

We rode in silence with Paul between us. By the time we reached Horstman House, Paul was asleep, leaning against his father's arm.

"He's had a big day," Daniel said. "I'll carry him up to his room."

"We've all had a big day," I said. "I'm ready for some rest too."

At Daniel's request, Helman pulled the car to the rear driveway near the back stairway. Then he held the door for Daniel to gather Paul in his arms.

"Thank you, Helman," Daniel said. "That will be all for tonight, and I'll drive tomorrow evening."

"Yes, sir," Helman replied, looking at me with his coldest stare. I tried to ignore his obvious efforts to intimidate me.

"Whew! This kid's getting heavier," Daniel managed to say while carrying Paul upstairs.

"Yes, he's changed a lot in the past three months. He eats better and he's really grown—in many ways," I said.

We reached the second floor near my room. Daniel tried to wave good-bye but couldn't, so he winked instead. "Good night, Wendy. See you tomorrow—or tomorrow night." He continued softly, "We'll leave for the play at about the same time if that's all right.

"It is," I said. "Good night."

Daniel smiled, and then trudged down the hall carrying the sleeping Paul in his arms.

So I was going to the play. Daniel had taken that for granted too. But, I decided, he really did want me along, so I wasn't going to worry about his failure to ask me formally.

I hurried to slip my key into the lock and was startled to find the door unlocked. I turned to call out to Daniel, but he and Paul were out of sight and probably out of hearing range.

I cautiously reached inside for the light switch, which usually turned on the bedside lamp. Nothing happened. The switch next to it turned on the overhead light, and I was relieved that it worked. I slowly surveyed the room, then stepped inside and locked the door. At first glance, all appeared as I had left it. Then I found the bedside lamp on the floor, the globe broken.

Picking up the lamp, I saw that the drawer in the table desk was slightly open. Had someone searched my room and accidentally knocked the lamp off the table? Nothing seemed to be missing. What could an intruder have been looking for—the threatening note? Did he or she want to destroy the evidence of the threat? Well, they weren't successful if that was their intent. The note was still in my purse.

I picked up the broken glass that hadn't completely shattered, because of the rug. Changing into my nightgown, robe, and slippers, I avoided stepping where the broken glass had been, in case there were small pieces I couldn't see.

Then, taking my purse and keys, I went into the hall and locked my door again. The house was very quiet, which was usual at that time of night, but when I walked toward the bathroom I heard a creaking on the third-floor stairs. I turned abruptly to look behind me and couldn't see anyone.

I hurried to the bathroom and locked the door behind me. I was breathing hard, and my heart was racing. I thought, *I can't go on like this.* Each time I became less wary of the threats against me, something happened to scare me to death.

I was actually frightened to return to my room and was creeping stealthily down the hall nearing my door when I heard footsteps again on the stairs leading down from the third floor. I fumbled with my keys, frantic to get inside, when I heard her voice behind me.

"Well, hello, Wendy. You're up rather late."

I whirled about to see Martha hooking up the chain that had recently been draped at the entry to the third-floor stairs.

I tried not to let my voice reveal my panic. "Oh, Martha—I'm so glad it's you. You scared me."

"Well, how silly. Why should I scare you?" she asked.

"Well—because I heard footsteps and couldn't imagine who would be coming down the stairs from the third floor at this time of night," I explained.

"I ordinarily wouldn't have been there at this hour," she said, somewhat defensively, "but I couldn't sleep and remembered I'd left my book upstairs."

I saw that she did have a book, so accepted her explanation. "Oh, I'm not suggesting you shouldn't be there. The noise just frightened me," I said.

"Well, you get a good night's sleep," she said, turning to her door.

"Martha, I—" I was about to ask her if she had seen anyone in or near my room while I was away—but then I thought better of it.

"Yes?" she asked, turning back to me.

"Oh, nothing. Good night," I said and went into my room, loudly clicking the lock behind me.

For some reason I stayed by my door, leaning back against it to settle down. Then I heard Martha's door close, followed by footsteps on the creaking stairs. Martha was returning to the third floor.

My suspicion level raised, but then I decided it was really none of my business when she went to the third floor. My door was locked, and I got the stool from the desk and, this time, wedged it solidly under the doorknob. I wanted no nighttime visitors. I'd continue my investigation tomorrow.

I felt I needed to pray. I knew I'd asked so many times for the Lord's help in guiding me, but had I been ignoring His attempts to communicate with me? Did He really inspire me to stay on to help Paul, or had I allowed my own desires and needs to get in the way of His wishes? Was I being warned by the Spirit to leave this place?

My thoughts were in turmoil, so I turned to my scriptures for the help and comfort which they so often gave to me. In my studies I had been reading 2 Nephi. I turned to the marker where I'd left off in chapter twenty-five and read the beginning of that chapter, continuing until I came to a familiar verse which right then suddenly seemed very meaningful to me. *For we labor diligently to . . . persuade our children, and also our bretheren, to believe in Christ, and to be reconciled to God, for we know that it is by grace that we are saved, after all we can do.* I paused in my reading to think, then repeated the last few words aloud. "After all we can do." That phrase seemed extremely important at that moment, and I wondered if I had done all I could do—to help Paul and Daniel bond with each other. *Is my growing closeness to them an opportunity to bring them to the gospel—to believe in Christ?* Had I really had faith that the Lord wanted them in His fold and that He'd protect me and help me in my efforts?

I moved to close my scriptures, but a page from the fifty-eighth section of the Doctrine and Covenants fell open. My eye strayed to a verse I had previously marked in that chapter, and as I skimmed the words, they caught my attention. I then read the entire verse aloud: "For the power is in them, wherein they are agents unto themselves. And inasmuch as men do good they shall in nowise lose their reward." This verse seemed to echo the advice I had just read in 2

Nephi—do *all* you can do, all the *good* you can do, and the Lord will save you and reward you. I thought carefully on those words and interpreted them to mean that there was still a need for me at Horstman House and that the Lord would preserve me in fulfilling it. I realized again that I was a free agent, and the Lord wanted me to make decisions based on His advice and on that agency. I prayed with those thoughts in mind.

Then I turned out the light and climbed into bed, wishing that my bedside lamp was working so that I could leave it on. But I thought of the locked door, also propped shut by the stool, and went to sleep thinking of the now-familiar verse of scripture that was becoming my support: "Be still and know that I am God."

Chapter Twenty-Six

Daylight was most welcome since I had lain awake part of the night, thinking, listening for sounds, and waiting for visitors who never came.

I tried to make it a routine morning—praying, dressing, fixing a cold-cereal breakfast for Paul and me, and going to the classroom for our half day of school. Despite the reassurances of the night before, I felt very paranoid and suspicious of everyone remaining in the house.

The house seemed unusually quiet. Then I remembered that Daniel had dismissed all but the old household retainers for the three-day weekend, only Martha, Blanche, Ingrid, Helman, and John remained. Also, the workers who had been making noisy preparations for the ball were gone, leaving all in readiness for Saturday night.

Paul and I walked the empty halls to the schoolroom. He had been in school throughout the summer when most children had vacation, but our extra efforts had resulted in improvements in his reading and mathematics skills. Although I didn't have standardized tests to evaluate his progress, my experience told me that he was now reading on a fourth-grade level. The one-on-one positive experience had paid off. He had caught up.

Almost more important to me were his improved health and outlook. He and his father seemed almost like buddies instead of the strangers they were three months earlier.

I had also been successful in enlarging Paul's experience outside the classroom and outside Horstman House. All in all, I felt a genuine sense of accomplishment—as a teacher. I found myself thinking of these things while Paul studied quietly.

Then, my thoughts returned to my own situation. When Daniel, Paul, and I were away from Horstman House, I'd almost forget the terrors of the place. But when we'd return, all those fears came rushing back or were added upon by more threats and strange happenings. I simply had to face it—I couldn't stay at unless Daniel followed through with his promises to help me learn who was threatening me. I decided that I couldn't stay permanently at Horstman House under any conditions. I hated the place, and I felt I'd done my part with Paul and Daniel.

Reflecting further on that realization, I summarized the situation at Horstman House. The beauty of the interiors and the glories of the grounds and architecture were diminished by the sinister aura which dominated the estate. The bitter spirit which abounded there overshadowed the happiness that I found in Paul—and, *sometimes*, in Daniel. I had helped Paul. I had helped Daniel. I had brought them together as father and son. I'd have to be satisfied with that. I'd have to find a way to tell Daniel that I was leaving.

Then I made the mistake of looking again at Paul, conscientiously reading the book I'd given him. After our trip to Huntington Gardens, he had become totally fascinated with the outdoors and wanted to study animals and go to the zoo. He was immersed in a little book entitled *How Animals Sleep*. When I had come here, I reflected, he looked like a serious, hurting, lonely child. The changes in him were so evident—he looked like a healthy, happy, optimistic, and normal boy.

He smiled at me, and I knew that I had come to love him—not just as a teacher loves her student, but almost as a mother loves a son. Then I felt overcome with frustration, wondering how could I leave him to the pessimistic training and treatment of Ingrid—or someone just like her. I couldn't do that to him.

Paul interrupted my thoughts. "I'm hungry," he said.

I looked at my watch. It was twelve-thirty.

"Yes, that cold cereal was no substitute for Blanche's breakfasts," I agreed.

"I have an idea. Let's find Dad and go out to lunch again," Paul suggested, putting his books in his desk.

"Okay, where do you think we'd find him today?" I asked.

"I don't know. Let's try his room. And if he isn't there, maybe he's in the library," Paul said.

We closed up the schoolroom for the weekend and walked together to Daniel's second-floor quarters, opposite Ingrid's office. I realized I'd never seen Daniel's living area, which was not too strange, considering our platonic relationship.

I was about to say to Paul that I hadn't seen much of Ingrid recently when she stepped out of her office. I cursed myself for thinking of her, seeming to have motivated her emergence from hiding.

"Good afternoon, Miss Nourse," I said in a properly formal manner, hoping to discourage further conversation.

"Good afternoon, Miss Nourse," Paul echoed.

"Humph," she said in reply. "I see that you are leaving the school-room early—*again.*"

I thought of completely ignoring her remark but said, "Well, as you know, the food service has been curtailed for the weekend. We thought it might be all right to come out for some lunch."

My sarcasm missed its mark. "Yes, Mr. Horstman informed me that you and your *pupil* were taking part of the day off," she said.

This time I didn't take the bait, preferring not to respond to her condescending manner. I simply said, "I'm glad that he informed you," and turned to knock on Daniel's door.

"Mr. Horstman isn't in," she said with a note of satisfaction in her voice.

"Oh, do you know where he is?" I asked, matching her calm.

"I'm sure that he had some important business—in town," she said emphasizing her words in a way that let me know again that Daniel's business was not my concern.

"Oh, well thank you," I said, more kindly than I felt.

Then I turned to Paul, and without a word, led him down the hall toward the back stairway. When we were beyond Ingrid's squint-eyed stare and her hearing, I said to Paul, "Well, since your father's away, we'll take my car and find some lunch on our own."

"Cool," he said, and hurried me along as if to escape from Ingrid's presence.

We propped the heavy garage doors open and squeezed into my car. Backing out of the garage and heading down the hill, I once again felt a sense of freedom. *My car*, I thought with pleasure. Just owning it gave me courage; I knew that if I really had to leave, I could just drive away.

We ate lunch at another sandwich place since Paul had decided that hamburgers were the greatest. It was fun to be together away from Horstman House, but I couldn't help missing Daniel.

When we were finished eating and were driving back, I felt a real need for a nap, partly due to the hamburger, I supposed, but also because of my lack of sleep the night before. "I'm suddenly very tired. I think I'd better take a nap before going to the play tonight," I said, yawning.

"Yeah, I'm kinda tired too," Paul said. "I'm not used to staying up so late—but it's fun."

"Well, the play will require some real concentration. It's pretty heavy."

"Heavy?" he asked.

"I mean, it's pretty serious subject matter, and the language requires careful listening," I explained.

"I can handle it," Paul stated with a newfound assurance that pleased me.

"I'm sure you can," I replied, smiling.

After being readmitted by Helman to the Horstman grounds, I garaged my car and closed the heavy doors. Then Paul and I went up the back stairway to our rooms. I watched him go down the hall, calling after him, "Be ready at six-fifteen—wear your tux."

"Okay. But I hope only one more time," he said, and laughed. Then he turned and was out of sight.

I went to my room and found the door locked this time. Then, again locking the door behind me, I removed my shoes and, thinking I'd fall asleep at once, lay down on the bed. But I couldn't sleep. I became more and more restless as the minutes passed.

After a while I sat up on the edge of the bed, listlessly examining the ugly rug with its tangled vine border. Those intertwining and knotting vines reflected my feeling of being trapped. I had to get out of that claustrophobic little room.

I put on my shoes, grabbed my purse, locked my door, and fled down the back stairs, almost gasping for air when I reached the outdoors. I breathed the fresh air and walked away from Horstman House, not really thinking about where I was going—just getting away.

Without planning it, I headed past the garage and in the direction of John's cottage, an area I'd avoided since the fire at the boathouse. John's little house looked as inviting as it had when I first discovered it. Again I wanted to knock on the door to find the friendly face I'd seen after John had rescued me. But our relationship had changed. In our very few meetings over the past months I had found him gruff and uncommunicative, as he was at our first encounter.

Reluctantly, I passed the cottage and made my way through the trees, planning to hurry past the ruins of the boathouse and to walk around the lake. But when I parted the branches of the fir trees I met with a surprise. All traces of the boathouse and the fire were gone. In its place was a beautiful little garden, encircled by stone benches. *Mary's garden revived*, I thought. And my thoughts were confirmed. On one of the benches was carved the simple tribute: "For Mary— From John."

It was a lovely spot, filled with pansies, petunias, and perennials—a lasting memorial to Mary. I was touched by this loving gesture.

I sat on a bench and thought it would be a pleasant retreat for anyone. Horstman House was hidden from view by the trees, and the area seemed peaceful and happy. The memories of my narrow escape from the boathouse did not intrude in this wonderful place. I said a silent prayer of thanks.

His approach was so quiet that I jumped when John spoke. "Ya found Mary's garden, then?"

I turned to see him standing behind me. "John! You startled me—yes, I found your memorial to Mary. It's beautiful and such a sweet thing to do. I hope you don't mind my being here," I said.

"No, I don't mind. I come here myself when I want to think—of her. I feel different about this place, now that the old boathouse is gone."

"Yes, I can sense it too. It's a peaceful place now."

"Yes, yes it is," he agreed. Then he was silent.

"Well, I'm glad I got to see this, John." I stood. "I'll continue my walk now." I started toward the dirt path through the trees.

"Miss Wood," he called. "I'm sorry—"

I stopped and turned. "Sorry, John? Sorry for what?" I asked.

"Sorry that I cleaned up the laundry basement before ya got to show Mr. Horstman what ya wanted him to see. I didn't think to check with anyone before we sent the workers down there. Mr. Horstman told me ya were upset."

I returned to the little garden. "Oh, I understand. How could you have known? Thank you, though, for telling me. Now I have one less person to suspect—"

"Suspect?"

"Never mind," I said. "It's not anything you can help with now."

"Well, I want ya to know that I've been watchin' out for ya, since your accident here and since Mr. Horstman asked me to. Ya may not know I'm around, but I've been checkin' on ya," he said.

"Thanks again, John. That makes me feel better." I paused, then decided not to say more. "I'll go now." I went back to the path.

"Are ya sure ya want to go that way? That trail around the lake hasn't been kept up. I wouldn't want anything to happen to ya."

"I really need to walk and I've never been this way. I'll be careful," I said.

"Do that." He pulled out his pocket watch. "It's about three now. Try to get back to the big house by four. I'll check to see if you're back. If you're not, I'll come lookin' for ya."

"Thanks again, John. But I feel I'm really in more danger in the house than out here," I explained, partly to see if he would reveal any knowledge of what had happened to me there.

He didn't respond, the way I wanted though—he just said, "All right, then. I guess ya know best." Then he went back to his cottage after taking another look at Mary's garden.

John was right—the path had been so seldom used that it was overgrown in places, and I had to duck and bend under tree branches which had grown out and over the pathway. I stepped in a hole and twisted my ankle, but the pain was temporary. *It might actually be good to sprain my ankle*, I mused. *Then I'd have an excuse for my klutzy dancing at the Saturday night ball.*

Birds chirped and twittered, skies were blue, the pines smelled wonderful, and the afternoon was warm. I thought of Paul again. Throughout his young life, all this outdoor beauty was within a short distance of his house, but he was never introduced to it or even allowed to discover it on his own. I hadn't realized all that was there, either, because my memories of the boathouse fire and the lake had kept me from returning. It was too bad that I probably wouldn't have the opportunity to bring Paul there.

The farther I walked from Horstman House, the better I started to feel. Then I heard something some distance behind me. It was cracking twigs. I stopped. The noise stopped. My first reaction was to scream. Was someone following me? I waited and heard nothing more. I was tempted to retrace my steps and confront whomever might be there, but I was more than halfway around the lake, and it was past three-thirty. I decided the best course was to continue on.

I walked more briskly now. The pathway on this side of the lake was less rutty and the trees were less dense, so I wasn't forced to dodge so many branches and I made better time. I was almost three-quarters of the way around the lake when I heard snapping sticks again, accompanied by heavy breathing. "Who's there?" I shouted, not daring to look back.

"Wendy, I've been trying like mad to catch up with you." I turned, relieved to see Daniel coming along the path, puffing and wiping his brow with a handkerchief.

"Oh, Daniel," I said. "I'm so glad it's you. I was about to take off running because I heard someone coming."

"I'm glad you didn't. John told me where you were going, and I started to worry. This isn't exactly the wilderness, but no one comes this way anymore. I was afraid you might have an—accident."

I thought he was wisely cautious in using that word. He knew it had become a sore point with me.

We walked on together, more slowly since he needed to catch his breath, and I felt more secure.

"Paul and I looked for you at lunchtime," I said, "but Ingrid said that you had business in town."

"Yes, I did. I've tied up some loose ends with my attorneys and a few other advisors. I'll tell you all about it later," he promised.

"Well, I don't expect to know all your business. I wasn't suggesting that. Paul—and I—just wanted your company," I explained.

"I'm glad to be wanted," he said, smiling.

We walked the remainder of the way in silence, simply enjoying our companionship. We left the lake, walked by the swimming pool, and then past the ruins of the guesthouse. I thought the remnant of that terrible fire still retained an aura of terror and grief.

Daniel must have sensed it too. He hurried toward the gazebo, not looking at the burned-out shell.

We sat on the gazebo bench to rest for a moment.

"Why hasn't the guesthouse been rebuilt—or torn down?" I asked, no longer able to hold back my curiosity.

"Well, at first, after the fire, I couldn't stand to think of it—I wanted nothing to do with the place. Then, later, I thought of rebuilding but kept putting it off. Then I forgot—or tried to forget—all about it. I took no interest in it anymore. And we had no guests, so it just became something that I ignored—something that I was always going to fix but didn't—" He had rambled on, almost like someone making a difficult apology. He paused, deep in thought, then said, sadly, "Actually, that's the story of my adult life—I've always been *going* to fix things—but haven't . . . until now."

"But you have fixed something—your relationship with your son," I protested.

"Yes—but I'd never have been able to do even that, if you hadn't come along." He looked at me with a sweet tenderness which touched me.

All of the anguish of the past summer seemed to vanish at that moment. I felt safe. I felt needed. I even felt loved. Then I felt eyes—watching us. I turned to see the drapery slide back into place over Bella's third-story window. I shuddered and looked to see if Daniel had seen the curtain move. Either he hadn't or he pretended he hadn't.

"I'd—I'd better go have a shower and get ready for tonight," I said, responding to the changed atmosphere.

"Yes, I guess you're right. I wish we didn't have to go to that play," he said.

"Will you have to make another speech?" I asked.

"No, I told Carolyn that I would come on one condition—complete autonomy and no more speeches."

"What will you do if she decides to ignore your wishes?"

"I'll get up and walk out," he said, and I believed him.

"Well, let's hope she remembers, then, because Paul and I would have to walk out with you. I'm not sure I have that much nerve." I said.

"I have enough nerve for all of us when it comes to Carolyn. It's a learned response."

"I keep wondering why you let her get you so involved in all of this. You seem to dislike it—and her—so much," I observed.

He paused for a moment before answering, seeming to consider his response very carefully. "Frankly, she blackmailed me into it."

"Blackmailed?" I was shocked that he'd actually made the charge, having previously thought he'd said it facetiously. "What do you mean?"

"I simply mean that she guessed—she *knew*—something she threatened to make public if I didn't go along with promoting her Great Bella scheme. I can't say more—-right now."

"Well, that does answer part of my question. I really couldn't understand how she could have persuaded you against your wishes," I said, repressing my desire to ask for details.

"No more talk about Carolyn," he insisted. He looked at me again, smiling. "I'll meet you and Paul at the rear portico this time—in my car at six-fifteen?"

"Okay, we'll be there." I started to walk toward the house and then stopped. "Thank you for coming to my rescue," I said playfully. I smiled and left him alone at the gazebo where we had first met on that night three months before; though it seemed longer because of all that had happened since I came to Horstman House.

What a strange—and revealing—afternoon, I reflected.

Chapter Twenty~Seven

After leaving Daniel, I walked down the same halls I had entered upon first coming to Horstman House. I went purposely to the dining room, where Paul and I had seen Bella's portrait in her role as Phaedra, The Glittering Counterfeit. I had come to accept that title as befitting the Bella I had come to know—or at least had come to know more about. She was indeed a counterfeit insofar as having been a wife, mother, and grandmother were concerned. She was not the real thing. Now I was going to see a revival of the play *Hippolytus,* produced in imitation of the production in which she had starred. I looked again at the portrait of an evil woman—both in the role and in life. Paul's question about some actors possibly being like the roles they play was true in this instance.

I walked the full length of the first-floor hall and went to the library, one of the only rooms in Horstman House where I had felt comfortable. I decided to spend a short time there looking for information on Euripides' *Hippolytus* so that I could answer questions Paul might have about that ancient Greek play in which Bella had played the queen of Athens.

I found several reference books and learned that theater critics and historians discussed Phaedra as a marvelous tragic heroine; one who was as vicious in love as she was in her hatred. In summary, I discovered that Phaedra fell in love with her stepson, Hippolytus, and destroyed herself in her attempts to live the dual role of loving wife to the king and rejected lover of her stepson. It had been Bella's opportunity to recreate another powerful and tragic woman.

I became absorbed in my research and reviewed again Lisa's collection of clippings regarding Bella's career. *Lisa really was obsessed with the Great Bella.* Among the clippings was a *Los Angeles Times* review of Bella's Phaedra. She was praised for her passionate and moving portrayal, and the production was lauded for its innovative use of masks of tragedy, as the Greeks had done. Apparently it was a "unique experiment in theater production." I wondered if the revival production would utilize the Greek masks.

Then I looked at my watch. It was almost five-thirty. I'd have to rush to get ready. I put the clippings in the map table, closed the lid, and returned the books to the shelves. Then I hurried to the elevator and to my room.

I showered quickly and tried to do something with my hair and face. Then I ran to my room, grateful that I had already set out my pale green evening dress which was designed and draped like a Greek robe—coincidentally appropriate for the event, and I wore the pearl earrings again.

Going into the hall, I was not surprised to find Paul there, his usual punctual self and all dressed up in his tuxedo.

"Just made it," I said, checking my watch.

"You look pretty," Paul said, always free with his sweet compliments.

"So do you," I told him.

We went together down the back stairway to the rear of the house where Daniel waited with his convertible's top up. He got out and opened the door for us. Paul went first, climbing into the backseat.

"It's a beautiful evening," I said.

"Yes, it is, but I left the top up so that the wind won't mess your hair," Daniel explained, smiling.

"I'm not sure the wind could do much damage tonight—might even improve it."

"You look beautiful, as usual," he said.

"Thank you, as usual," I responded. "You two men do know how to make a girl feel pretty."

Traffic was heavy, but we still made it to downtown Pasadena and to El Molino Street by seven-thirty. No searchlights or red carpet this time, but in front of Pasadena Playhouse valets waited at the curb. They opened our doors and drove away to park Daniel's car.

No photographers, either, I was relieved to see, and there was a more dignified and sedate crowd of theatergoers than at the film revival. But the Playhouse still seemed festive and excitement was in the air.

I remembered meeting Helman there three months earlier. I thought in amusement that no one would have guessed that I'd return a few months later on the arms of the two Horstman heirs.

The lobby was relatively small but impressive, and featured an heroic-size painting of Gilmor Brown, the founder and director of Pasadena Playhouse and School of Acting.

Daniel was greeted in the lobby by various acquaintances but didn't pause for introductions; instead he led us directly to our seats.

The theater itself was also comparatively small, but the seats looked comfortable, and the ambiance was warm and intimate. I was delighted to see, here and there, theater and film celebrities. I picked out Jennifer Jones, of course, and also saw Jack Lemmon, Betty Garrett, Judith Anderson, and several aging but beautiful women, who well might have been contemporaries of Bella. Carolyn Reinhart was nowhere in sight, I was pleased to observe.

We were seated in the center about halfway back—excellent seats, I thought. I sat between the two Horstman men and was pleased at how the evening was progressing.

The houselights dimmed, the chatter silenced, and Carolyn appeared in the footlights. A spotlight shone on her red feathered dress, and we were treated to another flowery greeting and thank-you speech. Daniel must have truly convinced her that he wouldn't join her in the spotlight, because she thanked her committee members, including Daniel by name, but didn't call on anyone to stand and be recognized. Carolyn took pains to emphasize that the dinner and ball on Saturday was an *invitations-only* affair. She finished her speech, and after a pattering of applause and a blackout, the curtain rose, the stage lights came up, and the drama onstage began.

The poetic language of the play may have been beyond Paul's understanding, but he appeared spellbound by the masks, the costumes, and the broad movements of the actors. The thrill of live theater was not lost on him. I also enjoyed the play and kept imagining how well Bella would have played the tragic Phaedra.

Fortunately, the Greek's aversion to showing violence onstage made the tragic sorrows of Phaedra and her ultimate suicide less frightening than it might have been in a modern, more realistically violent play. Paul's first experience with theater seemed a positive one, and I was grateful again to have contributed to his learning experiences.

After the curtain calls Daniel suggested that we hurry out, but that was not to be. Carolyn appeared from nowhere in her feathery and sequined costume and insisted that he come to the greenroom beneath the stage to meet the actors. In turn, Daniel insisted that Paul and I accompany him. Although I didn't relish Carolyn's company, I was excited at the opportunity to go backstage and to meet the cast—a starstruck girl's fantasy fulfilled.

The greenroom was a simple large rectangle, painted light green, and filled with people congratulating the cast members on their performance. Unlike an ancient Greek cast, which would have included only males, this was a co-ed group of actors, who appeared much less heroic and much more human without their masks. But it was fun to meet such enthusiastic young people who had dared to try their wings in a very difficult profession.

Daniel seemed anxious to get away, even though he was courteous to all. But I could have stayed much longer, basking in the stimulating aura of the theater. He dragged us away and upstairs, escaping over the protests of Carolyn. Once outside, Daniel gave the valet our parking stub and tipped him so well that he urged us to come back—*soon*. Then, putting the top down, Daniel drove into the warm and breezy starry night. I'd had a wonderful evening and told him so.

Paul added, "Me too, Dad. It was . . ."

"Fantastic!" I supplied, helping Paul to find yet another word to express his enthusiasm.

"Yeah, it was fantastic!" Paul grinned at me after using the new word.

"I'm glad you both enjoyed it. I'm just relieved another festival event is behind us. Anybody hungry?" Daniel asked.

"Yeah, I'm starved," Paul responded.

I realized then that we hadn't eaten dinner. "I'm starved too."

"I want a hamburger," Paul volunteered.

"You're going to turn into a hamburger," I said, varying a phrase which my mother had often used when I overdid something.

"It's late—maybe we had better find a short-order place," Daniel suggested. "Do you mind?"

"No, I don't mind. I just want food," I said.

"Me too," Paul agreed.

We located the same California burger place we'd eaten at earlier that week, and Paul practically shouted for joy. We were very over-dressed for the setting, and other customers stared while we looked for a booth.

"Guess they're wondering what the occasion is," Daniel said, laughing.

"California burgers all around and three large chocolate shakes," Daniel told the waitress.

"I want a root beer," Paul said.

"Okay, two shakes and a root beer," Daniel corrected.

"And I prefer strawberry," I said.

"Okay, make it one chocolate shake, one strawberry shake, and a root beer," he said. Then, when the waitress was gone, he added, "There I go again, making all the decisions without consulting."

"It's okay—in *this* instance," I said.

Then we sat quietly, all of us tired from staying up late nights and from the excitement of the past few days. Paul broke the silence with a very serious and unexpected question. "Dad, I know we don't talk about Grandmother, but I was thinking about her—the movie and the play made me think about her." He paused, looking down at his hands. "Why can't I at least meet her?"

Daniel waited a long time before speaking. I looked at Daniel. Then Paul looked at his father. Daniel was struggling to phrase his answer. "Paul, I'm so sorry. I've tried to explain this before. Your Grandmother didn't even want to see me when I was a child. I didn't know her as my mother, and it made me very sad—so I know how you feel. I couldn't change things then—I still can't—but in the next few days, I promise you, there will be some big changes in our lives—in *all* our lives." He turned to me, then to Paul. "Some of them will be good—some of them may seem bad, at least for a while. But—"

He didn't get to finish his sentence because the waitress brought our food. Daniel stopped talking while she placed it on the table and then left, with the habitual, "Enjoy your meal."

Paul asked, "But what, Dad?"

"But . . . I hope in the long run that what I have to do will make all of us happier. I'm going to tell Wendy all about it tonight and tomorrow night. Then I hope she can help explain it all to you. Okay?" Daniel asked, searching Paul's face and mine for acceptance.

"I don't understand," Paul said.

"I know you don't. Maybe you never will. I'm not sure I do. But I hope you'll come to accept what I've done—what I'm doing. I've made some big mistakes, Paul, in so many ways. But I'm going to try to make it up to you."

"Okay—I guess," Paul said uncertainly.

"Well, the one thing I *can't* do is change all the relationships within our family. But, thanks to Wendy, you and I have already changed. I'm going to be a better father—and that's a promise, too."

I wanted to cry, looking at the two of them, together—together in a real sense. Daniel's praise for me also touched me. But his promises both pleased and frightened me. I wondered exactly what changes he was promising. What did he plan to tell me tonight and tomorrow night? I wanted desperately to know and yet I felt very apprehensive. Was this feeling a warning or premonition?

Chapter Twenty~Eight

Daniel left us at the rear portico of Horstman House, then drove his car to the garage. Upon his return we went inside together and used the elevator since the main stairways were cordoned off and blocked by the temporary stage built for the orchestra that was to play at the ball.

We walked a very sleepy Paul to his room and said our good nights. But before going into his room, Paul asked, "What about my piano lesson tomorrow morning?"

"Whoops, we forgot about that problem," Daniel said. "The piano has been moved to the entry for the orchestra, and there will be too much going on tomorrow for you to concentrate on a lesson."

"That's good, because I haven't practiced all week," Paul admitted.

"I'll leave a note for Ingrid asking her to call your teacher early tomorrow to tell him not to come. In fact—maybe I'd better have her tell him not to come anymore," Daniel said, almost to himself.

"You mean I won't take lessons anymore?" Paul asked, suddenly wide awake.

I was as surprised as Paul by Daniel's suggestion, but Daniel spoke before I had a chance to express it. "No—I still want you to study piano, Paul, but not for a while. Okay?"

"I agree—you should keep playing, Paul. You don't want to waste your talent," I said.

"But—" was all that Paul got out before Daniel interrupted. "I'll—we'll explain everything to you later, Paul, after I've talked with Wendy. Okay?" Daniel hugged his son, and Paul grinned.

"Okay, Dad, but I'm not sure I can sleep now," he said.

"Oh, I think you'll fall asleep the minute your head hits that pillow," I said.

"Yeah, but I can't wait till tomorrow," Paul replied. "Good night Dad, Wendy." He closed his bedroom door, leaving me to get the details of Daniel's unexpected announcement.

Daniel didn't say anything immediately, however, so I gave him some motivation to get on with it. I stifled a yawn and said, "I'm tired too. I think I'd better get some sleep." I started toward my room.

"But we have to talk," Daniel said, following me and taking my arm.

"I have to admit that you've made me more than curious. You've been leading up to these revelations all evening."

"I know. I didn't mean to be so melodramatic, but I had to make certain everything had been arranged . . . before I could tell you—ask you—" He stopped right there, still leaving me hanging.

"Well, if we're going to talk, I have to sit down. My feet are killing me," I said.

"Where shall we go? Do you want to come to my place?" He laughed, then joked, "My place—or yours?"

I smiled, then suggested, "I'd be more comfortable on neutral ground. Let me change into something more comfortable and then . . . how about meeting in the library?"

"Seems appropriate," he said. "After all, that's where our serious talks began."

Daniel was right—the library was the scene of our first discussion about Paul, about Bella, about Lisa, about this house, and about him. "Give me fifteen minutes," I said.

"Okay. I want to get out of this monkey suit too. See you there." He smiled and went down the hall toward his rooms.

I paused for a moment, thinking that the minute Daniel was out of sight, the oppressive aura of this place seemed to return. I hurried to the bathroom, locking the door behind me. I was really too tired for a serious talk on any subject, but I had to find out why Daniel was being so mysterious. I looked both ways when I reentered the hall, then rushed to my room, again locking the door.

I hung up my dress and slipped into some loose-fitting jeans and a T-shirt. *Not too glamorous,* I thought, but I'd had enough glamour for a while. At that point all I wanted was comfort.

I grabbed my purse and keys, locked my door, and began the nervous walk down the hall to the elevator. The house was quiet, the only noise the shuffling of my slippered feet.

I was startled by a shadowy figure walking toward me in the semi-darkness. Then I realized, with relief, that it was only Daniel coming to the elevator. "You scared me," I said, thinking I'd used those words too often in the past few weeks.

"I'm sorry. I had to come back this way to get downstairs, you know," he reminded me.

"I know. It's just that the house is so quiet—almost spooky—with so few people here."

We opened the elevator door, stepped inside, and descended to the first floor. The lights were brighter there, and my fears lessened as we walked to the library, where Daniel turned on a lamp and went toward the table bar. "Do you want a drink?" he asked.

"You know that I don't drink, Daniel, unless you have a soda." I sat in a comfortable chair near the lamp.

"And you know that Blanche doesn't keep sodas at Horstman House," he said, apparently deciding not to pour a drink for himself.

"Yes. I know. Is there some ice water?" I asked.

"No, but I can get some from the kitchen," he offered.

"Oh, never mind. Let's just get this chat going—I'm really tired."

He returned and sat in a chair across from me.

"Well, maybe that will work in my favor—maybe you're too tired to say no?" he suggested.

"No to what? That's the question."

"Well, it's a very long story requiring a lot of explanation. But I'll save that for tomorrow night, when you've had a good night's sleep and a day to consider my . . . proposals."

"Proposals?" I asked, more attentive.

"Well, that wasn't the best choice of words. Requests would be a better way of saying it. I've rehearsed this in my mind—but I don't know exactly how to begin."

"Go on. I'm listening," I said.

"I just hope you won't—that you'll agree."

"I can't agree until I've heard to what—go on." I was growing impatient. Then I saw the pleading in his eyes. "I'm sorry," I said. "Apparently this is difficult for you."

"It is—I have so much to thank you for. Your coming here brought a breath of new life into our depressing world. I really believed my life was over—that I had no power to change anything." He paused, deep in thought.

"I haven't done all that. I've helped you change your relationship with Paul . . ."

"I've told you—I couldn't have done that without you. You pointed the way and made it seem possible. Your love and concern for him rekindled mine. I actually was afraid to love—anyone—ever again," he said quietly. "You showed me how to love him. How to reach out to him. How to forget my own problems and see my son's."

"Well, thank you. That makes me very happy, too—happier than I could have imagined." I paused, realizing the truth of that statement, then urged him on. "That said, what do you need now?"

"I need you," he said, pausing, then moving beside my chair. "But I realize that will—have to wait. Right now, I want you to go on loving Paul and teaching him and caring for him." He stood behind my chair.

"I have no problem with that—I really do care for him. Teaching him has been very rewarding, but—"

"There always seem to be 'buts' in our discussions—"

"But," I continued, with conviction, "I can't stay at Horstman House. I made my final decision today. I was looking for a way—for the right time—to tell you."

He looked shocked at my announcement. Then he sighed, moved around to face me, and sat at my feet. "I know that you can't stay here and I've taken care of that problem, if you'll agree." He waited a moment, then said, "I've bought a house—your dream house—"

"What?" I interrupted.

"Shhh!" he said, bringing his index finger to his lips. "Hear me out—please." He stood and raised me to my feet. "Come sit next to me." He led me to a sofa nearby, and we sat side by side.

"My dream house?" I asked incredulously.

"Yes, the house in San Marino that you loved. I told Mrs. Martin, the seller, on the day we saw the house that I wanted to buy it—lock, stock, and barrel. I've bought the house, the furnishings, the dishes, the towels—everything."

"But, I don't understand—"

"Hush," he said gently. "I'm trying to tell you. Mrs. Martin has already moved, taking only her personal possessions. The house is yours, if—"

I couldn't believe what I was hearing. "Yes—if?"

"If you'll take Paul there with you and be his friend, teacher, guardian—his foster mother." He rushed through his plea, letting it all come out.

"But what about Bella? What about this house? What about you?" I asked.

"Bella is the past. I *hate* Horstman House more than you do—the rest will have to wait. But I want to get Paul away from this house and—its influence. I want to get you away from this house. And, for now, I've arranged everything with my lawyers. The deed to the house is in your name—it *is* yours, if you'll accept it. I assure you, there are *no* strings attached if you accept the house, except that I hope you'll agree to take Paul there. It's completely paid for, and you'll still receive salary for your other needs. They've drawn up papers making you Paul's temporary legal guardian until—"

"What?"

"Until I can be a father to him again."

"This is all happening too fast. I love that house and would love to live there, but—there are some major considerations—I have some conditions I must clarify."

"Yes, go on," he urged.

"I've talked to you about my religious beliefs—my dedication to my Church," I said.

"I told you before that I have nothing but positive reactions to your members—to you."

"Yes, but if Paul is to live with me—if I am to be his guardian— he'd be living in an LDS home. We pray, we go to church, and we have strict codes of conduct that are part of my everyday life. I can't live otherwise, and I'd be influencing Paul in that direction. How would you feel about that?" I asked.

"I have no objection to his being taught Christianity," he said. "You wouldn't baptize him into your church without my permission, would you?"

"Of course not—but if he lives the gospel of Jesus Christ in our home—and he would be—then he will very likely end up wanting to be a member, to be baptized," I explained. "I won't take him—"

"You won't take Paul?" he asked dejectedly.

"No, no, you didn't let me finish. That's not what I'm saying. I love him like my own son—you know that," I protested. "I was going to say that I won't take him unless I have your permission, and your blessing, to raise him as I would raise my own son."

"Well then, that's settled, as far as I'm concerned. That's exactly what I want to happen. And someday maybe I—but I'm projecting too far ahead. The question is, will you sign these papers?" He withdrew some legal-looking documents and a pen from the inner pocket of his sport jacket. "See, here's the deed, in your name. The house is paid for. And here is the document making you Paul's legal, though temporary, guardian." He spread the papers before us on a low table. "As I mentioned, the deed has been transferred and is solely in your name. It's legal as is, and my lawyers have drawn up these papers making you Paul's guardian. They have witnessed my signature. As you know, since you've read all those news articles about us, I'm a lawyer, but I'm also a notary and can witness yours."

"You said *temporary*—then you *do* intend to be a part of Paul's life?" I asked.

"Of course—if the guardianship were ever to become permanent I'm sure the courts would have to be involved. These papers just make it so that I can turn over—can request—that you take care of Paul for a temporary period. Can you wait until tomorrow night for me to explain? When this festival is over, I'll tell you everything—I'll explain everything. You'll have to have faith in me and in my good intentions. And you'll have to be very patient for just a little longer."

"I'm not sure I even have enough patience to wait until tomorrow night. Why can't you just tell me everything right now?" I begged. I was in shock.

He stood and paced away from me. "Please—please try to understand. I just need another night—and day—to resolve some things."

He returned to sit beside me again. "Please, I know you'll take good care of Paul. I know you'll be a good influence on him. You've already proved that to my satisfaction. Now, will you please sign these papers and wait one more day for the rest?" He gave me the pen. I thought of Paul and the opportunity to leave Horstman House forever—then slowly and somewhat numbly, I signed my name.

He gathered up the pen and papers, put them in his coat pocket, and said, "Now, I'll walk you through this mausoleum of a house to your room. And after tomorrow night, you and Paul can move out whenever you like."

We both heard the library door close, but Daniel beat me to the door to search the hallway for an eavesdropper. I ran after him.

"There's no one here," he said. "I guess the library door was ajar and the breeze blew it shut."

I looked toward the exit doors at the nearest end of the hall. One of the outside doors was open, as Daniel had suggested, so I accepted his interpretation of the event—although I wasn't entirely sure. The wind may have blown the library door shut, but why was the outside door open in the first place?

Now that I had opportunity to leave—and to take Paul with me—I couldn't *wait* to get out of Horstman House.

Daniel took me to my room and thanked me again. I thanked him in return, still stunned by his generosity and by his trust in me. "Should I tell Paul tomorrow, or do you want to tell him?" I asked.

"You tell him. I'm going to be very busy tomorrow, tying up some . . . loose ends. I'm sure he'll be happy. He has a new life, too, thanks to you."

He took my hands in his and smiled at me nervously. Then he told me to lock my door and hurried away down the hall, leaving me shaken and confused.

Chapter Twenty-Nine

I knelt and said a prayer filled with bewildered thanks for the chance to leave Horstman House and to take Paul with me. I also expressed my concerns about the papers I'd signed and the possibility that someone was eavesdropping on our conversation in the library. I then fell asleep the moment I lay down, despite Daniel's revelation of his life-changing plans and my hurried decision to go along with them. I supposed late evening events and restless nights had combined so that sleep came easily.

When I woke late in the morning I didn't remember dreaming and felt better than I had in days. Then I thought of the unsettling happenings of the night before, which seemed somewhat like vague memories, and I asked the Lord for guidance again—was I doing the right thing in taking over temporary guardianship of Paul and in accepting the gift of a house?

I thought in amazement about the prospect of really owning a house. Did I actually agree to become a temporary foster parent? How could I tell Paul? Would he take the news well? And what of the things Daniel hadn't explained—particularly his need to be separated from Paul for some indeterminate reason and period? These questions dominated my thoughts when I went to the bathroom and then returned to my room to dress.

I wore a cool, gauzy pink dress and white sandals, still craving comfort on the warm August day. It was too late to fix breakfast, and I wondered how Paul had managed. Possibly he had slept in too.

I decided to find him to see if he wanted to escape somewhere for lunch. That would also give me opportunity to talk with him away from Horstman House about the major changes in our future. I hoped the news would make Paul happy. After all, Horstman House, even with its cold and restrictive atmosphere, had been the only home he'd known. How would he react to my announcement that he'd live with me in a new place—without his father?

Stepping out of my room, I could hear the activities on the first floor—chattering, shouting, dishes clattering, and even musicians practicing. I went down the hall to Paul's room and knocked. He came right to the door. "Hi, I was wishing you'd come," he said brightly.

"I slept in and feel so much better. Did you get breakfast?" I asked.

"No, I slept in too. I'm starved," he said.

"I'm ready for lunch, myself. Would you like to go for a ride?" I grinned. "But no hamburgers, please," I begged playfully.

"Well, okay, how about Mexican food?" he asked, and closed his bedroom door.

"I guess I can handle that," I conceded

We walked toward the back stairway together and out the rear door to the garage.

"Where's Dad?" Paul asked.

"I don't know for sure," I answered. "He just told me that he'd be busy all day and that you and I would be on our own."

"Okay, let's go," he said.

We found the heavy garage doors still unlocked and dragged them open. I guessed Helman had been too busy to find a key for the padlock. Or at least too busy to give it to me. We slithered between the garage walls and the car and squeezed into the front seat. "Wear your seatbelt," I suggested to Paul. "I'm driving."

"Oh, you're a really good driver," he reassured me.

After driving down the hill, I asked Paul if he remembered the location of the button to open the gates. He hopped out and proudly showed me that he did. When, after a brief interval, the gates opened, Paul climbed back in the car and we were on our way.

The exhilaration of leaving Horstman House returned. I thought of how happy I'd be when I went through those gates for the last time. Now, if I could find the right way to share that news with Paul.

We found a taco place just off the freeway and went inside.

"I don't know what to order," Paul said while we waited in line. "I've never had Mexican food."

"You really are expanding your tastes—hamburgers, Chinese, and now Mexican," I said, smiling at him. *Almost my son*, I thought with a strange ache in my heart.

"How about a chicken enchilada, rice, and beans—and I'll have the same? How does that sound?" I asked.

"I'll tell you after I taste it," he said, laughing.

"Remember, you're the one who suggested Mexican food. But I think you'll like it."

We picked up our food and drinks on a tray, a new experience for Paul. "Hey, this is neat," he said.

"Yeah, it's cool," I said, smiling at my use of Paul's phrase.

He led me to a booth. "Is this okay?" he asked with his usual good manners.

"This is fine," I said, noting that we were pretty much alone on that side of the restaurant. I needed to talk with him privately and candidly.

Because we had skipped breakfast, we both concentrated on our food for a while, eating in ravenous silence.

When he finished, Paul said, "That was great. I liked it better than Chinese food."

"Yeah—light on the vegetables. Right?"

"Well, there was a little tomato and lettuce," he said, smiling. "This is fun, Wendy. Thanks." He paused for a moment, then said in his serious, grown-up way, "*Everything* is different since you came."

"I'm glad if that's made you happy. We've come a long way in our relationship since that night . . ." I stopped, realizing that I was about to bring up an event that Paul probably wanted forgotten.

" . . . since that night you caught me in your room?" he completed my sentence.

"I didn't mean to mention that. I just meant—since we first met."

"Yeah, when you caught me there, I was so afraid you wouldn't like me—that you'd be mad at me," he said.

"But I did like you and I do. You know that now, don't you?" I asked.

"Yeah, sure I know." Then he made it easier for me to go on. He looked at his hands and said shyly, "And I . . . like you, Wendy."

I reached across the table and took his hands in mine. "Truthfully, Paul, I've grown to love you. You're more like a son to me than just my student." I paused and looked directly into his eyes. "Do you think . . . do you think you could accept me . . . as something more than a teacher, as—as your guardian—your foster mother—someday?"

His chin jerked up and he said loudly, "Could I! Are you going to marry my dad?" he asked.

"No, Paul. Your father has arranged for me to be your temporary guardian—a foster mother. I won't be your stepmother, but I will be taking care of you," I explained. I had tears in my eyes, and Paul looked surprised, confused, and excited all at the same time. I let go of his hand and reached in my purse for a tissue. "I'm getting a little blubbery," I said, handing him a tissue as well, to wipe his mouth with.

After a moment, he asked, "Is that what Dad was going to tell me?"

"Well, not entirely. There's more. I hope you'll be happy about the other things I have to tell you," I said.

"If it means you're going to stay, I will be," he said.

"Well, that's not it exactly."

"You mean—you're leaving?" he asked with panic in his voice.

"Yes—yes, I am." He stared at me, startled to hear that answer. "But, if you want to go, I'm taking you with me."

"What?" he exclaimed.

"If you'll go with me, your father has bought that wonderful house we saw the day we went to Huntington Gardens—and he wants you and me to live there for a while. I'll be your temporary guardian—your foster mother."

His eyes and mouth were open wide, but he seemed unable to speak.

"Paul, are you all right? I didn't mean to shock you with the news. Would you—rather live at Horstman House?" I asked, dreading his answer.

I was relieved when he found his voice. "No. I don't even like it there—I didn't know it till you showed me where other people live. Do you think that neighbor boy will still be there?"

"Well, I don't know for sure, but I'd be surprised if those people have moved too." I hoped they'd be there. It would help to have an LDS family next door.

"I hope he's there," Paul started, then rushed on. "But, I don't really care," he said. "That was a great place—the swings and the teeter-totter. And I bet I could even learn to swim."

"Why didn't you learn to swim in your pool?" I asked.

"No one ever taught me—and they told me I couldn't go in the pool alone," he said sadly.

I understood. I hadn't wanted to go there myself, with Bella looking down from above and the burned ruins of the guesthouse nearby. It hadn't seemed the inviting spot that a pool should be. Later, it had been another part of the threatening environment of Horstman House I had avoided, since a pool practically begged to be the scene of a disaster.

I pulled my mind from my troubles and answered Paul. "Absolutely, you could learn to swim. In fact, I'll teach you myself." His excitement was evident and I was joyous at his open acceptance of the move—and of me.

"But what about Dad?" he asked, suddenly realizing that I hadn't mentioned Daniel in the equation.

"Well, that's a little more complicated," I answered as best I could. "He hasn't fully explained it to me, but he said that we—*you*— are definitely in his future plans. He just said that he has to work out some things . . . some, well, problems. And I have to consider some things, too. Your father will need to—to agree to make some changes in his life. Then maybe we could go on from there—"

"Will he come to see us?" he asked, anxiously.

"Well, I would think so—but I really don't know what's going on, Paul. If I did, I promise I would tell you. Your father and I will talk again tonight, after the ball. Then I hope I can tell you more tomorrow."

"I'm always having to wait till *tomorrow*," he whined. "But I guess I can anyway," he added resignedly. "When can we move?"

"Your father says that the house is ready and we can move when-ever we want—after tonight of course," I explained.

"Well, let's move tomorrow. All I have to take is my clothes and books—oh, and my piano music. Was there a piano in our new house?" he asked.

"You know, I don't remember. But I do know that your father wants you to continue playing, so he'll make sure you have a piano."

"I want a small one. I don't know what they're called," he said.

"A baby grand?" I asked.

"Yeah, that's it. It would fit in our new house, too. A white one," he said.

"A white piano would look very nice in our new house," I agreed. I stood. "Shall we go?"

He followed reluctantly. "Yeah, I guess we have to go back. I don't want to, do you?"

"No, I really don't, Paul. I'm going to be glad to leave Horstman House too."

On the way back I decided I should break one of Ingrid's sacred rules; I had to ask Paul a question about his grandmother. "Paul, do you feel—does it bother you to leave your grandmother behind?"

"No," he answered, without hesitation. "I don't know her. She isn't even real to me. She's just in her paintings and her movie. I . . . I don't love her. I don't even know her—and I didn't know my mother, either. No one ever loved me before. You're the first one to be like a— mother," he said, looking away out the car window.

I felt his yearning and wanted to ease his hurt. "Paul, anyone who really gets to know you couldn't help loving you. It's just that some-times things happen to make some people . . . unable to do what they need to so they can let love begin—to let it grow. I guess things happened in your grandmother's and your mother's lives to keep them from learning to love. But it had nothing to do with you—you *are* lovable. Ask me. Ask your father. We both love you very much."

"Yeah, I know." He smiled hesitantly. "I'm learning to love people too. Just like my dad is."

"Paul, your father has always loved you. He told me that when I first came to teach you. He just didn't know how to let you know. No one ever taught him how to love, either," I explained.

"Yeah, I guess his life was a lot like mine when he was little."

"Yes it was. But you know now that he loves you—don't you?" I urged.

"Yeah." He brightened. "Yeah, I do. I guess you helped both of us," he said.

Chapter Thirty

Again we returned to Horstman House and entered those imposing gates for what I hoped would be my last time. After parking my car in the garage, I led Paul toward the nearest rear entrance and we climbed the stairs to our quarters.

On the way Paul asked, "Are you excited about going to the ball tonight?"

"No, I'm not, Paul," I answered truthfully. "I enjoyed the film showing and the play, but tonight's grand ball is not my thing."

"Then why are you going?" he asked.

"Well, partly because your father asked me to be there. And he bought me a dress to wear. I guess I don't want to disappoint him," I explained, both to Paul and myself. The truth was I had to talk myself into going. I really didn't want to mingle with Carolyn Reinhart and her crowd, so I'd just make an appearance, be with Daniel, and try to leave early.

"Dad said that I could come," Paul revealed, "but I'd have to wear that tuxedo and stay out of the way."

"Did he tell you that you'd have to do that?" I asked, surprised and a little perturbed.

"No, I guess I figured I'd just be in the way," he admitted.

"You won't. In fact, would you go as my escort?"

"Huh?" he asked.

"Would you take me to the ball, kind sir?" I requested more dramatically with a wink.

"Really? You want to go with me?"

"Yes, really. I'll feel much more comfortable if we're together. And I plan to leave as early as I can get away. How about it?"

"Sure. I'll go with you. I saw some of the food—it looks good."

"It does, and by eight o'clock we'll be very hungry. We'll eat dinner and have a good time together. Okay?"

"Okay," he said, smiling. "Thanks, Wendy."

"Thank you." I was relieved not to have to make a solo entrance. "I'll knock on your door at eight, then," I said. "I'm going to do some packing. Maybe you should do the same."

"But what do I put my stuff in?" Paul asked.

"Oh, that's right. We'll need some boxes. I believe the caterers left some in the kitchen area. I'll go take a look."

"Let me come too, and I can help bring the boxes upstairs," Paul said.

"Okay, but let's use the elevator this time," I suggested.

We took the elevator down and entered the busy first floor. People we'd never seen were going both ways to and from the kitchen. We had to jump into the flow to avoid being run down.

In the kitchen we found a still-distraught Blanche trying to keep the strangers from damaging her kitchen.

"Blanche, how are you holding up?" I asked sympathetically.

Blanche sighed. "I just keep telling myself that it will all be over soon. I can't wait. I just hope Mr. Horstman will never again agree to hosting an event like this one." She moved to a kitchen chair and sat resignedly.

"Blanche, do you know what happened to some empty boxes that were stacked here?" I asked.

"Yes, I told them to put them in the servants' dining room—out of my sight. I can't stand all this clutter," she said.

"Do you suppose we could have about six of them?" I asked.

"Well, they're not mine to give away. But I imagine they contained food items that will be eaten tonight. I don't think the caterers will be using them again."

"Well, if you say it's all right we'll take a few boxes, then," I said.

"It's all right by me. But why do you need boxes?" she asked.

Paul looked at me, and we exchanged glances.

"Blanche, I guess Mr. Horstman hasn't told you—Paul and I are leaving Horstman House tomorrow, or as soon as we can pack our personal things," I explained.

She stood, slowly. "Leaving? What do you mean *leaving*?" she asked.

"I'm sure Daniel—Mr. Horstman—will explain it to you. To *all* of you, soon. Paul and I are moving to a place in San Marino that Mr. Horstman has bought for us. He's made me Paul's temporary guardian."

"I'd better sit back down," she said, lowering herself to the chair. "What does that mean for the rest of us—for Horstman House?" she asked, obviously fearing for her future.

"I'll have to leave explanations of his plans to Mr. Horstman," I said quietly. "But I'm sure that he wouldn't close Horstman House and that all of you will retain your positions here." I tried my best to reassure her, without really knowing Daniel's plans.

"Well, I suppose you're right. But it just won't be the same without Master Paul here. Somehow, knowing that he was the heir to Horstman House created a feeling of permanence—a continuity and a sense of the future. Of course, it's not my business to question Mr. Horstman's decisions. It will just be—an adjustment," she said.

"I'll come back and see you, Blanche," Paul said. "I won't forget you. You're a great cook and you've always been nice to me."

"Master Paul, you've always been a real little gentleman. I'll—I'll miss you," she said, dabbing at her eyes with a handkerchief which had been tucked in her sleeve.

"And thank you, Blanche, for being a friend while I've been here," I said.

"I'd like to have done more," she said. "You and Master Paul brought life to this house. But I'm glad, in a way, that you're leaving."

I didn't know exactly how to react to that, but she clarified. "I mean, I'm glad you're strong enough to get away. This house has a way of usurping one's life. Some of us end up selling our souls for nothing but . . . *security*," she said bitterly.

Again I didn't know how to respond, so I simply said, "I hope you can find happiness, Blanche. We'll say good-bye before we leave."

"So, when did you say you're going?" she asked.

"I don't know for certain, but if we can get our things packed we may move tomorrow," I said.

"That soon? Well, I guess there will be some major changes here, then." She stood and moved to a counter, which she absently wiped off. "Does Ingrid know?" she said, turning back to us.

I paused before answering. "I really don't know. I assume that Mr. Horstman has told her. I do hope so," I said, realizing that I hadn't actually considered Ingrid's probable reaction. I hoped I wouldn't have to be the one to break the news to her.

"Well, good-bye for now," I said, holding Paul's hand and taking him toward the servants' dining room.

"Bye, Blanche," he said, but she said nothing—just kept staring at the wall before her.

We found the boxes and carried them up the back stairs rather than going back through Blanche's kitchen. We left three boxes by my door and took the remaining three to Paul's room.

"Do you need help packing?" I asked.

"Well, I've never done it before—but I guess I can do it. I might need help tomorrow, if I can't get it all in," he said.

"Just pack the things you really need for now, and I'm sure your father will arrange to get the rest for you later."

"Okay, but it'll be hard to know what to take and what to leave," he said, sitting on his bed.

"Pack your summer clothes and your toothbrush and a few favorite books and games. That should do for now," I suggested. "I'll check later to see how you're getting along. Okay?"

"I'm excited," he said. "This is like a real adventure."

I sat beside him on the bed. "It is. I hope you'll be happy, Paul. There will be a lot of changes. You may get rather homesick for a while."

"Not if you're there," he assured me. "But what about school? Will you still teach me?"

"I'm sure that will be the plan for a while. You know your father has some strong preferences for individual tutoring over public schools."

At that moment I looked up to see Ingrid standing in Paul's doorway, hands on her hips, and scowling in her customary way. "What is going on here?" she demanded.

I sighed and silently counted to ten. "Nothing that should concern you," I said, standing.

Paul stood too, both of us conditioned to respond to Ingrid's authoritative manner. "I'm just getting ready to pack," Paul said, innocently.

"And just where do you think you are going that would require you to pack?" she asked, dashing my hope that Daniel had informed her.

"Uh—apparently Dan—Mr. Horstman neglected to tell you," I said, gathering courage to explain the rest.

"He told me to cancel Paul's piano lessons today—and for the near future. Of course I objected, but to no avail," she admitted. "What other foolishness have you managed to convince him to accept?"

"Oh, this was not my idea!" I protested. "Mr. Horstman has—has made me Paul's temporary legal guardian and—foster mother." *There, it's out!*

She stepped in to confront me face-to-face, the veins bulging in her neck and her jaw set so that she talked through clenched teeth. "That is impossible. He would never agree to such a thing without first consulting me."

I didn't back down, strengthened by my knowledge of the legal papers I'd signed. "I assure you, it's true. The legal documents have been signed and Paul will be going to live with me."

She looked at Paul, who had moved behind me and was peering out at her from that relative safety. "Master Paul, you will not listen to this foolishness," she commanded. "I intend to find your father and get this matter straightened out. In the meantime, you will stay in your room until I come for you."

"Ingrid—Miss Nourse—I believe that you have meant well in your attempts to rear and discipline Paul. I give you credit for that. But you no longer have authority to discipline him or to give him instructions. That is now my job—and his father's role. Paul and I will be leaving tomorrow." I reached behind me and drew Paul between Ingrid and me, protectively folding my arms around him. "I'm sorry to have revealed this news so abruptly. I'm sorry, too, that it upsets you. But there is nothing you can do to change it," I said quietly, but firmly.

"We'll see about that, miss," she seethed. "I've been a part of Horstman House since Mr. Daniel's childhood. I will do *whatever* I have to do to preserve this family and their household!" She paused for a moment, looking at me coldly. "I should have sent you packing the first day you arrived here. I rue the day I didn't. But, contrary to what you think, you haven't won yet." She turned and went away. I noticed that her walk was determined, but slow, without the angry energy she usually exhibited in her exits.

We stood silently for a moment, letting the impact of Ingrid's words sink in. Then I said, "I'm sorry that you had to be a part of that scene, Paul. I didn't want this change to become a tug-of-war."

"What's that?" he asked quietly.

I was always surprised by Paul's educated manner and how incongruous it was with his lack of basic understanding of everyday life and terms. "I mean, I didn't want you to be pulled back and forth between us, because of your father's decisions," I explained.

"Well, Ingrid hasn't been as mean since you came. And it's been a lot happier here." He sat on his bed again. "She's just mad because she can't make everybody do what she wants, like she used to."

"You're right, of course. But I hope you know that she was really trying to do what she thought best for you," I said, trying to put the best possible face on her behavior, for Paul's sake.

"Yeah, I know—but it wasn't," he said, without hesitation.

"Well, let's get on with our packing. That should keep us busy until time to get ready for the ball. If you finish early, I suggest that you take a nap. I'm going to since we may be up late again." I kissed him on the cheek and left for my room.

"Okay. See ya," he said, already starting to pack his toys.

"Yep, see you at eight."

Walking toward my room, I realized I'd been very naive to think that everything would go well with this change. Our escape from Horstman House might still be possible, but Blanche's and Ingrid's reactions had clarified that there would be consequences. I had managed to convince myself that getting Paul to accept our plans was the only obstacle to our flight. But the reality was that our actions would create repercussions throughout Horstman House.

I rehearsed Ingrid's words in my mind, "*I will do whatever I have to do to preserve this family . . .*" The threatening aura of Horstman House returned, and I ran to my room, locking the door behind me.

Chapter Thirty-One

My locked door provided an illusion of safety from the threatening atmosphere of Horstman House, but I was very grateful that I was spending my last night there. I expressed my thanks for that blessing to my Heavenly Father.

I was surprised to find that it was almost five-thirty. It was too early to dress for the night's festivities. I decided to pack the things I needed and then to take a nap as I'd advised Paul to do. I sorted through my closet, packed my few clothes into my luggage, and left my new evening dress hanging there for later.

I didn't notice it at first but when I lifted the beautiful white dress on its hanger to admire it, I was horrified to see that the skirt had been slashed in at least a dozen places. *It's ruined!* I thought in horror.

I wanted to cry, but then my defenses rose again, and I realized for the first time, the threats and acts against me are motivated by more than a desire to get rid of me—someone was jealous. Someone didn't want me to wear that dress tonight.

I wanted to grab Paul and run away with him without waiting for more information from Daniel and without appearing at the ball.

My shifting emotions then moved to defiance. I would not let anyone—*anyone* at Horstman House—make me run away.

I opened my suitcase and removed the green dress that I had worn the previous evening to the play. Paul and Daniel would wonder why I didn't wear the new one, but I'd tell Daniel what happened when I got the chance, and I'd make some excuse to Paul. The green dress would simply have to do. Still, my thoughts were jumping. Someone with a key to my room destroyed the dress, and I had a definite suspect in mind, although the idea of Ingrid doing something so childish—and leaving evidence that could get her in trouble seemed preposterous.

My things were packed, so having replaced the globe the morning after it had been broken, I turned on the lamp, checked the door lock again, and lay down to rest for a short while. Sleep didn't seem possible, but apparently I was exhausted despite the shock of finding the damaged dress. I had a nightmare that I was being chased from the house, and that the time for me to escape was running out. I awakened with a start at seven-fifteen and had just enough time for a quick shower before dressing—in green.

That final trip to the bathroom, where all my problems had begun, coupled with my nightmare, added an urgency to my planned escape. While I showered I relived each harrowing occurrence—the hands pushing me downward in the tub, the fire in the boathouse, the threatening notes, the frightening phone call, the near fall down the basement stairs, the encounter in the darkened laundry, and now the shredded dress. I couldn't get away too soon. *Maybe Paul and I should leave tonight, after a brief appearance at the ball,* I thought. I then wondered about Daniel's plans to talk with me again. Could that wait?

I returned to my room and automatically finished getting ready, my thoughts in a turmoil. Then I hurried to Paul's door, anxious for his company.

Again he was scrubbed and shiny in his tuxedo when he answered my knock. The first thing he said was, "Where's your white dress?"

I didn't want to alarm him, so I simply explained, "I'm very unhappy that I can't wear it, Paul, but it's been damaged, so I wore this green dress again. Does it look okay?" I asked, trying to get past the problem.

"Sure—you always look pretty." he said.

That boy always lifts my spirits, I thought.

"Well thanks, Paul," I said. "You are the perfect gentleman." And I winked at him, enjoying his charming smile in return.

"I'm hungry," were the next words out of his mouth.

"I am too," I agreed.

We could hear the orchestra music coming from the first floor, a Viennese waltz. *This is a high-toned affair,* I thought. Stepping from the elevator, we found the first-floor hall filled with Horstman House guests moving back and forth from the dining room buffet to the drawing room and entry, which had become the ballroom. I could see several couples dancing, but Paul and I headed in the opposite direction for the food.

It was actually a relief to be among that crowd of several hundred people. I felt much more secure than I had upstairs in our sequestered quarters. Some guests said polite "hellos" to Paul and me, but I recognized no one. In fact, we were generally unnoticed in the throng. The guests were obviously well-off, but the stars and celebrities appeared to have skipped this event. Daniel was nowhere in sight.

The buffet was superb, featuring every conceivable main course, as well as wonderful side dishes. As usual, the seafood appealed to me, and Paul watched what I took and chose the same. Wine and champagne flowed freely, but of course we skipped that. With heavily loaded plates, we looked for a place to sit, finally settling on chairs at the far end of the dining room.

We ate without conversation, except to say things like, "This is so good," and "Did you try that?"

When we finished, I felt a prompting to suggest to Paul that we change clothes and head for our new home. But then I remembered Daniel's earnest desire to talk with me and decided we couldn't go without telling him.

"Shall we walk down the hall and listen to the orchestra for a while?" I asked, halfheartedly.

"Yeah, I'd like that," Paul said.

"Maybe you could even ask me to dance?" I suggested.

"I—I don't know how," he said.

"Well, neither do I—at least not very well. But maybe we could hobble around the outside of the dance floor, just once?"

"Well, okay, but you'll have to teach me," he said.

"That's what I am—your teacher," I replied, smiling at him.

"You're *more* than that *now*," he said, grinning back at me and taking my hand.

We reached the crowded dance floor, and I looked for Daniel but could see him nowhere.

"Well, Paul, may I have this dance?" I asked.

"Yeah—sure. I'll try," he said.

I showed him where to place his right hand in the small of my back and took his left hand in my right. "Just take two steps right and then two steps left—step, close, step—step, close, step," I demonstrated as I spoke. "And then repeat those steps again and again."

He was hesitant at first, but his natural sense of rhythm took over, and he was soon waltzing almost effortlessly, despite the differences in our height. He backed me without difficulty around the periphery of the dance floor, until we bumped into another couple dancing in the opposite direction. "Pardon us," I said, before turning to see who we'd collided with.

"Of course," Daniel replied, laughing when he recognized me.

I turned toward that familiar laugh. "Daniel!" I exclaimed. Then I saw his dancing partner—none other than the tenacious and clinging Carolyn, dressed in a black sequined and feathered gown.

"So nice to run *into* you again," she said, laughing at her own lame joke.

No one else laughed. Daniel looked quizzically at me, gesturing toward the green dress.

"I'll explain later—another *accident*," I said, pointedly.

"Yes, just another little accident," Carolyn echoed, obviously thinking that my reference related to our collision.

"Yes." I said.

"Paul, I didn't know you'd learned to dance," Daniel said.

"I didn't learn—until tonight," Paul explained. "Wendy taught me."

"Well, just something else to make us grateful for Wendy," Daniel said.

Carolyn seemed to want to change the turn of our conversation, saying, "Well, nice to see both of you. Daniel, will you escort me to the champagne?" She linked her arm through his and dragged him across the dance floor. He turned and mouthed, "I'll be right back."

But our reunion was interrupted by an unexpected and dramatic event. There was no fanfare or drum roll, instead the orchestra abruptly ceased playing. Then, in the hushed silence, the chandeliers dimmed, followed by a piercing shaft of light from a second-floor spotlight. The pristine whiteness of the circle shone on the second-floor balcony at the juncture of the stairs. All eyes were directed upward toward a glittering, masked figure theatrically posed and costumed as Phaedra.

Gasps emanated throughout the gathered crowd. Then there was a spontaneous burst of applause in reaction to witnessing the unprecedented reappearance of the Great Bella, breaking her long seclusion from her adoring public.

My gasp joined the others. I was shocked to see the woman whose life had affected all of our lives so dramatically. Of course, she was covered from head to toe by the tragic mask and Greek dress, but we all knew that we were experiencing a historic occurrence in the world of American theater—the reemergence of a legend from our collective past.

Almost imperceptibly the spotlight faded, and some of the group rushed against the orchestra platform and the barriers at the foot of each flight of stairs. Of course I wasn't suprised that the personage to whom they wanted to draw near had already disappeared into her third-floor bastion, having given them only a single thrilling glimpse of the Great Bella.

The first floor was lit again, and the orchestra resumed playing. No one danced for a while, consumed with conversation about the Great Bella's unexpected appearance at the ball in her honor.

Paul was as awestruck as the rest of us. He stared at the place where she had appeared, his mouth still wide open.

I decided to break the spell and bring us back to reality. "Well, Paul, you've seen your grandmother at last."

He turned to me with that sadly serious look in his eyes. "Yeah, but it wasn't *really* her—it was just the fake her, like in her pictures."

"I know that's true. But at least it gives you a sense of who she is— of who she *was*—and how she's still adored," I said. "Try to remember that when you think of her. You're the grandson of a great artist."

"Big deal," he said, surprising me with his anger. "I'd rather be a grandson of a great—of a good—grandmother."

"Well, as your father says, there are some things we can't change, even if we really want to. I wish we could for your sake," I said, sympathetically.

"Oh, I'm okay," he said less passionately. "Besides, who needs a grandmother when I have you—and Dad. I'm okay," he finished, the anger dissipating and clearly trying to reassure himself and me.

Just then Daniel barged through the crowd. "Let's get out of here," he said, grabbing each of us by an arm. He was greatly agitated and seemed almost panicked in his desire to leave. He rushed us past the library and out the door at the end of the hall. Then he led us to the gazebo, away from the crowd inside.

He sat down on the gazebo bench, and we followed sitting on either side of him.

"Well, I've made my appearance—and so has *she*," he said, bitterly, and we both understood his reference. "Carolyn will have to be more than satisfied by that unexpected climax to her festival. Now she's off my back—forever."

I was surprised at the anger which he was obviously suppressing. "Did Bella's appearance shock you too?" I asked.

"Yes—it did. I knew nothing about it. I found Helman on the second floor. Apparently he was enlisted to make the arrangements and to run the spotlight. He apologized for not informing me but said that he had been sworn to silence."

"Then, Bella's appearance upset you?" I asked cautiously, wondering what our tense and hurried exit was about.

"I don't want to talk about it right now. Paul, it's your bedtime, I believe. Can you make it to your room alone? Or do you want us to go with you?" Daniel asked.

"Oh, I can go alone. I'll use the back stairs up to Wendy's room so I don't have to go through all those people," he said. "Wendy and I are moving tomorrow, Dad, so I'll want to get up early." He looked at his father adoringly. "Thanks, Dad, for getting us a new house."

Daniel returned the loving look. "Has that made you happy, Paul—all the changes we've made?" he implored.

"Yeah, I'm happy—but you're coming too, aren't you?" Paul asked.

"Yes—someday. But it could be awhile. I have some problems I have to face—to work out." He hugged Paul, then stood and raised him by his shoulders. "I'm going to explain everything to Wendy, then she'll explain it to you in your new place. Okay?"

"I guess—but why can't you just tell me now?" Paul asked.

"Because I want to know you're both safe—that you're settled in your new house, before . . . everything comes out." He was having difficulty controlling his feelings. "If I can come, I'll explain to you myself. But if I can't, Wendy will help me. Is that okay? More than anything, I want you both to be happy."

"Okay, Dad. Good night, Wendy. Thanks for the dance—and everything." He waved good-bye, and headed back to the house.

We watched him go, and when he was out of sight, Daniel said, "He's taking the news well. I'm grateful to you, Wendy." Then, he asked, "Why didn't you wear the new dress?"

"Well . . . someone came into my room and slashed the dress."

To my surprise, Daniel said nothing, but I could see his mounting physical tension. He seemed to be steeling himself against a rising fury building inside him. Then he walked away deliberately to the other side of the gazebo—away from me. I sat alone for some time, trying to appear calmer than I felt.

The guests began leaving from the front entrance and driveway. Valets helped them to their cars. I watched this exodus for some time, saying nothing to Daniel until much of the traffic had slowed.

It seemed that the activity inside was also winding down, since the caterers had hauled their equipment and supplies from the kitchen to waiting vans and had driven away. Another indicator that the festivities were over was the return of Helman and John, their supervision of the temporary security and parking employees apparently at an end. The gates had been closed, and a deceiving quiet had settled upon the Horstman estate.

Daniel seemed to want to wait until the flurry had ended before responding to my information regarding the dress and before commencing our discussion. Although I wanted to hear what he had to say, I also felt anxiety because of his angry and pensive mood.

I tried to sit back and enjoy the late summer night—the stars, the moon, and the breeze. I reflected that the gazebo and its surroundings were indeed beautiful, so long as I avoided looking toward the silhouette of the burned-down guesthouse—a reminder of that terrible night of years before and that the serenity of the estate was a façade.

When he saw Helman and John leave the mansion and cross back to their respective quarters above and beyond the garage, Daniel seemed to realize that he could delay no longer. He had been standing away from me, looking toward the lake, so that he had to walk across the gazebo to approach me. He still said nothing, just watching me closely.

"Well, are we ready now for our conference?" I asked, trying to create a somewhat lighter mood.

He didn't answer but took my hands and brought me to my feet. "Wendy, I still have *no* right to say this . . . but—I care about you. Someday I hope you'll allow yourself to consider—"

As if on cue, to interrupt his plea, I heard a door slam loudly from the direction of Bella's third-floor balcony. Both Daniel and I turned to see a shadowy figure peering at us through parted curtains. Apparently Bella had overheard Daniel's words. *Why did she slam that door? Was it just an angry reaction?* I wondered. Was she jealous of her son's involvement with an outsider—any outsider? Or did she disapprove of me? Was she determined to keep the memory of Lisa alive? I couldn't understand her motives since she had rejected her son—and his son—so long ago.

"Apparently your mother heard what you said to me," I said. "She doesn't seem to approve," I added, trying to sound less concerned than I actually felt.

He was quiet again, taking me back to the bench and sitting beside me. Finally he said, "Wendy, I was about to make a proposal for the future, for *our* future—yours, Paul's, and mine. But I don't expect an answer. I realize all of that will have to wait until we know each other better—until some of your concerns about my background can be remedied—and until you've heard me out."

"I . . . uh . . ." I didn't know what to say. I didn't think he understood what resolving my "concerns about his background" required. But I didn't get a chance to explain because he continued intently.

"*Right now*, there are other things I have to tell you. This is the most difficult thing I've ever had to do. But if you'll just listen quietly, until I've finished, maybe you'll understand. And I hope you'll be able to—forgive me."

"But what have you done that I have to forgive?" I protested. "You've been very good to me. The only thing I wish you'd—"

"Hush," he said, placing his index finger lightly on my lips. "Let me talk now, or I'll never get this out." He continued, slowly and haltingly. "Wendy, the person you saw tonight in that garish mask— the woman you saw just now on the balcony—is *not* Bella. She is *not* my mother."

Astonished, I could only demand, "What are you saying?"

"Please let me explain—" he begged.

"No—just *tell* me. Who was it, then?" I insisted.

He took a deep breath. "It was Lisa—Lisa, my wife." His look of concern matched the horror in my face.

I rose slowly, not believing what I had heard.

"Let me explain," he begged.

I didn't want an explanation. I didn't want to hear more. I didn't need to know more. He moved toward me. "No," I said. "Let me go!"

I ran from the gazebo, barely able to see through my tears. I found my way through the side door and into the first-floor hall, still running from that awful truth. I couldn't think, I couldn't reason. I just had to get away—from Daniel, from everyone and everything at Horstman House. I found the elevator and opened the door, grasping for the second-floor button, still blinded by my tears.

I wanted to scream. The elevator rose too slowly, then stopped. I opened the door and stepped out. I took several moments to realize I hadn't been there before—I was on the third floor!

I felt I was in a nightmare, unable to control my thoughts or actions. I heard them conversing in whispered tones. Then I turned to see her—Lisa—*not* Bella—talking animatedly with—*Martha!*

I stood frozen for a moment, while the implications of what I was seeing set in. Martha, my supposed friend, had been Lisa's tool. She had conspired with Lisa against me.

Then, somehow I gathered my wits and stealthily and quietly moved in the opposite direction from my enemies. I prayed they hadn't heard or seen me.

I came to the top of the rear stairway, the stairs I had been forbidden to climb, and there found Martha's little sitting area—her television, her books, her easy chair—and her *typewriter*. On a low table, the old portable was in its open case, a clean sheet of paper rolled in and ready for use.

I crept to the machine, risking being heard, and slowly typed, "Leave This House."

Immediately I recognized that typeface and the uneven spacing—of the typewriter that had been used to compose all of those threatening notes.

I ripped the sheet from the typewriter, madly rationalizing that I finally had proof, when two strong hands came from behind and locked my arms behind me. I smelled a pungent odor on a cloth held tightly over my mouth and nose. I fought ineffectually and remembered falling to the floor—

Chapter Thirty-Two

I became aware of being lifted and wedged inside a cold, hard compartment. The biting odor from the cloth remained strong in my labored breathing. I struggled again but lost consciousness.

Some time later my uncontrollable coughing awakened me. I was lying on a cement surface in a very dark place. The air was foul. I heard a car motor running. Reaching out to find support for standing, I touched a metal surface—a car bumper. I was in a garage, and the exhaust pipe was spewing carbon monoxide.

I used the car to help me climb slowly to my feet. I was dizzy, nauseated, and still coughing. I fell against a heavy wooden wall, and it moved just enough to reveal a crack of moonlight. I tried to call for help between coughing spasms, but could hardly make a sound.

The crack admitted a cool whiff of air, and I fell against the door again, trying to breathe. I thrust my shoulder against the door with my remaining strength, but it wouldn't budge. I pressed my face to the opening and inhaled again. I tried once more to call out, then I prayed silently for help.

Then I thought, through my drugged and choking haze, *Turn off the engine*. I leaned on the trunk and body of the car, trying to work around to the driver's side door. I finally got there, but the car door was locked.

I fell to the floor, then crawled again toward the cracked opening, fighting to reach that breath of oxygen. I pulled myself to a crouching position, leaning on the door for support.

I heard loud voices—then metal on metal and a crunching, cutting sound. The garage doors flew open, and I fell out, gasping for air. I looked up to see the blessed faces of John—and Daniel. The help I'd prayed for arrived. Then nothingness descended.

I awakened from a groggy haze to find a plastic mask on my face, a stranger leaning over me, and another rubbing my hands and elevated feet. Involuntarily I tried to pull the mask away, but the stranger gently moved my hand and said, "Please leave the mask in place, ma'am. We're giving you oxygen."

I muttered some unintelligible words.

"You're fine, ma'am. You've had a close call, but I think you're going to be all right. Just relax and breathe naturally," the man urged.

Looking about slowly, I recognized John's living room. I was lying on the same sofa where he had placed me after the boathouse fire. *John O'Connor to the rescue again,* I thought. I saw that I still wore that long green dress.

Then I was aware of another voice. "Are you sure she's really going to be all right?" Daniel asked with genuine anxiety.

From behind Daniel, I heard another frantic question, "Is Wendy all right, Dad?" Paul was there, and somehow that did make me feel all right—almost.

"I believe so, Paul. Thank heaven we found her in time," Daniel answered.

I was aware of a gathering around me when the stranger, a paramedic I supposed, said, "Please, everyone, stay back for a while. We need to check her heart and her respiration. Give us a chance to do our work—*please.*"

Daniel and Paul sneaked a look in my direction, then Daniel hurriedly ushered Paul and John into another room.

"Maybe we should take her to the hospital for observation," the paramedic said, as if thinking aloud.

From beneath my mask, I protested weakly, "Oh, no, *no.* I'll be okay—please." I didn't want to go to a hospital or even see a doctor. I just wanted to rest—and then to get as far from Horstman House as I possibly could.

I closed my eyes. The paramedic said, "We need you to stay awake, ma'am. In a few minutes we'll get you up and have you walk around." He shined a penlight in my eyes, then took my pulse and blood pressure. He listened to my heart and lungs with his stethoscope.

"Well, your vital signs are good," he said. "How are you feeling?" He removed the mask so that I could reply.

I looked more closely at the young man who seemed so concerned about me. He had kind blue eyes and tight, curly brown hair. *A nice face,* I thought, and I replied, "I feel all right—just shaky and tired. I have a headache."

"Those are expected reactions to your accident," he said.

"What happened to me was *no* accident!" I felt as if I had yelled it, but by his mild reaction it was obvious I hadn't.

"Well, Mr. Horstman says that he plans to call the police, just in case you're right about that. Then you can tell them your story," he suggested.

"At last," was all I could say.

"Now, let me help you sit up," the paramedic said, lifting me with his strong arm behind my back.

His dark-haired assistant lifted my legs and feet to the floor, then steadied me to a sitting position. Then the room whirled, and I slumped to the side.

The paramedic replaced the oxygen mask over my nose and mouth, saying, "Just sit here for a while. When you feel like it, tell us, and we'll help you stand."

"Are you feeling any chest pain?" the other man asked.

"No, I'm just rather nauseated and dizzy," I said through the mask.

"How is your vision? Are you seeing clearly?" he asked, leaning in to hear me.

"Yes, I can see you fine."

"Can you see the far side of the room?" he queried.

"Yes." I looked in the direction that Daniel and the others had gone. "Yes, I'm seeing fine," I said.

"Okay," the paramedic said, and then cautioned, "If you should become disoriented or notice any memory loss or difficulty in breathing or moving, you'll need to get to an emergency room. Will you promise to do that?"

"Yes. I—I think I can stand now," I said, and each of them took an arm and helped me. I felt very weak but walked around the room with their assistance. Then they led me back to the sofa.

"I'm going to leave this oxygen tank and mask with you," the paramedic said. "I think you'll be okay, but keep breathing this oxygen for about half an hour and try to stay awake. I'll tell Mr. Horstman the symptoms to watch for—just in case."

"Thank you—thank you so much for getting here in time," I said.

"Well, you're welcome. But you need to thank those men who got you out of that garage and called us. Otherwise, it might have been more serious—even *fatal*," he said seriously.

"I will—I'll thank them," I said quietly. Then I gave a silent prayer of thanks to Him who had really saved me—grateful just to be alive.

He replaced the oxygen mask, then they gathered up their other equipment and left for the rear room, where Daniel, Paul, and John had gone.

A few minutes later I heard a rear door close—then Daniel and John reentered the living room. Daniel was still in his formal clothes but had removed the coat and bowtie.

"Wendy—I'm so sorry—for everything," Daniel said.

I attempted to answer.

"No, don't try to say anything right now. You need to keep breathing that oxygen," Daniel urged.

I removed the mask. "I—I have to say—something. Then I'll—put it back," I said haltingly between breaths.

"Okay, but—"

I interrupted him. "First thanks to both of you for—rescuing me—I want to see Paul for a moment." I stopped talking to calm down and catch my breath.

"Of course," Daniel said hesitantly. "Paul, will you come in here?" he called.

Paul peeked around the door frame, saw that I was sitting up, and then ran to my waiting arms. "I'm so glad you're okay," he said, hugging me.

"Don't hug too hard, Paul," Daniel cautioned. "She's had a bad—scare." I knew that he'd almost said *accident* but had checked himself.

"Paul," I said, "our move to the new house may not be possible for a while."

"I know—it's okay. I just want you to get better," Paul said.

"You'd better get that oxygen mask back on," John said. "We don't want to take any chances."

"Okay. Do you mind—if—if I stay here the rest of—the night, John?" I asked, still feeling a little panic and noting that my lungs were overstressed just from talking.

"Of course not, and I'll be right here watchin' out for ya," he assured me.

"That—that's good," I said, very relieved that I wouldn't be taken back to Horstman House and that John would be with me.

After an awkward interval, Daniel broke the silence. "John, do you have someplace where Paul could lie down? It's getting late—*early*—and, under the circumstances, I don't want to take him back to the house. But he ought to get some sleep."

"Sure, sure," John replied. "I've got a spare bedroom all made up. No one ever comes to use it, but it's ready." He took Paul's hand and said, "Come with me, young feller. Ya need some shut-eye."

"But—I want to stay here—with Wendy," Paul said, not budging from his spot at the foot of the sofa.

"I'll be right here, Paul." I paused, then took a deeper breath. "I'm too weak and tired to go anyplace." Another breath, then, "Get some rest. I'm okay."

"Well, if you're sure you won't go away?" he asked.

"No, not tonight—not without you—anyway," I answered. I fit the oxygen mask over my nose and mouth again.

"Now come along, young man. Do as your father says," John urged good-naturedly. They left the living room, Paul looking back over his shoulder all the way.

Daniel and I were alone. I still didn't want to hear his excuses—his reasons for hiding from me and Paul, that Lisa, not Bella, was alive. He had led me on, betrayed my trust in him, lied to his son . . . It was too much to accept, too much to believe, and too much to bear. I wondered how Paul would respond to the shock. I knew I couldn't handle it.

As if reading my thoughts, Daniel said, "We have to talk—I have to talk. Please let me explain this time. None of this would have happened if you'd have heard me out." He was angry, but I could sense it was out of a fear for me. Then his features softened and he sat beside me on the sofa. "I know there's no acceptable excuse for what I've done and I'm not asking you to forgive me now. Maybe it's too late for that but perhaps I can help you understand."

I started to remove my mask, but he stopped me. "No, don't try to talk. Just listen, please."

John stopped in the doorway after putting Paul to bed. "Excuse me for interruptin' ya, Mr. Horstman. I just wanted to tell ya that I'm goin' over to the big house to check on—things."

"I'd appreciate that, John, and if you will, please awaken Blanche, Ingrid, and Helman, and get them together in the dining room. Tell them I want to meet with them as soon as I can," he said, kindly but firmly giving orders. "Then," he emphasized, "will you make *certain* that Martha and Madame Horstman—Lisa—are together. I'll be coming to talk with them too, when—when I'm finished here."

"Yes, sir, I'll do that. The boy's sleepin' fine." He looked at me. "Anything else, sir? Ma'am?"

Daniel looked to me for response. I shook my head in the negative.

"No thanks, John. I'll be using your phone, though, if that's all right," Daniel said.

"Of course, sir." He gave us a tentative smile and then left by the back door.

Another of our long silences ensued, but this one wasn't caused by my shyness or by Daniel's moodiness. Daniel and I were being forced to face the facts of his past and of the future. If, indeed, we had a future, which I very highly doubted at this point. I felt as if I didn't even know him, and didn't know if I could ever trust him again. Besides, all of this, he still had a wife, and I felt horrible for even having had an interest in him. I was trying to control my anger when finally Daniel began, interrupting my thoughts. I resolved to keep quiet and listen, a response made easier by the awkward mask I was wearing.

"The only way I can think of to begin sounds very trite, but it's a long story," he said, possibly trying to add a lighter touch to a very serious topic. He tried to smile, but seeing my expression, he gave it up. "I'll try to be direct. Then, when I've finished, if you have questions, I'll try to answer them—okay?"

I nodded my agreement, anxious to get it over with.

"First, I want you to know that I didn't set out to lie to you. I didn't dream—before I came to know you—that any teacher would become more than that—to Paul or to me. But Paul did come to care for you, just as I did." He paused to sense my response, but I resolved to hold my reactions in check, so he continued.

"I have to review some facts of my past, which I've already shared with you. Not to find excuse for my actions, but so that you might understand why I—why *we*—did what we did." He stood and crossed the room to a window, his back to me. "I've told you my maudlin tale of living without the love of parents—of my mother." He turned to face me. "Oh, I know it sounds so classic—the unloved child, but it was true." He moved closer to me again. "Then, when I met Lisa, and she loved me—*pretended* to love me—I was happier than I'd ever been. But it didn't last. She became totally absorbed with Horstman House, with herself, and with my mother's fabled life." He sat beside me again. "I realized later that I should have gotten Lisa some help—help with her mental problems—but I'd lived with the pretentious aura of the Great Bella for so long that I could almost accept Lisa's adulation of her. It seemed almost natural—almost inevitable."

Again I nodded my acceptance of that observation, thinking of my own fascination with the fantasies of the movie world. My nodding seemed to encourage Daniel.

"She collected clippings regarding Bella, as you saw in the library, and she gathered Bella memorabilia. She began to dress as Bella had dressed in the twenties and thirties. She even found ways to integrate herself into the life of the *elusive* Bella," he said sarcastically.

He paused for a moment, reflecting and thinking. "The closer their mutual affection became, the further Lisa withdrew from me—and from Paul. I felt that Bella had won again. Bella had taken herself from me, then she drove away my father and, finally, in her insatiable need for attention, she had usurped my wife's affection. Of course, Lisa was actually the active conspirator. She moved away from me into the guesthouse, making it almost a shrine to the Great Bella. She duplicated the furnishings in Bella's quarters and transformed the guesthouse into almost a mirror of Bella's rooms. It all sounds too fantastic to be believed, I know, but in sum, she became another Bella—at least in her own eyes, and in mine. And Bella began living through her too, adoring the youthful image of herself."

I was horrified at the realization that Lisa had literally moved out of Daniel's house and life. He paused for my reaction, but I still did nothing, quelling my sympathy and my concern for him. I wanted to reach out and touch him—console him—just as I had wanted to at our first fateful meeting in the gazebo. But I didn't. I still needed some answers.

He must have interpreted my lack of action as a need to hear more. "I know that I should have done something—anything—to help her or win her back. But I was conditioned, you see, to accept that love was temporary—fleeting, at best. That had been my lifelong experience. Instead of taking action, I just went into a shell—into seclusion. Following my mother's example, I suppose."

I still said nothing. He seemed frustrated and exhausted and stood again. "I'm thirsty. Would you like some water?" he asked.

I simply nodded.

He left the room, and I heard glasses clinking and water running. *Should I run, too?* I thought. I was afraid that my sympathies for him would blind me again to what really had happened to me here. I reminded myself that I'd been used and lied to. I'd been threatened and physically harmed. I'd almost died.

Daniel returned with two glasses of ice water. It looked so good. I hadn't realized how thirsty I was. He placed his glass on a side table and brought the other to me. He carefully removed the oxygen mask and gently helped me raise the glass to my lips. "Don't drink too fast, now—and don't drink too much at once. Just sip it," he suggested.

I drank and then found it much easier to make sounds. I said, "Thanks, I think I'll hold the glass for a while."

"How is your headache? Are you still dizzy? Can you breathe all right?" he asked, anxiously.

Too many questions, I thought, and I still had too many of my own. "I feel better, physically," I said pointedly. "But go on. I understand what happened to you and to Lisa. But about what happened to me?" I left the question dangling.

He sat on the sofa again and I kept sipping that wonderful cold water. "Go on," I urged.

"Well, I spent most of my time thinking about myself and how I'd been used and hurt. I—I'm afraid I began neglecting Paul's needs—I repeated Bella's behavior in that, too. I withdrew from Paul—from everyone. I immersed myself in my work and lived like a

. . . well, a bachelor. I was lonely and unhappy, so I selfishly didn't care if everyone else was the same. This all happened before you came into the picture, of course, but it set up the situation for all that followed, including what happened to you." He paused, and my frustration grew. He could have told me these things weeks ago when he knew I was in danger.

"Keep going. I'm trying to be patient," I said, "but I've had a hard night."

"I know that and I'll be as brief as I can, but I need you to understand the whole story," he said, and then continued. "My behavior only fueled the friendship between Lisa and Bella. My mother had painted in oils as a diversion, so Lisa began to paint, too, encouraging Bella to take it up again. She was even able to lure Bella from her third-floor hermitage, bringing her down the elevator and frequently, in the evening after the house was quiet, taking her in a wheelchair to the guesthouse. They painted, drank, and enjoyed each other's mutual admiration."

I interrupted him with several questions. "Why didn't you join them? Wasn't that your opportunity to get to know your mother— when she finally emerged from her cocoon?"

"I did try that," he said, "but Bella sent me one of her impersonal typed notes, telling me that I was not welcome at the guesthouse when she was visiting there."

"Are you certain the note was sent by Bella?" I asked, thinking of the typed notes I'd received from Lisa and, I now realized, delivered by Martha and Helman.

"I—I didn't suspect that. As I told you, Bella had always communicated through her typed notes."

"Well, it's clear that Bella—that Lisa—has *continued* the practice," I observed, somewhat ironically.

"Yes, I realize that, now. The typed threats against you came from Lisa. I *should* have taken them—and the acts against you—more seriously. I know that now, but Lisa had been playing games like that for years, at times even threatening me in her notes. She *is* insane! But I had grown so totally accustomed to her pretensions and her tricks," he explained. "She never followed through with her warnings—not since the guest-house fire—until you came. And I thought she was so obsessed with her role that she'd never come down again. I was just too consumed in grief and self-deception to know what I was thinking. But I guess she was truly threatened by you—her counterfeit world was threatened by you. She didn't want me and she didn't want Paul, but she wasn't about to let anyone else into our lives," he said bitterly.

"I've already understood and believed your version of the abuses against you and Paul. I know that you've both suffered at the hands of Bella and Lisa. That's the main reason I've stayed here, to help Paul, and you, but—"

"Yes, we always come back to those 'buts,' don't we? I'm trying to answer your questions—all your objections," he said. He took my hand in his. "But this next part is the hardest for me to explain—to justify," he said quietly.

"I'm still listening," I said.

"Well, we went on that way—living apart—for too long, and I frankly tried to put Lisa and Paul out of my thinking—out of my feeling." He paused, took a deep breath, and then went on. "I stopped paying attention to the comings and goings of anyone at Horstman House. I just let the staff—Ingrid, Martha, Helman, John, and Blanche—take care of everything and everyone. I paid the bills and stayed away. When I was here, I kept as much to myself as possible."

"I understand that and the reasons for most of it. I still can't totally accept your rejection of your son. But I guess we've already dealt with that—together," I said, removing my hand from his grasp. I was feeling a little panicked by the closeness and said, "I think I'd better replace the oxygen mask."

Daniel helped me, seeming concerned that he'd kept me from following through with the paramedic's instructions. "I'm sorry. Is this too much for you right now?" he asked.

I lifted the mask again. "No, it will be too much for me if you don't tell me everything. But, please, get to the point. Why did you pretend that Lisa was dead? And why did you set up Lisa as a counterfeit Bella? Why didn't you just tell the police the truth?" I asked.

"Well, I think the anger and grief and guilt made me a little crazy, myself," he admitted sadly. "But most of all I still loved her. I still loved Lisa, despite all she'd done to me—to Paul," he answered. "Also,

I still felt sorry for her. She had no one but us. She was raised by many sets of foster parents. Of course, when I married her, I had no idea how deranged she was."

He stood and paced the small living room while he talked. "Lisa and Bella had become soul mates. In Lisa, Bella had an adoring fan to bolster her all-consuming ego. Oh, I suppose Lisa also lessened Bella's self-imposed loneliness. And Lisa had totally submerged her own identity in Bella's. She was already making plans, I assume, for Bella's—accident."

"Accident—that word again," I said, in a warning voice.

"I'm sorry," he said. "But Lisa made every effort to make the fire look accidental and she succeeded in that. You read the newspaper account of the cause of the fire—the *accidental* spilling of the turpentine into the fireplace."

"Yes, but who saved that clipping? Did Lisa also save clippings of that event?"

"She even did that. The newspaper report represented the culmination of her planning—her own ritual death and her assumption of Bella's character and role were complete. It made it all seem real—in her mind—and in the thinking of the outside world. Now, she *was* Bella!"

I yanked the mask from my face. "But why did you go along with her madness? Why did all of you cover up what she'd done?" I demanded, warring between sympathy and disgust.

He waited a rather long time to answer. Then I realized that he was attempting to control his feelings. Finally, he was able to say, "Because I was a—coward. A total coward. I helped create the lie to avoid charges against Lisa—against our family. I couldn't face the notoriety, the headlines, the prying, the courtroom scandal that would have resulted, if Lisa's—if my wife's—murdering my mother had been discovered."

He cried quietly, then, seeming to release all the emotions which had been building through years of maintaining the lie they had created.

I couldn't resist his tears. Pushing the mask aside, I reached out to him, and we cried together.

When he regained control, he asked, "Then you haven't totally given up on me?"

"I really thought I couldn't forgive your deception, but I know now that you wanted to tell me, you were simply afraid that I *would* turn against you, if I knew. I can see that you tried not to—to express interest in me, because you knew you weren't free. I'm grateful for that unselfishness on your part. And I'm sorry for what you and Paul have suffered. But your holding back the truth from me almost cost me my life, Daniel."

"I know that—and I can't forgive myself for that," he said. "I had made up my mind to tell the truth, to reveal our conspiracy to every-body—you, the police, even Paul, if I could find a way to avoid permanent damage to him. I'd planned to call the police as soon as I'd told you everything. Also, as you know, I saw my lawyers and arranged to make you Paul's guardian. What you don't know is that I changed my will, naming Paul as my sole beneficiary and giving you power of attorney, until Paul is of age. I bought the house for you and arranged for your move there with Paul—all in preparation for what I would have to face when I finally told the police about our cover-up of Lisa's crime." Again he took both my hands in his. "Can you see that with your help, I was planning to try to undo all the harm I'd caused?"

"Yes, I can see that now. You told me that I'd be required to be patient—and understanding. I know why, now. But I still can't quite figure how Lisa, how all of you, were able to bring it off—the conspiracy, as you call it, to cover up Bella's murder."

"Well, that too is a long story. But remember, Lisa had planned well. When I confronted her, after the fire, she told all—actually laughing at her own cunning and at Bella's gullibility. She exulted in her accomplishment—she had become Bella. Her plotting took place over many months. During one of his visits to Horstman House, Dr. Richardson mentioned that a bottle of liquid ether had been taken from his bag. Lisa admitted on the night of the fire, that she'd used the ether she'd stolen from Dr. Richardson to put Bella to sleep—so that she'd feel no pain, she said. Then she dressed Bella in contempo-rary clothing. Lisa's own clothes. She placed her wedding rings on Bella's finger. Then she poured the turpentine from the oil painting supplies along the carpet so that when she lit the fireplace the flames would spread across the rug and then to the drapes and furniture. Before anyone became aware, the fire was an inferno. Lisa had escaped to Bella's third-floor rooms, taking Bella's wheelchair with her. I saw her there watching the blazing fire from the balcony. Of course, at that time, I thought I had seen Bella, my mother, up there.

"By the time we reached the fire department and they got here, the guesthouse was a pile of charred remains. The firemen and Dr. Richardson, in his office as coroner, declared the fire and the death to be accidental. Dr. Richardson pronounced that an autopsy and further investigations were unnecessary since he knew Lisa—the deceased—and the family so well."

Chapter Thirty-Three

The oxygen therapy was beginning to work, giving me energy to dig for some crucial answers. In fact, I fired off a barrage of questions, leaving Daniel little chance to respond.

"Then who knew the truth about Bella's death?" I asked. "How did they learn it? And how did you convince them to keep the secret?"

"Hold on," Daniel urged. "I owe you answers to all those questions and more, but how about one at a time?"

"Okay, start with number one—who knew?" I demanded.

"First, let me explain how *I* learned what happened. Okay?" he requested.

"Okay," I agreed.

"Well, the police came just after the fire was extinguished. As I said, they relied on Dr. Richardson's assessment and didn't make any charges. They gave me Lisa's ring and other jewelry, then left with the firemen and the doctor. I went to the gazebo, looking at the ruins of the guesthouse and trying to make sense of it all."

"How awful for you," I sympathized, realizing that at that point he really had believed Lisa was dead and his mother still living.

"It *was* awful," he agreed. "I hadn't had a life with Lisa for a long time, but the thought that she had died so violently was devastating. I blamed myself for not doing more and, at that time, I felt it had all been such a waste. Then I thought of Paul and felt a renewed love for him—but I still didn't think I could face the responsibility of caring for him and of telling him someday all that had happened."

"But he needed you all the more," I protested.

"I know that—but as I said before, I didn't know how to be a parent. It all seemed so futile."

He continued his story. "I was sitting there, feeling sorry for myself, when the permanent staff came to try to help—Ingrid, Helman, Martha, and John came together. I asked Helman to contact a funeral director to arrange a private service. I asked Ingrid to check on Paul and asked John to keep watch on the burned ruins of the guesthouse and the remains of—the body. And, ironically, I asked Martha to explain to Bella all that had happened. Instead, of course, she found Lisa upstairs—alive."

"What a terrible experience for all of you," I said, "and then to find out . . ."

"Yes, they all went about their tasks, and I wandered into the house to the library, for a drink. I had just sat down, when Martha came rushing in, yelling the incredible news that Lisa was alive—upstairs! I ran into the hall and to the stairs, taking the steps two at a time. I suppose Martha went to tell the others, because one by one they followed me to the third floor, gathering in the hall outside Bella's rooms."

"Then, no one knew . . ." I thought aloud.

"Before they got there I had already confronted Lisa. She laughed hysterically at my shocked reaction. I don't remember her exact words, but she didn't deny what she'd done. As I told you, she actually boasted of her cleverness in winning Bella over and in assuming her place."

"What about the others?" I asked.

"They were as stunned as I, but Ingrid, in her usual way, immediately took charge. Martha kept saying she should have known, but Ingrid shushed her and commanded that *no one* speak the truth of that night, inside or outside the estate! She reasoned that we needed time to think and plan. And I just went along, too numb to take any action myself. She ordered Martha to stay with Lisa and told Helman to station himself outside Bella's—Lisa's—door. John asked me what I wanted him to do, and I just answered that he should do whatever Ingrid told him. I just let her take over."

"Then that was the beginning of Ingrid's control over your house and everyone in it," I assessed.

"Yes, I guess you're right," he said. "I just went to my rooms and sat awake all night. The next day, Ingrid gathered us together in the library and laid out her plan to protect the reputation of the Horstman family and the Great Bella. She painted a picture of the suffering Lisa would undergo in prison or in an asylum. She predicted an avalanche of police detectives and reporters destroying our privacy and our lives. Somehow Ingrid's plan seemed the easiest and best solution—and I just went along."

"There's one person you've left out. Where was Blanche during all of this commotion and your deception?" I asked, letting a hint of bitterness creep into my voice.

"Apparently both Blanche and Paul slept through the entire night's experience. Then she was told only what the outsiders were told—that Lisa had died in the fire," he explained.

"But how could the truth be kept from her all those years when she was living right here in your house?" I asked, incredulous.

Daniel focused for a moment before answering. "I'm ashamed to admit that we kept the truth from her by the same means we kept it from everyone—from Paul and from you. It was fairly easy to continue the pattern that Bella had established for so many years. You know the rules—no initiation of contact with Madame Horstman, no one allowed on the third floor, and very limited access to the estate by outsiders. All we had to do was continue those procedures and make certain that Lisa stayed on the third floor. That was Martha's job, and John's assignment when Martha wasn't there. It worked, until . . ."

"Yes, I know, until I came," I admitted. "Maybe I should have stayed in my place instead of stirring up the old . . ." I almost said "flames," but caught myself in time to say, "troubles."

"I don't blame you for that. At first, it was simply annoying to have you calling me to task regarding my treatment of Paul. But later I saw your determination to help him as a means of helping both of us. You reawakened the potential for a relationship between us. And you helped me find the way—" He paused. "I—I've thanked you again and again for bringing life back into our house. You did that!"

"Yes, and I also brought to life all the hurts and festering wrongs of the past. And I almost died in the bargain," I observed wryly.

Daniel looked away.

"I'm sorry to bring that up again, but I am a victim of those two scheming women," I said. "When I left you tonight, I found Martha and Lisa together on the third floor, undoubtedly deciding how they could finally get rid of me. They saw me, came after me, and tried to kill me. I know that Martha helped Lisa—there were two of them. One held my arms and the other held the ether over my mouth and nose. They've worked together to harm me."

"I know you can't help blaming Martha—I don't expect you to forgive her for helping Lisa harm you. But I'm at fault regarding Martha, too. Lisa dominated Martha's life, just as Bella had. They both played on Martha's loneliness and her great need for security. It doesn't excuse all Martha may have done, but again, maybe it helps you understand. I'm sure that Lisa threatened Martha with loss of her home at Horstman House—just as Bella had—to get her to do what she did."

"Oh, I understand. Martha befriended me then cut off that friendship when Lisa gave her orders. And I thought you—or Ingrid—had made Martha and others ostracize me. But what about Blanche? Why did she become so cold toward me?" I asked.

"Because she learned about Lisa—that she was alive and undercover upstairs. She found out right after the incident in the boathouse. I had a meeting with the staff, you remember, and somehow in the discussion of the fire, your escape, and the need to protect you, the *real* identity of the third-floor resident slipped out. Blanche was shocked—then angry," he said.

"And she was never the same after that," I added.

"No, she had more conscience than the rest of us. She feared for you—but didn't dare to tell you, to warn you," he said guiltily.

"Well, at least I know that I had one friend here," I said.

"You have more than one friend here—Paul is your friend, John is your friend, and believe it or not, I'm your friend," he pleaded.

"I believe you now, but there were times when I really wasn't sure."

"I did you a great disservice in my selfish desire to keep you here for Paul—and for myself," he confessed. "And covering up Lisa's actions was wrong! I've lived with that knowledge every day—the knowledge that I didn't have the guts to do what was right. Somehow I couldn't face the fact that Lisa would be in a prison—or a mental institution—for the rest of her life. But in not confiding in you, I placed you in danger. I realize that all too well now, and I'm sorry. But I hope you know that I didn't really think that Lisa cared what I did—"

"Then Lisa didn't react when you brought Carolyn Reinhart here?" I asked, seeking some kind of final reassurance that Carolyn wasn't important in Daniel's life, and that he wasn't lying to me anymore.

"No, but remember, Carolyn never lived here, never stayed here. She was just a dinner guest. You, on the other hand, were becoming a real part of our lives, and not just as Paul's teacher," he explained. He stood and walked to the doorway, probably to check on Paul.

When he turned back I said, "Yes, I realize now that it was Lisa—not Bella—who observed us from the balcony on several occasions."

"She did," he said, turning back to me. "I heard about that, of course, through Martha and Ingrid. But I really didn't think that Lisa could be *dangerously* jealous of you—of me—of someone she didn't really care about. I thought she was simply trying to keep the attention on her."

"Well, just one more question about Carolyn?" I ventured, standing slowly so that I wouldn't keel over.

He came to me. "Are you okay?"

"Yes, it feels good to stand." I suddenly became aware of my appearance. "Look at this dress. I look a wreck," I said.

"You're beautiful, even in that dirty dress and with smudges on your face," he said, helping me keep my balance.

"Flattery won't work. You still have to provide more answers. You said that Carolyn *blackmailed* you into agreeing to the Bella Horstman Festival. What did you mean?" I asked.

"Just what I said. During one of her appearances here, Carolyn let her snoopy nature take over. She excused herself from dinner to go powder her nose. But instead she took the elevator to the third floor and, unobserved, went to see Bella. Instead she saw a much-too-young Bella talking with Martha in the hall. She returned in a hurry so that I didn't suspect that she'd been snooping about."

"Then how long has she known?" I asked.

"Oh, she didn't tell me right away. She kept her suspicions to herself until she could use them to advantage. Her festival presented that opportunity," he explained.

"I need to sit," I said, feeling overwhelmed with information and walking to the sofa. He followed and sat by me again.

"But after she presented her proposal—to keep quiet if I'd help promote the festival—I'd almost decided to confess to everybody. Her blackmail only pushed me closer to that action," he said. "The festival itself clinched the decision. I decided I couldn't go on with the pretense." He paused, reflecting again.

"Then that phony appearance at the ball—of the Great Bella in her Greek costume—was the final straw," I observed. "I was stunned too, but like everyone else, I thought it really was Bella. Who could have helped Lisa arrange all of that?"

"That was my question also, and I found out," he answered. "Lisa had convinced Martha and Helman that her appearance in costume would enhance the festival and that no one would know she wasn't Bella in that Greek headdress. In fact, they told me that they thought it would further convince everyone that Bella still lived, reinforcing the charade. Of course, if they had asked me, I would never have allowed it."

"Then Ingrid wasn't involved?" I asked.

"Oh, I suppose she knew. Helman doesn't do anything without consulting his wife." He suddenly looked sheepish, obviously realizing he had let another cat out of the bag.

"They're *married*?" I exclaimed, not totally astonished since it explained some things. Helman's responses to Ingrid had always seemed more like those of a henpecked husband than those of a dutiful yet equal servant.

"Yes, they're married, though they've maintained their separate quarters—for appearances. As you know, appearances are all important to Ingrid—and Helman takes her orders like everybody else," he said with a smile, the first I'd seen that morning.

"It's nice to see you smile," I said.

"Well, this has been a difficult twenty-four hours for all of us, but especially for you." He looked at me fondly. "I was so worried that—that you might not make it," he said.

"And that brings us to my final question," I said. "How did you and John come to find me last night?"

"You ran away from me at the gazebo and I sat there for some time wondering whether to chase after you or if it would it be better for your sake, to let you go. Then I knew I couldn't just let you leave. I had to convince you not to leave us, not to leave me, without knowing the whole story."

"So?"

"So, I went after you. First I went to your room, but you weren't there. Then, I went to Paul's room on the off chance that you'd gone to get him or to say good-bye. He woke when I opened his door, so I had to explain that you had left. Of course, he was upset and insisted on looking for you. Then I waited while he dressed," he said.

"And all that delay gave Lisa and Martha time to dope me with ether, I'm guessing. But how did they manage getting me downstairs without using the elevator—without your seeing them?" I wondered.

"I think they must have stuffed you in the dumbwaiter, then lowered you to the laundry level. After the paramedics came, John and I found a big laundry cart in the bushes by the garage. I'm assuming they loaded you into that and wheeled you to the garage," he said.

"I vaguely remember being stuffed into a small space, but that's all, before I woke up coughing. Was I locked in my garage—where my car was parked?" I asked.

"Yes, apparently they dumped you onto the garage floor. They must have taken your car keys from your purse, started your car, and then locked the car doors. They closed the garage doors and locked the padlock so that you couldn't escape, if you woke up," he reasoned.

"But how did you find me?" I asked, amazed at the lengths to which Martha and Lisa had gone to get rid of me.

He moved closer and held my hand again. "When Paul and I couldn't find you in the house, we came out to see if you had driven away. John was already at the garage door with his tools. He pointed to the locked padlock and said that someone was coughing in there, the motor was running, and that he was about to cut the lock. We heard the muffled call for help and realized it was you trapped inside. John cut the lock and you fell out. He had already called emergency services, so the paramedics got here in a hurry."

"Thank heaven," I said.

"Thank John," he countered. "If he hadn't gone into action Lisa might have succeeded in her attempts to get rid of you permanently. And you know the rest of the story," he said.

"Yes, at last, I know the rest of the story," I agreed.

Paul wandered sleepily through the doorway, rubbing his eyes and yawning. "Wendy, are you okay?" was the first thing he said.

"Yes, come here and give us a hug," I said, and he came to my waiting arms. Then he hugged his dad.

"So, everything's okay?" he asked, looking back and forth between his father and me.

Daniel answered, "Everything's okay, Paul—at least for now."

Paul looked up at me. "I woke up and didn't know where I was. Then I heard you talking and remembered—if you're all right, can we move to our new house?" Paul begged.

Neither of us knew how to answer that one. Finally, I said, "Maybe not now—but soon, okay?"

The decision was taken out of our hands when John burst in, yelling, "The big house is on fire! I've called the fire department. I think everyone's out, except . . ." He saw Paul then and changed his reference, ". . . except *the third floor*. That's where she—that's where the fire started. The main stairways are still blocked, and I tried to get up the back stairs, but the fire has spread there too."

Daniel ordered, "Stay here!" and ran out, followed by John.

I wasn't about to stay there, however, and Paul shared my determination to see what was really happening. Together, we walked as fast as I could manage toward Horstman House, which looked like a huge black monolith silhouetted against the rising flames and the nighttime sky. We could see fire in all the third-floor windows. Daniel, John, Blanche, Ingrid, and Helman were lined up facing the building, helpless to do anything until the fire department came. We joined them, hypnotized by the flames and the roar of the fire as it ate through the aged timbers of the roof and upper-story walls. The heat became unbearable, and we backed away from the rear drive onto the lawn.

Then we saw them—Lisa and Martha—on the third-floor balcony, trapped by the fire. Daniel ran forward, as if to try to help, but the heat was too great. He backed away toward Paul and me. I warned Paul to look away, before he could recognize his mother, then covered his eyes, turning his face into the folds of my long skirt.

Lisa looked down at all of us gathered there together. Then, still playing the role of the Great Bella, she slowly turned away and regally strode back into the flames. Martha also looked toward us, and then, head bowed, slowly followed Lisa into Horstman House—her only home.

Epilogue

NOW

I sat in my favorite big chair in the living room, reading the final pages in my 1976 journal when a tall, grown-up Paul entered. "Hi, Mom," he said.

"Oh, Paul, how nice to see you, dear. What's the occasion?" I asked.

"Nothing special. I was on my way from work and decided to drop by to see how you're doing," he said. "You reading those old journals again?" he teased.

"Yes I am, and I'm not apologizing. Why do you think I wrote in them?" I asked.

"I guess so you could read them later," he answered and laughed.

"Exactly," I said. "This journal brings back a lot of memories and feelings."

"Not very good ones, I bet," he suggested.

"That isn't entirely true, Paul. Think of what might have happened if we hadn't come to know each other? What if—"

"I know, Mom. What if we hadn't moved to this house in San Marino? What if you hadn't saved Dad and me from that big, gloomy place?" he teased. "You don't need to remind me again. It's just that it's behind us now, thank heaven, and sometimes I think you spend too much time thinking about those days. Are you still having those nightmares about it?"

"Shush." I smiled. "They come less often, and I do not *obsess* about those days. It's just good mental exercise to remember how it really was.

I think reading helps me sort out memory from reality—it'll probably help my nightmares diminish. Enough about that. How was your day?"

Paul looked doubtful. "Whatever, Mom," he said with a shake of his head. "As for work, you know Dad's a slave driver," he answered.

"Yes, but you like working with him. You know you do."

"Okay, but I *have* to complain so you won't think I'm finally growing up," he teased, sprawling on the sofa.

I warmed at his teasing but hushed him with another question. "How are the kids?"

"Great. Of course Joanie thinks I spoil them, but she does too. She's a great mother," he said, smiling.

"And a great wife," I added.

"Yes, we're lucky, I guess."

"No, you're blessed, and you've made the right choices," I said.

He sat up and looked in the direction of the kitchen. "Something smells good. What's cooking?" he asked.

"It's roast beef. Want to stay for dinner? You could call Joanie and have her bring the kids over," I proposed.

"No, I better not. She's planning a night out. Our regular Friday night date, you know. She has a babysitter coming at seven-thirty, so I'd better get home, I guess."

He stood and crossed to kiss me on the cheek. "Where's Jill?" he asked, looking around.

"Oh, your sister has a new friend—a boy she met at Pasadena City College. We haven't met him, but she's promised to bring him home tonight after their study date," I explained.

"Yeah right—'study date.' She's too young to be going out alone with a boy," he said half seriously. "How old is she now—fifteen?"

"Oh, for heaven's sake—she's twenty-three, Paul!" I paused to mentally double-check; my memory had been known to slip of late, I realized with amusement. "She was born two years after your dad and I married in '78 . . . Twenty-three. I was right."

"Well, twenty-three is still too young to be dating," he said, laughing at my need to calculate. "Just make sure he's good enough for her," he cautioned. "I don't want her going out with just anyone."

I reflected on how grateful I was that they'd always gotten along. We really didn't know how Paul would accept his sister's birth, but after a while he'd gotten over the only-child syndrome and they'd become close.

"Well, I'd better go," he said.

I rose to see him to the door. "I know," I said, "why don't you ask Joanie if she'd like to come with the children for dinner on Sunday after church? And I'll ask Jill to invite her new friend to come, too. That way we can size him up and give him a hard time."

"That's a great idea," he said with a mischievous smile. "I'll call you."

I thought, *That's great . . .* and smiled. That phrase would always be part of Paul—of us.

I hugged him and sent him on his happy way. Then the phone rang. "Hello, Horstman residence," I answered. "Oh, yes, Brother Simms. Daniel hasn't come home yet, but I'll have him call you. Yes, yes, he mentioned that he needed to contact you about home teaching. Yes, fine, I'll have him call. Good-bye."

I checked the roast and put two potatoes in the oven to bake. Then I returned to my journal to finish reading those final entries. As I read, I remembered the images vividly.

The firemen finally came. They pumped water from the pool and lake but were unable to save the third floor—or its two occupants. Fortunately, the first and second stories were heavily damaged by smoke and water but were otherwise left intact.

The police had arrived with the fire department, and when the fire was out, Daniel arranged to confess his cover-up of Bella's murder and his having harbored a criminal—his late wife. He took all the blame for the cover-up, avoiding implicating his loyal staff in a conspiracy.

At first I was upset by this, remembering Ingrid's icy and commanding role in the whole charade, but Daniel explained his reasoning. He helped me better understand exactly how intensely loyal the staff was to the Horstman family name—almost more so than to Daniel alone. I had noticed how old-school the running of Horstman House was, obviously, but I had not understood how that affected the psychology of the estate servants over the years. Daniel pointed out that they were almost traditionally British in their loyalty to the family, and that Ingrid and the others had simply done what they thought absolutely necessary to protect the family and their own honor—inextricably tied to that of Horstman House.

Besides that loyalty, I came to realize that they had been conditioned over the years to follow the most bizarre of orders at Horstman House, and had endured both Bella's and Lisa's abuse for too long. Daniel reasoned that perhaps if he'd been more able to take charge after Bella's death, Ingrid would not have gone to such measures. But he hadn't been, and under the circumstances she had probably thought it a necessary and expected response to protect Daniel's name.

The strange circumstance all of them had adapted to—the feeling that one's identity was tied up in the success and happiness of their employers—was almost enough to justify Martha's strange behavior in my mind. Her actions, and especially her final act of loyalty, haunted and confused me for years after the fire.

Daniel had his day in court and was found guilty of withholding evidence in the murder of his mother. His subsequent jail sentence was suspended by a judge who sympathized with his losses and the motivations for his ambiguous actions. On parole, Daniel was ordered to complete two thousand hours of community service over a one-year period, and I saw to it that he found no difficulty in finding a place to serve; through my bishop, I introduced him to the LDS Church Welfare Services.

Daniel completed his year of service for the less fortunate and was humbled in learning how difficult life was for many people. He prayed with the other welfare workers each day and was taught the gospel. And through it all, he became a less self-centered man.

He also found time to supervise the salvaging and rebuilding of Horstman House, minus the third floor. He planned to donate the estate to the city of Pasadena for a museum after the art works were cleaned and restored. Of course, John and Helman assisted, and Ingrid gave orders. The three of them stayed on to be employed at the Horstman Museum once it was established.

Immediately after the fire Paul and I had moved to our new house in San Marino, along with Blanche, who also wanted to leave Horstman House and asked to spend the rest of her days with us.

Daniel bunked with John in the spare room at the cottage. He visited us in San Marino regularly and *on time*, for lunch or dinner, and we planned fun field trips together.

Paul continued homeschool but gained a new friend in Tommy, the boy next door, who begged him to go to public school the next year. Eventually, Daniel caved in.

We attended church every Sunday at our ward chapel, and, with Daniel's permission, Paul was taught by the Mormon missionaries. Blanche came along as an investigator from time to time, and she too finally joined the Church several years later.

The day after the fire Paul had come upon me and Daniel and asked, "Dad, is Bella—is Grandmother dead?"

Unable to phrase an answer, Daniel looked to me.

I said, "Yes, Paul—I'm sorry. Bella *is* dead—your grandmother is dead."

I had made a decision at that moment to hold back a portion of the truth. Bella had died—but Paul didn't have to know just *when* she had died. We shielded him from the publicity surrounding Daniel's trial at that time, and when he was old enough to understand, we told him the *whole* story. And the *whole* story—all I learned from it, all that came of it, and all that still mystifies me— has often occupied my mind since. I will never quite know how Martha could have done what she did—or Bella, or Lisa, for that matter. But I did discover that the Lord kept His promises, and I knew that bearing that testimony would be my final act.

ENDNOTES

1) In chapter four, I based the title of Bella's portrait, "The Glittering Counterfeit," on the writings of Euripides. The text is paraphrased from the play *Hippolytus*, translated by E.A. Coleridge.

2) In chapter twenty-five, the exact scriptures Wendy reads are to be found in 2 Nephi 25:23 of the Book of Mormon, and Doctrine and Covenants 58:28.

About the Author

C. Paul Andersen received his Ph.D. degree in theatre production and dramatic literature from Brigham Young University. He taught in several Utah high schools, at BYU Hawaii, and at Dixie State College, where he was Director of Theatre and Dean of Fine and Performing Arts.

He founded Pioneer Courthouse Players Repertory Theatre Company and produced, directed, and wrote plays for the company for seventeen years. He also directed the Old Barn Theatre in Kanab, Utah, and consulted with other southern Utah communities in founding their summer theater programs. He also served the community as a member of the Board of Directors of the Dixie Center.

Upon his retirement from Dixie State College, C. Paul Andersen received a citation from Governor Michael Leavitt for his lifelong contributions to theater and the arts in Utah. Now he spends his days writing fiction and has three novels in the works. He and his wife, Kathleen, have four children and twelve grandchildren. They live in Roy, Utah, surrounded by their family and serving in various Church callings.